N
E
S
W
Château Encalor
Tel Sonda
Château Delnor
Al Wafra
Shriveled Forest
Northern River
Villendralier
The Snoozing Sloth
Vast Woodland
Tel Pata
Etarish
Onolon Grove
Château Londror
Gallant Valley
Barren Tundra
Mount Quall
Southern River
An Razi
Numalosh
Tassa Lake
Château Nessongor
Tel
Kastallon
Land Where Castles Lie

Daughter of Kastallon

Matthew Blackburn

First Edition

Fulton Books
Meadville, PA

Published by Fulton Books 2024

ISBN 979-8-89221-529-9 (paperback)
ISBN 979-8-89221-530-5 (digital)

Printed in the United States of America

To Andrew, who is my biggest critic and the
one who introduced me to fantasy.

This would not have happened if it weren't for you.

Chapter 1

The Big-Beaked Bird

The morning sun shone through the crossbars of a window in the orphanage, rays of thin light blanketing the floorboards of the bedroom built for nineteen other children. Although they warmed the room slightly, her mood did not reflect the joy they represented. She lay uncomfortable in the bedsheet's attempt at comfort. She heard the soft cooing of sleeping children in their beds next to her and around her. She was usually the first one out of bed every day anyway.

Willow Dennings was a girl of ten still trapped in a building made for children without parents. As far as she was concerned, it made sense. In her ten years of life, the only people who could be considered as parents were the headmaster himself, Mr. Linmer, and the directress, Mrs. Veraminta. Each night, the directress would instruct Willow and the other girls to clean themselves, clean their beds, clean the floors, and then finally, when the work was over, tuck themselves in for bedtime. Each day, she would wake them up at dawn to get ready for any chores or possible interviews.

Willow always woke up ten minutes before the ceiling light would click on, and Mrs. Veraminta would shout, clapping her hands loudly, "Wake up, girls! Wake up! The sun has risen, and now you must rise. Get up! Up I say. Up! Up! Up!"

Mrs. Veraminta was not as nice as she appeared. With her graying hair tied tightly behind her and her bland dress with faded gold buttons, the woman tried to radiate modesty, but her harsh voice mimicked nails on a chalkboard. Willow wanted to cover her ears but never did out of fear that the directress would force her to clean the bathrooms with no help and only a sad rag to accompany her, so she endured the barrage of noisy commands.

Perhaps today could be the day, she thought, *the day that all of us long for, the day where we can have a real family and not be stuck here in this place, this temporary space.*

She hoped the words in her mind would ease her, but they were just words. Willow looked around her bedroom again and sighed.

Breakfast came and was earned only if the directress said that your hair was proper, your dress was unwrinkled, and your shoes were tied with the right knots. Fortunately, ten years with the same repetitions helped Willow recognize what was acceptable and what was not. She kept her uniform on the same hanger in the same order in the same closet over by the door in the corner. Her initials were sewn into the fabric inside the cotton overshirt she wore day by day. It was the same with the plaid skirt that cut off at the knees. The sad part was that her clothing never fitted her just right due to her being the size of girls a couple of years older than her.

"Look how skinny she is," one of the girls would say as she got dressed.

Another right beside that girl would follow with, "Skinny like a tree branch!"

Willow could never find the right words to say back without seeming mean. How did you respond to that treatment? She could not lash out in anger, because the directress would snatch her wrist, which hurt terribly by the way, and drag her to the room at the end of the hall, the room where no light entered. She had heard stories of it before and was thankful she hadn't shared in their experience.

But she remembered the headmaster's words when she came to him with tears in her eyes and sorrow in her heart.

"Now, now, my dear Willow, whatever is the matter?"

His voice was soft and kind like a mellow harp playing a beautiful melody.

"There are girls who make fun of the way I look," Willow cried.

"Oh, you poor girl. What are these things that they say, my child?"

"They say I am like twigs from a tree—thin and lanky."

"Ah, but you see, Willow, they forget that even the thinnest of trees still produce the most beautiful of blossoms when they reach springtime," Mr. Linmer comforted.

Willow felt her mouth widen into a smile as the tears stopped.

"Don't let them bring you down, child. Now run along and take your books with you. I'm sure the directress will be more than happy to see you with them," Linmer chimed.

Willow clutched the two worn books she was given for her daily instruction from the academic director, Mr. Eckley, as she followed in step in the line leading to the classroom. Just on the other side of the hallway, the younger boys were lining up to go to the bathrooms. Like the girls, each of them wore the same uniform, only for them, it was a bleak gray sweater and those brown felt pants with darker shoes too.

They were a few grades below the girls, so it made sense that they went first. One of the boys, a rather cute and hyper boy, could not contain his laughter as he waited beside the open door to the boys' privy. "Beat you at marbles, later" were the words she made out before the lad disappeared into the bathroom. Something about the way he said them made her blow air from her nose.

She shook her head as the line continued into the classroom.

*****

Willow sat at the simple wooden table with a ceramic plate of dinner staring her in the face. The food sitting on the white circle was a small slab of meat, a bit of carrots, and a spongy roll of bread. Her appetite had been stifled the moment the ingredients were placed on her plate. She fiddled with the carrots with her fork, trying to stack them from biggest to smallest.

The smallest carrot was nearly on the top when a familiar voice rattled her ears.

"Is someone sitting here?"

She looked up and saw a small boy with pale skin and the bluest of eyes. Dots of freckles patterned his nose and under his eyes. His teeth were surprisingly nice and straight and white as they greeted her from his grin. He had his plate in one hand and his metal cup of milk in the other.

Willow realized he was talking about the empty seat on the other side of her table. She glanced at him again.

"N-no! Go right ahead," she insisted.

The boy nearly jumped out of his shoes.

"Yippee!" he cried. "All the other boys took the seats on the other side."

The boy plopped down into the hard wooden seat and scooted himself closer.

"Aren't you not allowed to sit with the girls?" Willow asked. She found herself holding the roll in her hand as she spoke.

The boy took a few gulps of his milk.

"Says who?"

The boy chuckled, gnawing at the meat on his fork.

Willow glared at him with caution beginning to rise in her stomach. She took another bite of the roll, chewed it quickly, and swallowed it. She watched him scarf down chunk after chunk of his roll. Whoever this boy was, he ate like an animal.

Has Mr. Eckley not taught him manners? she wondered.

"Says Mrs. Veraminta. She always keeps the boys and girls separated at lunchtime. It's a mystery she's not over here now, scolding me for letting you sit here," Willow murmured.

"She's not here right now. I was lucky to leave the line when she stepped out. That's when I saw the boys in my class taking up all the seats. This one was empty," the quick-eating boy managed to croak through his stuffing of carrots.

Willow checked the room from corner to corner on the side where the servers were. Headmaster Linmer was providing supervision in the middle between the girls' tables and the boys' tables. He paced with his hands clasped behind his back. As for Mrs. Veraminta, the orphanage directress, this boy had called it right. She was not in the room.

Where has she gone? She is always in here with us, Willow pondered, still surveying the room, hoping to catch a glimpse of the withering woman.

"I guess that is pretty lucky," Willow said, finally touching the slimy meat on her dish.

There was some sort of sauce adorning it that almost helped it look appetizing, but the stench of it was nauseating. The roll had been bland too. That also didn't help.

"Name's Leonard. Leonard Leobo. Most call me Leo for short," Leo said, wiping the milk mustache off his lip with the sleeve of his sweater. "What's yours?"

"Willow. Willow Dennings."

"That's a pretty name," Leo replied kindly.

His boyish mannerisms were in full flaunt. It was common for kids his age.

"Thank you."

"Why are you so tall? I saw you out in the hall earlier, and you stood out—literally."

Willow was reminded of the words Frances and Ruth had teased her with earlier in the day, but Leo's words didn't have the same edge to them. It was like they were sincere yet curious.

"I don't know. I've always been the tall one here," she said.

"Really? That means you must be the oldest!" Leo said, wide-eyed.

Willow shook her head with closed eyes, her hair bouncing in the motion.

"I'm actually the youngest in my class by month. My birthday is in November, and everyone else has spring or summer ones."

The words would have clumped in her throat had they not escaped so quickly.

Today is November 13, she remembered.

The first time she was told what day her birthday was on had been when she was six, when she saw Clara, a ditsy girl whose birthday was in late summer, receive a neatly wrapped gift at lunchtime. She opened the gift and took out a cute red bow that she wore to this day. Willow remembered, that day, she asked Mr. Linmer about birthdays at recess.

"What is a birthday, Headmaster?" she asked.

Mr. Linmer squatted down to her level and met her eyes with his. His hair was beginning its transition from gray to white.

"It is the day when children like you were brought into the world, dropped here wrapped in linens by a graceful stork."

Willow recalled his smile being gentle and welcoming, as it always was.

"When is my birthday, Mr. Linmer?"

"Come. Let me show you," Linmer said then.

She recollected the events of that afternoon all those years ago. He showed her to his office and let her see the book that kept record of each child who was instated into the orphanage, finding her name and seeing the date next to it. November 13, 1910, was written in black ink in the ledger. The month and numbers were etched into her mind that day.

"How do you remember all this stuff, Headmaster?" Willow asked, sitting on his thigh.

Mr. Linmer's smile returned, and he placed her gently back on the hardwood floor beside him.

"Why, I write it down of course!" he said. "Why don't I write it down for you?"

"Really?" Willow gleamed.

"Certainly! That way, you will always remember it."

Willow watched as the headmaster took a sheet of paper, tore it, and scribbled the date on the scrap in large lettering so she could read it.

Willow glanced at the bookmark sticking out between the pages of one of the worn books she had in the lunch chair next to her. The year 1910 was exposed. She was glad Leo couldn't see it.

Before he could spew something else, Mrs. Veraminta rang a handheld bell to begin the dismissal.

*****

The day had concluded once the evening benediction from Mr. Linmer was over. He had spoken about good deeds and the importance of doing them, for you never knew who might repay you in turn for your help. Willow always enjoyed hearing him speak, letting his voice console her as a break from the expectation-fueled barking of Mrs. Veraminta and Mr. Eckley. She had admired him and wondered and wished why the other adults were not of the same kindness seen in the headmaster. Perhaps there was a reason, but Willow didn't know it.

She watched the busy streets through the crossbars of the same window she awakened next to each morning. There were the cars trotting down the road, the kids just like her riding their bikes on the sidewalks or sides of the road with glee, and the men and women walking with one another past storefronts filled with various toys and trinkets. Oh, the torture that came with placing an orphanage next to a toy shop! The only toys they were allowed were different-colored letter blocks and carved wooden animals.

Dressed in her white evening gown and her wavy hazel hair resting on her shoulders, Willow sat back in the chair she had pulled from one of the many desks at the front of the room. Most of the other girls were asleep while she remained awake. There was something almost serene about being the last one to fall asleep and first one to wake up.

She brought her knees to her chest as she sat. Her abnormally long feet hung off the end of the seat but did not fall from the tight grip she kept on her shins. She had hoped that a family would come in to see her today, a potential light in a cave of shadows, but no one had come, not for her, not for any of them. It was as if they were all cursed to spend their days in a place where their basic needs were met—simulated normalcy.

Before she could rest her head on the caps of her knees, something rustled outside. She blinked quickly, trying to discern whether the noise was fact or fiction. She turned her head around her right shoulder, listening if someone else had heard the noise. Nothing. She craned her neck to the left with the same goal in mind. Still nothing. She faced forward again, placing her feet back on the cold floor.

It must have come from outside, she assured herself, staring blankly at the crossbars again.

The streets looked normal. The men and women walking looked normal. The world did not seem any different from what she had seen hours ago. The people walked the streets, the moon shone white, and the automobiles raced and stopped as usual.

She scratched the top of her head, still wondering what in the world made the racket. Had it been a sudden brush of one of the many branches from the green-leafed trees next to the building? Was it the falling of ice sheets from atop the roof? It had snowed the previous night, and the frozen blankets were still in their defrosting stage, as the weather had not reached above freezing the whole day.

Willow stood nervously and drew nearer to the windowsill, trying to get a better look at the world outside her window. Again, there was the same rustling sounded as if quick little wings were flapping furiously.

Pigeons and songbirds don't make nearly that much noise, she remembered, seeing the clear image of the summer birds in her mind's eye.

Then in a muffled sort of way, she heard the sound of a high-pitched chirp. Her brow furrowed as it continued. It was as if one of the more annoying girls were moving a creaky door back and forth without entirely closing it, bringing forth a wretched squeak/squawk sound. Willow blinked rapidly, still unsure if the weird noise was still going. As if done instinctively, she turned the locks of the window and thrust the glass open, the crossbars moving with it, the chill of the cold, biting air nipping her cheeks. She shivered.

As she peered out into the night from her window, nothing seemed out of the ordinary—nothing except the toucan perched on the lamppost, gawking at her with its bright blue eyes. Willow closed her eyes, rubbed them briefly, and opened them again to see if the strange bird would disappear. It seemed her eyes were not lying to her. This was not a hallucination of the mind or a conjured image stemming from lack of sleep. The black-feathered bird with its sunrise-colored beak was as real as the nightgown she was wearing.

Without a moment's hesitation, the toucan flapped its way to the wooden windowsill, sending Willow reeling backward in fright that she nearly tripped over the chair she had been sitting in minutes ago! Another round of chirps left its curved opaquely orange beak.

"What are you doing, strange bird?" Willow asked as if the bird understood her. "You cannot, under any circumstances, be here in my room! Shoo! Shoo!"

She whisked her hands in a flutter motion, attempting to scare the bird away from the sill. The exotic avian shook its head and lingered, unfazed by and unafraid of Willow's gestures.

"You had better fly off now, birdie, before Mr. Linmer finds you! Or worse, Mrs. Veraminta finds you! Only the worst of children know what would happen should she get ahold of you!" Willow said, panicked.

The bird seemed to straighten up at Mr. Linmer's name and chirped once more. Willow blinked rapidly again, trying to understand the bird's behavior. Did it understand her? Did it comprehend English? Suddenly, the toucan took flight again, this time gliding over to the door across the room, which was the exit door of the second-floor bedroom for girls her age.

Oh no, no, no! Why, why, why? Willow feared silently.

She made her way over to the small bird, who sat very still and looked right up at her as her feet paused. Her eyes were almost as wide as the bird's.

"What do you want from me?" she asked, kneeling down to the bird's level and trying not to scare it from her appearing much taller than itself.

The bird pointed its big beak toward the round copper knob of the dilapidated door. When Willow put her hand on it, the bird nodded like a boy! As she pulled it open ever so slowly so as to not allow any creakiness or wobbliness to wake the other girls, the big-beaked, black-feathered little bird hopped and hopped in excitement. No sooner had the door been wide open than the toucan soared down the staircase to the bottom step, waiting.

"Oh, little bird, I'm not supposed to be out right now! You'll get me into trouble, and I'll be sent to the room at the end of the hall.

That dreadful room!" Willow cried, still inside the room, peering into the dimly lit hallway.

The banister was covered in a thin velvet cloth leading down each step down to the floor of the foyer. A decadent rail followed the wall a few feet above the stairwell as a guide for those treading up and down the stairs. Each day, she would take the journey down them to her studies and to lunch when it was time. But at nighttime, it was rather unsettling and scary with no light bounding in from the bedroom.

Willow turned around to see if any other girls had heard the bird's trip down the stairs and felt a brief moment of relief when none of the other beds had been disturbed by someone leaving them.

How can they not hear it? she wondered, turning back to the ajar door.

A lump of anxiety grumbled in her stomach as she held a hand to it. From the time she was able to discern what kind of place she was in and the day-to-day events that transpired inside of it, Willow never once looked for or caused trouble. She was nothing like Frances or Ruth, who could constantly escape trouble due to their cuteness or being coy, yet they misbehaved on the daily. She wasn't like Leo, who seemed to be a boy of high mischief, as she remembered how loud his laughter had been in the hallway hours ago.

She was a girl who just wanted to get by, to do the right thing so she could earn the right to go back to sleep at night, though she tried very hard most of the time, and wake up ready for her duties the next day. Now this bird was beckoning her to follow it.

How could I let this happen? If I had just shut the door and kept in bed, the bird would not have flown in! she cursed to herself.

Finally, she took a candle from the desk next to the doorway and lit a match from the box of matches in the drawer, the gritty tip igniting with just two strikes of the box. She held the match in the wick of the waxy candle and watched as the withered string came to life, accepting the trade of fire from the match. Willow quickly blew out the match and waggled it wildly, trying not to let the smoke waft. Luckily, the candle was already in its holder, a blackened metal stool with a carrying handle integrated into it.

She wrapped two fingers around the handle and took the candle with her. Now the hallway was just a tad brighter with the glow of the small flame. Her shadow was a dark silhouette against the faint orange glow cast on the wall.

Willow closed the door as gently as humanly possible to ensure that the click would not be enough to wake Mrs. Veraminta on the first floor.

Here goes nothing, she dared.

One tiptoe after the other, she went down the stairs, keeping sure to steady herself on the railing connected to the wall. The toucan was still at the base of the stairs and, at the sight of seeing the tall girl, opened its wings in joy! Once Willow traversed the final step, she watched as the toucan waddled into the dark foyer. Even with the dimmed lights in parts of the room, the shadows still dominated the space.

But she was not alone. She made out the shape of a man standing in the middle of the room, his figure quite easily perceivable without the need to draw the candle closer. The toucan chirped again and hopped once more as it stood next to the figure. Willow took a brave step closer to the standing shadow, nervousness clumping in her throat. Another step forward and she could tell the man had a cane in his left hand and a bowler hat atop his head. Then the figure turned around.

"Ah, Willow! I've been expecting you. What took so long? Was it Juniper's fault?" he said cheerfully.

Willow nearly dropped the candle from shock.

"Mr. Linmer?" she gasped.

Chapter 2

Secret of the Century

Although Willow was tall for her age, she felt dwarfed by the height of the headmaster, whose chest met her eyes. In the dimmed lighting, she could faintly recognize Mr. Linmer's soft smile, white stubble, and impeccable suit. The cane in his hand was nothing more than an average stick, pointy at the end and curved bark where the hand rested. It was as if the cane wasn't fully finished compared to the length of the actual walking stick. Whether that was the case was puzzling for Willow. She was still trying to understand why the headmaster was stalking the foyer in the dark, let alone why this bird had decided to fly through her window on the second floor.

"I'm so sorry, Headmaster. I'll go back to bed now!" Willow said, expecting the old man to criticize and scold her for disobedience. But in fact, the opposite occurred.

"My dear girl, have you no sense? When have I ever made the choice to punish you? To raise my voice to you, child? How out of character that would be," Mr. Linmer chimed.

"I…I don't understand, sir. I am out of bed, and it is late at night. Shouldn't I be sent to the room at the end of the hall, where there is no light?"

"You'll have to speak with Mrs. Veraminta about that. But I don't think we shall be around long enough for her to notice," said the headmaster, winking.

The confusion then set in for Willow, who was bewildered by the words leaving Mr. Linmer's lips. Had it been Veraminta in the foyer, she would have become very angry toward the little bird, and she would have been dragged back up the stairs, possibly by her hair, all the way down to the room at the end of the hall and left there until the afternoon arrived the next day—no food, no drink, and no company. It was the worst punishment for a child, especially a lonely one. Needless to say, she was relieved to see the headmaster.

"What do you mean?" Willow asked, still clutching the candle's handle.

"There is much to be told!" Linmer began. "Let us talk more in private, shall we?"

Mr. Linmer's office had not changed in six years, which had been the last time Willow had to visit him. Its orientation had not changed. The furniture was the same wooden chair-desk combination, and the wall of bookshelves behind it didn't look that different, save for perhaps a few new books here and there. The office's floor was a darker wood than the foyer's, giving a contrast to the atmosphere between the rooms. Linmer's desk was neatly organized with different cases for various papers divided between adoptions, reprimands, and any other business in that order. A few windows, tall and thin, were on the left of the room with views of the gated walkway out front decorated with bushes and shrubs.

As Willow followed the headmaster inside, the toucan, Juniper, if that was what Mr. Linmer said its name was, trotted right beside her.

"Would you be so kind as to place that candle in the orb on my desk?" Mr. Linmer said, gesturing to the clear round ball safely secured in a three-legged apparatus next to the cases of paper.

To the girl, it resembled nothing more than a small spherical vase for perhaps a plant or bundle of flowers. Yet Willow nodded, looked, and placed the candle, taking it off the handle first, into the orb through the circular opening on its top. Suddenly, now the room was much brighter with the flame's light emanating into each corner. Juniper's beak was agape for a few seconds at the sight.

Willow watched as Mr. Linmer planted his cane against the desk and sat gently in his sturdy seat behind it. She, however, took the leather chair to the right of the two opposite of him. Before he spoke, Linmer removed his hat and set it in front of him.

"Ah, that's much better!" Linmer said. "Let me start from the beginning."

Willow had known Mr. Linmer ever since she was young enough to think and remember faces and names. A wave of calmness washed over her as he spoke.

"Long ago, in another land far from this wretched hole, there was a castle that used to be full of life, passion, excitement, and yes, even magic. Its name was Château Ensalor, the largest castle in the land and the most expansive of the Four Houses. It was ruled by the duke and duchess for many years in a period of peace and abundance. No calamity consumed them. But that was before *they* arrived from the Isle Far and Wide. The invaders! How lucky you were to escape them," Linmer explained.

Willow gulped.

"They? Who are they?" she asked, a bit of fear rising in her words.

Linmer shook his head, memories of the events that had transpired ten years ago beginning to come back to him in vivid recollection. Willow could see the sorrow knocking on the door of his face, his conscience hesitant to open it. Further explanation would ease her, and she hoped the same could be said for Linmer.

"The Gilded Caliphate, a deadly clan of conquerors, murderers, and slavers. They forced the duke and duchess into exile, banishing them and stripping them of their magic and cutting off their connection to Shimmer," the headmaster detailed, his fragile lips quivering.

"Forgive me for the questions, sir, but what is Shimmer?" Willow begged.

From the books she was allowed to read, which were checked and reviewed by the orphanage literarian, some of them mentioned dust and debris that floated about in the space between Earth and its galactic neighbors. She wondered if that was what he was talking about. It was hard to conceive with no previous image for reference.

She tried to picture what it might be like using pictures from the science books that Mr. Russell showed her, seeing ideas of greens, reds, and touches of blue or orange. Even the word was foreign to her too. How could stars turn to dust, and how could dust come from stars?

"A question for a later time, dear. It is not polite to interrupt those who are speaking, especially those retelling stories. Now soon after they were banished, the world lost its fertility and bountifulness, becoming a barren, dry, cracked land where nothing grew for years. Some of the natives even scattered in search of food, shelter, and water. The Caliph Nahla, cursed be her name, destroyed both the royal thrones where once the former two sat and constructed a dastardly, ugly, distasteful seat, upon which she sits now. Luckily, there is hope for us all."

"What do you mean, Headmaster? I mean, this is quite a lot of new information."

"That is where you come in," Linmer said with a grin. "You are more extraordinary than you have ever been told, Willow. More than the Caliph. More than me!"

"More than you?"

"Yes, more than me!"

"I don't understand," Willow muttered.

"Oh, good heavens, I have forgotten about this disguise of mine. Allow me to give you a proper introduction, child," Mr. Linmer said, rising.

Upon his standing, Juniper motioned for Willow to rise and back up a few feet with her wings, hopping backward as Willow stepped gently away from the headmaster's desk. Once they were a safe distance away, a spectacular sight beheld them. The headmaster, Mr. Linmer, whom she had only known as a kind, thoughtful, wise old man, suddenly had a sprinkle of light glowing from his chest. He took up his cane from its position against the desk and tossed it from one hand to the other and back again as if he was putting on a show for the girl.

The next thing she witnessed was a powerful strike of the cane against the shaded floorboards, a quick spatter of sparks expelling from the contact between cane tip and floor, and simultaneously, his well-kept suit transformed, a rolling strand of yellow light moving up from his shoes to the collar of his shirt into a marvelous display of purple, blue, and yellow robes held in place by a simple eight-strand rope that had two pouches hanging on either side of his waist.

His cane transformed from the oddly unfinished mixture of remodeled wood and tree bark into a long, splendid, elegant silver staff that bore a burnished amethyst gem on its upper tip, a gem whose sparkle was nigh as shiny as the flare inside the see-through orb. Right before her eyes, the bowler hat still stationary on the desk transfigured into a pointy large periwinkle hat with a wide rim.

Willow had never seen such an amazing spectacle in all her ten years of life. She stood speechless as the wizard standing in the glow of the candle inside the orb stroked his long gray beard, which had apparently grown from the stubble she remembered seconds ago!

"You're a…a…," Willow stammered, still in awe.

"A wizard! Yes, indeed!" the glittering sorcerer declared, followed by a hearty laugh. He whisked his pointy hat off his desk, floating around until it landed right on his pate.

Juniper squawked at the sight of the wizard, prancing to and fro in joy. Willow did not know what to think of this new knowledge that the headmaster was actually someone of grand magical standing and found it rather difficult to wrap her head around it. As she had done with Juniper upon first sight, she rubbed her eyes to see if the grandeur in the room was only a dream; and as before, it was nothing of the sort. A wizard in bright robes with a mystical staff was really standing in this tiny office lit only by a small candle, but even it seemed inferior to the dazzling image of the mage.

"Let me be more clear, my dear," he asserted. "I am Merlin, magistrate of Château Ensalor, master of all things magic, conjurer of spells and incantations, and your regal guardian from here on out. At your service!" Mr. Linmer, now Merlin, welcomed.

Willow stood puzzled and somehow astonished along with it. She wondered what would happen should Mrs. Veraminta accidently wander into the room to not only see a child out of bed so late at night, which was disobedience, but also to notice the grand sage that used to be the old cotter she knew as the headmaster. Would she faint from shock? Would she even see the wizard at all?

If the bird can see him, then surely it must be real, she guessed.

Willow felt the sudden urge to bow, to kneel as if in the presence of an angel from heaven or the king of a country.

"No, no, child! Do not seize my subservience. You do me a great dishonor by implying that my light shines brighter than yours," Merlin demanded with a stamp of his staff. More sparks flew.

"But I am just a girl, a nobody. You're a wizard! A real wizard!"

"And you are a daughter of that once great land! Willow, you belong to one of the most remarkable families in my country. Why else do you think you stick out from the rest of the children? Why do you think you lay awake in the evenings and rise earlier in the mornings? Your body is not adjusted to the time and ways of this world. It longs for a return to its homeland."

"My homeland?"

"That is correct," Merlin regarded. "Without the presence of the duke and duchess, magic cannot thrive. That is why you must come with me."

Leaving the orphanage had only ever been a dream, a fantasy. Most of the children were content with their situation, abandoning hope in whatever potential savior could rescue them from the dreary world of the four walls around them, children like Frances and Ruth, like Leo. How were they so happy with the bleakness and repetitiveness of it all? Perhaps they possessed a better sense of ignorance, allowing them to cope with the sadness she assumed ruled their hearts.

Willow was sure she did not have anything like that. It was sadness that prevented her from trying to go anywhere, to refuse the current circumstances that life had placed her in. And yet now an opportunity presented itself in a form that most would conclude was a daydream, a result of poor nourishment, or an imbalance of the four humors.

"Now don't bother scurrying back upstairs to get your things. You have everything you need in that suitcase over there," Merlin said.

He used his newly transformed staff to point at a rather average-looking suitcase propped against the bookshelf. It was nothing more than a wide trunk with leather straps and studded accents connected by two buckles that would unlock the case with just a tap. But both had to be unhooked before it would fully open itself.

"Wait, Mr. Lin—I mean, Mr. Merlin, sir!" Willow said, as the wizard seemed to be preparing for something, looking around for a specific thing.

"Oh, it's just Merlin. Ha ha!" Merlin chimed cheerfully as he patted himself with his free hand.

He released his grip from the staff, and to Willow's surprise, it remained standing in the exact spot it was when it left the confines of the wizard's hand.

"Could you explain why I must go with you, Merlin?" she asked, holding her hands close to her body in a nervous manner.

Juniper's gaze matched Willow's. That is, they were both looking at Merlin, who stopped only to see their eyes waiting for his.

"Take a look at Juniper," he instructed. "Hold your arm out at an angle, like this."

Merlin gestured with his arm as if he was to look at a timepiece that was not there. Willow followed suit. Juniper the Toucan, with a brief release of energy, jumped up and flapped and perched on her arm.

"She is your companion, the animalistic symbol of your family," Merlin continued. "She, like myself, has watched over you ever since you arrived here, Willow. It was your parents' last instruction for me—to make sure you were looked after and to see that Juniper stayed by your side wherever you went. Though I might add, she has popped in and out from time to time."

Juniper felt light on Willow's arm. She used her beak to stroke it in a downward, side-to-side motion as if she was cleaning it. This was actually an affectionate act, not a hygienic one. Willow watched with an open yet happy mouth at the deed.

"Why haven't I seen her until now?" she asked.

"In a different world," Merlin started, "boys and girls like you are unable to see their companions until they reach a certain age.

Don't you remember what day it is? Surely you have not forgotten since the time I wrote it down?"

Willow blushed from embarrassment at the question. Each morning, she crossed out a day on a calendar she had copied from the one in the lunchroom, counting down the days until her birthday. This had only taken her a few years to undertake, as Mrs. Veraminta did not allow paper and pencil at that time—unless, of course, it was for doing any missing work. Willow felt bad every time for lying to her, but she was glad she could keep track of her birthdays.

"My birthday is today," Willow added, stroking the white feathers on Juniper's neck.

"Precisely!" Merlin affirmed with a subtle nod. "To answer your question, you must come because you are the only chance we have at bringing peace back to the land."

"Who is we?" Willow asked.

Merlin then strutted over to her, staff in hand and a hand on a pouch. He sniffed once he stood still inches from her.

"The answer to that question, girl, lies at the shore of South Beach, near the Narrows Bridge. That is where the Wayfinder will be waiting for us."

Chapter 3

Meeting the Wayfinder

The world always seemed so small from within the orphanage walls, to Willow at least, and most days, it didn't bother her that she could not see everything through the crossbar window of her second-floor bedroom. Staten Island had been the only place she had known. Periodically, Mrs. Veraminta would allow the children to play in the gardens and cramped backyard, watching over them like a hawk stalking prey. She would see them jumping and clapping and running around until they became out of breath, tired from the unordinary exertion. She despised most fun things, as she found them to be a waste during the day when work could be done or some other stimulating, tedious task until the evening came. That was when she believed the rest was earned.

Sea waves were a new sound to Willow's ears, the sloshing and whooshing from the tide coming in and out respectively. It was yet another thing she had missed out on because of that mean old woman. What was most interesting was how the sand felt beneath her slippers, soft and pillowy grains of powdered dirt clumping with each step. Some of it was even getting inside of them!

The moonlight was just enough for her to make out the difference in the sand where the tide reached its highest point before withdrawing again into the ocean. One side was the same tan grains; the other, a muddy, squishy, slippery paste. She could see the glint of the moon reflecting off the surface of the foamy water. It was as far as the eye could see where the night sky, full of billions of stars, met the horizon of the murky flood.

Willow carried the suitcase Merlin had shown her from inside his office an hour ago. The trek that began with the closing of the gates at the end of the driveway of the orphanage had been a mighty prolonged one. She tried so hard to not stop and stare at the new-found buildings throughout the city. Although they avoided most of the public attention by sticking to the shadows, she could still hear the bustling of each block, the busy streets of each borough. It was a lot to take in at once.

"How much farther?" she asked, nearly stumbling in the lumpy sand.

"Not much. We must make sure the sun is completely asleep and the night has made its first yawn. Only when the stars are dancing can the Wayfinder appear," Merlin reassured.

He kept a light grip on Willow's hand and carried his magic staff in the other, using it like a walking stick. His robes were just short enough to not catch the grains of sand as they walked. The cold air was enough to produce a shiver as Willow saw her breath in the air, white and wispy. For het first time at the beach, it was a rather unsatisfying one, what with the sand, the air, and perhaps even the water being colder than normal. She did not want to find out for herself. She turned a cheek to Juniper, who had roosted on her shoulder for the adventure, and found that even her beak was chittering.

"Ah yes, here should be swell!" Merlin said, then paused.

Willow dropped the suitcase on the sand and pulled her coat tighter, trying to keep in as much heat as possible. She looked up and saw that most of the lights from the city were gone, only a faint glow hovering over the tops of the buildings behind them. They had stepped away from the sand and onto a small, rocky path jutting away from the main coastline. The water was shallow enough that she could see small pebbles beneath its surface, as well as larger rounder rocks that could cause her to slip if she wasn't careful.

"I don't see anyone here, sir," Willow determined, shivering again.

She saw that the land of the path stopped and descended into the water. How deep it was she could not tell. She made sure to stay as far from it as possible.

"Patience is key, my dear. He will come soon," Merlin responded, holding on to the staff with both hands.

A few minutes passed, and Merlin took in a deep breath through his nose, drawing in as much of the salty air as possible. Before he let it go, he smacked his lips three times. *Smack, smack, smack.* Then he swallowed and then let the breath out in a matter of seconds. Willow and Juniper shared a glance and turned back to the wizard.

"He is close. Probably a few miles away."

Merlin followed up with a grin and stroked his rather long beard. The wizard appeared to be unfazed by the cold weather.

Willow wanted to ask the sorcerer how he could tell that the mysterious Wayfinder was getting closer, but she felt as though if she did, it would be answered with a rather confusing parable. So she decided to just say nothing and try to keep warm in the cool air. Another tide came in with a slosh ringing in her ears. In the distance, the Narrows Bridge carried cars between the island and the continental cities, their headlights like little dots of yellow zooming between the suspension cables of the bridge. Willow had always wondered what the island would look like from the bridge. Perhaps she would be able to someday. Maybe.

"He can't be far now," Merlin began. "Let's let him know where we are!"

"How are you going to do that?" Willow inquired, petting Juniper with her finger.

"He will need a beacon."

"What's a beacon?"

Willow had not heard the word before. Was it an animal? Some kind of food? Before she had time to process the thought, the long-bearded mage raised his silver staff in the air with both hands. The wizard then bellowed a strange phrase, speaking louder than his normal softer tones.

Once the magic spell left his lips, the gem protruding from the tip of the staff glowed bright with its purplish hue as if a star from the night sky itself had been imprisoned inside a crystalline cell. Willow had to shield her eyes from the spectacle, and Juniper used both of her feathered wings to hide hers. The waters before them began to ripple rapidly, a slow illumination of white trickling forth from the shoreline.

To Willow, it appeared like milk flowing into the water from the land. She had never seen anything quite so strange in her ten years of life. Her eyes widened as the milk seemed to surround the small jutting they were standing on.

"What's happening?" Willow tried to yell over the sound of the splashing, splattering waves.

Merlin replied, his posture unchanged, "Magic, my dear. Magic! This is the beacon!"

In the back of her mind, Willow hoped no one else could see what she was seeing out of fear of the authorities being involved. She didn't want Merlin—or rather, the man she formerly knew as Mr. Linmer—to be taken away because of something she was needed for. That idea made it feel like if he got in trouble, it would be her fault. Yet at the same time, there was a fear for them as well, a fear that if a bystander were to catch them, should they be the authorities or not, they could get hurt! She didn't want to think about it right now.

She almost wished she hadn't opened the window to let the bird in, to follow it down the stairs, to see it jump for joy at the sight of the headmaster. She wanted to get out of the cold and into her warm bed. At least that was one good thing that came out of the orphanage.

Before long, Willow could see something stirring in the water and heading toward them. A hump in the water was continually getting larger and larger as it drew nearer and nearer. A spout of water was expelled from the surface yards away from them, a thin jet of water that split into smaller droplets as it ascended, then splashed back down when it reached its peak.

"Ah, here he is! Get ready!" Merlin said excitedly.

The spell must have worn off, Willow thought as she saw him lower his staff, and with it, the water settled, and the purplish haze from the gem faded away.

Willow braced for something big, as the lump in the water was right on their heels! There it was, before her eyes. A massive blue whale surfaced like a submarine in the water, its bluish-gray skin and wrinkled chin only inches away from the shoreline. It was using its tail and giant flippers to tread water and stay afloat. Merlin went over and placed a gentle hand on the beast, keeping his staff in the other. The whale seemed to like him and appreciate his kindness.

"Greetings again, Balaen. Ten years is too long apart, my friend," the wizard said.

Willow noticed one of the whale's eyes, and it blinked at her.

"And who might this be, Merlin?"

Balaen talked without moving his enormous mouth. It seemed as though his voice was escaping through the blowhole atop his head. Willow was pretty sure she was blushing, because she was astonished that a blue whale, the largest animal in the world, was speaking to a wizard who petted him.

"Oh, quite right! This, my filter-feeding friend, is our hope in bringing life back to Kastallon."

"Ah, the One Who Unites. She's not at all what I imagined," the whale spoke.

"Skeef did not mention appearances, but I am certain she is it," Merlin reassured.

"How can you be certain, oh conjurer of spells?"

"I have watched her carefully ever since she was brought to this realm," Merlin said.

Willow craned her head as she listened.

"You mean you knew about this the whole time?" Willow asserted, her brow furrowed.

"Precisely, Willow. As I said before, 'twas the last command of your parents. That is why I put you here, so that you would be safe and hidden from any potential detection," Merlin stated.

"I see she is acquainted with her companion," the whale confirmed. "Perhaps she may be what Kastallon needs."

"Um, Merlin, sir, what is Kastallon?" Willow asked as she tugged at the wizard's dry robes.

Merlin took his glance away from the whale and turned it to the girl and the bird.

"It is where we are going, my dear. Your home!"

The sorcerer winked.

At the notion, Balaen rested his massive wrinkled chin on the small patch of shore the two of them were standing on and opened his gigantic mouth. Willow could see the remaining water from a previous meal still gurgling about inside. She looked upward and saw rows of fibrous, stiff tendrils hanging down from the top of the whale's gaping jaws. It was baleen, the type of filter-feeding teeth that most whales had.

"Don't be shy, Willow. He won't bite," Merlin said, stepping onto the whale's fat tongue with a squish.

Willow was nervous about entering a sea beast's mouth, much more about whether they would be swallowed whole! But it was Juniper who calmed her, as the bird was quite mellow about seeing the whale's open gob and filamentous teeth.

"So…so we get to K-Kastallon in a whale?" she asked anxiously. She was still carrying the suitcase that had accompanied her since they left the orphanage.

Merlin tried to ease her nerves.

"He is a Wayfinder, one of the few remaining in service. He is the only way to get from our realm, here on this island, to the Land Where Castles Lie. Please be at peace, girl. Balaen has carried more than a girl, a bird, and a wizard before. Take my hand and climb aboard!"

Willow looked back as the wizard extended a hand to her. Even with its cold weather, bustling streets, and mostly dirty infrastructure, Staten Island was home. It was the only place she had ever known. It gave her food, water, clothes, and even a warm bed to sleep in each night. Sure, the management wasn't the best, but it was management nonetheless. At least someone was looking after them.

She had only ever made one real friend, even if she had only spoken to him for a brief moment in the lunchroom. Seeing his face in her memory wasn't quite enough to stir tears, but she began to wonder what would happen if he never got to talk to her again, if he never got to sit at the table and goof off again. What if she never got to hear that silly, boyish laugh again?

She looked again at the wizard standing on the moist tongue of the blue whale and the bird perched on her arm.

These are my friends now, she thought. *No matter what, I will come back for Leo. For a boy with that much happiness, he doesn't deserve the place he's in. If we can stop whatever it is that Merlin and Balaen said is bad in their land, surely I can take Leo with me when we come back. It's what he would want.*

"Are you ready?" Merlin asked, his hand still waiting for Willow's.

Juniper then flew off her arm and settled on the wizard's staff.

"Juniper seems eager. What say you?"

Willow took a deep breath in and let it out, finalizing her decision. But before she could move, she asked her final question.

"What will happen to the orphanage if you are gone?"

Merlin chuckled.

"Oh, my dear, I feared you might feel attached to this place. Though you may miss them, Mrs. Veraminta will keep them in check."

Whatever happens, I will come back for you, Willow thought, taking Merlin's hand.

Chapter 4

A Barren World

For a whale's mouth, the temperature was surprisingly comfortable. It was not too hot—or rather not so hot that it was miserable. It was not too cold either—or rather not cold enough to freeze to death. It was a comfortable medium of the two. Sure, there was a constant wetness and sloshing of standing water that dampened her slippers and gown when she sat, but it could be worse. It could have been that the water was much, much higher that she struggled to keep her head above the meniscus of the mouth, and they drowned, but Willow was thankful Balaen had done this sort of thing before. She kept her hands clamped on her arms and her arms resting on her knees. Juniper was nestled in her lap snuggly. Was she snoring? Did birds even snore?

Moments ago, they left the rocky and sandy beach of Staten Island and ventured in the water underneath the Narrows Bridge, carried in the maw of a whale proportionally larger than any average whale seen in the Atlantic. The very concept of her situation was crazy. How did an orphan go from watching people walking and holding hands in the street to sitting in the jaws of a sea beast with a toucan and a wizard? It was not your average night in New York, that was for sure.

Willow felt her eyes begin to droop, her vision beginning to get hazy and swirly. It was probably the warmth of the baleen mixed with the hum of the bird in her lap that contributed to her newfound drowsiness. Or it could be the fact that if she were still in her bedroom at the orphanage, it would be well past her bedtime.

Something inside her wanted to sleep after all those consecutive nights deprived of sleep. On the contrary, she did not want to knock on slumber's door and make a pact. She wanted to be fully aware of the world she was about to see, a world where headmasters became wizards and where she apparently belonged. Apparently, she also had a family there. At least that was what she assumed from the spiel Merlin told her. Yet there was a dreamlike quality to her surroundings. It was probably just fatigue talking.

Sooner or later, she found her head drooping and her eyes giving in to their sagging. A gradual numbness began to take over, her mind slowly dozing off, and she slept like she had never slept before.

*****

"Willow! Juniper! Awake now! Awake I say!"

The urgency in Merlin's voice sounded genuine. A brief shaking from the wizard jolted Willow awake. Juniper squawked and hopped up.

"What? What is it, sir?" Willow said, startled.

Merlin had knelt to match her gaze.

"Balaen is about to begin surfacing," the wizard said, using his staff for balance.

Willow rubbed her eyes with her damp hands. They were wrinkled from the salt water still in the whale's mouth and from prolonged exposure to it.

"What does that mean?" she asked.

"It means we are about to come out of the water!" Merlin replied, standing. "This is your first time experiencing wayfinding, so I wanted to warn you before you panic from the sudden shift. You will feel everything begin to weigh down on you, and the forces at be will try to drag you down into his gullet. When that time comes, you will need to grab hold of his baleen and grasp tightly. Fortunately for Juniper, she can fly."

"What about the suitcase?" Willow asked, looking for it.

"You mean this one?" Merlin said, gleefully holding the same suitcase from before in his other hand. "Oh, there's more to this old thing than meets the eye."

At the release of his hand and a snap of his fingers, the trunk began to float as if some unseen strand of twine was keeping it suspended in the air. A low haze of purple was underneath it.

"See? Nothing to worry about," Merlin said.

Then when Balaen's mouth began to rumble and gravity's pull increased as the beast himself began to ascend in the water, the wizard said, "Now quickly, grab hold and do not let go!"

Willow sprang into action, using her damp fingers to wrap her hands around the brushlike teeth of the whale. It was surprisingly comforting with how soft they were. It was like hugging a paintbrush. She kept an eye open and examined the color of them as the rumble and effect of it heightened. They were a bright yellowish white, completely ivory near the base where teeth met gums. The tips of them were almost wispy and loose. That was what made them feel relatively soft to the touch. Never in her ten years did she ever conceive the thought of being able to touch the teeth of a blue whale, let alone exist inside of its mouth. She considered herself lucky.

The rumble and swell of the air continued and continued until finally, there came a point where it all stopped. No shaking. No pressure. Things returned to the way they had been before the surfacing began. The hovering suitcase collapsed, and Juniper stopped flying. Willow hadn't realized both of her eyes had been closed until she opened them from the newfound light inside Balaen's jaws. But it wasn't the purplish light of Merlin's staff or even the light of a low-level fire. It was sunlight beaming in from the whale's open mouth. But something about the way the sun felt against her skin made it seem as if it was not the same sun that shone through her orphanage window in the mornings. There was a subtle change in heat, and it was not as bright.

Willow released her grip from the baleen and stepped again on the squishy texture of the tongue. Balaen gurgled. Merlin, who hadn't changed his posture or position during the surfacing, clapped his hands in delight. Willow nudged closer to the wizard and picked up the suitcase beside him. She felt Juniper perch on her right shoulder gently and stroke her hair with her beak.

"Step closer to Balaen's lips, Willow," Merlin encouraged.

Willow did as the wizard demanded and treaded closer to where the water began to slip in slightly. If her slippers hadn't already been soaked from the standing water earlier, she would have reacted more to the water swallowing her ankles. She had good balance just behind the whale's lip. Beyond the opening of the mouth, she could see a large continent in the distance. Even farther beyond it were mountains visible to her eyes, mountains that stretched high into the sky.

"Where are we?" Willow asked, looking up at the sky, which was, of course, a shade of silver darker than the normal white clouds of Earth's sky.

The expanse above was now a gloomy gray—not exactly white but not close to black.

"My dear, I welcome you to Kastallon. That continent you see far away is the Land Where Castles Lie, the very same land where the wretched Caliph sits in her wretched throne," Merlin said.

"Why is the sky so...pale?" Willow asked, a touch of fear in her tone.

"Because, my child," Merlin answered, kneeling beside her, "the magic of this realm is far gone. Even I, one of the last conjurers, am feeble as long as the Caliphate controls Château Ensalor. Until the Two Thrones are restored and the true rulers of the land sit in those seats, spell-casting will be harder to do. That is where you come in, Willow."

"The One Who Unites?"

"Exactly!"

"I don't understand. I'm not special. I'm not a wizard like you. You're telling me that I am the one to restore the thrones, but I don't know how I am to do that!" Willow cried, feeling a tad bit overwhelmed by the information.

"Once we get ashore, there is a person who can explain it far better than I can," the wizard proclaimed. Then to the whale, he said, "Balaen, take us to the western shore."

*****

Dull sunlight twinkled in the grains of sand on the shore of the western region of the Land Where Castles Lie. Willow stepped onto the pillowy ground, noticing the familiarity between the sand of Staten Island and the sand of Kastallon that she stood on now. There were no seagulls, no cars to make noise in the background, and certainly no street lamps to light the path when night fell. All she could see was sand, a few patches of dying flora, and cracked earth as if a drought had swept through the land and stripped it of life and flourishing.

In the distance from the shore they had landed on, Willow saw some merchants riding strange six-legged animals. At least she assumed they were merchants from the packs of goods and trading materials (salt, silks, and other items) hanging from their saddles. There were horns protruding from their animals' scaly skin. Willow had never seen any animal of the sort, not even in her wildest dreams or her most frightening nightmares. Luckily, they were at a distance, taking the path carved out in the dirt.

"Where are they going?" Willow asked, still peering at the small convoy.

"Château Delnor, the Stronghold. Those are Buhz soldiers. Best steer clear," Merlin instructed, motioning for Willow to move.

"There is another castle?" Willow inquired, carrying Juniper on her arm and the suitcase in her other hand, sticking close to Merlin.

"There are four in total," he said.

"Four?"

"Yes, four, one for each of the High Houses of the First Rulers: Ensalor, Delnor, Londror, and Nessongor—north, west, east, and south respectively."

Willow tried to grasp the idea that one land needed four castles but only one of them for the rulers who reigned. She had heard of fairy tales where there was a king and queen who had a daughter, the princess, who needed saving from a knight. They were found in some of the books she read in the orphanage library. They were very interesting reads, but she felt ashamed to read them, as she felt she was the only one interested in those kinds of tales. Then she wondered if Leo would like them too, and as she thought of the boy she left on Staten Island, a few drops of sorrow set in her eyes.

Whatever happens, I will come back for you, she remembered, the words still in her mind and heart.

"Well, Merlin, aren't you going to show her the way to Al Wafra?" an unfamiliar voice squawked.

Willow stopped in her tracks and nearly dropped the suitcase.

Merlin turned to the bird.

"She needn't go there just yet, Juniper. She must meet Pinner first."

"Well, I don't think she's ready for his wildness, for lack of a better word," the bird said again, flapping her wings briefly.

Willow looked at Merlin, then at Juniper and back to Merlin and then again at Juniper, sharing her confused look between them.

"You can…talk? A toucan that talks?" she said, puzzled.

"Oh, where are my manners?" the toucan began. "I am Juniper, herald of House Drinith and your personal companion."

The bird bowed with one wing under her chest and the other extending out behind her with royalty. Willow gulped.

"I believe she still doesn't fully understand, dear Juniper," Merlin assured.

"It is like this, Willow. Since we are in Kastallon, I can speak just the same as you and the wizard. When I am in Earthrealm, its birds' biology forbids me to utter words. Does that make sense?" Juniper explained with her eyes set on the girl.

Willow took in another deep breath and let it go slowly.

"I'm in a world where wizards exist, creatures have six legs, and birds can talk. Tell me I'm dreaming!"

"I am not the only animal to speak, you know. Those bukavacs yonder can speak too. Dreadful creatures, I say, but they can form sentences," Juniper replied.

"We can walk and talk at the same time, can't we, friends?" Merlin said in an urgent manner.

Willow and Juniper turned to him. The bird talked first.

"Now just a moment, Merlin. We have not decided where she will visit first."

"She needs a better explanation, and Pinner can give it to her," said Merlin.

"And I think she needs to find food and water first. Don't you know she hasn't eaten or drunk anything since we departed?" Juniper ordered.

It was true. The last meal Willow remembered having was lunch with Leo. She remembered how unappetizing the meat was and the soggy vegetables too. How Leo managed to keep the slop down was incredibly baffling.

But as she stood in the soft sand in the presence of new friends, her stomach growled loudly. She placed a hand on it as if it would tame the sound, but alas, it did not help.

"Is there anything to eat in the suitcase, Merlin?" asked Willow, beginning to place the small box in the sand and click the tabs.

"I'm afraid not, only clothes meant for you to wear to not be seen as a total stranger in the Land Where Castles Lie. Don't worry, I made sure that they would fit you quite comfortably and were crafted from the finest cloths," the wizard responded, leaning on his staff.

The contents of the suitcase matched what Merlin had said. An autumn tunic and silver belt, olive-green trousers, and brown leather boots were packed neatly in the frame of the case. Behind these items was a cloak a shade of brown darker than the boots, also packed neatly in the frame.

"It is settled, then. The girl is hungry and requires nourishment," Juniper demanded.

Merlin stroked his beard and carefully considered the next words out of his mouth.

"I suppose you're right. Suppose I should pay Pinner a visit and tell him of your coming. Oh, he will be absurdly delighted to meet you, Willow. Perhaps you will see him later. For now, take this pouch, and Juniper will show you the way to Al Wafra, the main village area not far from Château Delnor. There you will find an amazing assortment of foods I'm sure you've never seen before. Now off you go! I shall meet you both where the river flows between the Enchanting Grasslands when I return from Pinner's cave. I do hope you take care of yourselves."

Without another word from the bird or the girl, Merlin pierced the soft sand with his staff, a puff of smoke rising from its tip, and he was gone in a flash!

Willow felt the weight of the small pouch in her hand. It was nothing more than a sackcloth bag tied with brown string.

"What do you think it is?" she asked the bird.

Chapter 5

Al Wafra

"Open it, and let's find out!" Juniper said, gliding down to the cracked, dry ground on which Willow stood.

The suitcase Merlin had given her stood still beside her. She wondered why the wizard would leave her with such a mysterious item, let alone with a talking bird and a case full of strange clothes. Seeing no other option, Willow squatted down and placed the pouch gently on the ground. Juniper leaned in closer, and she carefully pulled the tied rope loose with her fingers. She held her breath, anxiety seeping into her brain for a second.

To her surprise, the sack was full of a sparkling purple-bluish powder. The only thing Willow could compare it to was the sugar that was kept in small packets at breakfast for the orphanage workers to use for their coffee, save for the very obvious violet hue it displayed.

"Ah, wonderful!" Juniper said, hopping around. "I was afraid it was all gone!"

Willow stared at the powder in the bag. Seconds passed, and she decided to pick it up and hold it in her hands, closer to her gaze. She wanted to try and count each little twinkle in the grains.

"What is it?" she asked the bird.

Juniper leaped, fluttered, and landed again on the girl's left shoulder and peered down at the glittering dust.

"That, my dear, is Shimmer! It is a rare commodity only found in the Land Where Castles Lie, and only those who have a connection to magic can use it correctly. Merlin must have kept it with him all these years, waiting to give it to you when the time came. How marvelous! All we need now is a conduit," Juniper replied happily.

"What is a conduit?" Willow asked, then remembered how many questions she had been asking. What else would you do if you were in a place you knew nothing of?

"Forgive me, Willow, for I must remain patient with all the questions you will have. A conduit is a tool that wizards use to channel magic from Shimmer and cast all sorts of spells. Remember that staff that Merlin carries with him all the time? That is his conduit. And that crystal that the staff sports? It is one of the last remaining Shimmer crystals in Kastallon.

"Thank Skeef the Caliph has not discovered where the others are. Now let's tie that back up and keep it in the suitcase," Juniper continued as Willow's stomach continued to growl. "We need to get you some food."

"I could use some bread or chicken," Willow said, saliva beginning to coat her lips.

"Believe me, Willow, there will be so much more than simple foods in Al Wafra."

*****

The sun shone high in the sky as it beat down on the wasteland around the pair as they walked the path in the grayish dirt, it itself being a lighter shade on the ground. Lots of pebbles of different sizes and shapes littered the landscape around them. Ahead of them, the path branched out into different routes that led to different places.

To their right, some abandoned buildings Willow assumed used to be houses stood like tombstones. They had been constructed from smoothened clay and had their doors and windows carved out to let the cool air in. But all life had been stripped from it, and the wind escaped its windows, wounds in the home's body.

To their left, the land seemed to stretch as far as the eye could see before dropping off into the sea. No trees birthed color in their eyes, no animals scoured for prey, and no clouds occupied the sky with their whiteness.

Moments ago, Willow had found a comfortable spot to slip out of her nightgown and try on the new clothes the wizard had packed for her. Fortunately, he was right about how the clothes hugged her arms and legs and torso like a hand fitted in a good glove. She had thrown the cloak over her shoulders and buttoned it at its collar, letting it drape behind her.

Had it not been for Juniper warning her to keep the hood up to cover her head, she would have been much hotter and miserable than she almost was walking the bland path. She felt small beads of sweat forming on her brow and forehead, beads that began to dampen her bangs.

An hour had passed since they departed the shoreline, and soon, the stone buildings and draped tents and wooden overhangs of Al Wafra were in sight. A large archway between two limestone pillars, one that if walked through would lead into the marketplace, stood before them, guarded by two men in gold-and-black armor. A bit of fuzz lined their collars from their cloaks. Their raven helmets sported crooked horns like ant antennae. From the looks of it, they were guarding perhaps the only entrance into the tan-walled city.

Willow felt Juniper nudge her with her beak.

"It would probably not be a grand idea to give them your name. Today, you are Winnie, not Willow. Until it is safe, use that name," the bird said in her ear.

Willow then approached the two soldiers guarding the entrance.

"Excuse me, sirs, but may we pass?" Willow asked nervously.

In her mind, she wasn't sure how the men would react to Juniper's presence. But for the moment, nothing had stirred them. She also hoped that carrying a trunk around wouldn't seem suspicious, and again, she found it, too, had not concerned them. In fact, it seemed the men did not hear her question. They neither moved nor responded to it. Instead, they stared sternly at the horizon and gripped their spears and shields tightly.

Seeing this, Willow decided that if they didn't move, she would. She stepped forward between the soldiers as if to begin down the tunnel path, hoping they would remain stoic. But when she stepped, their spears crossed and blocked the space between them.

"How rude!" Willow said with a tint of harshness in her throat. She gawked at them with a look that meant confusion and frustration.

One of the guards looked at her, turning his helmeted head toward her, a mirthless visage glaring at her.

"State your business, girl! No one enters the city without proper cause," the gilded man said, speaking with a gritty tone and slight rasp.

But suddenly, his glare became perhaps sincere when he realized who she was. He bent down to her level.

"What is a child like you doing in the desert alone? Are you lost? Where is your father?"

He turned to the other soldier.

"Say, Tosh, what do you make of this little one and her bird?"

The other soldier replied with less worry than his comrade.

"Quite a unique bird, Jad. She seems harmless enough, I think."

Tosh shifted to Willow.

"What is your name?"

Willow knew the question would arise sooner or later. She went with what Juniper had suggested that she do.

"M-my name is Winnie," she said.

"And where is your father, Winnie?" Jad inquired.

This was when Willow did not know how to respond. The question had never been asked back on the island and, as such, had not been a problem. What would she say? Should she be honest or stick with the lies Juniper had told her to use? Mr. Linmer—or rather, Merlin—had always told her, "Lying will get you nowhere. It is for the mischievous and foolish." With two soldiers having armor resembling hornets staring her down, lying felt like the only thing that would keep her from being in the middle of nowhere. So she decided to lie again, though she knew it would leave a poor feeling in her stomach later in the night.

"My father is, er, inside the city! He told me to meet him here once I finished my morning chores."

Well, it's not a complete lie, she thought. *I did have morning chores to do.*

"I do hope prayer was included in those chores."

Tosh's tone seemed demanding, as if, if she told him the practice had been omitted from the routine, he would swiftly bash her with his shield. Leaving the thought to dwell in the back of her mind, she nodded nervously in response.

"There's a good girl," Jad said, tapping his spear on the ground. "Now run along and find your father. I'm sure he will be more than happy to see you. He may be somewhere in the marketplace. Find him quickly now!"

"Thank you, sirs! Thank you!" Willow said as she passed them by, heading down the tunnel into the corridor.

Her steps were louder now with her boots clapping against the cobblestone. The sun's light faded, vanished, until it was seen and felt again on the other side of the shadowed entrance. Not only that, but the sound of the wind receded and was replaced by the many voices of those inside the marketplace, some carrying baskets and others sackcloth bags full of goods.

Willow had never seen so many strangers in one place than she did in this bustling marketplace. There were colored fabrics she had never seen before that draped over the tops of the vendors' stations to keep the sun from glaring onto their heads and potentially spoiling the food. On the sides of the main pathway through the city, men dressed in full-body robes sat with their canes against the stone walls, some relaxing while others were minding their business or enjoying a meal of bread and juice. People were trading goods back and forth. Fruits, vegetables, spices, clothes, and even antiques were up for grabs. This made her want to clutch the trunk she carried in both hands instead of leaving it to dangle in one.

"That was close, Willow. But I applaud you for your sharpness. Now, then, we need to head for the baker's place. I'm sure there is fresh bread already made," said Juniper.

Willow nearly missed the conversation, as she was still taking in the commotion around her. Everyone was practically wearing the same garb, save for the change in colors—some red, some green, and some brown or tan. But the most common was white or black. It was the merchants who surpassed that level of dullness.

"Right. Um, where is the baker? I've never been here, so I don't know where to go. I'm sure it is not far from here," Willow said back, blinking.

"That is why I am here, dear. I will fly ahead and guide you. But be warned. Keep your guard up. Do not lose sight of your destination. It is too easy to get lost in the crowd."

"Fly high, then. That way, I'll always know where you are."

So the two chose to follow Willow's plan. Juniper the Toucan, rose into the air above the scuttering plaza and began to glide using the air current produced by rising warm air. Willow did her best to time her glances from the crowd up to her friend in the sky. It was mostly simple since the customers stayed at their places with the vendors and traders. A narrow path was artificially made from the space where people weren't standing. Willow put the hood of the cloak over her head so as to blend in with the people wearing theirs. They took the trail under an overpass, hanging a right, then a left and continuing straight again.

There hadn't been much interference yet. But some of the people in the crowds began to clap their hands and raise their voices as she approached the baker's place. As she stood on the cracked stone steps of the baker's place, she turned around to see what the commotion was, the smell of freshly baked bread tempting her.

Why, it seemed a parade had strolled into town, and it was not just any parade. It was a parade of carts and people and flower petals flying and animals carrying people, donkeys and horses mostly. They were very celebratory with their songs and dances, which were integrated into their traversal of the streets. Willow could hear them singing and made out a few of the words.

O come ye and do your part
Take the stroll by foot or cart

The journey to Ranha is upon us!
Flock to us now and join the throng
For Fikra's might be ever strong
The journey to Ranha is upon us!

There could be heard instruments providing music with the voices of those in the parade. She then proceeded to move along the main pathway with several people beginning to join in. They would drop what they were doing and slip right in and find the rhythm with which to blend their bodies to. It seemed that all commerce was halted as the parade moved through, as Willow witnessed that even the merchants and vendors ceased their operations and assimilated.

"Does this happen all the time, Juniper?" Willow asked as Juniper perched on her left shoulder.

The paced line of joyful singing trudged along the marketplace and into the plaza, which was surrounded by clay buildings, some having domed roofs and others a straw and wood combination. Whatever this was, it was enough to entrance the entire community.

"According to the law set by the Caliphate, every five years on the third day of summer, the Horn of Fikra is sounded from the walls of Château Ensalor, the signal to begin the pilgrimage to Ranha. Once the horn at Ensalor is blown, each of the three other castles will sound theirs in succession, prompting all people in all of the nearby towns, villages, and even cities like this one to stop their trading, selling, buying, and mingling and prepare their bodies for the journey. Men, women, and even children take up this task. They pack their things the night before, from what I have observed, and take it with them for the day.

"They pack everything except for food, stowing away a special flask of drinkable water in their bags and purses and sacks. After leaving their home, they begin northeast to Pallee, where Ranha lies secluded in a glade of trees. It seems the parade of pilgrims has reached Al Wafra. Though I cannot say that I understand the occurrence, it would be wise to not stand about watching and not participating, Willow," Juniper rambled.

"Wait!" Willow said, surprised. "You said they don't pack any food? Why not?"

She turned back to the bakery, through the windows, where she could see the baker himself beginning his closing routine of snuffing the fire, replacing the ingredients, and dismissing his workers.

"Won't they starve on a trip that long by foot? Are they out of their minds?"

"I am afraid it is not out of the ordinary for the participants," Juniper said. "The reason they go without food is because it is the first act of respect toward Fikra, the Caliphate's goddess. Their philosophy wills that those who honor her by staving off food on the expedition become better servants and more deeply rooted in the faith. It is seen as a civil duty during this time."

Before the bird could say another word, Willow's stomach guided her decision-making. She pulled open the wooden door to the bakery and stepped inside. Now the smell from before had intensified, causing saliva to build in her mouth. Around the room, there were wood and metal buckets full of different loaves of bread. Some were a dark brown with grains on tops. Most of them were the original oval-shaped tan loaves. The worktable had been littered with flour. The oven was nothing more than bricks layered in a pentagonal fashion with a square-shaped hole for depositing ready-to-bake loaves of gooey dough.

The baker finished up his routine as the last robed worker passed by Willow and exited through the open door carrying his packs and things in a clumsy jog. As the baker, a rather rotund fellow with a long hazel beard and bald head dressed in his green robes and donning an apron, pulled the strings of his sack tight, Willow approached him urgently, nearly knocking the chap over from fright.

"Excuse me, sir, but could you spare a few loaves? I am dreadfully hungry and have been since I arrived in Al Wafra."

Willow seemed to have a begging tone. The baker began to catch his breath and find his feet, removing his hands from the dusty table.

"My, my, dear girl, you've given me a shock!" he said firstly, then added, "I am afraid we are closed for the afternoon until further notice. Unless you are blind, deaf, or dumb, I don't have to tell you the reason why I'm leaving."

"Oh no, sir, I am aware of the circumstances. But seeing as you will not be returning for a while, wouldn't it be fair to lend me some of those delicious-looking loaves?"

"Do you have any coin?" the baker inquired, grabbing his sack, his voice gritty.

"No," Willow said, embarrassed. "I'm just a girl."

"No coin, no loaves."

The baker began to head for the open door, but Willow caught him before he could take another step to the threshold.

"Oh, but please, sir! Please!" she cried.

"You won't need it on the journey to Ranha, so I suggest you scram!"

"Now that isn't any way to speak to a child! How very rude of you!" squawked Juniper, who had been listening to the exchange the whole time.

"Oh, now your pigeon talks too?" the baker said and burped, not bothering to cover his mouth.

Bubbles of anger began to well in Willow's chest, and she felt her face begin to get hot. For the moment, she ignored the fact that she was hungry, but her stomach still gurgled.

"She is not a pigeon, you oaf!" Willow said, speaking loudly, and quickly regretted it.

All her life, she was taught never to speak out of turn, to use her manners, and to be respectful to adults and to those who gave her their time. The only problem was that although Mrs. Veraminta tended to be spiteful, demanding, and overly strict, she was never rude to the children like the baker was. There had been moments, however, where Willow would have been satisfied by shouting back at the directress with all the frustration she had stirred. But such an act of open rebellion against her would have resulted in her being dragged off to the room at the end of the hall, where the light never reached. She was lucky she had goodwill and a stronger mind. But she was no longer in the orphanage. She wasn't even sure it was still Earth.

"You had better watch your tone before I take your tongue!" the baker said with balled fists.

He was quite a burly man, an intimidating specimen for sure. His face began to redden with rage, his temper like that of the previously stoked flame of the bread oven.

Aware of her rising attitude and frustration, Willow took a breath in and let it go. She kept her focus away from the plumpness before her and scowled at the floor.

"I'm sorry," said Willow. "We just need something now before we get on the road. We have a long journey ahead, don't we? What's the harm in eating now and forgoing food later?"

She looked up at him with sincerity that only she knew was an act.

"This is my first pilgrimage, sir. It would be rather unpleasant if you were the one who refused to feed a helpless girl before and discover later that she departed from hunger."

"Fine, girl, but I need something in return. That's how it works around here. You take, I receive. An eye for an eye," the baker replied.

Willow then noticed that he began to gawk at Juniper in a rather uncomfortable fashion.

"Perhaps I'll take that bird from you in exchange."

"She is not a part of the bargain!" Willow said. "No bird is worth a few loaves of bread."

"Ah, but it would seem that it is no ordinary bird. Dare I say that I have never seen such a peculiar bird in all my days."

"I will not give her up!"

"Then I guess you will travel with nothing but the air around you!" the baker said, closing in on the threshold of the open door.

The parade's jubilation increased in volume as more and more of the people of Al Wafra poured into the line of singers, dancers, musicians, and tamers. The entire city was ripe with sound. Yet Willow could still hear the rumble and grumble of her empty stomach over the many noises of the paraders. If she didn't act now, she would certainly continue to be very hungry, even after she left the walls of this desert town.

"Wait!" she cried. "There is one more thing I can offer."

She set her trunk down on the table in the center of the bakery. The baker moved away from the threshold with anticipation.

"And what might that thing be, child?" he said.

Willow clicked the tabs on the trunk, and the lid thrust open with a chink. Using her hand, she lifted the lid and revealed her previous clothes.

"I don't see anything but worthless clothes for an even worthless girl!" the baker scorned.

He watched as Willow replaced some of the clothes, placing them atop the lid, until she removed the sackcloth pouch that she had received from Merlin.

"What is that?"

"Why don't you look for yourself?" Willow answered, untying the rope that sealed the pouch tight.

As the final strand was unraveled, the baker approached the bag presented before him, and the same purplish glow of Shimmer befell his eyes, and he gaped in awe of the rarity.

"Where did you get your crummy little paws on this? This… this is illegal! Do you realize how many loaves this could buy you?" the baker whispered as if even the tiniest mention of the violet powder would alert the guards at the entrance of the city, and they would arrest him on the spot!

"How many?" she asked after gulping.

"Enough to never have to bake another loaf in your whole lifetime!" the baker whispered again. "I'll tell you what, girl. You hand over that pouch, and you can have my entire stock."

It sounded like a good deal, especially for a hungry child. For Willow, having bread in abundance and never having to replenish it once many loaves were eaten had to be the best thing that could possibly happen to her.

She considered the way the potbellied baker was ogling the precious powder inside the pouch.

If I hand it over now, I won't be hungry for a while. But this is Merlin's gift to… me. What would he think if I traded it for some meager loaves of bread? she thought, and her lips curled.

"Well, are you gonna hand it over?" the baker urged.

Willow licked her lips and took another brief look around the room.

So much bread, she observed. *Enough to never have to bake another loaf again.*

She bound the rope of the pouch together and…

"No!" cried Juniper as she leaped into the air with a screech.

She made a quick glide from the shoulder of her partner to the open bag and seized the pouch by the opening in her beak, flying around the room over pots of flour and sugar, nearly knocking over containers of yeast and water.

"Hey! Give it here, you insolent bird!" the baker yelled as he swiped in an attempt to catch Juniper in his meaty hands.

Juniper flapped enough to avoid each swing of his palms.

"Just take some and go, Willow! I'll catch up with you!" Willow heard the bird call out to her, still dodging the fat man's lashes. She had never seen Juniper move with such swiftness.

She's right, Willow thought again. *It's our only option. Now is the time to act!*

With a quick shuffle of her feet over to one of the wood and metal buckets, Willow took two small loaves of warm bread in her hands. Not knowing what to do next, she tried to get a steady gaze at Juniper with her eyes, but she was too fast for her to keep up. Instead, she called out.

"What next?" said Willow, standing in the same spot as before.

Juniper curved around the table and under the window, close to the brick ceiling.

"Wrap them up in that cloth next to the wine bottles!" Juniper answered, again moving out of the way of the baker's hands.

Before she could move, Willow heard the gritty voice of the baker.

"You'll do nothing of the sort!" he said, shifting his attention to Willow.

He stomped over to where she stood by the door, and Willow moved. But before the baker could lay a finger on her, Juniper dived down hastily, pouch still in her beak, and with all the strength that her lesser talons could muster clamped her pointy toes onto the man's vulnerable head. A shriek of pain escaped from his agape mouth.

The baker, jostled by the fresh sting of bird feet, ran to the left of the girl, where most of the kitchen utensils were. Several pots and pans and rolling pins and spoons and knives and other assortments of baking tools lined the walls and countertop but suddenly were thrown about as the baker crashed into them, trying to unlatch Juniper's talons from the flesh of his pate. Fortunately for him, it worked.

Seizing another opportunity, Willow took the white cloth that lay bunched up next to a couple of fine wine bottles topped with cork and wrapped up the two loaves in her hands, stacking them inside the wrapping. She then dashed out the door with Juniper gliding after.

"Thief!" the baker cried out to the public from the open door. "Thief I say!"

*****

Willow had never had to run so fast in all her days at the orphanage, let alone steal from a stranger. Usually, the only activity she was able to have was during recess outside with Mrs. Veraminta watching them, scowling. But it was never a full-on sprint like she was doing now. Back then, it was just a friendly game of tag or a few minutes on the swing set, which was her favorite thing at the playground, although it was not of the greatest quality. The chains were rusted, and the seat was worn. But those didn't matter to her as long as the thing worked. As for stealing, it was forbidden and would be a one-way ticket to the same room each of the children so desperately avoided.

The adrenaline in her veins overcame the coming swell of guilt building in the back of her mind. Right now, the only thing that mattered was not being caught by anyone and meeting the wizard at Pinner's cave, whoever that was. She felt her legs begin to burn with each step of her run. Her breath picked up, and it seemed it would never return to normal even if she paused for a moment to wait for Juniper. She wondered if the bird even made it out all right.

Suddenly, she heard a familiar squawk, though it was quite muffled, coming from above the crowd she shoved through. It was annoying to have to bump and move through waves of the people in the parade. Each one scoffed and ridiculed her as she pushed past them with desperation.

"Sorry!" she apologized. "I'm sorry! Pardon me! Sorry!"

Regardless of any pursuers, Willow wanted to leave. Thankfully, her disturbing the parade was not enough to pacify the continuing performance of the procession.

Then a sense of dread overcame her. There, ahead of the parade, on the right side of the growing crowd, in between two separate vendors, who were surprisingly unfazed by it, stood a figure dressed in raven robes with an uncanny mask obscuring its face. It was a most terrifying mask. Made of iron and leather it was and smeared with yellow-and-black accents. Its wide, vacant mouth stretched from ear to ear; its eyes were like the night and hollow. No nose holes were present.

There was never an image more frightening that she had ever seen, not even in the depths of dreams her brain imagined. The figure began forward, and Willow felt her heart drop like a stone in her chest. Its gaze met hers. A shiver of sheer terror tingled the back of her neck. In the chaos, Willow felt Juniper return to her shoulder and drop the pouch in her other hand.

"What is that thing?" said Willow. "Has it been here the whole time? Why aren't the others worried about it? What are we to do?"

The exit was in sight: a limestone archway between two buildings built of tan stone with windows, balconies, and no doors. But the crowd they were in the midst of seemed to tighten as if more and more people gathered into the crowd for the parade.

"Run!" squawked Juniper. "That is a Specter, one of the Caliphate's spies that roam the land, searching for enemies of the state! Magical executioners they are!"

Using the rhythm of the parade, the two shuffled their way closer and closer to the corridor, the alleyway, from whence the archway led. Simultaneously, the Specter watched them with an unbroken stare, a menacing glare, and kept a slow pace diagonal to their destination as if to meet them at the archway and flank them. The crowd, ever oblivious, continued their trancelike dance.

Then it appeared that the parade was turning to the right of the corridor by which they sought to leave, and a blip of worry beset them with the thought of failing to break away from the throng. This direction, which turned out to be where the mass was headed, was, in fact, in favor of the Specter.

Where did this monster come from? Willow thought quickly.

She pushed between more dancers and singers, limbered between a few men on horses, and squeezed past a troupe of musicians, covering her ears.

Almost there, almost there, she assured herself.

At once, the Specter raised a frail arm, the hem of the sleeve draping down to its waist, and opened a hand with wide, gloved fingers. A few green sparks flew from the fingertips, crackling. Then a glow emanated from the palm, a steady green darker than the sparks, and the figure gripped his chest tightly. The verdant gleam increased the longer its palm rested there. Then with a flick of its wrist and extension of its arm, a flash of green light flickered, and two creatures sprang forth from the figure's hand as if a portal had been opened, and the exit was out of its hand. The creatures flopped around in the dirt, covered in a clear slime.

Through the thin gaps between the pilgrims, Willow caught brief glimpses of the foul things. Only a mere two feet tall with olive-green skin and messy black hair, the minions made a sound of gurgling and choking. Finally, they stood up on their thin but stiff legs and peered into the crowd with their lifeless large eyes scanning.

Soon, the minions took off at a surprising speed for their size once Willow crossed into the alleyway as the crowd of pilgrims entered the curve around the block. Juniper watched as the minions jumped all the way up and over the dancing people into the alleyway after them.

"They're coming!" she squawked. She flapped again to keep up with Willow's hurried pace.

Past sandstone walls and through the marble archway they went as the chase began. The minions' feet made very wet squelches in the dirt, leaving mud in their footprints. The city's streets, unknown to Willow's memory, felt like a labyrinth, a maze. Each turn and alleged shortcut only furthered their confusion of the entire neighborhood. Luckily for them, no one else was there to get in their way, as they had all joined the parade moments ago. There was no one to slow them down or stop them.

Seconds passed, and the ugly things were right on their tail, slowly beginning to close the gap that had previously been just shy of three yards. The horrible sound of their gurgling was once again heard in Willow's ears. To make matters worse, they began to chomp and gnash with their sharp, uneven teeth inside their angled beaks.

"What are they?" Willow cried. "I don't like them! Make them go away!"

"I wish I could," Juniper yelled, flapping madly. "I don't know what to do!"

Ahead of them, next to a few empty vendor stations, lay a wheelbarrow full of strange-looking fruits or vegetables. Their skins were beginning to dry in the hot sun, making them wrinkled and rather unpleasant to look at. Beyond it, the secondary marketplace stretched down the long street to much similarity of the previous plaza area.

"This place is endless!" Willow called out in frustration.

She was advancing fast toward the wheelbarrow's spot. Coming upon it, she summoned whatever remaining strength she had—she was growing tired by the second—and pushed over the wheelbarrow, spilling the weird food all into the street of dirt, particles of brown, black, and beige sticking to them. Willow then continued into the marketplace as the horrific creatures stomped all over the squishy fruit-vegetables when they passed over them, each one becoming a mashed mess under their clawed toes.

Then it seemed as if she could hear them speak! Their voices were fraught with fell rasps, their intonation very jumbled and throaty.

"Come here, come here!" they said. "Eat! Eat we want! Lick the meat! Suck the blood! Chew the bones! Yum, yum, yum!"

Their voices were atrocious and disgusting. The sound of them made Willow sick to her stomach.

On they went after her, still with their razored fingers raised. Willow's legs burned, her feet sore from running. She wished she were back home, if you could call an orphanage a home, where she could just sit and talk to Leo with his milk mustache again. It was nice to actually have someone other than the headmaster to talk to for once. But Leo was at home, and if she wasn't quick now, she wouldn't be going home.

At the other end of the street, Willow saw a grid gate made of steel and chain. It was completely shut, meaning no one came in or out. Two paths diverted away from each other in a straight line, left and right. Thinking on her feet, she decided to curve to the right with Juniper trailing her. The green minions were gaining on her now. It seemed their stamina knew no end. Could they really keep going and going without stopping or pausing? Above them, the sun continued its sweltering stare, and the sweat began to build up in her tunic, her bangs sticking to her forehead again. The cloak she wore wasn't helping, but it did keep the sun off her face and neck.

She curved to the right, past a few wooden barrels stacked against one of the walls in the alley, and then she saw it. All hope of escape vanished; her fear and dread intensified. There, at the end of the turn, was nothing but a dead end, a wall, a dry, dusty sandstone wall with no special features or qualities. Yet it seemed to mock her and laugh at her knowing full well that it was the reason those minions would get to her now. She was defenseless against them. She had nothing save for the Shimmer and the bread she stole.

But then something changed, something in the air. Or was it only the sound in her ear? She heard the sound of hooves fast approaching.

Clip-clop, clip-clop, clip-clop.

They were coming from down the street, past the portcullis. Willow saw dust picking up as whatever it was ran closer and closer. Soon enough, she could see a rider atop a horse, but it wasn't just any natural horse. It was a zebra with its exotic striped body of black-and-white. The rider's saddle was a rich leather. The reins he gripped in one hand; a shamshir in the other. The curved nature of the thin sword meant it was designed for cutting and slashing. As he raised the weapon in the air, Willow felt a sense of hope return!

The minions, who had finally turned the curve, were unlucky with their timing. The rider came through past the corner, and with two swift strokes of the sword, he dispatched the green mongrels from their miserable existences, a few spills of blood ejecting from their wounds.

The minions' lifeless bodies slumped over onto the dirt, the last of their gross, unsettling gurgling fading out. The rider brandished his sword, quick movements meant for show, before he sheathed it inside its curved scabbard. He shushed the horse and, with a click, ordered it to walk over to where the girl and the bird were, stacked against the wall.

Lowering his facial covering, the rider spoke with a midrange voice. Willow could tell that he was not as old as he appeared.

"Are you all right, miss?" he asked, keeping his hands tight on the reins. "You do realize that way is a dead end, right? You should've made a left, not a right."

"Yes," said Willow blandly. "I know that now."

Chapter 6

Pop Goes the Thief

The afternoon sun had found its place in the sky. Sounds of the parade began to fade out in the distance as if the crowd of pilgrims was making their way out of the city. The wind blew softly through the windows of the surrounding buildings and through Willow's hair. The zebra looking down at her snorted loudly, clopping once more.

The rider, dressed in his form-fitting black tunic and gray boots, removed the hood of his cloak and ruffled his blond hair with a gloved hand.

"You don't look familiar," he said. "Why were those Kappas chasing you? It can't be because they were hungry. They'd have sought thicker prey."

"Was that supposed to be a compliment?" Willow said sarcastically as she moved away from the wall and picked up the bread still wrapped in white cloth. She wasn't sure how to take the rider's comment.

Juniper fluttered back to her shoulder.

"An observation, more or less," the rider said, his hands returning to the reins. "Those things aren't normally seen inside a city like this. Their stomping grounds are found in the south, where the marshes dwell. These must have wandered in perhaps."

The rider glanced down at the Kappas lying stiff in the dirt, slashes on their necks draining blood that stained the ground. He knew what they were from their anatomy: beaked mouths, green skin, and hard shells on their backs.

"They didn't come from there," said Willow, drawing nearer to the zebra.

Then Juniper, who moved to her forearm when she gestured, spoke next.

"Those Kappas were summoned by a Specter," she chirped. "We saw it when we were moving through the parade. We tried to slow them down, but alas, they backed us into a corner."

"Well, then, I believe a thank-you is in order," the rider said, lifting his chin and grinning.

He was a fair lad. He was just beginning to grow stubble on his chin and a few hairs above his lip. Time had not taken its toll too much yet for him. His eyes were a soft hazel.

"I cannot thank someone if I don't know their name," said Willow.

She was always told to use manners with strangers. She was thankful that the orphanage taught her that much at least. Yet it seemed that she remembered that some of the other girls her age had not paid attention.

"If you must have a name, then the name you shall call me is Rowan. No more, no less," the rider said. "This is Racer, my loyal steed. You will never find a faster horse."

Rowan grinned and gestured to the zebra, who grinned awkwardly. Then he spoke too!

"It is a pleasure to make your acquaintance."

Racer's voice was mild and polite. He bowed his head, and the black hair of his mane drooped down with it, and once his pleasantry was over, he raised it back up to normal. Indeed, he was a handsome horse, and his stripes made him all the more brilliant. It almost put Juniper's bright beak to shame.

"Tell me," Rowan began, "what business do you have in Al Wafra? And what would a Specter need with you?"

He dismounted and patted Racer, keeping his gaze on the girl and her bird. Willow stepped closer again, clutching the wrapped bread under one arm and holding the pouch of Shimmer in her other hand. She wasn't sure if she needed to be honest or if she should lie again, though the latter would only make the stone in her stomach, which had been there since she lied to the guards earlier, worse. Seeing as how Rowan saved her, it might be okay to be truthful.

I guess it wouldn't hurt to tell him everything, she thought. *But I should keep my name different.*

"I," she started, but the truth was hard to spit out, "stole some bread from the baker."

Willow bowed her head in shame and stared at the ground.

"That's why we were running."

"That explains the chase but not why a Specter summoned minions. Are you a fugitive? Do you know if the Caliphate would be looking for you? Specters usually target those who have escaped their grasp or people they know have a connection to magic. They are drawn to them. They can sense magic like a hound sniffing the trail of a deer. But you don't seem like anything of that sort. Are you carrying something like that? A wand or weapon imbued with it? Surely it can't be the bread you stole. There is nothing magical about this land anymore.

"That baker may be suspicious, but I can assure you that there are no arcane qualities about him. Would that there were, he would quickly be found out, and the Specters would drag him from here to the north, bringing him before the Gilded Caliph herself. What about that pouch of yours? You seem to be holding on to it tightly? What secrets does it contain, hmm?"

Willow was reluctant.

"It's none of your business what's inside it! It was a gift."

She held the bag close to her chest like a newborn pup.

Rowan's curiosity was not dissuaded. He snatched the pouch from her with one swift swipe as if he had practiced swiping for many years. Willow winced and immediately tried to take the pouch back but was thwarted by Rowan's strong palm against her face. It stank actually from the sweat that had built up from handling the reins.

"Give that back! It does not belong to you! It's mine! It's mine!" she cried, but the rider in black held the pouch at a distance.

When Juniper tried to peck at him, Racer stepped and blocked the way. As a zebra, he was much taller and bulkier than a toucan, so it was quite easy for him to protect his master. Juniper backed off.

"Seems you cherish this little item of yours," said Rowan. "Let's have a peek inside."

He began to untie the string around it.

"What could it be? Gold? Sticks? Food? Maybe even a precious heirloom you want to keep safe? Perhaps I will take it as a rew..."

His words were cut off, and his mouth gaped when his eyes feasted on the revelation inside the pouch. The same purplish glow illuminated his face, his pupils shining with violet. Then Racer witnessed the surprise therein, and he, too, was agape, tilting his snout in wonder. A tear almost came to Rowan's eye before he quickly closed and retied the string as tight as it had been before. With his grip loosened, the pouch was hastily retrieved by Willow.

"Where did you get that?" Rowan asked with a hand on his hilt. "How did a scrawny, messy child get your hands on that? I'd wager that you stole it. A thief! Yes, that is probably it. Now, girl, hand it over. You have no idea the power you hold in your hands!"

With his left hand clutching his sheath, Rowan reached out his right with an open palm beckoning for the pouch.

Willow wasn't sure how to react. The young man wasn't exactly shouting down to her like Mrs. Veraminta would have. But Juniper certainly wasn't having it.

"Now back off, you! She has had quite the tumultuous day, and you are shouting at her! Imagine if you were in her position. How would you feel?" she clacked, pointing her beak in a rude fashion at the fair-haired young man.

"I would feel worse knowing I was a thief!" Rowan retorted, his right hand moving to the hilt.

Willow felt like running, but the act would be futile with the zebra against her.

"I did not steal the Shimmer!" she declared. "It was given to me by a wizard, a very nice, old, helpful wizard who dropped me off here. There! That is the truth! The pouch was a gift. A gift!"

She wanted to sob, but her anger beat out the embarrassment inside her, and she began to walk away from the rider and his horse with Juniper on her arm.

Rowan's demeanor suddenly shifted at the mention of wizard.

"Just a moment," said Rowan. "What was the name of this wizard who gave you this pouch of Shimmer?"

Willow paused, her back still turned away from Rowan and Racer. Although they had saved her from the minions, what evidence had they given that they could be trusted? He hadn't put his hands on her, nor had he posed a major threat to her. His sword still slept in its sheath.

"Should I tell him, Juniper?" whispered Willow, hoping Rowan couldn't hear.

Juniper looked back at Rowan briefly. The man was rubbing his chin with patience and contemplation. The bird then returned her gaze to Willow.

"I believe we can trust him. Go ahead," she replied softly.

Willow turned around and stood in place, taking in a deep breath and sighing long and slow. She crumpled her lip in worry. She was afraid that if she mentioned Merlin's name, perhaps he would become a target, and she would be to blame. But what other choice did she have?

"His name is Merlin," she spoke.

*****

The white moon began to bare its light to the land, casting a gentle glow onto the decrepit trees and rocks and earth. Even the wilting grass growing feebly in the reddish dirt felt its touch. The path ahead was one of smooth sand that was distinguishable from the landscape around her. A mile out from the path trod a dried, fruitless riverbed with nothing but pebbles, bits of twigs, and shells to line the soggy basin. Ahead in the distance, a woodland of desolate trees stood united in their sterility, their dying bark beginning to peel off their stalks. The world around them felt like a body suffering from an incurable disease or like a widespread city decaying and fading away.

Willow wasn't exactly comfortable sitting behind Rowan as Racer trotted along the sandy path. She had wrapped her arms around him and held him with a moderate tightness. Juniper perched on Racer's lower back just before his tail began its descent. Although the sun made the air warm and her body hot, the air now was cool with the wind blowing once more.

Rowan kept his gaze to the horizon, focusing on safely navigating them through the desert. The trail wasn't foreign, but he had never ventured in the night. He would always rest when night fell and set up his tent a ways away from the main road in case any bandits or other mystery folk decided to strike. He was used to silence when he traveled, though occasionally, he would detail with Racer the many stories he was told as a child. But now with a new face, the silence was awkward and discomforting.

"You haven't told me your name," he said, but then he hoped she was already asleep so he could feel less antsy. Then he felt her head lift off his back. "You know mine. It's only fair that I know yours, don't you think?"

Willow blinked rapidly and then held her eyes open halfway. She was drowsy from the brief nap she had taken since she was finally able to sit again. That had been a few hours ago, when sunlight still warmed her back and Juniper flew beside them. She yawned.

"Willow," she said. "My name is Willow."

"And where do you come from, Willow?" spoke Rowan, still clasping Racer's reins.

"I come from Staten Island. In America."

"America? I've never heard of that name. Is it a city or town or village? Is it in Kastallon?"

"I don't think so," she muttered sleepily. "It's a country."

"A country?" said Rowan. "And who is the ruler of this country called America?"

His pronunciation of her nation's name made Willow giggle slightly.

"Woodrow Wilson," she said clearly. Her drowsiness was wearing off.

"Ah, King Woodrow of America. The name does not inspire hope."

"He's not a king," said Willow. "We call him president."

"Pre…si…dent? What is a pre…si…dent?"

"It's like a king, but without all the power," said Willow. "He can give orders, but those orders have to be checked by other officials, like judges or representatives. If he were to say 'I want all of the roads to be painted yellow,' then that order would be sent to the other two groups, and they would have to agree in order for it to happen. The president cannot do things without the consent of the others. My teacher told me that. He said, 'That's how we keep a balance of power.' It's how we avoid what they call tyranny."

"If all the roads," began Rowan, "were painted yellow, it would be too easy for someone to follow your trail, not to mention it would look rather displeasing to the eye. They should stay the natural color they are. This way, you can cover your tracks and get away."

"Are you always covering your tracks, Rowan?" Willow inquired.

She looked behind her and saw the tops of the walls and twinkling lights of Al Wafra disappear as they continued. Rowan fell silent at the question and remained silent for a brief moment. Then he began again.

"I have to. Ever since the Caliphate invaded ten years ago, I haven't stopped covering my tracks. The Caliph saw to it that my village was destroyed when they would not submit to her way of life, to her religion. I remember seeing the flames spread and consume my father's house. I still remember the words that he used his last breath on, and they stick like thorns in my ear.

"'Run! Run, my son! Take Racer and go as far as he may take you!' I haven't stopped running since. You might think that was my first time in Al Wafra, but you would be wrong. This is as far west as I've been in a while. Al Wafra has changed little since she moved in. Cursed be her name! I remember when it used to be full of life, bursting at the seams with greenery. Now look at our land, lifeless and dull. Pitiful is what it is. I digress.

"I've had to live life—for the past decade, that is—as what is called a nomad," said Rowan before he covered his mouth to let out a quick cough.

"What's a nomad?" asked Willow, rubbing her eyes.

The moonlight was right above them now, and the sand twinkled a more gentle dance as opposed to its sunlit one. Juniper was still nestled behind Willow, softly cooing through her nostrils.

"A nomad is a man or woman who has no home, someone who wanders the land, taking shelter only in the places known to keep them safe. But now the former safe places are corrupt and now send watchers in the night to check every corridor, every basement, every attic, and every cupboard for those giving nomads refuge. There was once a time when it was not only Racer and myself. Yes, three it used to be.

"Two years ago, I met a girl who was also forced to live life on her own, though her family cast her out when she did not agree with the new faith. We met in a tavern on the road between Etarish and Villendralier called the Snoozing Sloth. We shared a few pints…"

"What's a pint?" Willow interrupted, not knowing that she had done so.

Rowan scowled.

"Are you so dull that you don't know what pint means?" he said sternly. "And that you know not to butt in when someone is talking? How incredibly rude! Honestly, did you…"

His words trailed off as Willow's gaze shifted to the horizon ahead, where the beginnings of a spooky, shadowed woodland began to rise from where sky met soil. But in the distance between Racer's front legs and the first barren root of that dry, dead forest stood an old woman.

"Look, Rowan. Look!"

Willow pointed with her right hand. Juniper blinked her beady eyes open and let out a yawn.

"You did it again!" Rowan said, angrily grabbing the reins.

Racer reared back on his haunches and came to a standstill.

"What is it, boy? What's the matter?"

Rowan patted the soft black mane slumped on Racer's neck.

"There's a woman on the road ahead," said Racer, snorting. "She's just standing there, no one else. No mount. No supplies. Seems she's alone."

In the dead of the night, when only the moon and its lunar light allowed the world to be seen, the old woman began to step forward at a slow pace. In their eyes, she moved weakly, as if she had been in the desert for ages. Barely they could see the sand trail left behind her as she trod, a rounded path in the grains that piled up a few centimeters on the sides as she trudged. The night wind blew a decent breeze, enough to send Willow's cloak tossing behind her. She held on to Rowan a bit tighter than normal.

"Stay here," Rowan said, swinging his left foot over and dropping onto the sandy path they stood on. He patted Racer gently. "If anything happens, you run."

Rowan stroked his mane briefly. He then turned and began to close the gap between the crone and himself, keeping his hand steady on the hilt of his shamshir.

"Steady there!" he said, raising his free hand. "What is your business on these roads? I can't think of a reason why someone like you should be out all alone at a time like this. What brings you out here?"

Rowan was now only a few yards away from her. Underneath her hood and cloak, he could see her tattered clothes, wrinkled face, and withered gray hair that dangled in front of her ears.

She's walking with a limp, Rowan affirmed mentally.

Then the old crone croaked, her voice melancholy, "Is that a horse I see? Oh, bless you in the name of Fikra! I've been walking back to Al Wafra for two nights now, but"—she glanced at her legs, then back at Rowan—"I don't think I can make it with these feeble sticks for legs. Please, kind sir, could you carry me back to the city? I would really like to see my family! If you can, I can pay you in gold."

If he didn't have company, he would have probably sped past her on Racer, not batting an eye toward the fact that she was an older woman. Travelers at night weren't his business. If they were in trouble, it was their problem. Back then, his only concern was taking care of his horse and himself. Anyone outside of that was either an ally or a threat. He was no white knight, no perfect soul or saint, who exchanged time for gold. This gammer was no different.

"There's no room on my horse for you," said Rowan, stopping his stride. "I'm afraid you will have to pray for your legs, dearie. We cannot all be granted strength. Now I must ride on, and you will have to move!"

He walked back to Racer and put a foot in the saddle. But before he could clamber aboard, the old crone chimed in once more.

"You would mean to abandon a widow in the desert?" she cried.

It seemed she moved up closer to the party when Rowan turned back.

"How heartless can you be? I have nothing!"

Rowan drew his shamshir sword.

"Back away if you want to keep your life!"

He now stood firmly in his stance, feet squared and shoulders primed. He held the curved sword in one hand and kept the other tight on its scabbard. The tip of the blade came nervously close to her neck.

"You will tread no farther," said Rowan. "You will step aside and let us pass. Our mission, which need not be explained to you, is one of significant urgency, and I will stop at nothing to see it through—not for a helpless child and certainly not for a dead woman either."

The old woman backed off. But then she began to do something neither Rowan nor Willow and the animals would have guessed. She began to smile, a most heinous, unsettling smile.

"Men like you deserve to be lost, deserve no redemption. Fikra has no place for you in her eternal garden. It will not be blemished by your tainted soul," she said, her words trailing off into a skin-scratching cackle. "Arise now, friends! Take from them what we are owed. Tribute to Fikra so that we may not be hungry. May she curse this fiend for his dishonor."

At the sound of *dishonor*, piles of sand around them took form, and their grains began to sift down to reveal humanoid figures wrapped in beige and dark brown linens as if to camouflage into the sand. They carried knives and small razors; one of them carried a whip. The bandits then began to surround them, prowling. Willow could hear their snickering and jeering like a crowd of hyenas.

Rowan kept his sword ready, holding it in a fighting stance. His eyes scanned each of the bandits with their rags and rugged weapons.

No way could I take them all, he thought, his eyebrows furrowing.

Willow clung tightly to Racer's saddle; Juniper took a defensive stand atop her.

"What do we do, Rowan?" Willow cried, her eyes wide and alert.

Rowan swung his shamshir in an attempt to ward off one of the bandits who were edging closer to them.

"Get you back!" he said. Then to Willow, he added, "There's too many of them! We need a distraction, something to affect them all at once."

The old woman's cackling ceased, and she spoke once more with a sinister tone. The bandits continued their slow trudge closer and closer.

"Take what is owed, my friends. Kill them and lay their bodies for the pheasants. Leave the horse! We shall gut it and feast upon it. Its bones shall grow our crops, and the marrow will feed our children! Go now. Have at them!"

Racer understood the crone's words clearly and whinnied loudly, raising his front legs in defiance. Upon their descent, he used his hind legs to kick away one of the ragged bandits.

Other thieves brandished their weapons, and Rowan struck back! The clang of metal against metal rang in Willow's ears. Rowan swung his shamshir again and thrust it into the chest of an outmaneuvered bandit, blood soaking it when he drew it back.

Watching the fallen bandit slump to the sand threw the other thieves in a rage. Their movements became swifter, and their daggers were furious! Rowan was almost overtaken when Racer knocked another bandit away with his strong hind legs.

Then Rowan remembered something that had surprised him hours ago, something about Willow.

"Willow! Where is the Shimmer?" he yelled over the battle, kicking another bandit away, the ragged figure tumbling down.

Willow felt for the pouch. It was still tied to her belt securely from before. She sat up and made space for Rowan as he mounted again. Two of the bandits were gone, and there were but a few seconds of air to limber back to Racer.

"Here! Here it is!" Willow said, holding the pouch out to Rowan, who sheathed his sword and gripped the reins in one hand.

He made a quick sound, and Racer took off! His hooves left shallow prints in the sandy path. But the bandits did not give up. They began to run with a peculiar speed, nearly matching Racer's pace. Willow looked back and saw the old woman mumbling something under her breath and twitching her fingers in an uncanny fashion.

"Lend it here," Rowan said as Willow plopped the pouch in his free palm.

The bandits soon began to close in, swiping at them. Willow was pretty sure she felt a tiny sting in her back from the swing of a dagger, and she winced. Rowan pulled the string open with his teeth, revealing the purplish powder, and held the pouch close to his lips. Willow could not make out his whispering, but she faintly heard it as she clung tightly to him.

Suddenly, she smelled smoke! Something was burning, smoldering, and igniting! She peeked around Rowan's shoulder and saw the burlap of the pouch falling to cinders, and a swirling ball of blaze and heat formed in his hand. The entire process was only seconds long. Rowan heaved the burning ball of fire over his head and...

Boom!

Crash!

In an instant, the bandits were blown away. Sand and dust and ash were scattered behind them, leaving only embers and streaming steam behind them. As the sand fell, Willow peered once more behind them. The magical old woman was fading from view as wretched roots and tattered bark enclosed the horizon.

They had escaped into the shadowed woodland.

Chapter 7

The Whisper of the Wind

Rowan awoke. His eyes blinked as the daylight shone against the thin cloth of his tent. Shadows of leafless branches were painted on the swaths. But he felt like something was missing. No, *someone* was missing. He went through the events of the previous night and remembered the bandits and the explosion, and he remembered setting up the tent so that he and the girl could...

The girl! he thought, and his nerves spiked.

He tossed away the blanket and quickly cinched his boots on and jumped out of the tent through the limp opening. Outside, he saw nothing but dead or dying trees wrought with desolation. The very grass underneath his boots was grayed and withered, crunching with each stride. The sky above was the same gloom from before, and the sun hid itself behind drapes of clouds, periodically revealing itself in mere passing.

Rowan gulped and closed his eyes, listening closely to the forest around him. He heard no squeak or growl of animals, no tweet or chirp of birds; the wind itself did not rattle through the twigs and thin boughs surrounding him. Quietness and tranquility had taken over. Death—or perhaps only the absence of life—had established its dominion.

Ahead of him, the forest widened, and a path could be seen among the dried, perished forest floor. Footprints made their way into the forest, and Rowan decided to follow them. He looked back and found Racer lying peacefully next to the tent, his head resting softly on the ground.

"Just stay put," whispered Rowan to the horse from afar. "I have got to find her."

Of course he was talking about Willow, as she was not inside the tent when he arose. He briskly fetched his cloak from inside the tent and began to follow the tracks in the grass.

*****

Walking in that shadowed woodland was eerie, to say the least. Without the normalcy of chittering or cooing, the forest felt abandoned, empty. If the trees could speak, Rowan assumed they would cry out for water and reach their arms out, begging for mercy. But alas, the trees adhered to their stoicism and rose like blackened stalks emerging from the earth, their roots surfacing through the ashen turf. Rowan compared them to long fingers stretching from a wooden arm.

"Willow!" Rowan called out, cupping his mouth with both hands.

To his surprise, there was no echo to ring through the forest. It was as if his voice traveled only a few feet like it would in a small, enclosed room. He looked around and saw that nothing had stirred in response to his call—no rustle or pitter or patter. He cupped his mouth once more.

"Willow!" he said.

Then in a softer voice, as if to himself, he muttered, "Where have you gone, girl?"

He walked for a few more minutes through the ghoulish, foul forest, finding nothing but the same as he had seen before: dead, decaying flora showing little signs of life. A few small stones lay about the path like they had been rolled or moved in an odd fashion. In his mind, Rowan felt that she had run away. Or worse, something might have taken her! Had the old crone followed them into the woods? He considered the possibility of it but felt the odds of it were slim. The explosion surely took her out and left nothing behind but sand.

"Willow! Come back! I am right here! Follow my voice!" Rowan called again, yet no response followed. But something did hear his beckoning, something monstrous.

A few seconds after the words trembled away, a fierce shriek sounded above him in the leafless treetops. Although the tops of the trees were without green, the sun still gleamed through the thin cracks. But there was a shadow that covered it briefly as it flew across the canopy. Rowan saw it clearly, though silhouetted, the shape of it at least.

It was birdlike—ten times the size of the average bird, however. It was slightly humanoid but bore the appearance of a great owl. Large, terrible talons descended down from the canopy, and mighty wings fluttered, stirring up the ash and dirt around him. Then he saw the face of the beast! Black eyes like inky orbs stared him down as the creature shrieked once more from its short, sharpened beak!

The beast swooped over him, and the air around him nearly took him away. Rowan flung himself into the grayed grass just in time to avoid the grasp of its clawed feet as it glided back to the treetops. Rowan saw this retreat as the perfect opportunity to gather his feet and flee. Doing so, he snatched up one of the small stones in his hand and darted farther into the forest.

A few minutes passed, and once again, the dreadful bird screeched over him. He gripped the hard rock in his fist and passed more trees on his run. What was this monstrosity? What did it want with him? Where did such a beast come from? Questions were left unanswered as he sprinted, his legs carrying as far as they could. It seemed the path ahead continued forever.

"Away with you!" he yelled to the feathered beast.

He watched the creature begin its turn in the air and descend once more. Rowan turned and stood his ground as the beast soared toward him.

If I aim true and straight for the eyes, perhaps I can disorient it, he thought as adrenaline fueled his focus. He had never seen anything like this horror in his lifetime.

He raised a shivering arm in a position cocked to throw the stone. Again, the creature drew nearer and nearer, screeching and shrieking very loudly. The closer it came, the closer the targets were. The great bird moved with a surprising elegance, spreading its elongated wings out widely.

Steady, he told himself. *Steady on.*

He was grasping the stone so tightly he thought he felt its slight sharpness beginning to pierce the skin of his palm. He ignored the pain and kept his gaze finely tuned to the approaching fiend.

The great bird came within ten feet of Rowan before he launched the cobble with all the strength remaining in his arm and witnessed it slam into the left eye of the bird, who cried out in pain from the impact. The bird fell directly to the ground and writhed like an upset infant, its wings dropping feathers like leaves falling in the winter.

Rowan, still empowered with adrenaline, took off once more down the path, away from the wriggling mass. The agonized squealing began to fade as he ran. He panted more than he expected, taking in rather deep breaths.

The path he trod began to curve left, and ahead, he saw a fairly wide hole that had formed in a dell beside an empty stream. A pebble-covered shore jutted out ahead of it. Seeing as though the creature was far from defeated, only temporarily disabled, now was the time to seek shelter. Rowan darted into the blackness, stepping across the pebbles and mud. The light from outside barely streamed in and gave the cave's interior a dim glow. He had stumbled a few feet inside before he collapsed onto the cold, damp ground of the cavity with his back against the mossy wall.

He had not had to run that fast in months, so his body was not used to the exercise. From within the safety of the cave, Rowan could hear the roar of the creature outside. He tried to steady his breath, but his heart was racing too fast. Then something stirred in the dimness of the cave, something that sounded like shuffling or the quick movements of an animal. Still locked in his fight-or-flight, Rowan turned sharply toward the back of the cave and squinted his eyes to see what it could be, blinking a bit. There seemed to be nothing there at all.

Must have been a rock suddenly falling from the wall, he thought as he continued to calm down.

But when he returned to his original position, a sorrowful noise emerged from the same area, a noise like that of a crying babe. Rowan stood and trod farther into the cave. The light from outside was barely there, but his eyes were quickly adjusting. Blinking rapidly and then stopping, he found that it was a person sitting with arms wrapped around legs, sobbing. The person was keeping a head down on the arms. Rowan frowned nervously.

"W-Willow? Is that you?" he asked softly. He was trying not to scare the child further.

The cloaked head raised and revealed Willow's face, drenched in tears and red—or at least he figured it was red—with emotion. She had probably been crying all morning. Then her eyes went wide, and she jumped up to embrace him tightly. She began to cry even harder into Rowan's black tunic.

Not knowing what to do, Rowan simply said, "Let's get you out of here, girl."

He led her out through the hole in the dell and sat her down in front of a tree that was next to the empty riverbed. He could see its roots sticking out into the dry basin below. Willow's crying had stopped, but her mood remained the same: saddened. She maintained a steady frown and slightly turned-up eyebrows as she talked with Rowan. A period of silence followed. Finally, Willow gave in and began to speak her mind.

"I want to go home," she began, sadness still coating her words. "It is obvious that I do not belong here. The people are mean and selfish. There are creatures flying about that want to eat me. I don't like it here."

She paused for a second, then added, "Why am I even here? Merlin should never have taken me away from the orphanage. What was he thinking?"

She put her face back into her arms and rested them on her knees. She wanted to cry, but it seemed the tears would not come.

Rowan stood abruptly.

"Do not question the choices of Merlin the Magical!" he said.

Then remembering the word *orphanage*, he changed the next words to leave his lips.

"What do you mean orphanage? Is that a city in America? A town perhaps?"

"It is a depressing place. I used to call it home," Willow replied.

"At least you had a home," said Rowan. "At least it is still where you left it. Still standing, I mean. But if Merlin himself brought you here, to Kastallon, then you must have a purpose."

He scratched his chin.

"What purpose?" Willow asked, looking up at him. "I have no special powers. I can't do whatever it was that you did with the Shimmer last night. I don't belong here. I can't be the One Who Unites. I'm just weak and helpless. I want to go home."

"Wait," said Rowan. "You know about the prophecy?"

"Prophecy?" said Willow, sniffing again. "What's a prophecy?"

"A prophecy," said Rowan, "is a prediction given by someone in the past. It is merely a foreshadowing of something or someone to come. Usually, deities or telepaths give prophecies, as no mortal man or creature knows what lies in the future ahead. Has Merlin spoken to you of the prophecy of Skeef? Surely he's told you that much."

"No," puffed Willow. "And I don't much care anymore. We need to find the Wayfinder so he can take me away from this horrible, scary place. I just want to lie in my bed again, where it is warm and cozy and tolerable in the least, much better than this terrible world. Won't you please take me to him? It's a big blue whale that—"

"Yes, yes, I know what he is," said Rowan. "Balaen is the last of his kind, and should he be caught, the Caliph will turn his blubber into margarine for cooking. We cannot allow him to be seen while the Caliph still sits on her wretched throne. You said you couldn't be the One Who Unites. Then you have heard of the Skeef's prophecy!"

"I don't care about that stupid prophecy," said Willow loudly. "I don't want to be whatever that is! I want to go home!"

She stood and stomped her foot like the immature girl she was. But no sooner had her foot struck the ground than her ears picked up an uncanny whisper that seemed to flow in the wind, a whisper that was calling her name. Her face turned a fresh pale color.

Willow.

"Did you hear that?" said Willow nervously. "Something is calling my name."

She looked around and through the trees around her. She even looked back into the cave they had exited. Nothing was there. No one was there.

"I believe you are hearing things," said Rowan, crossing his arms.

But then the sound returned to Willow's ears once more. This time, the whisper's beckoning was stronger.

Willow. Come.

Trancelike, Willow turned and stepped into the empty basin and began to follow its path through the forest. Rowan had his eyes closed last he spoke, and so it was a surprise to him when he opened them again to see Willow pacing away from him down the way of the river. He began to trail behind her.

"Willow!" called Rowan. "Where are you going? What do you hear?"

His attempts to grab her attention again were futile, as the girl continued to wander. Soon, a breeze befell them, and the boughs swung in the wind, almost dancing to a tune they could not hear. The dry basin curved to the left, and more roots of the trees poked through the soil along its sides. Willow didn't notice them. What she did notice, however—and it seemed to worsen her trance—was the seemingly growing opaqueness of the breeze; the wind was slowly taking on a golden hue in thin wisps and streams around them.

A larger trail appeared in the basin, and Willow kept on following it. Rowan noticed it too, and his eyes widened at the sight.

"Willow," said Rowan, "what's going on? This seems… unnatural."

But Willow did not hear him. She continued to follow the golden lights. Rowan did the same. Soon, they came into a part of the forest that was no longer dead or dying or covered in the bleak shadow that consumed the rest. No, this part of the forest was a glade, an open space of green grass surrounded by trees. But there was color, and lots of it. There were different-colored flowers—some red, some blue, some yellow, and some white; there were butterflies fluttering around peacefully, and even the sun could finally be seen high in a sky of blue, which was a shock to them, as all they had seen of the sky was a gloomy, dreary gray.

There in the middle of it all was a small white lamb lying still with its head down and legs curled underneath it, sleeping. The golden streams of the wind were flowing into it as it lay there. Willow was the first to see it, and when she did, she suddenly felt an overwhelming sense of calmness within her, as if all her worries and troubles had been lifted. Rowan soon caught up with her, which was not very hard, as she had stopped when she saw the lamb, and he, too, saw the lamb and felt the same feelings. But he knew exactly what he was seeing.

"I can't believe it," said Rowan.

He wanted to say more but could not find the right words. Instead, he knelt in the short grass beside Willow, who was still standing. Then the two of them both heard a gentle voice within their heads as the sleeping lamb suddenly awoke.

"Welcome, children," said the voice in their heads. "Be at peace and fear not. Be not dismayed or taken aback. You have solace here. You may rise."

As soon as the voice trailed off, Rowan rose and stood beside Willow.

"What is this feeling?" said Willow. "It is like a feeling I have never felt before. It feels as though a heavy weight has been lifted from my shoulders, like all the dirt and muck has been washed away. Rowan, what is this?"

"I am the Numen of your father," said the voice. "The Numen of Merlin, the Numen of Ufton, and the Numen of Lorcrish. I have seen your sorrow and know your suffering."

A few minutes later, there emerged from the tree line in the background a pair of dryads, olive-skinned women wrapped in roots and vines. They approached the two of them in a very stoic stride, pacing themselves with each step. Rowan gawked at them, as he knew that beholding a dryad, especially with the current state of the land, was a sure sign of luck in the highest degree. When they reached their desired spot in the glade, they stood on either side of the lamb, who now stood on all fours. They were almost like nature's angels.

"Why did you bring me here?" asked Willow in a soft voice, putting her hands together below her waist.

The lamb took a few steps forward and kept about six feet of grass between it and the girl. It smiled and blinked as the voice in Willow's head began again.

"My dear Willow," said the voice, "as Merlin said before, you are the daughter of a great family in Kastallon. I have heard your cry and have summoned you to bring you peace, to reassure you of your purpose here. As you are both aware, by now, a curse has been placed on this creation of mine. It is the Caliphate, Willow. They do not belong here. They are conquerors from the Isle Far and Wide that is to the west of this land, this land called the Land Where Castles Lie.

"As for you, you are the answer to this invasion, this oppression. You *are* the One Who Unites, the one who will usurp the Caliph and restore this great land to its former glory. It is my will."

"But how do you know?" said Willow, and the lamb's countenance suddenly fell to a nigh angry scowl.

The dryads crossed their arms in disappointment.

The voice boomed again, saying, "Do you doubt me?"

Willow faltered.

"Are you of so little faith that you do not believe? Was not I the one who gave you safe passage to the orphanage? Did not I send Rowan to save you from those who would see you eaten and left for buzzards?"

"M-Merlin never mentioned you," said Willow dejectedly.

"And yet now you see and still do not believe?" said the voice.

Then the lamb suddenly bent its legs and jumped a short height in place, and a bright light shone into her eyes. Suddenly, she began to see memories that were not hers, visions of the Conquering and the destruction of the Two Thrones. Very faintly, she could see two figures disappearing into the darkness as many armies began to consume the castle behind them. In another, she saw Merlin carrying a bundle of cloth into the mouth of Balaen before slipping to the watery abyss.

Once the visions subsided, Willow fell to her knees. Rowan stooped down to steady her back to her feet.

Willow's eyes began to moisten. Then after a pause, she asked, "What must I do?"

"I will show you the way to Tel Pata, the hidden cave where the sage Pinner dwells. There, your regal guardian awaits your arrival with much anticipation. Now before I send you on your way, allow these words to seep deep into your very essence. Know that I will be with you wherever you go. Know that I will protect you. Know that any promise I make will be kept. Whenever you feel you are lost in the dark, the whisper of the wind will comfort you and guide you, for that whisper is me."

As the final words of the voice rang and faded in her head, the dryads bowed before striding away with the lamb; and where the lamb strode, so did the beauty of the glade with it. Soon enough, though, the lamb began to fade into that golden wind, which began to streak itself through the forest as if to show Willow and Rowan the way out of that shadowed woodland. Willow gathered herself and began to march forward, following the golden light.

Willow wiped her eyes and turned back to see that Rowan had not stirred.

"Come on," Willow said cheerfully. "Let's not keep him waiting!"

CHAPTER 8

A Twinge in the Web of Spies

A dark shadow loomed over Chateau Ensalor, the once proud beacon of royal hope in the northern region of the Land Where Castles Lie. Where there used to be thriving oaks standing tall and strong now resided frail stalks of feeble bark and boughs. The formerly nice and neat stone path to those huge wooden doors now rested in shambles. As for the castle itself, it was an enormous structure with many halls and many pointed towers. Many staircases within led to the second and third floors with their halls and chambers. Though the stone giant stood silhouetted, flickers of light still passed by the windows of the many halls as if people were carrying torches and taking turns monitoring them for trespassers or intruders.

But the most important room in the entire building was the grand and glorious throne room. Through the huge wooden doors and into the main foyer were two more doors that, once opened and walked through, would lead guests and residents into the wide, open space. Lining the space from top to bottom and spaced out evenly across the room were thick pillars meant only for decoration. What would have been a vibrant design of various shapes on the floor was now disheveled and in ruins. The side walls of the interior throne room were lined with many windows, some of which had holes in them, and were struck with the tip-tap of rain. (It was only raining in the north, however, as it was prone to storms of the sort.)

There at the farthest area from the door, so as to make a path from doors to the back, was a twisted, mangled throne blacker than night itself. Upon that wretched throne sat an even more foul and cruel woman. She was known as the Wasp of Kastallon, the Ninth Mother of the Gilded Caliphate, and otherwise named Caliph Nahla of the Buhz Dynasty.

Her hair was a most unsettling ebony; her eyes a terrifying red. Her skin was cold and gray. She dressed herself in a vibrant display of gold, black, and orange with many rings on her arms. Atop her pate, she bore an orange diadem that sprouted angled stalks like antennae. In her right hand, she carried a large scepter with a red crystal at the top. It seemed to glow with an evil haze.

On either side of her throne lay two rows almost like pews in a church, and in those pews sat her Synod of Viziers with their golden robes and turbans. Each of them sat patiently awaiting the command of their Caliph. Ahead of them all, however, standing on the steps leading to the throne itself, were five menacing figures, each with their own unique attribute. They were the protectors and servants of the Caliph, infamously known as the Five Vexes.

From the left, if you were standing before the ensemble, stood Zak, the Sacred Vex, who sported a vertical ring in his helmet. He wore light iron armor. Next to him was Sal, the Caped Vex, who, of course, sported a cape flowing behind his heavy iron armor. Beside him stood Saw, the Silent Vex, whose mouth was wrapped to prevent noise from escaping his lips. He favored light leather armor. Continuing to his left was Hada, the Devout Vex, who had an affinity for magic. He was the only Vex wearing stolen wizards' robes. Lastly and certainly the strangest stood Raj, the Stoic Vex, whose face was rather difficult to read and whose reactions were very, very minor. He held a small black box with shallow scribblings and writings carved into it. Each of the Vexes wielded a different weapon attuned to their fighting style.

Together as a whole—the Caliph, the Viziers, and the Vexes—they watched as the wooden doors opened, and in strode three witches, each dressed in robes, hoods, and cloaks. The three of them were equally wrinkled and equally powerful. The Caliph stood, and when she did, the entirety of the Synod rose with her. The witches stopped a few yards from where the steps began. The whole room was silent with anticipation.

"Welcome, my Seers," said Nahla with a bold voice. "Long has it been since your previous summoning, and your arrival is most appreciated. I take it your birds have gathered quite the important information. What news do you bring?"

She cocked her head back in a smug way.

One of the witches stepped forward and spoke, and although her voice was not loud, the chamber echoed from only her talking.

"Your ladyship," said the witch, "I bring word of strange events that have occurred as of late, a twinge in the web of spies. Only days ago did we spot the last remaining Wayfinder off the western coast. We did not see who strolled out, but we know that if he surfaced near the land, he was definitely carrying cargo. That being said, things in Kastallon have not been the same since his surfacing."

"Indeed," said the witch to her right. "Sister Kestrel speaks the truth. But I have witnessed a most deleterious threat just outside of Al Wafra. The moon was newly risen, as the night had just conquered the day. My minions and I set out to intercept what one of our Specters had seen inside the city. We lie in wait for just the right moment, taking refuge in the sands beside the main path. Minutes passed, and before long, we could hear the subtle vibrations of hooves drawing closer and closer, accompanied by two voices, one young and another younger, a young man and a girl.

"Seeing them, I hoped to stop them, which I did by disguising myself as a hapless traveler in dire need of safe passage back to the city. But the foolish young man refused, and yet I expected as much from him! My brethren and I pounced, and soon, their swords clashed with his! But here is the unexpected part, your ladyship. Here I tell you that they wielded Shimmer!"

The whole room gasped.

"The young man used it to cast an explosion spell that decimated my entire platoon! I managed to flee at the right moment, and they vanished into the Shriveled Forest."

"This," said the last witch, "is where my story matches with Sister Cliona's that you have just heard. When the moon retired and the sun took its place, one of my Strix nearly caught the same young man running through the forest. The girl, according to him, had awakened before him, and though my Strix had not seen her, it appears our suspects eventually met inside a cave within a dell next to the empty riverbed."

"Stop!" said Nahla, raising a hand. "I shall hear no more. You speak of a girl traveling with a young man. What is the nature of this young girl? Surely you know that much with your roaming eyes across the land."

The Caliph reclined back into her throne.

"Yes," said Kestrel. "She is most displeased with her circumstances. She has begged the boy to leave and find the Wayfinder again. She is defenseless, helpless, weak."

"You say this," said Nahla. "But it does not explain why this foolish young man, who apparently has a connection to magic, would defend this girl. Why would he risk his life in a skirmish in which he is outnumbered? Hmm? Must there be something special about this girl?"

"Allow Sabrine," said the witch next to Cliona, "to share a most peculiar detail in this little tale of ours. Would you like to know what another Strix witnessed in the heart of that forest?"

"Out with it!" said Nahla aggressively. "No games or questions."

"At once," said Sabrine. "Deep within the Shriveled Forest, one of my birds told me, a strange phenomenon occurred. There, in a glade not far from the eastern exit, this phenomenon temporarily transformed the environment back to its original state. Lots of color was seen again, and those disgusting flowers were sprouting up everywhere. The bird saw the girl follow a golden stream of wind into this glade and, from the frail branches where it perched, watched as they conversed with a small, weak, pathetic lamb."

The whole room gasped and began to murmur in low voices.

"You mean," said Nahla, "to imply that the children spoke to him? He whose name shall never be spoken in this castle again?

Impossible! No one has seen him or felt him since our regime took over the land. How can we trust the utterings of a bird?"

"Have faith," said Kestrel this time. "Our Strix cannot tell lies. It is not in their nature. And their eyesight is pure, unfailing. What they see and say will always be the truth."

"Yes," said Cliona, stepping out. "I second that statement, your ladyship. These creatures are very talented and trustworthy. They are and will never be against you."

A clap of thunder nearly shook the room, yet the inhabitants therein were not roused. The Caliph took a deep breath and covered her mouth with her hand in thought. Inside, she was trembling, and it was taking every single ounce of willpower to hide her inner feelings.

"So," said Nahla carefully, "what you are saying is that you believe your Strix, these birds, have found…the One Who Unites? That the prophecy I have so annoyingly heard for the past decade is, in fact, true? And you believe it is this girl?"

"Why else," said Sabrine, "would he summon her when she is at her lowest? Moments before the encounter, she was begging to be returned back to—oh, what was it? What was the word the girl spoke? Ah yes, back to the orphanage."

The Caliph stood and stepped forward from her throne. She proceeded to step down the steps leading to her throne, and the Vexes parted to let her pass through them. Then after she was past, they returned to their original places. The Caliph took a few more steps closer to the witches and stopped a yard or two ahead of them. They noticed her brow was furrowed, and her countenance unsettled. She was very perturbed by the witches' news.

"So it is true, then," said Nahla. "The One Who Unites is not from our world.

"Ah," said Cliona, "but we have the wisdom to suggest that she is a Kastallonian. The daughter of the former duke and duchess, whom you so excellently dispatched long ago."

"How is that possible?" asked Nahla. "They have no children, no heirs. They are naught but two feeble people with nothing to claim but their lives. It has been so long since then. How could that be possible?"

She raised her scepter at them, and the Vexes took battle stances. They stood fast, ready to either destroy the witches or protect the Caliph.

Kestrel smirked and bowed her head briefly.

"Perhaps we should let their former magistrate, the mysterious Merlin the Magical, explain. We have felt his presence too since the whale surfaced. Long has it been since his essence was felt in Kastallon. Our spies have not seen him, but that does not mean he isn't lying around in the Tels with his brethren."

The Caliph and the Vexes, who still stood vigilant, backed off and maintained their original positions. None of them uttered a word, and neither moved till the Caliph commanded it. For the Caliph, she lowered her scepter and gave a deep, frustrated sigh. A moment passed, and she began.

"It is settled, then," said the Caliph. "Find the wizard and make him squeal. Show no mercy. I want every drop of knowledge squeezed out of him like a boa strangles a rat. We shall find this girl and slay her. For as long as the duke and duchess remain dethroned, our power shall not falter!"

When her words had ceased, she tapped her scepter hard on the floor.

"Now," said Nahla again, "I've no further need for the three of you. You may return to your towers."

The witches turned around and made for the door with the same slow pace that they had entered with, step by step by step until the door closed behind them. The Caliph then began her return to her seat, and the Vexes repeated the same sidestep movement as before.

Just as her bottom met the throne's seat, one of the viziers to her left stood. He was a stout man with a thin black beard that curled at the end. He bowed to the Caliph.

"Permission to speak, your ladyship," said the vizier.

The Caliph nodded.

"Thank you, your ladyship. Should we find the wizard Merlin, what of this girl who we assume is the One Who Unites? What is to become of her?"

"The wizard," said Nahla, "will lead us right to her. Once I have her in my presence, she will regret the day she ever stepped a single foot back into Kastallon. As for that assumption, we must assume that she is such and should not be taken lightly. We do not know her motives, only that she has spoken with the lamb. She is just a child, a puny, tottering delinquent who is not a match for the strength in me.

"Witness this scepter, my Synod! See how it glows with the vitality of Fikra! Do you doubt her power? Do you not believe she will prevail? Did my sisters not descend from the Summit of the Great Wasp and inherit her influence? Should your faith in me fall, by association, your faith in Fikra falls. And if that be the case, this entire chamber is full of dead men."

The vizier sat back down with haste. To defy the orders of the Caliph meant to defy the orders of Fikra, and that meant certain death.

The Caliph then spoke again.

"Let that be a reminder to you all," said Nahla. "I only wish we could find the sniveling worm and gut her here and now. I would do it myself, of course after making her squirm."

Sal, the Caped Vex, did something unexpected to the lot of the entire chamber. He removed his helm and turned to the Caliph to kneel. None had seen his face before and were rather surprised by his handsome visage. His face was clean-shaven, and his hair was tied back. He paid respect to the Caliph with his different-colored eyes—one blue and one green. His voice sounded extremely different without the muffling from his helm.

"My Caliph, Wasp of Kastallon and Ninth Mother," said Sal, "allow me to find this worm and bring her to this very room. My horse is swift, and my blade is true. I will strike down anyone who would stand in our way. Would you grant me this honor, your ladyship?"

"Why should I?" said the Caliph. "Why not dispatch the Gilded Legion across the land and devastate those who do not submit? What makes you better fit than an entire army?"

The Caliph crossed her legs and relaxed in a smug, comfortable sort of way. The Synod of Viziers had their gazes fixated on the still-kneeling Vex. The other Vexes also turned and waited with anticipation for the response to follow the Caliph's questioning.

Sal, not even breaking a sweat, clenched his teeth behind his lips before he said anything.

"Because," said Sal, "I know how to find her."

CHAPTER 9

In the Cave of Pinner Vemtal

It was noon by the time Willow and Rowan finally made their last steps out of the Shriveled Forest. They were following the golden streams of wind that Skeef had made for them, and they continued southeast into a wilting grassland. Ahead of them, however, the empty river basin continued to stretch for miles. In the distance south of them, they could see the hazy view of the Bell Mountains with the tallest of them being Ittermount. The summit of that great rock was hidden in the grayness of the sky's gloomy sea.

As they walked, the only thought in their heads was how in all of Kastallon were they going to explain what they saw to Merlin. Soon enough, though, Rowan swore he could hear the clopping of hooves closing in behind them.

"Someone's coming!" said Rowan, making a grab for his sword and panicking when he realized that he had left his scabbard in the tent he had made when they first entered the forest.

He patted his waist desperately.

"Confound it! My sword eludes me. Get behind me, Willow!"

The tree line of withering conifers they had just come out of was still visible, and they turned to brace themselves for the coming visitor. Willow, seeing that Rowan was a whole head taller than her and more, hid behind his broad stature.

"What could it be?" said Willow. "Didn't we blow up the witch in the desert? I mean, I did not see anyone else inside the woods."

She gulped.

"I've not the slightest," said Rowan, still bracing. "Whatever it is, be prepared to run as fast as your legs can take you. Do not delay. Do not hesitate."

Rowan balled his fists and made himself ready for a scuffle. Anticipation began to transform into worry as the rustling and clopping began to draw nearer and nearer.

They are too light to be bukavacs, he thought. *Those are horse hooves.*

Then a familiar voice rang out from among the tree line.

"Rowan! Willow! We're coming!" said the mild and polite voice, though it was stressed.

The voice was followed by the swift appearance of a zebra ridden by a toucan, racing out of the brush and crunching on the fallen, scattered twigs. Trot after trot, Racer and Juniper soon caught up to Rowan and Willow, who were happily agape. Rowan embraced Racer with arms around his shaggy neck while Juniper perched on Willow's arm and cooed.

"It is nice to see you again," said Willow with a smile. "I was wondering where you were, you and Racer both. Did you happen to see a lamb on the way? We had a chat with him before he showed us the way out."

Juniper found her way to Willow's shoulder.

"Certainly not," said Racer as Rowan mounted him once again, putting his feet in the hanging stirrups. "We were more worried about finding you two than seeing some small lamb. Let's not go back to that awful place, shall we?"

Willow was then pulled up onto his back with help from Rowan. She was glad to see that all of Rowan's things—sacks, canteen, scabbard, and all—were hanging tidily on either side of Racer's brown saddle.

Rowan held on to the reins with one hand and patted Racer's neck with the other.

"Even if it was not that long ago," said Rowan, "it is good to be back."

The sun was high above them as they continued southeast into the grassland, though the grass was not as green and plentiful as it used to be. The sands of the west began to trickle off into a reddish dirt landscape with very little flora. In the distant east, there were winding hills and rolling valleys that seemed to go on into another foggy forest area. Willow tried not to focus on them and keep her attention on the path ahead, the pebbly, dry path ahead.

*****

It was not long after they began down the path away from the woodland that they struck up a friendly conversation. The company was happy to be reunited and assured themselves not to separate again. Though they had slept some, they were still altogether tired but still happy. The sky, albeit gray, gloomy, and very cloudy, had a few streaks of sun shining through it. Rowan drove while Willow kept her arms around him with Juniper sitting nicely behind.

"How long were you in there," asked Willow, "before you realized we were gone? I mean, surely you did not sleep the whole time. Did Rowan not tell you where he was going?"

"Well," said Racer, "it is actually a funny story, that. From what I can recall—and perhaps Juniper can vouch for us too—it was just dawn when I was awake next to the tent that Rowan had propped up between two trees. I was having quite the loveliest dream about running through the wide, open space that used to be before it was called the Barren Tundra. But the tent was a rather simple tent with its green and olive drapes held together with rope and pikes. I stuck my head inside the opening of the tent and sniffed. Now usually, Rowan has a certain funk to his clothes. The boy has not bathed in a few months."

"Now just a moment, you," said Rowan, offended. "We have been on the run. You cannot expect me to just find a flourishing river in the western tundra."

"Regardless," said Racer, "I could not smell you near me, and I was afraid for you. I removed my head from the tent and searched frantically in the area we'd chosen. I saw neither you nor Willow and feared you had abandoned me! I turned around, and Juniper was perched high up on one of the branches of a nearby tree. 'Do you see them?' I said to her. 'Can you see anything?'

"'I see nothing but trees for many yards,' said Juniper from the branch. 'This fog is not making it any easier! I suggest we go through the woods to find them. They cannot have left the woods, for it is quite easy to get lost in here.'

"Juniper flew back down to meet me. 'Who knows the true way out of this maze of a forest?' At that moment, she sat on my back, and we strolled through the forest, following the path before us. There were many winds and twists and turns, and we feared once again that we would be hopelessly lost forever.

"Suddenly, there was a gust of wind and a very dreadful noise above us. We had never heard anything quite similar to this noise in all our furry and feathery lives. I took off in a strong and quick gallop through the forest, passing tree after tree and root after root, until we came to a dell with a grand hole in its side. We took shelter and hid from whatever was stalking us from above. We were not far inside, as I could see the beast's talons right outside, riddled with wrinkles and equipped with terrifying black claws as sharp as daggers.

"We watched as the beast hunched over and pecked at the dirt and dead grass. It was a rather large owl of some sort with a mangled beak and large, unsettling eyes. It appeared to be taking in the air around where our feet had previously trod. We held our breath for as long as we could so as to not startle or alert the creature to our hiding place."

Racer was still trotting along on the pebbly path in the reddish dirt and kept passing fallen chunks of stone on either side.

"Wait," said Willow. "You said you were inside a cave too? Rowan and I hid there, hiding from the same beast! I cannot believe you were actually able to catch a glimpse of it."

"Shhh!" said Rowan, holding a finger over his lips. "I want to hear the rest of the story. It is not good manners to interrupt a storyteller's tale."

Willow nodded in apology.

"Now," said Racer, "once the beast fled, we deemed it safe to exit. The two of us could hear the sound of cracking branches and blowing wind as if the beast was taking off once more, hopefully to fly far, far away from us. We took off once more, trying to find a way out of that foggy land, and we suddenly started seeing these golden streams in the air, acting like a guide through the forest. It was as if the very wind itself had transformed because it sensed we were lost."

"Actually," said Willow, "that was Skeef. We met him in a glade somewhere in the heart of the forest, and the glade was not at all affected by the darkness from the rest of the woods. In fact, there were lots of flowers and grass and butterflies and other animals too! There were these green people covered in vines and leaves that I—I really do not know what to call them actually."

"Ah," said Rowan. "You're thinking of those dryads. They are rather magical beings who only appear when the air is pure and the light is true. To be fair, it is quite good luck to happen upon them, for they are rare sights in these times. We should be considered blessed!"

"Shall I finish?" said Racer, who was a bit tired of interruptions.

The two apologized, and Racer continued again.

"Now we followed the streams of wind through the river basin, and we had to hurry, for they were quickly fading away as they went. It was quite a peculiar event, that. Anyways, now we have come to the end of this tale, as moments ago, we saw you two happily strolling along right through the edge of the forest in this region. I was so ecstatic to finally see you and Willow again that I came running as fast as I could! I reciprocate your appreciation of our reunion."

Racer waggled his head and shook the black hair of his mane.

*****

The sun was beginning to set in the west behind the ocean, turning the gloomy gray clouds a vibrant reddish orange and shining a straight reflection on its surface. Yet the same clouds began to clump together and grow in a scary, darkened mass of black vapor. What began as tiny sprinkles of wet drops progressively turned into heavy, fat drops of cold, hard rain. The dirt path the company trod suddenly became sloshy with mud and gunk, as they were soon drenched by the monsoon. One might say they were inside a monsoon!

"A storm!" said Rowan loudly. "We must find shelter quickly!"

He flicked the reins, and Racer started to gallop as fast as his sturdy legs could take them.

"Do you know the way to Tel Pata?" asked Willow. "That's where Skeef said Merlin is waiting for us! Can you get us there?"

Willow squeezed Racer's ribs with her thighs and clutched the hood of her cloak tightly. Rowan flicked the reins again, and Racer continued his hasty gallop.

"Well," said Rowan, "the thing about the Tels is that one does not simply *find* them! Only those with a deep knowledge of magic can find their way! We would need Merlin himself to show us the way! Alas, look!"

Rowan held a hand over his brow both to shield it from the rain and to catch a better glimpse of the golden streams once again. Long and wispy, they came from behind them and went on and on ahead of them into the promptly blackening world around them. A deafening boom of thunder rattled them to their bones as Racer followed the streams, whipping up mud and grime as he went. The weather was against them!

The wind howled through the biting rain. There seemed no end to it, as the streams began to curve slightly to the south, away from the northern river, which before they turned away from it began to be filled with water once more.

Soon, the terrain became rather hill-ish and slippery. As the rain fell, the golden streams began to gather to a single point on one of the hills, a rather short and steep hill just a few yards ahead of them. It seemed as if the streams were leading them right into the hill, as there was no hole or entrance into it, no door or crater. But Rowan knew exactly what it was.

"Skeef is guiding us!" said Rowan. "That must be the entrance to Tel Pata! Leave it to the Creator to aid his children when they believe! Make haste, Racer, make haste!"

Another flick of the reins, and Racer hastened with the golden streams.

As they drew nearer to the steep hill, the streams began to intensify and glow brighter and brighter, and the grassy nature of the hill began to crumble, concaving. Bit by bit, it fell away, and the earth within began to solidify and form strong stairs. The company soon reached the newly formed entrance, and the stairs began to descend farther and farther into the hill.

As soon as Juniper's tail feathers crossed into the cave, the outer lips of the entrance set their closing in motion. It was as if the very hill itself had opened up and swallowed them whole. Willow clung tightly to Rowan despite how sopping wet they both were. She could feel Juniper shivering and hugging her lower back with her body. Darkness was soon all around them, and no light entered forth into that chasm.

Then once the mouth of the cave was completely shut, the storm was dampened and could only be partially heard from behind the dirt and stone. A muffled thunderclap let them know that it was still right over them. But they were more elated that they were now finally out of it.

In the darkness, Rowan patted himself all over, feeling to make sure he still had his cloak, sword, and other belongings. He was thankful they had not blown away in the chaos. He shook his head, and his hair fluttered like a wet mop, spraying little droplets of rainwater onto the walls.

He used one of his hands to slick it back so it would not obstruct his vision by hanging down in front of his face, though he could barely see a thing anyway. He dismounted, and his feet, to his surprise, landed on solid steps of stone. A dim glow began to emit from where the bottom step reached dense dolomite, the same stone that made up the walls around them. It was a light brownish color with tinges of gold and black and drops of silver.

"Hello," called a familiar voice from the room at the end of the stairs. "I shall assume that you know magic, as the Tel would not have let you enter without it—unless, of course, there are many of you, and one in the company knows magic. Now, then, friend or foe?"

As the company descended the stairs, Rowan holding on to Racer's reins with Willow still mounted, they began to see that the staircase of stone was actually quite wide—wide enough to fit a cart through! The light that began as a dim glow increased to a comfortable level and was as if the room was lit with hanging lanterns.

Once inside the room, the company noticed that it was quite a spacious room. The light therein was cast from gleaming stalactites in the ceiling. Each of them glowed with bright yellow chunks dotted around them. There were bookshelves integrated into the wall with an array of different-colored books and volumes; tables, chairs, and desks with several peculiar artifacts, one of which was a strangely curved horn, lined or hung about them. In a corner next to one of the bookshelves was a great chest locked by a great lock. It was made of carved wood and fastened with metal. Several bumps ran across the metal as decoration.

Throughout the room, Willow noticed that there was not a speck of dust upon any of the decor or furniture. In the center of the room, within a circular outline on the floor, there was a group of chairs lining the outline of the shape. These chairs were made of sturdy wood and accented with fine leather.

"Welcome," said a strange man in a ragged black robe, carrying a twisted staff.

His beard was short and was equal parts white and silver and scraggly all around his chin. The man's teeth were uneven, and he bore pockmarks on his cheeks. His head was bald and covered with moles.

"It seems we have been expecting you according to the old man over there."

He pointed to a figure donned in purple with a pointy hat and exquisite staff gently steeping his tea in a chair next to one of the shelves.

"Merlin!" said Willow, running over to him.

Merlin stood and embraced her warmly with a gentle smile. Like she had known before, his caress was warm and comforting.

"My dear Willow," said Merlin, "I have missed you! Are you hurt? Were you followed? You must tell me if anything happened, or else I shall give way to worry."

"I am fine," said Willow. "I do not believe we were followed, but we did encounter the storm outside. It was really wet and nasty and muddy, and the thunder rang in my ears and—"

"A storm, you say?" said the strange man. "We have not had rain since the Caliphate waltzed in and destroyed the Two Thrones. The Caliph, cursed be her name, has placed a dreadful spell on the weather, and the very land itself has withered and dried up. But now it seems to be receding for some bizarre reason."

The strange man found his spot in one of the chairs around the circle in the middle of the room. But Merlin, who released Willow, caught Rowan in his gaze and froze. In the back of his mind, memories began to flood. He remembered the young boy with a shining smile who was very excited to be under the wizard's tutelage. He remembered his mother and father and how encouraging they were with the boy's affinity for magic. Then the bad memories arrived. He remembered when Rowan disappeared after the Caliphate moved in.

Merlin then moved to Rowan, and both of them froze, their essences wrought with disbelief.

"Rowan," said the wizard.

"Merlin," said Rowan, and he embraced the wizard tightly.

A moment of joy came over them on top of the relief that sprang from seeing each other. He saw a slight twinkling in the wizard's eyes as if tears had begun to well up in the man's baggy, wrinkled eyes, in which bushy brows topped. The wizard then removed his hat in a very solemn fashion.

"I thought you were gone," said Merlin. "I was beginning to wonder what had become of my apprentice! Why, the last time I saw you, my boy, you were but a little lad running about my chamber, wishing me to teach him everything from my spellbook. I certainly remember when you earned your first Pip after learning your first spell."

"'Twas one of the happiest moments in my life," said Rowan, "because I had a great teacher. It is good to see you once again, master."

Rowan bowed his head briefly and looked up at the wizard again before finding his seat in the circle of chairs. Merlin followed suit and gestured to Willow to do the same. Seeing that the room was rather commodious, Racer and Juniper found a comfortable spot next to one of the bookshelves with the zebra resting his head gently on the floor and the toucan lying politely on his back. The company was now in their chairs.

"Now, then," said Merlin, "allow me to introduce you all to a good friend of mine and the grand warden of Chateau Ensalor, Pinner Vemtal."

The strange man bowed his head with his eyes closed briefly.

"Pinner, this is Willow Denning, my apprentice Rowan, and their guardians, Racer and Juniper respectively. You can trust them with your life."

"Well, I would hope so," said Pinner, blinking rapidly and twitching slightly. "For children, they took their precious time. But it is nice to finally have company after a decade of loneliness and solitude. Why, in that time, I seem to have mastered the art of tea-making. Would anyone like any? It is lavender and mint."

Pinner gestured toward the iron teapot sitting steaming slightly on the table behind Merlin. The smell of the floral elements brewed wafted in the space therein.

"No, thank you," Willow said politely.

Rowan declined as well. He sat with his legs crossed and his hands in his lap. As for Willow, she sat very ladylike with her legs together and hands stacked on each other.

"This is a beautiful house that you have. I do not believe I've ever seen a space so large. It seems nearly endless!"

"Oh," said Pinner, "this is not my house. 'Twas not built to be anything of the sort. It is merely a hiding place. The Tels of Kastallon serve only as a place of research and prayer. They were discovered by the first Astrons in the early days of Eon Primary, when I was but a bumbling, wee tot. As I said earlier, one may only find and enter the Tels through deep knowledge of magic. You cannot simply dabble in the arcane arts and call yourself a wizard. It takes dedication, discipline, and determination."

"Precisely," said Merlin, "which brings me to Willow, my friend. She is the key to restoring the throne in Ensalor and driving away the enemy that sits upon its remnants. In order for her to have a chance at uniting the rest of the realm, she must learn our ways. After all, her family has an affinity for magic—not as much as us but enough to quickly progress."

"Affinity?" said Willow. "What does that mean? And what do you mean not as much as you? I believe I do not understand."

Her lip went to one side, and she squinted.

"Now, now," said Merlin, "it is not polite to interrupt. It is best for me to tell the story from the start. Would you like to hear what I have been up to since last we met?"

"That I would love to hear!" said Rowan, who now relaxed in his chair.

"If there is one thing," said Merlin, "that us Astrons preserve, it is our memory. Before I arrived here in Tel Pata, a lot has happened. Now the decision had been made to send Willow on her way to Al Wafra to fetch nourishment, and I used a disappearing spell to move locations. When I reappeared, I must have been imagining the wrong forest, for I reappeared inside the Vast Woodland where Château Londror dwells, with its parapets and towers and stone walls and famous moat around it full of spikes and sharp rocks.

"I was not close to the castle, but I was sure it was not far. Inside that woodland, what with its slowly darkening leaves and growing fog from the downs beyond in the hills not far from the tree line, I was lost as lost could be. Not only was it the place I did not wish appear in, but it was also a place I did not wish to stay!

"I began to traverse through the trees, glade by glade, with all the speed I could muster, passing fallen limbs and dried, crunchy leaves long separated from their home tree. I passed several spots where the roots were growing aboveground, and they made the path I trod extremely hazardous. There were no birds to hear, but most of the greenery and flora on the floor was beginning to waste away.

"Although the spell may be receding, its festering influence still holds a presence in the land, and perhaps the Vast Woodland will not hold out much longer. The Purloinian enchanters have worked tirelessly to keep the petrifying spell at bay, but alas, I fear they are reaching the peak of their strength, and they will begin to falter. I reserved the observation and continued through the forest. The only thing on my mind, besides the ever-declining forest around me, was getting to Tel Pata, for I needed to see my old friend.

"Eventually, I found myself back in the spooling hills where the northern river runs. There the fog began to thin, though it was still a massive haze among the downs. I kept my path straight and narrow, daring not to tread away from the riverside. Though it was not thriving, I was happy to see the basin once more. It was the one last guide I had with the usual landmarks hidden in the haze. Hours followed, and I began to see the lower hills just beyond the southern mountains. This is where I made haste, and within minutes, I arrived at this very hill by which you all entered.

"As Pinner has said before, one does not simply enter the Tels without a deep understanding of arcane knowledge. Seeing as, obviously, I am Merlin the Magical, I held out my hand and spoke a spell only known by the ancient sorcerers who were the first priests of Skeef. The hillside then caved in, and the same stairs by which you descended moments ago appeared. When inside, I saw this funny-looking warlock sleeping at his desk. 'Wake up!' I said to him, and the fool jolted awake and dared to send a swift magic blast at me. Quickly, I countered it with a simple wave of my staff."

He grinned.

"That is not how it happened," said Pinner, who was offended. "You decided to tickle my backside with a mild zap spell!"

"Oh, come off it," said Merlin with a chuckle. "Where was I? Oh yes! As soon as Pinner was awake and he realized who I was, he was laughing, and we shared a brief greeting. He sniffed like a dog would a patch of strange grass and spoke. 'Do my eyes deceive me?' said Pinner. 'Could it be that after all these years, Merlin the Magical has once again returned to old Pinner Vemtal?'

"'It is no curse, I promise you,' I said. I was quite happy to see him after all. 'So, dear friend,' said Pinner, 'I assume you have come to me laden with news of the One Who Unites, yes?' He was so fixated on the news and could hardly contain himself.

"'Your assumption has not failed you,' I said. 'She is the one I brought with me out of the chaos and agony that consumed her home a decade ago. She is more than capable, but some training and conditioning, mentally and physically, would do her some good. Right now, she is with her guardian, Juniper the Toucan, on their way to Al Wafra. I insisted on bringing her straight here, but the bird and I could not come to terms with our disagreement.'

"'A shame,' said Pinner. 'I would have loved to see how much the little one has grown. Where did you keep her? A place that was safe, I would hope.'

"'Certainly,' I said. 'We traveled to a land far away from here in a realm called Earth. There I took up the role of a lively, nurturing headmaster at the orphanage she stayed in. She was looked after, fed, bathed, and taught the things of that world that would keep her sharp and disciplined.'

"'What?' said Pinner. 'You mean to say before me that you did not hide her anywhere in the Land Where Castles Lie? What would her parents think if they discovered such knowledge?'

"'I'm afraid they already know,' I said. 'It was their final wish before the entire realm collapsed and fell to the will of the Caliphate. With my coming back to Kastallon, it seems that ever since I stepped out of the mouth of the whale, I have not felt their presence as I would have before. Have you heard anything from the duke at all?'

"'I have not,' said Pinner. 'There have been no pigeons to find their way to this cave, nor have I intercepted any during my evening strolls. Perhaps it is best not to worry for them and keep striving to find them. I am sure they are still out there somewhere, or perhaps, they have ventured beyond the Western Waves.'

"'That is impossible,' I said. 'They would have never made it to the shore with the Gilded Legions spreading across the land. They would have been followed and chased and surrounded before meeting their doom like deer hunted by a pack of wolves. But as sorrowing as it is, they may already be gone, whether it happened as I have guessed or not. It is uncertain.'

"'There now, my friend,' said Pinner. 'Let us not dwell on the unfortunate. Allow your spirits to be lifted with the knowledge that the One Who Unites has come at last. Tell me, how is she to find her way here if you are not there to guide her, and she alone knows no magic?'

"'Now there's a question,' I said, 'that I know not the answer to. I did bestow upon her a pouch of harvested Shimmer, but I do not believe I told her it was such.'

"'Then for our sake,' said Pinner, 'and the sake of the realm, let us hope that she learns quickly. Come now, my friend. Sip some tea and tell me of your adventures as a headmaster in this place you call Earth. What is it like? Does it have a king?'

"As much as I would love to share with you the recollection I gave to Pinner of the events I experienced as a faux headmaster, I believe it is in the interest of time to save it for another meeting. For if I were to, we would still be here for another year or two. For now, let us strategize."

He breathed in and then let it out.

"I concur," said Pinner. "Now that we are gathered here without the prying eyes of our enemy, a battle plan is in order."

Pinner then got up from his chair and moved to the chest in the corner, using his twisted staff as support. He seemed a feeble old man—and looked a lot older than Merlin to Willow's eyes—the way he hobbled on shaky feet. With the tap of his staff on the lid of the chest, it slowly opened itself as if an invisible hand had commanded it.

Willow could not see clearly what was inside of it from where she was sitting, but she guessed from the books she read at the orphanage that it was loaded with ancient treasure or other artifacts. The old man reached in and retrieved a rolled-up parchment held together by a fine thread. He tucked the scroll under his arm and snapped his fingers; the chest closed back tightly. With a light sidestep, he found his way to the others, who were still planted in their seats, watching the ebony-robed elder.

"This," said Pinner, "is a map of the world we find ourselves in. You will have to forgive the fact that it is a dated old thing, and some of the newer landmarks are not all there."

Pinner untied the thread and allowed the paper to open on its own. To Willow's bewilderment, the map floated in midair right between the chairs they were gathered in. On it she saw a coastline with several curving lines symbolizing rivers stretching out from it. There were forests and mountains drawn on in black ink with the names of locations written in a language that was not English. There was a lake to the south near more forests and mountains, and across the eastern side, there were rolling hills and valleys. It was unlike the atlases she had been shown in her history classes, which displayed a colored outline of the many countries and continents of Earth. This map, however, was just black ink on faded parchment. She felt like she could look at it for hours.

"This is a map of Kastallon?" asked Willow. "It seems enormous. How do you get anywhere without cars or buses? Where are the roads and the buildings?"

"When it was drawn," said Pinner, "the illustrator was persuaded that buildings would prevent the map from reaching its completion and would not look as good. So they were omitted. Now let's have look here at the—"

"And what of the buildings in the actual world?" added Willow. "When we were traveling here, I did not see any signs of neighborhoods or cities or even villages. Where have they all gone?"

"They were destroyed," said Rowan, speaking up from his seat, "like my village was. The Caliphate began a crusade in the early days of its reign where the Five Vexes and their armies visited each city and village and town, and those who did not submit to their way of life were burned to the ground, every last one of them. They called us traitors and dissenters who had accepted punishment on behalf of Fikra, their goddess. As far as I know, I am one of the only survivors."

"How dreadful," said Willow.

A brief moment of silence followed.

"So that is why," said Merlin to Rowan, "you had to leave so hastily when you did. I see now I was wrong to think it was for something not quite like that. I thought you had had enough of me. You remember what I am speaking of, yes?"

"Yes, master," said Rowan. "We were having an argument at the time, and I was thinking something along those lines when I felt an inkling of fear. It was as if a voice was calling out to me, saying, 'They are in danger,' and I knew I had to fly at once. I am sorry, master, for my early leave."

"You are forgiven," said Merlin. "I believe I've had enough poignant memories for today. Let us return our attention to the map. Pinner, if you will."

Merlin gestured to him as if suggesting for him to speak on his behalf.

With a finger, he pointed to the top-left corner of the map, specifically at a small dot next to a set of mountains.

"Here is Château Ensalor, where the Caliph sits on her wretched throne. It is the largest castle, as it has a city within its walls. You must pass through the Jondii Mountains to get there, but they are more canyon-like than mountainous, unlike the Bell Mountains to the south. The castle itself is set upon a hill, and the buildings below it climb up it. It is made of very sturdy stone and armed peak to foot with Caliphate soldiers. The path from here to there is a treacherous one. But in order to reclaim the castle, we must muster an army."

"My thoughts exactly," said Merlin. "When the Purloinians realize that the One Who Unites is now in Kastallon, they will rally. They will take up their swords and shield and horses and enchanters and march north, giving their all with the goal of restoring this broken land."

"Easy," said Rowan. "I shall ride there at once and inform them. It cannot be that far from here to the Vast Woodland, where you, Merlin, were hours ago."

He gestured to the eastern side of the map at an opaquely black dot surrounded by hundreds of white dots. There were hills around the black dot with a bit of empty space like a glade.

"That," said Merlin, "is where you are wrong, my boy. We cannot simply go and inform them with nothing to show. The Purloinians are very visual believers and will have to see Willow for themselves. Do you not remember the prophecy that was given to the first priests and to the realm when first Skeef disappeared? Perhaps this will jog your memory.

"'Now in the days of the White Lamb, when an enemy of the west shall be upon us, the One Who Unites will be born, and a decade of tribulation shall be wrought. Only when they return to Kastallon will the divided become one, and the enemy shall be thwarted. A blade gifted by the ancestor shall be wielded; a winged being of white shall fly. Signs of restoration will be seen: the desert becomes saturated, and the dark becomes light. Such is the prophecy of Skeef, our lord and protector.'

"You see, we cannot just tell them. They must see the item I have mentioned and witness the changes listed. As it seems now, the rain is just the beginning."

"Well said," said Pinner. "Speaking of the item in question, good Merlin, allow me to grace our savior's hand."

Pinner got up again and returned to the chest with normal gait. He fetched a fine leather sheath and belt from within it, and the chest closed once more. He then stood with what seemed like solemnity as he peered at the weapon. A hilt of steel and dark wood protruded from the flat end of the sheath, which was itself wrapped with a thin twine. A purple gem glittered in the center of the hilt just before where the blade would begin. The hilt's pommel was pyramidal in shape.

Willow, to her surprise, felt drawn to it. There was like a strange itch on the nape of her neck as if a ghostly hand had begun to tickle it with pointy fingers. She gulped and continued to peer at the sheathed sword.

Seems dangerous, she thought, her eyes glued to the item in Pinner's hand.

"Impossible," murmured Rowan. "Only the Driniths hold claim to that sword."

"This," said Pinner again, "is called Pnevma. It was your mother's sword and her mother's before her, forged during late Eon Primary, when the forges beneath Numalosh were still active. Its blade is made of a fine alloy called Emunian iron, harvested from the ore deep within Mount Cauram farther south of those forges. That gem you see is a Shimmer gem, one of the last few seen aboveground. Though it is weaker than the gem within Merlin's staff, it still holds mighty strength. Your mother would be proud to see you wield it. Go on. See for yourself."

Pinner held out the scabbard.

Willow, who had never even touched a sword or weapon before, cautiously allowed Pinner to place the sheathed sword in her open hands delicately. To her left, Rowan eyed it very closely. Perhaps he felt jealous that his shamshir was not magical or could not become a conduit for magic. Once Pinner's hands drew back, Willow nearly dropped the sword upon feeling the true weight of it all.

In her mind, it was like holding a really heavy book, especially one of the encyclopedias she had seen in the orphanage library. She placed a careful hand on the hilt, which was icy cold to the touch against her newly warmed hand, and kept the other firmly on the sheath. She gulped just before slowly drawing the sword, which needed barely any force to do.

In the glow of the stalactites, the blade flashed. It was not a very long sword but could not be considered by even the most experienced soldiers a dagger either. It was perfectly suited for her, as long as needed for a girl of her height, which was not much, as the others were much taller than her. It was a blade that she knew many of the younger boys back home would gawk at, asking her to hold it.

"It is," said Willow, "heavy, but not so heavy that I will always drop it."

She sheathed the sword with a click and tried to hand it back to the old cotter, who kept his hands clasped together as if he was prepared to give a speech, but he simply insisted on her keeping it.

"No," said Pinner. "It is yours now. Take it and use it well. With the blade passed down from the ancestor, we are one step closer to seeing the thrones restored. The only task now is to get Willow here to Château Londror to persuade the Purloinian baron, and he will join us against the Caliphate. Perhaps there is hope after all. But we cannot just wander without aim.

"The Gilded Legion has many soldiers spread across the land with battalions in every place but the east. The enchanters' incantations have ensured they do not cross the tree line. Going north is a death sentence no matter how expertly planned the journey."

"What about that place there?" said Willow, pointing to an arrangement of circles not far from their location on the map. "It looks to be a forest. Maybe we could camp there and then cross the river? It almost seems too easy."

"An astute observation," said Merlin, "though it would be best to tread as far away from the Gallant Valley as possible. Pinner claims there are rather unpleasant tribes there, which may slow us down. Etarish is a good checkpoint. Lots of houses and taverns make good for a night of comfort. I will say, though, that should we cross into its borders, we will need to hide in plain sight."

"What do you mean?" asked Willow. "I thought the enchanters, if that is what you called them, kept the Legion at bay?"

"Not exactly," said Merlin. "Remember what Pinner said about the towns that did not comply? They were burned to the ground and destroyed. Etarish is among those that assimilated and conformed to their ways, perhaps becoming a cornerstone in their culture, though not as significant as Ranha. In order to not be seen as adversaries, we shall need disguises."

"What's a disguise?" asked Willow again.

Pinner lost his mirth.

"Did they teach you nothing?" said Pinner. "It is something you wear to hide your identity, a mask almost. Wizards especially are forbidden in Etarish since we are not viziers. Any sign of Skeef's magic will be a quick arrest and quicker execution. They do not tolerate men like us, not one bit. That is why I went into hiding, you see. I may be old, but I am still as cunning as a weasel!"

"Well put," said Merlin. "It is settled, then. Upon first light, we shall pass through Onolon Grove and over the river into the Vast Woodland so as to be greeted by the Purloinians. The high walls of Londror will be our landmark, ensuring us that we have reached the castle. There, too, will be a bridge, as the castle is surrounded by a deep moat. The rest is up to you, dear girl."

The old wizard smiled the same smile that Mr. Linmer used to shine when Willow was feeling down or upset. But it was in a different light now. Sure, it was still the headmaster she grew fond of, but now he was a fantastical wizard full of magic and power. Willow was still making sense of all of it.

*****

Night fell inside the Tel, or so Willow guessed. The downpour raging outside was actually comforting to her. It reminded her of the nights when a storm would pass through the city on Staten Island, and rain would strike hard against the sturdy glass with loud, forceful rasps. Pinner had shown her to her room just down the hall past the staircase they had entered from. It was a simple room: a bed made of mahogany and a chest of walnut similar to the chest that Pnevma was stowed away in. She propped it up beside the chest instead.

"You don't belong in a chest," said Willow as if the sword could understand her.

The gem embedded in the hilt glistened in the low glow of the single stalactite above. She gave a tender smile. Then a knock came to her door, and when she opened it, there stood Merlin once more, carrying something of an odd curved shape wrapped in a fine vermillion cloth.

"Merlin!" said Willow. "I thought you were going to bed too?"

She rubbed her eyes gently with one hand and tried to keep the other eye open to look at the wizard, who was still giving that friendly smile. He was not wearing his pointy hat, so his long white hair was stringy and wispy.

"I came to give you one more thing," said Merlin, gesturing with the shape in his hand.

Willow was still trying to guess what he was keeping hidden underneath the mysterious cloth.

"I want you to have this, but only use it when you fear there is no way out, that there is nothing or no one around to help you."

He began to unwrap the object in question, and slowly, it was revealed to be a bugle carved from the horn of a ram. It began small and spiraled slightly into a larger opening. Willow wasn't sure what to think.

"This is the horn of Saint Ufton, a former friend of mine. He claims it was bestowed to him by the previous avatar of Skeef, the Gray Ram. But hark, one blow of this instrument will, without a shadow of doubt, bring help from somewhere in the user's immediate surroundings or farther. Keep it safe, and always keep it with you."

"Thank you," said Willow as she took the horn and placed it on the chest next to Pnevma. She then returned to the square door. "Is that all, sir?"

"Yes," said Merlin with a quick wink. "I wish you a very restful, good night."

As soon as the wizard left, the door was shut, and Willow found her way to the bed with haste. She pulled the brown fur covers over her body as she lay, trying to relax. Drowsiness was setting in, and she found herself quickly falling into a deep, comfortable slumber.

Chapter 10

The Journey Begins

Willow awoke. She knew she was awake, but her eyelids refused to do their jobs. Lying there, she felt astonishingly at peace, protected by the dirt and stone that surrounded the hidden hostel she and the others found themselves in. The fur covers were a nice touch, she thought, and were warm enough for her sleep to be pleasant. The bed itself was not exactly on the same level of comfort as her bed from the orphanage, but it was enough.

She sat up and rubbed her eyes gently and pushed the bangs out of her eyes. Although she was not tired, the absence of sunlight was worsening her grogginess. She had been somewhat used to the cyclical nature of Earth: the setting of the sun before night and the rising of the moon as night fell. Even though she lay awake with the moonlight glaring through the glass, it was comforting to know it was actually nighttime outside. The same could be said for daytime. Inside the Tel, the only light was from the glowing stalactites above. They weren't burning stars, but they shone sufficiently to see the room around her.

The moment she shifted herself to the edge of the side of the bed with the covers drawn away, a most familiar scent wafted into the room from underneath the door. She sniffed deeply, and a satisfied smirk blossomed from ear to ear. It was the smell of cooking bacon! On holidays at the orphanage, breakfasts would include this crispy delicacy served with eggs and toast, and the aroma of it always reminded her that today was a special day. She wondered if whoever was cooking it now was also making it with eggs and toast. She decided to look for herself.

Up she got and opened the door swiftly. In the corridor, she looked left and saw the hall extending into another space; to the right, she saw the stairs again and the library they had spoken in the night prior with its shelves and chairs. The hallway itself nearly reminded her of the orphanage hallways, especially the hallway where she first saw Juniper. Then she began to wonder where the big-beaked little bird got off to and if she was able to sleep at all.

Following the hallway to the left, she found that the floor itself was soft, as if someone had gone in before and patted it all down to make it smooth. It was still dirt but packed together like carpet. The hallway was not long, but she passed a few more vacant rooms before reaching the space at the end, which was revealed to be a kitchen area similar to the bakery. There she saw Merlin dressed in a gray gown with minute vertical stripes sewn into it frying bacon in a small pan on a metal stovetop.

"Good morning," said Willow. "Is the bacon for a special day?"

The moment she eyed it, her mouth began to salivate with hunger, and her stomach gurgled a bit. Merlin smiled gently and flipped the reddish strips over with a fork, and the grease crackled.

"Is today not a special day?" said Merlin. "The One Who Unites begins her journey today, and in celebration, I am making bacon. How much would you like? There's more in Pinner's storage if this is not enough."

He gestured to the five crackling strips in the pan.

"No, no, that's plenty," said Willow, whose mouth was still watering.

She went over to the dining table just ahead of the cooking station, which was nothing more than a wooden table ahead of a large fireplace with several pots and pans and dishware and cutlery. The dining table was a fine square wooden table with four wooden chairs surrounding it.

"Where are the eggs and toast? That was also usually served with bacon on special days."

"Ah, my mistake," said Merlin. "Let me get them started."

He snapped at the pot hanging over the fire and at some of the cutlery too. To her wonder, Willow watched as a few eggs were taken out of the basket next to Merlin, cracked into a bowl, stirred with a spoon, and placed into the same pot from before as if there was an invisible person doing all the work. She stared with a raised eyebrow as the instruments returned to their original positions once the eggs were cooking.

The only thing she thought of to say was, "Will I be able to do that?" Then her mouth stayed open as she remembered Merlin telling her of her potential for magic. The concept of it all was still very difficult to grasp. What happened in Mr. Linmer's—now Merlin—office and the explosion that Rowan caused were still among the crazy things she was trying to make sense of and fully wrap her head around.

The smell of the bacon intensified.

"Years of practice," said Merlin. "But that is merely a command charm that only works for nonliving things. That type of magic is particularly too advanced for a beginner like yourself. Don't worry, dear, you will get to that point progressively."

He then took a wooden plate from the stack next to some pots and transferred the bacon to it. A few steps toward the table, and the bowl was placed in front of Willow happily.

"The eggs will be done momentarily."

As she took a bite of the bacon with a crisp snap, Willow admired the room. It was not cluttered like the baker's had been and was a lot more concise with its arrangement. Everything, whether it was cutlery, dishware, or cookware, had a designated place in the kitchen. Once she finished the final strip of bacon and swallowed—she was taught not to speak with food in her mouth—Willow licked her lips to savor any final flavor left from the meat.

"How much does Rowan know?" asked Willow pensively. "He used that pouch of Shimmer you gave to me as a gift to create an explosion, which drew away some bandits on the road away from Al Wafra. Does he know how to use command charms too?"

Merlin paused. He did not back away from the pot hanging over the fireplace; instead, he opted to replace the lid. He placed his hands on the wooden table and pressed somewhat hard. Willow could see something was bothering the old man.

"Did I say something wrong?"

"No," said Merlin. "I am just…recovering, it seems, from seeing him again. I thought I had lost him forever."

The wizard turned around and sauntered to his seat.

"It is best to begin from the time I accepted him as my apprentice. He was a bright little lad full of excitement and determination. His parents—very good they were—did not question his connection with magic. They embraced it. They were actually quite surprised to see that he had it given they were not magical themselves. But as he grew, so, too, did his strength and willpower. He was a very, very fast learner. We would train day by day, meditating and practicing or reviewing spells—some he knew, and some he did not.

"As for the other students at Numalosh, he was their role model. His quick progression and charisma made him quite the popular pick for them. They admired his discipline and how easy it was for him to put on a show of talent, how fascinating it was for him to ace challenges or hardships. It was not until that fateful day a decade ago when the skies grew dark and the wind suddenly stopped dead in its tracks. They came from the southwest and quickly decimated our defenses.

"But that was not all. More had marched up from the southern roads as well, and word had been sent by a messenger, who was one of his family's friends, by horseback to Ensalor. The desperate man informed Rowan that his village northeast of the Numalosh was in danger, and that was the last I spoke with him before the thrones were destroyed.

"Seeing him now is almost like seeing a son returning home from war. He is taller, stronger, and hopefully, wiser than last we met. It is good to see that he has kept Racer in good condition. He was a gift to the boy from his parents, who'd purchased him from a trader claiming to be from across the sea. He is certainly one of a kind in Kastallon, I'm sure. But it does make him a target. The enemy could easily spot those black-and-white stripes. As for his knowledge of magic, he knows only as much as I have taught him and perhaps any else that he's taught himself."

At that moment, with the clink of Willow's fork on her plate, Rowan stepped into the kitchen, dressed in only his black tunic, which hung freely over his dark gray trousers. His hair was very tousled—he had just woken up minutes ago—and he yawned mildly.

"Good morning," said Rowan. "I smelled cooking meat, and I had to see which it was."

He then looked at the reddish crumbs on Willow's plate.

"Ah, the smell was bacon. Is there any left?"

Rowan transitioned to the old stove, where the small pan lay with three strips still warm. He took one and bit into it, crunching it with his mouth closed.

"There will be eggs soon," said Merlin. "Give it another minute or so. Tell me, my apprentice, did you sleep well?"

The wizard watched Rowan pull a chair out and plant himself in it. He was still holding the other strips in one hand.

"Like a stone, master," said Rowan, "like a stone. I have always dreamed of visiting the Tels. But I also knew my knowledge was not as vast as your own. I hoped that one day, you would eventually take me yourself, but we both know what happened."

"Quite right," said Merlin. "Yet you persisted in these times. I am very proud of you. I hope you will show me your progress. Willow tells me you used the Shimmer I gave her to create an explosion in the desert beyond Al Wafra. That is an advanced spell for such a young wizard."

"Well," said Rowan, "I had an excellent teacher. But in the years since we parted, I occupied my time in search of any surviving spellbooks written by the old sorcerers and priests of Eon Primary. My first suggestion was the archives in Numalosh, but I did not dare tread near where the Caliphate kept high-ranking soldiers. From the bell tower of An Razi, you can see the giants chained to the forward pillars. So I continued my search, going from town to town and forest by forest, looking for any record of the old texts. But alas, there came none. I feared I would never find anything of the sort again, and I fell into a great sorrow.

"I kept you in mind, though, master. My only solace was knowing that you were still out there, wherever you were. It kept me hopeful. I continued to hide from the Caliphate, resting only in the wilderness. I had to steal to find food, and once again, my hope began to fade when the rivers started to dry up. That is why the storm we ran into last night was a blessing."

"Of course," said Merlin. "The monsoon raged on as the night prolonged. To my knowledge, it did not stop until the sun was fully in the sky hours ago."

"As for that spell," said Rowan, "it was an experiment. I knew the spell for a fireball, and I combined it with a simple enlarging charm. I figured, with the amount of Shimmer in the pouch, it would be enough. Come to think of it, it almost seems as if you knew it would be enough."

"Now, now," said Merlin, "I do not know the future. But a wizard must be ready for anything, and that pouch was the only harvested Shimmer I had left. Consider it a favor from Skeef. But combining a spell and charm is something that separates the intermediates from the beginners. I am truly proud of you, Rowan. I could not be more impressed with your performance. But another mystery is to be revealed. How did your path cross with Willow's?"

The old wizard coughed a dry cough and covered it with a fist over his mouth.

"Well," said Rowan, "that was but two moons ago. The day prior to my being in Al Wafra, I was exploring the Ruscis Hills to the west of Lod Rimona, where former Shimmer mines used to thrive with the sound of pick and shovel. My reason for being there treads along the idea of recovering any Shimmer that could have been passed over. But alas, the crystals have all dried up, and the carts have been dismantled, and the picks melted down to cold, clumpy steel. On a surprising note, however, they did not rake up the tracks by which the carts would traverse. These tracks went throughout the caverns and shafts and were hammered into the dirt with thick, strong nails.

Perhaps they were lazy and did not deem the deed worthy of their attention.

"I ventured deeper into the northernmost mine. All around were walls of limestone with slabs of quartz and clay scattered around. I followed the tracks into an area where hanging stalactites dripped cold drops of water onto their erecting friends on the ground, the stalagmites. These were on either side of the main tracks in the room, which led farther into a tunnel ahead. It was quite the wondrous sight indeed, but I decided 'twas not enough, as it bore no Shimmer or clues. I continued down the tunnel that I mentioned, and eventually, the light began to fade. Luckily, I had this with me."

Rowan then revealed a necklace strung with rope from beneath the hem of his shirt under his neck. It was a simple leather string supporting a white shard in its center that shone slightly. He held it up as he talked.

"My luster gem. It was given to me by my mother before I entered servitude with Merlin. I always keep it on, because she told me, 'You never know when you will need it.' So now I always have a way to see no matter how dark. These fancy things give off a glow when in darkness, and to counter the amount of darkness, it increases with the intensity of shadow.

"As I progressed through the mine, my gem glowed. And when I entered into the main harvesting area, all was revealed from the light of this pendant. I saw bones and clothes and carts and chunks of fallen stone left behind. I began to be completely assured that this mine was wholly abandoned.

"But suddenly, there came a heart-dropping patter in the forward hall. It was the sound of taloned feet coming ever nearer. Nay, it was the sound of fluttering wings! There soon appeared a swarm of Ahool emerging from that once thriving hall. They bore awful reddish wings with short snouts full of daggerlike teeth, and they were covered in horrible black hairs. I knew not what I did to disturb them, but I sought the entrance to the cave. Perhaps they were drawn to my luster gem.

"I ran and ran, following the tracks and retracing my steps, until I leaped out of the wide stone crater of the mine, blessing the ground with my body as I covered my head with my hands. I felt the rush of their wings in the wind around me and wondered if they were to return in my absence. I cared not, though, and dashed back to Racer with help from fear and adrenaline. Together, we fled from that empty, worthless quarry and found our way through the tundra once more. Hours later, we crossed through those limestone pillars, and there I saw the girl being chased by dread Kappas."

"It was swift," said Willow. "He dispatched them with great speed."

"My brother's sword is never dull," said Rowan. "It was bestowed to me but two years ago, when he began his journey farther east. He told me, 'Where I am going, dear brother, I shall not need protection.' He told me he was seeking the Mosshaven, where the water flows freely and the clouds never gather. I have done my best to keep it as sharp as ever."

"Ah yes," said Merlin. "I remember many journeys to that fair country to the east. Most never make it past its golden gates and verdant trees. They are very selective about who they allow in and often remain neutral in times like these. They've not been much help. Getting there is often a daunting task, but the reward—that is, beholding the grand temple and city—is worth the danger."

Merlin stood and clapped his hands.

"I believe that is enough reminiscing for the moment. Memories are a precious thing, but time is of the essence currently, my friends. You must prepare yourselves for the journey that lies ahead of you."

Rowan cocked his head to one side and furrowed his brow at the wizard and spoke.

"What about you, Merlin? Will you not be joining us on this expedition?"

Willow looked at Rowan and then at Merlin with anticipation. She knew in the back of her mind that she would not make the trip by herself, but she desperately wanted Merlin to come with. This was the first time she had seen him or been in his presence in two days. She always enjoyed his company and hoped the next words to leave his lips would be related to his staying instead of going.

"I have no further business," said Merlin. "My path runs parallel with yours, friends. Pinner is wise, but I have doubts with his navigation. Someone has to get us to Londror, and that someone is me. Besides, we all have some catching up to do."

Internally, Willow's heart was gladdened, and her wide smile proved it.

*****

It was noon when the company decided to exit the Tel and leave its magical protection. Outside, the grass was beginning to grow taller, and the leaves of the trees became splotches of green and yellow. Even the turf on the hillside was greener than it was before the monsoon raged. The cloudy, gloomy sky soon allowed rays of sun to pierce through onto the landscape below.

To the south, the mountains stretching into the heavens no longer looked arid and desolate; instead, they began to gather mounds of snowfall and clothed themselves in it. To the west toward Al Wafra, the sand was beginning to fill with mud and flora, and the trees soon followed suit. The entire world seemed to be undergoing a strange yet magnificent change. But this still seemed a slow process.

Willow took a deep breath in through her nose, and the air already smelled cleaner and purer than it had the night before. Instead of the dry, bland, burnt smell that hung in the wind, there was a rather sweet scent, like the aroma that followed soon after the rain ceased. The dew of the morning light no longer remained, and instead, the trees and grass blew gently in the wind's breath. Juniper fluttered onto her shoulder and cooed excitedly. Next to her, Rowan guided Racer by leading his reins with one hand, and the zebra's head bobbed as they walked.

Half an hour passed before the company decided to break the silence of the trek. The sun was not too hot, but it was also not too cold, and there was no wind to blow against their backs. They carried only what they needed for the long road ahead. In their packs were tins of food, which was only mere breads and cured meats that Pinner stashed in the Tel's kitchen area, and flasks of several kinds of

Pinner's teas. Some included mint, chamomile, chai, and sweetened. The breakfast that Willow had eaten earlier was holding her over. She wondered if the wizards needed food to survive like the rest of them did. She watched them carry on with tarrying or struggling as they led the way next to the shallow riverbed.

To the company's left a mile away, there stood a seemingly growing greenwood. Its leaves and grassy floor was beginning its rebirth, but stains of ash gray and black still remained. It was not as dense as the forest they had visited two days ago, but it was a forest nonetheless. If they looked carefully enough, they could see the eastern downs with their many rounds and the conifers and mosses therein. It was an expansive valley, but it was too far away to be sure. Willow squinted to try and see through the stalks of the woods, but nothing of value was seen.

Merlin was the first to speak.

"So, Willow, you must tell me of these Kappas you encountered. I trust they were unlike anything you have ever seen."

The wizard scratched his neck with his free hand.

"Of course," said Willow. "I was scared silly. I did not know what to do other than to run! But as I have mentioned before, it was Rowan who I have to thank."

"It was the least," said Rowan, "that I could do. You were about to give up and perish."

Merlin stopped, and the whole company stopped with him.

"You mean to tell me that the One Who Unites, after affirming her of this title, chose to cower like a cornered cat?"

"I...," said Willow. "I was unsure of myself at the time, sir. I am still but a stranger in a strange land. People were mean. There was this dark figure who summoned the beasts, and I did not want to be captured, if that is what would have happened to thieves."

Merlin's eyes went wide from unanticipated surprise.

"Thieves? You mean to say in my presence that you stole something? Whatever did you steal?"

He leaned in a bit.

"Bread," said Willow. "There was a baker, and I was hungry, and he would not spare any since I had no gold to buy any. He tried to take the Shimmer, so I ran."

Willow's tone was apologetic with a twinge of regret.

"To be honest," said Juniper, "I was the one who told her to grab some and wrap it in some cloth. But it was the Specter that sent the Kappas after us. It was tall, dark, and donned the same uncanny mask as the rest. It was there within the throng of those beginning their pilgrimage to Ranha, which, according to the baker, is what subjects of the Caliph are required to do."

"I am aware," said Merlin. "I thank you for your honesty, Juniper. But what is a Specter doing in Al Wafra? Those assassin-spies are only dispatched under extreme circumstances or for high-level threats to the realm. They kill quickly, quietly, and efficiently. You should consider yourself lucky to be alive. However, its presence there does raise suspicion. How would it have known of your existence there?"

The company was quiet as they continued their trek through the grassy plains. Soon, a few robins and sparrows flew freely and briskly above their heads, tweeting a very pleasant song. This song was something that filled Juniper with joy, and she ruffled her feathers with excitement. She launched herself into the air from Willow's shoulder, the wind behind her frisking her hair from the takeoff, and began to flap and glide around them.

"Oh," said Juniper, "how I have missed this! The sensation of flying in the sunlight!"

She flew perpendicular to the company's path and sought one of the baobabs in the distance growing tall and strong. Its bark was a fresh tan and sturdy; its leaves, a faded green and sprouting. Juniper flew around the tree and up into the small branches before heading back across the field to the company. She kept a paced glide next to Racer, who bobbed his head so as to acknowledge her impressive flying. She squawked a happy squawk and found her place on his saddle.

The next half hour was quiet as the company pondered on Merlin's question. They considered their places at that point in time. Merlin had used a transportation spell, and Willow had stirred up trouble within its walls. But neither of those things was due cause for the response they received.

Merlin rubbed his bearded chin and considered the possibility that the Caliphate knew somehow of Willow's existence. The weather was changing no doubt, but the monsoon came a day after her leave of that desert city. In his mind, he made note to meditate on this strangeness.

*****

The afternoon sun began its descent below the western horizon, leaving a stunning reddish-yellow glow behind it in the newly white clouds. The sky, which was now steadily becoming a brightening blue instead of the same gloomy gray, was beginning to darken, and stars like grains of sand invited themselves to the gathering of dusk. Even the night sky beyond the city on the island could not compare to the vastness and greatness of this evening canvas painted with dots of starlight.

A cool draft flowed around the company and took up some strands of Willow's hair in its breath. The daytime seemed to pass them all by, and to her, the repetition of story after story of Rowan's and Pinner's tales was what carried the sun below the horizon. She enjoyed hearing them, but parts of them, the tediously descriptive parts, hastened her eyes to close from boredom.

Then Pinner's voice snapped them open.

"Hark! We have come upon Onolon Grove. See there the old sequoias that lie in the heart of this greenwood."

About five miles out through the forest, there stood a group of tall, strong sequoia trees within the middle of the forest. Their bark was a brownish red with their branches high in the sky and covered with evergreen leaves. Between the needle-riddled stalks of the smaller pines, their enormous lower trunks could be seen.

"Those trees have been here since the realm was in its infancy, being planted by the first pioneers from across the Western Waves. To much relief, they have withstood the spell brought forth by that cursed Caliph."

"A sight to behold indeed," said Merlin. "Trees like that are sacred to the natives of this grove. They see them as kings or rulers of the woods, who owe their allegiance to Skeef himself."

"Fascinating," said Willow. "Who are the natives of this forest? Did they survive the smothering of Kastallon?"

Her curiosity was something that fueled a smirk to the old wizard's face.

"I believe," said Merlin, "the answer will find us in the forest."

He stepped over a few small rocks on the path and around some surface roots.

Pinner continued to lead the way with his twisted staff and consistent gaze ahead, only moving his eyes to and fro as if to contemplate the correct way forward. Soon, their path was lit by moonlight piercing through the hazy clouds. Around them, little blips of fire popped in and out in random order.

Willow thought it was magic until Rowan changed her mind. His voice was ripe with giddiness.

"Fireflies. They have come to aid our vision in these woods. Lead on, fair bugs. Lead on!"

And so the company, with Pinner at the helm, trod the dirt-filled, dusty path through the forest with the fireflies and their periodic light to show them the way. The pines swayed peacefully in the night wind, performing a solemn dance celebrating the coming normalcy from the Caliph's fading magic.

A few feet away, up in one of the taller pines north of them, the hoot of an owl perked their ears, and the ambience of chittering bugs was on all sides. Peace was finally upon them. Racer murmured quietly when he saw the small flying things shine and dim themselves in their own fashion, for he had never seen them before. Rowan sent forth his hand, extending his index, and one of them nestled onto it. He brought the bug close to his eyes, and when he did, it shone once more and took flight again. His grin told Willow that part of his inner child resurfaced within him, and seeing the fireflies again was like seeing a friend who had been away for some time; now they were reuniting.

Willow turned her head, however, and swore she could see a pair of small eyes peering through some of the shrubbery on the forest floor. She squinted hard, and when she did, a slight rustle shook its leaves. Suddenly, it felt like a rock had sunk all the way to her stomach. She turned to the others to see if they had witnessed the same, but their attention did not stray.

She adjusted her gaze back to the spot where she had seen the eyes. None was seen. Though she could not see that which she had seen before, she still felt as though she was being watched. She paused and stood for a moment. Juniper did not notice she was gone, and so on she rode with Racer. Willow, though, quietly went over to where she had seen the eyes and waited.

I wonder, she thought.

She tiptoed in front of the bushes and made way for the one next to the other and waited. She held her breath as she saw booted little feet hobble behind the bush. To her surprise, the footsteps made no noise and barely a print in the dirt. Then the feet rose to their toes, and as they did, Willow hunched down to try and see inside the bush itself. There, inside the thistles and thin branches of the bush, were two beady eyes staring right back at her with inquisitive flare.

A cry was heard, and the feet behind the bush stumbled over. Willow drew Pnevma and cut through the leaves and stems of the bush with the intent to kill. Each slash removed more and more plant matter into the dirt until the thing behind the bush was revealed, huddling itself and shivering with fear. It was a small person. He wore a tiny red tunic and tiny gray trousers; his feet were covered by tiny leather boots. Atop his head was a cone hat that barely fitted on the poor thing's head.

"Put that thing away before you hurt someone!" he cried, shielding himself from her sword as if even to look upon the blade meant instant death.

Seeing as the little man was of no apparent threat, Willow sheathed her sword and went to her knees, trying to appear less threatening than she had already been. The little man sat up and, when he noticed her sword was away, stopped shivering. Now Willow could see he had a beard of brown under his round nose that stretched down below his belt buckle, which was made of silver fastened to a length of leather.

"I am sorry," said Willow, "if I frightened you. My, but I thought you were a Kappa."

The little man stood up, and he was eye level with the kneeling girl. His stature was only three feet from the tip of his hat to the bottoms of his boots.

"By my beard, what a dreadful accusation! Don't you know a Gnome when you see one?"

His offended tone felt embarrassing to Willow. She gulped, but simultaneously, she felt like laughing. The Gnome stood with his hands on his hips in an attempt to look serious, but Willow only saw a small man in a silly hat.

"I have never seen a Gnome before," said Willow, trying to stifle the laugh welling in her throat. "Where I am from, there is no one your size prancing about."

At this point, she covered her mouth with her hand to hide her widening grin. The mirthless Gnome was not impressed, nor was he happy with being seen as a joke. He began to tap his tiny foot.

"Oh, come now," he said. "You're not too tall yourself! Why, I bet I could best you in a brawl."

The Gnome raised his fists. Willow nearly fell over when he started swinging!

"Merlin! Rowan! Mr. Pinner!" shouted Willow. "Come look who I have found!"

In seconds, the company came to her position and gaped at her discovery. Merlin was the first to speak out to the defensive Gnome.

"Now, now, Rasmorn, there is no need for violence. The girl means no offense. She is simply not accustomed to your kind yet. This is her first visit to your abundant green. Given the time, I am sure she will find you quite respectable. Hear my words and be at peace."

Willow stood and rejoined them. Rasmorn felt a bit crowded with the four humans towering above him.

"Well," said the Gnome, "don't expect me to like her!"

Rasmorn crossed his arms across his chest and turned up his nose with a humph like a spoiled boy, although he was middle-aged in Gnome years. Soon, more rustling came around them in the shrubbery and bushes on either side of the forest path. Willow was the only one to flinch from the noise. She placed a hand on the hilt of Pnevma, but Merlin stopped her with a quick gesture of his hand.

Firmly, he spoke.

"All right, all of you, reveal yourselves."

And at that moment, more and more Gnomes began to pour out of the bushes, dressed in different colors of clothes and different lengths of beards. The men wore tunics similar to Rasmorn's, but theirs were either blue, green, or yellow; their beards were either white, brown, blond, red, or gray. Each of them was the same height but not of the same body type. Some were fatter, and some were skinner; some were happier, and some were angrier.

As for the women, they wore short dresses with wooden shoes, and their hair was tucked under limp cone hats. Their dresses were either purple, pink, or a lighter blue. They had smaller noses than the men did.

Regardless, Willow had never seen a crowd of little people before and knew not what to think of it all. She skittered behind Rowan when they began to draw near them. Then a larger Gnome emerged from between them all with his hand behind his back, trying not to stumble on his lengthy bleached beard. He was only slightly taller than Rasmorn and the other Gnomes, but his wideness was greater. Round and fat, he waddled closer and closer to Merlin, his large nose peeking out from under his tall cone hat. His voice was quite gurgly.

"My, my, it has been a while, wizard!"

The fat Gnome sniffed and scoffed. Merlin squatted down with support from his staff and shook hands with the Gnome.

"I believe you are right, Caflan," said Merlin, whose grip was light so as not to break the less-strong bones of the wizened Gnome. "I see you have sustained yourself in these unnatural times. I hope, for your people's sake, that you have not eaten too much."

Caflan gave Merlin a look that might have been read as full of anger or offense, but seconds later, a loud, hearty laugh erupted from both men.

"Still the ever clever Merlin! Come, come! You must enlighten us with the tales of your adventures."

The dotard Gnome gestured for the company to move forward down the grassy path.

The forest was alive around them as they walked deeper and deeper into the forest. The fireflies followed them with each stride. The Gnomes were antsy—they didn't have visitors often—and were running ahead of the company. It was such a wonder to see those little men with their little legs skipping and striding and clapping along the way. A song soon began, being led by Caflan, and from what Willow could make out, it went something like this:

Hear the wind blowing in the trees
See the animals roaming free
O the sky above is full of clouds
The ground below we do not crowd
With all our might and gnomish hope
We form this clan, our plentiful trope!

The night is here, and food awaits
Grab the bowls and forks and plates
To those who happen upon this trove
We welcome you to Onolon Grove!

With the ending of the song, the company found themselves seemingly closer to the heart of the forest, but not quite where the sequoias stood. Although the bark of the pine trees was thick and sturdy, they could not hold a candle to the bulk of those tall, looming trees four miles away.

The Gnomes' village was nothing more than mere stone constructs made of cobble bricks and mud built in a clearing of trees. They were not tall enough or wide enough for any of the human travelers to enter into. Each one was a curved stack of bricks with a blackened open doorway betwixt two small torches.

In the center of the glade, there stood the tallest of these constructs: ovular and wide with layers of bricks stacked atop one another. Attached to the rightmost wall of the construct was a colossal chimney whose smokestack reached higher than the wizards.

To the company, the construct looked no different from a dwelling fit for people of their size. The doorway was only slightly taller than the top of Willow's pate. To the right of the dwelling lay a large campfire—large for Gnomes, that is—full of dried logs and twigs and branches and a roasting spit conjured from stripped wood and long, thin grass twine. Willow wondered what it was and why it was above the firewood. She did not ask, because she assumed she would find out soon.

Caflan and the Gnomes of Onolon Grove encircled the campfire and sank to their knees. The company found their spots somewhere between them while Racer and Juniper put themselves closer to the dwelling.

Caflan's voice was strong but still littered with gurgly tones.

"Bring forth the fire! Make alive this fair firewood, and let us dance and sing in honor of our guests!"

At once, there came two younger Gnomes from within the dwelling carrying small torches. They were gnomish women, smaller than the men. Their dresses were ceremonial robes of white instead of the common colors, and they bore no cone hats. Instead, that which adorned their heads were flowery circlets made of chrysanthemums and geraniums.

They made a paced stride over to the campfire, slow and steady. It was not so terribly slow that one would consider them to be taking their time, but not fast enough to rush themselves. Within minutes, they were directly close to the campfire, and Willow watched as they cast their burning sticks into the dried tinder. The logs below the roasting spit burst into flames with a bright, warm glow. A din of gnomish claps and cheers was heard.

Seconds later, several butchered carcasses of rabbits and small poultry were presented and placed on the spit. Two of the gnomish men stood and began slowly turning the spit as the chattering began among the gathering.

"So," asked Caflan, "what brings you all to this fair woodland grove? I take it, it is most likely not your stopping point. Before the time of the Caliphate, visitors would pass by several times and camp with us. But since the land was cursed, none has shown. Seeing all of you now warms my soul."

He began to munch after taking a roll from the bowl being passed around them all.

"Many thanks," said Merlin, taking a roll. "Our business here, yes, is brief. We will stay the night before we venture onwards to the eastern river, and then our business lies with Chateau Londror. The girl, Willow, must get there with haste."

"Ah," said Rasmorn. "You seek the Purloinian baron. From what I've heard, Zohar, son of Avidar, is no longer seeing guests. A couple months back, Baron Avidar fell to Gilded soldiers in a squabble near Lod Rimona. Terrible deathmatch, that."

The crackling of the fire seemed to add an ominous element to the Gnome's recollection.

"Days after his passing, doves were sent out from Londror to the remaining allies of the Purloinians. It is a miracle they were neither shot down nor seen. It was told that his body was stolen from the battlefield by Gilded soldiers and made into decoration for the battlements of Ensalor with his head being toted back to Londror in a sack, mane and all too. His teeth were plucked out, and his eyes harvested. A bloody nightmare it was. If I were Zohar, it would take a lot for me to find sleep again."

"How frightening," said Rowan, finally receiving a roll from the communal bowl. "Such events would surely transform one into a recluse."

Willow did not know what *recluse* meant, and she was sure she did not want to know. She was already trying not to picture the gruesome organless head of Avidar. She reluctantly took a roll from the bowl. It was a soft, squishy ball of warm bread that had a smell better than the bread served at the orphanage. But she couldn't seem to eat with the description she had just listened to. Instead, she tried to compose herself and kept the roll on the wooden plate she was given minutes ago. Then a strange feeling began to grow within her as she looked around the others.

It almost felt like a family, a family with many brothers and sisters (little ones of course). Merlin felt like a grandfather while even the tallest of Gnomes were perhaps uncles and aunts. They were probably the closest thing to parents she could understand. Hearing both of the wizards discuss the fate of her parents was another addition to her low appetite. Not only was she hopeful to find the parents Merlin told her of in his office days ago, but she was hoping to bring Leo too.

She was afraid her time with him would be too little to make a connection. But the bread reminded her of that moment in the lunchroom, where she watched him scarf down the grease-slathered slab of meat he had been served. Ever since she had been told she had parents, she had wanted Leo to see them and maybe even experience what it was like to have them. She felt that if they were alive, perhaps they would take him in too, and he would be her honorary little brother.

A fine thought it was, but it seemed unlikely now. A discomforting truth had enveloped her, the truth that her parents were no longer in Kastallon, and the dream of being a sibling, let alone a daughter, was vaporized with a single utterance of words.

She tried again not to think about them as the aroma of cooked meat wafted throughout the band of tiny men and the company. To her surprise, she felt her mouth water.

"By the looks of these, it would seem they were freshly slaughtered," Merlin observed as he accepted his portion of the rabbit meat with a kind smile.

It was still steaming. Rasmorn—or rather, perhaps Gnomes themselves—must not have learned manners, as he began to talk with a mouthful of bread and juicy meat. Willow looked away and focused on the chunk of roasted chicken next to her untouched fluffy roll.

"Quite miraculous actually," Rasmorn said and finally swallowed. "Just the other night, our hunting party was about and beheld the forest creatures roaming around as usual. 'Twas a sight unseen in a decade, since the spell had been laid upon the land. In fact, I was hoping the reason why you and your company have arrived was to explain the recent changes."

Merlin licked his fingers and savored the taste of the rabbit as he chewed. The cooked skin was not too crispy or too soft; it was just the right balance of the two. He picked up the fluffy roll and bit into it with a slight crunch from the baked outer shell. Once he swallowed, his voice was kindly like a gentle rain falling on leaves in the early morning.

"I think we should let the girl explain it herself."

He gave a look over to Willow, who was finally taking tiny bites of the meal on her plate. A sudden silence then swept over the gathering, and only the crackling of the fire and quiet munching from the Gnomes was heard. Caflan wiped his mouth with his sleeve, leaving a stain of rabbit grease. Willow took a hesitant glance up from her plate and back and then began to blush. She had realized that the crowd around her had ceased speaking, and all their tiny eyes were focused on her with anticipation. She gulped.

"Um," she said, the redness filling her cheeks. "W-what was the question?"

If no one spoke up, she was sure tears would begin to well. A second passed, and Merlin chimed in.

"Willow, tell them the truth about why the world is changing. Speak from the heart, and only from the heart. Your perspective is of more value."

The Gnomes, entranced by the wizard's words, shifted back to the girl with a quivering lower lip. This was unexpected.

Speak from the heart, she thought. *All right.*

She cleared her throat with a fist over her mouth.

"From what I have been told by both Merlin and the grand warden Pinner, I am what you all believe to be the One Who Unites."

She paused and placed her left hand on her scabbard tightly as she used the right to unsheathe Pnevma from it. The sharpened blade glistened in the firelight before them, and the purple Shimmer gem glowed faintly as if filled with an essence of sorts. The Gnomes, except Rasmorn, were in awe of the fashionable weapon. A few of them murmured as Willow held it high above her.

"This is the sword of my mother, Pnevma. From the words of Skeef, it was prophesied that I would wield it. It was also prophesied in the same that the world itself would change when I am come to this land of yours. The desert would wet, and the forests would blossom with life once again. But I have greater news to tell. I have met with Skeef!"

At the mention of Skeef, the entire gnomish mass filled the clearing with an astonished gasp. Once again, nothing but the ambient chittering and skittering was all to be heard.

A few seconds later, Willow began again.

"It was yesterday actually, when the sun was still high in the sky. Rowan"—she pointed to him—"can verify what I am about to reveal. We were in the midst of the Shriveled Forest in the northwest. We had escaped a band of bandits and an evil witch who tried to capture us! Luckily, Rowan there is a wizard-in-training, and he used a bag of Shimmer dust to summon a mighty inferno to blow them all away.

"As the morning progressed, we found ourselves lost and afraid in the forest, being chased down by a giant owl monster. Rowan found me in a cave, and then we saw the golden lights of the wind beckoning us to follow it farther and farther into the woodland. Perhaps a while went by, and then we arrived at a glade in the middle of the whole thing, only instead of the dreary stalks of trees comprising the rest of the forest, the landscape therein was ripe with life, teeming with animals and flowers and sunlight! That was when I saw him.

"There, sleeping gently and silently on a patch of grass serving as the epicenter of the golden lights, was the White Lamb with his snowy coat of white. He greeted us and told us to be at peace. I, for one, did not believe what I was seeing, but the Lamb insisted that everything was true, and what I was seeing was, in fact, real. Then he showed me a vision of the past, and I soon pardoned all doubt in him. To sum it up, I have spoken with the White Lamb, and hope remains so long as I remain, it seems."

She sheathed her sword and secured it with a faint click. The Gnomes sat quietly—some with tears in their eyes, others with an explicit countenance of awe or disbelief. Had this girl really seen the White Lamb? Questions similar ran through their heads. They began to glance at one another until finally Rowan stood.

"It seems you value a second opinion," said Rowan. "As the girl said before, I can assure you that this information is the truth. I was there when the White Lamb appeared before us in the clearing, sleeping soundly and peacefully. It talked to us with its mind or rather a feeling we felt. It was as if our own thoughts were creating words in our ears as the Lamb eyed us and tilted its head. Though I have heard merely stories of the legends of Skeef, I do know he only appears as cloven animals. The dryads were there too, green and swathed in vines."

All gnomish eyes were on Caflan now. Rasmorn, who had just scarfed down the last of his poultry, even turned his nose to him. The old Gnome rose from his seat with a faint grunt and raised a hand to silence the growing murmurs.

"Good Gnomes of Onolon, great news has come to us tonight!" said Caflan. "These travelers, including my old comrade Merlin, are our distinguished guests. There is no further proof that we need to believe that this girl, this Willow, is the One Who Unites. She carries the sword and was summoned by Skeef himself! Let us lift our voices once more!"

A din of cheering sounded, and each Gnome dispersed from their seats around the fire, dashing quickly into their tiny homes of cobblestone. At once, they each returned, taking only sets beyond the thresholds, holding lightly their pillows. It seemed, Willow observed, that they were beginning preparations for sleep. Each gnomish little family—two parents and one to three children each—was joining hands.

The sight warmed Willow's heart, and she smiled not only from the wholesome images but also from the knowledge that rest was coming. She had been on her feet all day, and though her heels were not aching, she knew that if they tarried any longer, the pain would arise.

Soon, a soft song began to ring through each branch and each budding leaf of the trees in the grove, a song wishing for peaceful snoozing and a refreshing awakening. Willow closed her eyes and allowed the words around her to penetrate deep in her mind.

O fertile ground with dirt so soft
Be mine sole and comforting altar
To bear my burdens and carry my thoughts
To make sure my dreams do not falter
Give us slumber as we close our eyes
To fall asleep and rest our minds

May the sky be blue and forever clear
As we awake with ones so dear
May the wind be gentle and the air be cool
As we begin our rituals
O may the harvest be long and bountiful
May the night be swift and danger be little

O fertile ground with dirt so soft
Be mine sole and comforting altar
To bear my burdens and carry my thoughts
To make sure my dreams do not falter

Then the song was over, and each gnomish family disappeared behind the darkened doorways of their cobblestone abodes. The company was guided by Caflan into the dwelling. Inside, it was very similar to that of the Tel save for the tables and bookshelves. In the farther reach of the four walls, there lay a space littered with pillows and other plush objects intended for sleeping.

Willow removed her cloak as she lay down and used it as a blanket. She then drifted off quickly to sleep.

Chapter 11

Between the Behemoths

Willow was shaken awake. When she opened her heavy eyes, the blurriness slowly began to reveal the shape of a man with a long ivory beard. Her mind was hazy from grogginess, but she could tell that the wide eyes staring back at her were indeed Merlin's. She could never forget the old man's kind eyes, blue like the morning sky. His whispered voice, however, was drenched with urgency.

"Awaken now. Hurry, hurry! Gather your things, but do it quietly. They are not far from the edge of the grove. How they found us I know not."

She didn't know precisely who they were, but the idea that it was a regiment of Gilded soldiers was not off the table. She rubbed her eyes quickly and rose to her feet. Rowan was nowhere to be seen. The large room of the dwelling was beginning to slow in its rotation, though she knew it was only her brain making her think it was rotating.

She looked down and realized her boots were still on and sought with her eyes to find the sword housed in the scabbard. She glanced at the fireplace and saw no trace; she glanced at the cupboards, and again, there was nothing but a few crumbs. She turned around to assure herself she hadn't placed it behind her before she slept; she saw nothing still! Where could it have gone? Last she remembered, she had secured it inside the scabbard strapped around her waist.

"Come now, my dear!" said Merlin, his hand firmly clenched around his staff.

She took up her cloak and clipped it together just below the neck, the brown drape flowing just above her heels behind her, which provided a fair amount of warmth. Over it, she strapped the rucksack on her shoulders. Before heading out behind Merlin through the door, she made one last look and conceded the idea that the weapon was somewhere in the dwelling.

Outside, the Gnomes were gone; the campsite was an empty, lifeless shell of what it had been hours ago. The wind was still, and the sun was not far from its eastern burrow, beaming rays onto the tree stalks and underbrush. The faint sound of marching boots and neighing steeds could be heard in the distance from the northeastern tree line.

Whoever they are, they do not know we are here, Willow guessed.

"Where are Caflan and Rasmorn and the rest of the Gnomes?" Willow asked, confused. She saw no trace of tracks in the leafy floor of the forest.

"Look carefully once more," said Merlin in a soft voice, trying to keep his volume to a minimum without going so quiet that Willow could not hear him.

Willow squinted briefly as she looked to her right in the tree line where the clearing and woodland met, and to her relief, she saw the same tiny boots like she had seen last night, only there were many upon many of them now. They were all hiding. From what she was unsure. Then a rustling came from behind the dwelling, a sound of heavier footsteps than those of a Gnome or a young man. Something was dragging behind it too, for whatever it was could be heard crunching in the leaves.

Merlin craned his neck to glance behind Willow, and suddenly, he saw red. There, bent over and supported by a twisted wooden staff, was the black shape of Pinner, tiptoeing slowly as if he was cautious of something unseen, carrying Pnevma still in its scabbard in his left hand. The sight of him nearly forced Merlin's tone to anger, yet the wizard held in his fury. With restraint, Merlin moved to him and kept his voice low. Willow could still hear an angry cadence, something very uncommon for the headmaster.

"What do you think you are doing with that?" Merlin scolded. "It does not belong to you. It has no relation to you!"

Pinner simply smirked and refused to blush, as one did when caught red-handed. Instead, he formed an excuse for his behavior in his mind, and the words came through his crooked teeth.

"Why, Merlin, my friend, I was simply admiring its beautiful craftsmanship. Whoever the smiths working the old forge in your home certainly are excellent with their work. Would not you allow me to bear a few minutes more? I do terribly love a good sword."

"As I said before, Pinner Vemtal, the blade is not your own. I suggest you return it to its rightful owner, or I shall smite you where you stand!"

Although Merlin was not talking very loudly, Willow felt a lump of fear in her throat for the dotard. She had not known him for long, but in that time, she hadn't taken him for a thief. *Smite* she had heard from some of the old books, and each time it was mentioned, someone was hurt. She kept her eyes focused on Pinner.

With a semblance of reluctance, Pinner placed the blade in Merlin's outstretched hand and took a few steps back to his former spot.

"My thanks," said Merlin rather blandly. "It seems I shall have to keep my eye on you as our journey prolongs. But answer me this, if you can. Have you seen Rowan, the young man with fair hair, and the zebra named Racer?"

At this moment, a fluttering of wings was heard. The sound came not from larger wings like that of a Strix or any other large avian but from Juniper the Toucan. Quick she came as she glided down from one of the pine branches high above the clearing. Willow saw her and presented her arm, and the bird touched down gracefully onto it, but her expression was quite the opposite. Merlin then turned to her but made sure that Pinner stayed within his peripheral vision, for his lividity had not been soothed or quelled.

Juniper spoke with both anxiety and dread.

"Sorry I did not come sooner. Rowan will be back soon with Racer. They went a bit ahead and through the forest to scout the path forward. But I'm afraid I come bearing dastardly news. There are Gilded troops about two hours' march away. They are being led by a general in a brushed helmet. I don't think I have ever seen him before."

It was a long road from Ensalor to Onolon, being at least three days' march by foot. How this general rallied a battalion in half that time was astonishing, and Willow began to fear for the company's lives.

"It seems this general has gone town by town through the night and camp by camp, calling troops to order," said Merlin, putting both hands on his staff in an inquisitive fashion. "It is not possible for an army of that quantity to descend upon this grove that quickly."

He turned around to peer into the bushes and conifers surrounding the clearing. Before he could call out to the Gnomes, an alarming rustling and cracking came from the tree line in the same direction where Juniper came.

Holding the hilt of her sheathed sword, Willow readied herself. Had they already entered the forest? Had they really wasted this much time? She peeked slightly at Merlin and saw small beads of sweat forming on his brow. He was both nervous and vexed, and perhaps such emotion was burning him up, yet his gaze was primed solely on the tree line.

Then Willow remembered something at the last second and relieved her grip. The sound was not of many boots or rushing hooves. It was a singular rider tramping and clopping through the glade. She plodded forward a bit. Suddenly, this rider emerged, and her premonition was correct.

It was a horse of black-and-white with ebony hair flowing while its mouth was bridled. Sitting upon this horse was a young, fair-haired man in a charcoal tunic, whose shamshir was bouncing with each stride. His umber cloak was draped across the horse's backside.

"Rowan!" cried Willow with joy.

The rider threw back the hood of his cloak and revealed a face full of worry. His usual grin was now overtaken by a distressed, mirthless frown. Willow's glee vanished.

"We have to move," said Rowan, his voice wrought with urgency. "Now."

He presented a hand to Willow, and as she took it, he pulled her aboard Racer, swinging her left leg over his back. As she had done before, Willow wrapped her arms round Rowan securely. Merlin and Pinner then positioned themselves next to them.

"We cannot leave the forest with our previous plan," said Pinner. "They will only cut us off once they catch us moving east. A terrible chase it would be."

"Then what do you propose?" asked Merlin, still disappointed in the old sorcerer. "South would take us to the Gallant Valley, and likely, we will meet more soldiers there. Obviously, north is out of the question. That only leaves the west."

Merlin scratched his beard.

A thought presently came into Willow's mind, a vivid but a tad hazy memory of the map inside Tel Pata. She remembered the Bell Mountains southwest of Onolon, how they towered above the horizon as they journeyed from the Shriveled Forest. They were like giants' legs reaching down from the clouds, giving the illusion that something massive was upright upon the land. She wondered if those were an option. If there was a cave in the forest in that dell, there most likely had to be one big enough in the mountains.

She blurted out her words.

"What about the Bell Mountains? Surely that way is an option."

She gulped, as she hoped she had not said the wrong thing or presented a pointless idea. But the wizards considered it for a moment. (She could tell by their pondering faces.)

"Well," said Merlin, "the Garmouth runs through them, as does the Southern River. Yet there is always the possibility of danger. I've heard stories upon stories of beasts and barbarians watching every speck of that path. Seems our only option in our current state."

"There is danger everywhere," said Rowan. "The One Who Unites is a target wherever she goes, a target that extends to us as well."

A lump of fear welled in Willow's throat, but it soon dissipated when Juniper said, "But that is why she has us."

She chirped and flapped her wings triumphantly.

"If we can handle a witch and her minions, certainly we can take on anything that follows. She has the sword, remember?"

Willow placed a hand on Pnevma, still sheathed. She was happy to have her own protection instead of relying on others. It didn't seem fair to her.

"It is settled, then," said Pinner. "We shall retrace our steps and go around the mountains before going through the Garmouth. Then we shall hastily follow the river away from the valley and cross over into the Vast Woodland, where Londror lies. It will be difficult no doubt, but we shall manage. Skeef will be with us every step of the way."

Willow thought for a moment that she could see out of the corner of her eye the shape of the White Lamb somewhere in the forest, but it was just the sunrays glistening off the branches. She wondered if she would ever see him again, for she longed for that sense of peace she had felt before. It felt as if every step, every decision, was cause for another morsel of anxiety, a fear of failure.

The company began a few steps back through the forest where they entered from but quickly halted when two voices cried out from behind them. Still aboard Racer, Rowan shifted to see what the exclamation was. All their eyes were drawn to two tiny Gnomes, a man and a woman, jogging toward them. The leaves from their hiding spots were still bouncing, so it must have been seconds after they began. The man was younger than Rasmorn, for his hazel beard was not quite as long. His tiny tunic was green as opposed to Rasmorn's red, and his cone hat was not as tall. The woman was dressed in a light blue skirt with her hair tucked behind her. Her cheeks were flushed as she ran.

"Wait!" they called in a hurry. "We want to come with you!"

Willow was confused as to why two small people not even as tall as her would want to take such a perilous quest. In the woman's hand, she saw a rosary of several spherical wooden beads strung together. They dangled and bounced in her jog.

Merlin, seeing them, stepped a few paces forward to meet them.

"Valner, Rossa," he said, "now is not the time for bravery."

He squatted to meet them on their level.

Valner huffed and puffed before he spoke.

"We understand, Sir Merlin. But we are young and not as feeble as Caflan. We cherish excitement and crave adventure. Would you not allow us to join your journey? We have protection, and we shan't get in the way!"

Valner revealed a needlelike small knife from the belt wrapped around his tunic. Rossa did the same, but hers was not as long.

"This," said Rossa, "is for the girl."

She procured the rosary and reached high to hand it to Willow, who awkwardly reached down from upon Racer and accepted it.

"It is a special necklace," Rossa added, "made from the roots of the tallest sequoia in the grove. It carries the same immunity to curses that those trees have. It will protect you and guard your mind from wickedness."

The rosary would not fit around Willow's neck, and if she had tried, it would have been a choking hazard. Instead, it fitted nicely around her wrist.

"I thank you," said Willow. "But it is Merlin's decision to have you accompany us."

Merlin smirked with pride as he turned to face Willow, a pride that only a father had for his child, only he was her headmaster, not her father, when said child reached a good milestone.

"Actually, my dear," said Merlin, "you are the One Who Unites, and we are your company. That decision lies with you."

Merlin stood and retook his spot next to Racer. In the distance, to the northwest, the sun began to cast golden glimmers on the first soldiers' armor.

A decision had to be made, and quick. Sure, these Gnomes were small, but small meant they could fit in places the bigger ones could not. Smallness made for silent, sneakier movements. They would be great scouts, as it would be harder to detect them.

Willow's lips wrinkled and twisted in a contemplative frown. The sound of marching boots and stamping hooves and neighing horses drew nearer and nearer. Smallness had its perks, but there was also a single detrimental disadvantage: weakness.

The Gnomes were a simple folk focused on living simple lives. They were not fighters or warriors. They were not leaders or those capable of leading. They were farmers and singers. Sure, they hunted for their own food. But that food was harmless and incapable of defending themselves. It was not impressive enough to be called hunting.

"I have made a decision," said Willow quickly.

The Gnomes held their hands to their chests in anticipation. There was hope in their eyes, and the company could see it.

"They shall come with us."

*****

A few hours had passed since the company evacuated Onolon Grove and had taken the two Gnomes with them. By now, the sun was at its highest point and beat warm sunshine down on them as they walked. It was a steady pace for all of them, and Pinner assured them that they would be at the base of the first mountain on the northern side by nightfall. For now, they were close to a tributary branching away from the Southern River. It was nearly full now with the riverbed being completely hidden. The banks were soaked, and grass and cattails grew from their edges.

Willow had never heard of anything back home called Garmouth. It sounded as if it was giving the name for an animal's consumption orifice, but from what Pinner had said about it, she guessed it was some wide opening, and what followed was a path no one should ever tread. She tried to keep the fear at bay by remembering that she was with good company. She had Merlin and Rowan and Juniper. That was all she needed. The rosary, too, was a good defense for her spirit. Rossa said it was constructed from the wood of one of the sequoia trees' roots. It was a nice little trinket, but she thought of it more as a souvenir for Leo. She figured it might fit him better anyways. Maybe.

By now, the company had been on an unending stride, and Valner, whose legs and ankles were beginning to ache, began to moan with exhaustion. Rossa patted him on the back. They both carried smaller packs compared to the others.

"May we stop to rest awhile?" said Valner. "My poor tiny feet cannot take much more trodding. The sun's light is waning now, and soon, twilight will be upon us. Should not we set up a bivouac at this time?"

He was the first one to stop and drop to his knees. The rest of the company felt pressed to stop too, so they did, all except Pinner.

"What is the meaning of this?" Pinner objected. "We cannot stop now! We must reach the base of the mountain by nightfall. If we stop now, it will be noon before we reach it."

He stomped his twisted staff into the dirt.

"Oh, come now, Pinner," said Merlin heartily. "I think we can spare a few hours. Besides, I'd say this lot has had enough adventure for the night. Rest is crucial, you know."

He rested a gentle hand on the old man's shoulder.

"Why don't you help the Gnomes set up the camp, hmm?"

"Then he can help with the song!" urged Rossa with excitement. "The more, the merrier!"

She and Valner set down their packs and unloaded them with meticulous hands. They set out plates and forks and spoons, as well as tinder for fire-making and a pot for cooking things. Willow watched them as she was helped off Racer. Juniper flew down and used her beak to pick up tinder and place it in the bundle that was beginning to form.

Valner took a wooden mallet from his pack and began to drive a tall stake into the ground. *Whack* went the mallet. *Whack, whack, whack.* A few seconds of whacks, and the stake was secure. Then this process was repeated a second time with a separate but equally tall stake. These stakes were unique, as the tops of them, which were usually flattened or rounded, were instead carved into a U shape meant to hold another thin log meant for hanging cookware or roasting meat. Willow saw the pot and guessed a soup was in the works for tonight's meal. Then she realized her stomach was growling at her, and she covered it with a hand, thinking it would somehow hide her hunger. The sound only furthered the Gnomes' growing joy.

Gnomes, on top of being simple, were selfless folk too. They enjoyed helping others and making friends and sharing meals or drinks with people they liked. Most of the time, Gnomes ate four times a day; and seeing how Valner and Rossa only ate breakfast, it was understandable they were quite famished at this point.

Rossa procured a cutting knife from her pack and unwrapped a few carrots and potatoes she had taken from the dwelling's supply.

"How about a good, hearty potato soup?" she asked.

The others' response to her question was more stomach rumbling with wide-eyed salivating. She then began to dice the vegetables on the wrapping that they were packaged in, which was a malleable hide.

A few more minutes passed, and the soup was cooking in the pot over the campfire. Willow had fetched water, and Rowan, who allowed Racer to graze, had helped Merlin and Valner set up a few tents for the night. They were nothing but drapes supported by more stakes and rope. The ground beneath them had been dug to make for a flatter, more comfortable spot for sleeping. Willow wondered if this was what was referred to as camping. The bivouac was a few yards from the river.

Rossa took some small wooden bowls from her pack and passed them out, giving one to each of the members of the company. One by one, they took the spoon from the pot and ladled a portion of the soup into their bowls. Willow had never smelled anything quite as aromatic. Even the sight of it—the chunks of carrots and potato and the bits of herbs and spices—seemed to increase her hunger.

She took the metal spoon in her hand, but before she could scoop soup into her mouth, the Gnomes stood and cleared their throats. A song started, and Willow could hear the words clearly as they sprang into dance with their singing.

Food is a very wonderful thing
It fills and soothes and satisfies
You can keep it tied up with just a string
Food is what we all now severely cling

Food is a very beautiful thing
It makes for a good, warm, happy night
You can bake it, fry it, flip it, wrap it tight
Food will keep you going without a fright

Food is a very amazing thing
No matter the day, no matter the time
A bit of soup for now made with thyme
Food will help continue the forward climb

The company applauded as the Gnomes bowed, huffing and puffing from the activity.

"And now," said Rossa, "please partake!"

She sat back down and dived into her share of the soup, shoving scoop after scoop of the creamy puddle. The rest of the company followed suit, and soon, satisfied grunts in approval came after. The sad part was, there was none left for seconds.

"That was the best bowl of soup I've ever had," said Willow, forgetting her manners. But none of the company thought anything of it. "Can you make more?"

Although her stomach was no longer roaring, her appetite was not quenched. She got up and presented her bowl to Rossa.

"Oh, my dear, I would. But the moon, it seems, is upon us, and it would be quite uncomfortable to sleep on a stomach too full," said Rossa. "Better to let this bite simmer before eating any further."

Even if she were to argue, it would have been pointless. She was not starving, but she was not exactly full either. She went back to her place by the fire and plopped down with legs crossed. Valner saw this as he smirked and grabbed his pack. He unbuckled the thin strap and reached in to find another morsel wrapped in the leathery cloth same as the vegetables. But knowing Valner, this time, he pulled out two pieces of something that had a sweet, sugary scent. It was a bit crumbly—it must have been jostled around during the trek—and some of the crumbs rolled off the wrapping into the dirt. Once both morsels were open, Valner moseyed over to Willow and presented one of them to her.

"Here," he said. "Have this."

Willow took a peek at the morsel sitting delicately in the Gnome's hand. It was a cubed slice of a cake of some sort, dark brown and spongy. She assumed it was chocolate cake, like that which could be seen in the bakery near the orphanage. She would see it from time to time when Veraminta would, although seldom, allow them a field trip to the gardens or the museums, and she would catch a glimpse of the dessert, as well as the pound upon pound of other sweet delicacies, such as doughnuts, pastries, pies, or éclairs too. But this piece of spongy goodness was unlike any of those she had seen before. Her curiosity overcame her fear of what it might be.

"What is it?" asked Willow, taking the cake slice and holding it close in two hands.

"Gingerbread," said Valner, still grinning. "Us Gnomes love to bake it for special occasions. Also because ginger root grows natively in Onolon. It's sweet and flavorful!"

Valner then began to eat his portion heartily.

Willow considered taking the whole for herself, but she looked over at Rowan sitting grumpily next to the fire, wrapped in his cloak. His bowl was freshly empty, and the spoon was still slumped to one side of it.

Perhaps he hasn't had something sweet in months, years maybe, she thought.

Remembering what Mr. Linmer, now Merlin, used to tell her—"A sharing heart is a caring heart"—she stood and took a few steps over to where Merlin's apprentice sat alone. She broke the piece of gingerbread in half.

"I want you to have this," said Willow. "It's gingerbread. Valner gave me a slice of it, and I remembered I never thanked you for saving me in Al Wafra. I guess this is how I can repay you since I don't have any gold."

Rowan's face turned into a warm smile.

"I've no need for gold."

He accepted the cake.

"This is one of the nicest things someone has done for me in a while. Thank you."

Willow sat next to him and nibbled on her piece of cake. Indeed, it was sweet and flavorful, but the flavors combined were those she had never tasted before: cinnamon, nutmeg, and cloves. Before long, she realized she had scarfed it all down.

It was a good night. There were no soldiers, no angry bakers, and no Strixes or Kappas, just a warm fire, good food, and good company.

Several minutes passed, and a yawn was produced from the mouth of Valner, a deep, drowsy yawn that was contagious, for Rossa and then Pinner did too. The moon's ascension had reached its peak, and the stars revealed themselves. They were tiny white lights on a canvas of shadow as if a painter had flicked a white-and-silver mixture onto his first coat of black. By now, both Rowan and Willow were lying on their backs in the soft grass.

Rowan pointed at one of the clusters of stars, just above where the tips of trees ceased. They were in almost a strange Y shape.

"See that?" he said. "That's Norlik, the Praise Constellation. My mother would tell me stories of how it was one of the first constellations to appear before Eon Primary."

He pointed to another cluster, this time in a shape mimicking a trapezoid.

"That one there is Vida, the Sleeping Constellation. It is the indicator of midnight."

"How many are there?" asked Willow.

"As many as the eye can see," Rowan replied. He then replaced his arm with the other behind his head.

Willow stared restlessly at the night sky, which was surprisingly clear.

"Do they have constellations in the world you were raised in?"

Rowan's tone hinted toward curiosity and sincere inquisitiveness.

"Yes," said Willow. "From what I remember from Merlin telling me, there was Orion the Hunter shaped like an hourglass, the Big and Little Dippers shaped like spoons, and Capricornus shaped like an upside-down triangle. There are probably several more, but I don't remember them."

"Interesting," said Rowan. "I would very much like to see them. Stars are one of the many things I like. Merlin tells me they are the fallen souls of those who have gone beyond and that constellations are the little shows they put on for us to let us know everything is all right."

"Sounds comforting," said Willow. "It's almost like heaven."

"Heaven?" asked Rowan.

The word seemed foreign to him like a word in another language.

"What is heaven?"

Willow wasn't sure how to answer. She had heard some of the adults talking about heaven in their conversation when they passed their lines in the hallways before class time. She had found—or rather, one was given to her—a dictionary, and she had looked up the word. What it told was that heaven was along the lines of "a place in the sky for several religions" or "a calm, peaceful situation," but neither of those seemed to match up with what she meant.

Rowan saw her confused face lost in thought, and then he, too, thought for a moment. Then it dawned on him.

"Like an afterlife?" said Rowan.

"What's that?" asked Willow.

"It is said that when we die in this world, there is a better, more dreamlike reality we enter into. Something like life after death, a rebirth."

Willow remembered her grammar lessons and understood that the pairing of *r* and *e* before a word meant to start something again.

"Another birth?" she asked, taking it literally.

"Don't think about it too much," Rowan said and chuckled. "Rest now, young one. We've a busy morning ahead of us, and you will need all the energy you can get."

The two of them then drifted off to sleep to the sound of the crackling fire and the soft chittering of the critters in the distance.

*****

Morning came, and with it came the bright song of birds long thought gone by the people who enjoyed listening to them: thrushes, meadowlarks, whip-poor-wills, and orioles. As the company walked along the base of the northernmost mountain of the Bell cluster, they could hear these songs and watched as some of the birds flapped and glided through the air, their yellow, brown, and blue bodies majestic and graceful with every movement. Willow had never seen any of them before. She only knew of the common robins and sparrows that would occasionally drop by on the windowsill or produce a song when they were outside for recess.

Juniper was not out of her sleepy stupor yet, and she was, like she had been lately, perched still as a stone on Racer's back with her beady eyes closed. Pinner, as usual, led the company as they trod around the base of the mountain.

"This summit," said Pinner, "is the mountain known as Knotvall. It is the first mountain to be seen if you were to view it from Ensalor. In the northeast, they call it River's Peak."

Suddenly, Pinner paused; and as he did, so, too, did the company. Ahead of them, they could see the river of the mountain's namesake flowing with a gentle current glittering in the sunlight, little white beads twinkling on the waves. Its grassy banks were damp as the shallow water passed over the many large boulders lying motionless in the stream. To their left, they could see the forested foot of Knotvall shrouded with cedar trees with leaves halfway finished regaining their greenish tints.

"Praise the White Lamb!" cried Rowan, his face that of unrepressed joy. "Years have passed since the river has seen its full flow. It warms my heart to watch the current."

"No time for reflection, boy," said Pinner. He took a few steps closer to the bank after walking past Rowan mounted on Racer. "Watch and learn, prentices."

Both Willow and Rowan watched as the black-garmented man raised his staff of twisted wood in both hands, spoke something in a loud voice in a language Willow did not understand, and struck the riverbed with the lower tip of the staff. For a few seconds, nothing happened but the splash made by the staff. But upon the fifth second, the water with its gleaming wetness began to split as if the wind had sliced the stream in half like the stroke of a sword. The current remained, but there was now a clear, pebbly path of damp dirt and flopping fish between the two sections of river.

Willow, as with the eggs and the explosion in the desert, knew not what to think of it. All she could think was to simply be amazed with a gaping mouth, letting an awed sound escape.

The Gnomes jumped for joy; Merlin nodded in complete understanding, for he knew this was exactly the right strategy for crossing. There was no spell for conjuring a stone or wood bridge. There was no spell for drying up the water without making it permanent. Pinner had used a division spell to part the stream like the one he had used during the Exodus of Ensalor years ago.

"After you," said Merlin, gesturing to Willow and Rowan to go forth.

Pinner said nothing as they passed him since he was the one who had to keep the spell intact.

A few seconds later, Merlin passed Pinner, crossed the uncovered riverbed path, and stepped onto the grassy bank on the other side. Pinner then held his staff above his head as he crossed before letting the stream reconnect once more, the action happening as smoothly as if nothing had happened. Willow watched the two halves gently collide, and the stream was one again.

*****

Sweat began to drip down her back and stain her tunic too. Willow and the company had been trekking for a while, ever since they made their way around River's Peak. It was a constant march in the soft, grassy path as they came closer and closer to the Garmouth. None of them felt like talking since talking used energy, and they needed all they could get to keep going. Juniper had taken a few brief glides ahead to scout for danger, and each time she did, there was nothing to report. There had been a moment, though, in the scouting where they feared more troops had cut them off.

"Wait! Wait!" Juniper had said, jumping off Racer's rump and flapping wildly ahead of the company. "Don't you hear that?"

None of the others had heard even a mouse's scamper. They had watched as Juniper flew higher and higher up the mountains' side to their left, squinting to keep her in view. She had stayed in place for a tad, as if she was scanning, and then she alighted once more in her previous place. The big-beaked bird had seemed to be all right.

"Did you see anything?" Willow had asked.

"No," replied the bird. "Must have been the breaking of a boulder. The rain from days ago must have loosened one of them."

The company had breathed a short sigh of relief.

They were lucky to have escaped Onolon without meeting any of those gold-and-black-armored folk. Perhaps they would have stood a chance. But chances with low positive outcomes were never worth taking.

Soon, their path began to widen into a gorge, large stone canyons below mountains with a shallow stream winding through it, the grassy plains turning to pebbly shoals. The water was gentle and flowed the same as the river had before. Willow was sure she had never seen anything quite as tall as those mountainous walls that rose on either side of the stream.

"I present to you all the Garmouth," said Pinner with a smirk.

The company had occupied the leftmost side of the shoals and began to stride forth onto the pebbly beds.

"This should keep us hidden for the time being," said Merlin. "You cannot fit an entire battalion through here."

He coughed.

"Shall we press on?"

The question was addressed to his companions with a hand gesture.

Rasmorn moaned and rubbed his knees.

"My good wizard, I regret to remind you that we little folk are not accustomed to long marches."

Rossa placed a hand on his shoulder.

Merlin's visage turned sour.

"It is rather frustrating to ask for adventure and then complain to your host that you are tired. Should we have refused your offer?"

Rasmorn quickly straightened up.

"No, sir," he said. "We—"

"We understood that you were on your way to the Vast Woodland and hoped the journey, albeit wondrous and adventurous, would be short," Rossa interrupted. "We were not expecting hours upon hours and miles upon miles. Gnomes are used to brisk walks and long evenings. Traveling throughout the day is rather tiresome."

"Fortunate for you," said Merlin, "we must stop for a moment to catch our breaths. But in the future, it would be wise to not put on airs your suggestions and take the journey as it comes."

"Yes, sir," said Rasmorn, thankful.

By now, the warm wind blew moderately through their cloaks and thin sleeves. The craggy giants stood like watchful sentries as the Gnomes and Rowan began to set up the bivouac. Rossa once again created the bipod cooking apparatus and set to cooking right away.

Merlin pulled Willow aside near the stream and handed her a drinking flask.

"Go ahead and fill it up," he said. "It was something that I meant to give when we first stepped foot in this land, but at the time, I was too worried about Pinner to remember."

The flask itself was a leather pouch similar to the pouch of Shimmer but slightly smaller and more rounded. It was as long as the horn he had given her earlier. Willow accepted it.

"That's okay. I had some from Rowan when he first took me in," she said as she lowered the pouch into the stream and watched the clear purity flow into it.

Water did not drip through leather, and she was sure to keep it tightly bound with string.

A moment of silence passed as the two took in their surroundings. The mountains of Ittermount and Mount Quall and the space they occupied between them—it was like a wilderness painting Willow might have seen hanging on one of the halls in the orphanage. The trees scarcely found on the shoals near the base of the behemoths were sturdy black oaks with leaves of yellow and green shades. They were like the watchers or scouts that reported to the sentries, and the wind meant they were gossiping about the travelers. The sky was finally back to its normal light blue happiness, albeit beginning to turn pinkish as the sun began to set.

The sound of the gentle current created the background as they talked.

"Why did you never tell me about this place until my birthday? I…I understand that I couldn't see Juniper till I was ten, but would it not have been sound to tell me earlier?"

Willow did not look at Merlin when she spoke. She kept her head down and eyes focused on the earth beneath her.

"Perhaps," said Merlin, "I did not want to frighten you with details you would not have understood. I wanted you to see the magic for yourself, to see Juniper, so that you would know it was true, every word of it. You would know the difference between a story a father might tell his children at night and a very real place unheard of in Earthrealm's history."

"I think I can handle it now," Willow said, finally looking at the old wizard.

Merlin saw something in her eyes he had never seen before—not in his office, not inside Balaen, and not even in the forest hours ago. There, in the bluish hue of her irises, was a spark of determination, a fire slowly being stoked by the bellows of potential.

"I believe you're right, dear," said Merlin.

With a wave of his hand, the words began to flow from his mouth with an eloquence unmatched even by the best orators and storytellers.

Chapter 12

Thunder across the Sea

A decade ago, in the final days of Eon Primary, Château Ensalor was the cornerstone of all magic and commonwealth in the Land Where Castles Lie. It was the largest, wealthiest castle of the four castles, those being Ensalor, Londror, Nessongor, and Delnor. People, including beings such as Gnomes or giants, cherished their time within its walls and considered it a privilege to be granted an audience with the duke and duchess. They were the fairest and most just in the land, and they descended from a long lineage of nobility, stretching back to Fredwin and Bella.

Before the collapse, I remembered them as some of the greatest friends and rulers I ever had the honor of serving. I was magistrate after all, and Pinner grand warden. The four of us together established the First Chapter of Skeef, a group meant only for times of emergency. Luckily, we only ever had to gather a handful of times—famine, natural disaster, and teetering on the brink of civil war to name a few. Thankfully, each of those conflicts never reached a prolonged period, nor did they ever happen after their first occurrences.

The duke and duchess, early in their reign, were also some of the fiercest warriors to ever take the thrones. Their prowess on the battlefield was a great deterrent for those who would seek an attempt at rebellion, knowing full well that any smattering of uprising would be thwarted by the armies of Ensalor, and their wrath would be terrible yet swift. That being said, they were not ready for the might of the Caliphate.

It was a cold morning. First light had just broken through the clouds. The birds were chirping and singing their songs like every other normal morning. Even the wind was calm and blew mildly through the boughs of the courtyard elms. All seemed as it were, and the day began with the same peace known year-round. But I could tell something did not feel right.

I greeted the sovereigns, as I did every morning when they entered the throne room for their breakfasts. The duke was chipper, taking many spoonfuls of eggs and many cups of milk as he sat at the end of the table nearest the Two Thrones. There were servants and handmaidens about.

"A grand morning to Your Excellency," I said, bowing.

"And a grand morning to you, Merlin, my friend," said the duke after downing another cup of milk to wash down the bread.

I looked at the duchess and saw that she sat in discomfort, a poor expression befalling her beauty.

"My lady, whatever is it that has wrought you malaise today?"

I took a few steps in her direction. She was using her fork to peruse the food on her plate instead of taking it to her mouth.

"It is nothing, Magistrate," she said weakly. "Simply nothing."

I frowned.

"Surely there is something bothering you that is causing you this irritation."

She did not seem in the mood for conversation, as her silence indicated.

"She did not sleep soundly in the night," the duke chimed. "'Twas a half slumber of tossing and turning."

The duke sipped the brown nectar in his silver chalice.

The rest of the meal was deafened by silence. I wanted to question the duchess, but I hypothesized that any further prodding would only worsen her unease.

Soon, the afternoon arrived, and the daily summons were in full swing. The duke and duchess were in their usual dress of red and blue respectively—a red tunic and robe underneath a coat of mail and a cloak of fur and a fine gown of blue underneath a cloak of fur. The duke was with his diadem, and the duchess, with her circlet. Though it seemed she sat comfortably, I could still sense the unrest within her.

Hours and hours went forth, filled with discussing the barons and aristocrats from the other castles and even a mayor or two from the surrounding towns. They demanded more food or a change in procedure, and for most of the discussion, the duke took over. My guess was that he knew the duchess was not in the mood and would not be for the rest of the day.

Later, as night began to descend, I was returning to my chamber after spending a few hours in my study and could not help but overhear the exchange inside the royal bedchamber. I made sure to not touch or knock upon the finely carved wooden door. The stone hallway therein was lit by torchlight, and the stairs leading to it were mere feet away. I leaned in closer and applied my ear to the door ever so carefully.

"Don't want to talk about it."

It was the duchess's voice.

"Will you please save it for tomorrow, when I may perhaps be in a better mood."

I could hear her shuffling the bedsheet.

"Why not now when we have privacy?" the duke asked. "No one is here to listen but myself."

I nearly scoffed at the irony.

"Won't you please tell me what has been bothering you today? It is completely out of character and unusual for you."

His words were sincere, and I knew they were. Never once did the duke just say things. If there was one thing that the duke loved more than his royalty and his sword, it was his wife and friend, the duchess. He would go to the grave for her.

The duchess sighed a deep sigh.

"Something has happened," she began. "I do not know if we are ready for it."

If I could have pressed my ear any more to the door, I would have.

"I...I should have bled today," she continued. "Today should have been the day to call the maid to have the linens washed, but this morning, it was not so. I've had such a deep feeling in my stomach all day, and I was unsure if it was what I assumed it was. I was not sure if I wanted it to be what I assumed it was."

"What did you assume it was?" asked the duke, his voice low.

"I believe I am with child," the duchess spoke, a shiver of terror in her words.

I let my ear come away from the door, my jaw agape with unbelief. I gripped the staff in my hand as I nearly stumbled from shock.

The duchess is with child?

I trembled.

*****

Nine months passed, nine months of good moods and bad moods, neither of them having more say than the other. I watched her progress, her abdomen growing larger and larger. There were days when she needed help getting out of bed, according to the duke, and she had her handmaidens help her when she did.

She changed her diet too in order for the coming child to have the proper health. She took longer walks down the halls and through the courtyards of Ensalor. When she made appearances in the lower city, people made way to make the path less difficult for her. She seemed to take her pregnancy well for a woman who had never been before. The duke took every precaution he could take note of from the nurses, handmaidens, and even local mothers of lesser status.

While the duke supervised his wife, I found that her secret was not what I sensed was wrong. No, there was something darker, much darker.

One evening, I took it upon myself to leave the castle's shelter and wander to the Jondii Mountains. It was a path of complete silence, meditation, and contemplation. Several thoughts jumbled about in my psyche. I sought the wisdom of the Gray Ram, who was usually seen there.

I journeyed a few feet up the northwesternmost peak and set up a small camp for the evening. I placed my staff against the hard stone wall of the flat spot I had found. I took twigs and dried leaves for tinder and made a fire by snapping my fingers, a simple trick for an old conjurer. Minutes passed, and soon, I felt a presence I had not felt in ages, a presence of overwhelming peace and comfort, as if I had been placed in the softest blanket or the quietest glade.

He appeared, Skeef, in all his shagginess and majesty. The Gray Ram clopped down from somewhere farther up the mountain. His horns curved downward behind his head before widening slightly outward; his wool was curly and soft with the pallidity of storm clouds. I could not keep the joy in my soul from showing in my smile.

"Greetings to you, my friend," said the ram. "What brings you to these crags?"

"Master," I said, my tone solemn, "something has transpired, the likes of which I am uncertain how to handle. I do not feel as I should. I confess that something is bothering me."

"Your feelings do not fail you," said the ram, his mouth unmoved, though his voice rang in my ears. "Look to the west. You will find the answer to your inquiry."

I stood and turned my attention to the western sky, for I could see from the height where I stood the distant shores where the Western Waves raged. Nasty, angry clouds began to form, and I could hear thunder across the sea. Sharp, jagged streaks of lightning split the air itself. If I had never felt fear before this moment, I certainly felt its cold fingers running down my spine as I watched.

There, where the foam met sand, wicked ships began to run aground. From the heights, I could see the gold-and-black stripes of their sails and the vivid sigil of a wasp with its outstretched wings. Piles and piles of armored soldiers spilled forth from the boats. They carried swords and shields and pikes and bows. There were legions of them marching into our land from the western shore. My jaw gave way at the sight, my eyes wide as valleys.

Then my fear culminated into a mass of sheer terror when I saw her step off one of the hundreds of boats, a tall, strong, armored woman carrying a large scepter glowing red with hatred. Her helmet bore a crown with many spikes like a tiara.

"W-what are they?" I managed to croak. "Where did they come from? Why are they here?"

There were several more questions scrambling in my head, but those were the ones that slipped out first. The ram joined me in my gazing.

"The Gilded Caliphate, invaders from the Isle Far and Wide. They are conquerors thirsty for new land. The tall one is Nahla, the Ninth Mother. Her soldiers are fearless, loyal monsters armed to the teeth and trained to kill."

Then the next words to ring in my ears were words I would never forget.

"They will take everything."

I froze, and my soul went numb at the thought.

*****

The Caliphate was swift in its northwestern march to Ensalor. In the wake of their path, nothing remained save for blood, fire, and destruction. The militia of the cities who would not bend the knee were decimated while those who surrendered were spared. Cowards, all of them. The duke did not take kindly to traitors and vowed to execute those who betrayed Kastallon once the enemy was dealt with. He had never known defeat in years and put his faith in his determined army.

There was one small problem: the duchess would not be joining him. She would find herself in her bedchamber, joined by her handmaidens, as the birthing process strained and tested her. Her cries of pain could be heard from the battlements where we stood watching the legions approach, the mountains behind them now.

"We must hold the gate!" cried the duke beside me. "Wait until they are within range."

To either side of us, archers lined the parapets of stone, ready with arrows nocked. Below us, where the portcullis was sealed, hundreds of brave Kastallonians held fast with their swords and shields, ready to defend the castle with their lives. I began to wonder why Pinner was absent.

"I wish you would have warned me sooner," said the duke rather intensely. He drew his sword and readied it as a signal for the archers.

I could not respond for fear of misspeaking. I was still terrified, as I already knew the outcome of this last stand.

Soon, the legions were upon us. But suddenly, they halted. A gap began to form as soldiers stepped aside to let pass a tall figure on a dark, overgrown steed. I recognized her spiked crown. I let the name Nahla slip from my lips.

She spoke with a powerful contralto.

"Rulers of Kastallon," her voice bellowed, "hear these words, for they may be your last should you fail to heed them carefully."

Her legions halted, giving an air of suspense. I, as well as the duke and his men, held our breaths.

There must be thousands of them, I thought with fear.

"You will relinquish your stake on this land to me, transferring all power to the Caliphate, in the name of Fikra the Indomitable," the Caliph continued. "Accept, and you may live to watch your children grow old with full bellies and high spirits. Refuse, and the halls of your castle will drown in the blood of your men."

She drew a mighty claymore and held it strongly with a single hand.

The horses and armored soldiers of the Caliphate were yards away from the towered gate. Our men behind the portcullis lay in wait. The sky above seemed to match our chances: grim and dreary. Soon, heavy drops of rain began to pelt the metal shield with loud clinks. Whatever decision the duke was deciding, he was taking an unbearably long period to make it. I stood next to him in fear that the Caliph would grow impatient quicker than we hoped. Already, her mind seemed made up regardless of what the next words from the duke were.

Finally, the Duke cried out, a shining sword still held firm, "Men of Ensalor!"

A brief roar of shouts within the castle responded, overpowering the loudness of the drops against iron.

"This foul wench seeks to take that which you call home, to claim for her own the land your grandfathers and their fathers before them built with their sweat and blood!"

I began to tremble once more. I had plenty of encounters before this in my time, encounters with wicked beasts and bouts with those doused in evil. But never had such trepidation lingered and consumed me with its dark influence. Was it the seriousness of her threats? Was it the countless spearmen and swordsmen at our doorstep? Was it the anxiety I held for the duchess and her coming child? Was it a potential shred of doubt for the duke?

It was none of those things, not even close. It was the reality of abandonment, the shadow of predestined failure. The grand warden was missing; the duchess was indisposed. Even now, we were but ants competing for territory with orb weavers, and we were caught in their silky web.

"Hear these words, devil, and take them back to your abyss!"

The duke's tone was commanding.

"Ensalor shall not fall today! Your march from the sea ends here. The power of Skeef will not fail us!"

Another round of shouts and battle cries followed.

"Open the gate!" cried the duke, brandishing his sword. "For Ensalor!"

I watched as the archers let their arrows fly into the mass of warmongers before us, some of them getting the timing wrong and succumbing to an arrow in the neck. The rest, however, stood strong with shields raised. Below us, a mild tremor rumbled as the gatekeepers began to raise the forward portcullis by turning the chain-bound spindle with iron-wrought wheels. Slowly it came, buying time for the archers to down more and more of the Caliphate troops.

Why are they not moving? I wondered.

But no matter how many of the front lines fell, more of them swarmed to take their place. Nahla raised her claymore in waiting, the swordsmen around her banging their shields with the flat parts of their swords, the spearmen pounding the ground with their pommels.

The portcullis's ascension was halfway. Twang went the bows beside me as the duke watched their flights. Then he clasped a firm hand on my shoulder, his voice loud in my ears.

"Hold them fast, Magistrate," he yelled. "Let none pass!"

At the final word, he rallied a few men clad in armor and chain mail from across the battlements and stormed down the stone stairs. I wanted to stop him, but his foolishness and valor had already taken him. I watched as he joined the ranks of his men below, his sword firmly bound to his hand.

Then it all happened so quickly that minutes passed before I could comprehend. Nahla lowered her massive sword, and her soldiers then advanced around her. A din of shouting and clamoring followed. Then as if in response, the duke and his men charged forward in a determined sprint. There were yards and yards of grassland between the two armies, and with each passing second, they were closing the gap. My eyes were centered on the duke. I had to be sure that I knew where he was when the evacuation started, something all of them were completely and hopelessly unaware of. Another tremble of fear forbade my feet from taking action.

On and on, I watched as the forces of Ensalor and the blighters from across the sea clashed sword and shield, the neighboring archers continuing their volleys. Nahla, cursed be her name, wiped out an entire formation with a single stroke of her sizable sword. Then the thought occurred to me as I watched her down another five or six men. She was the only one mounted atop a horse. That made her a target, a tall, armored, quick-moving target.

For the first time since the attrition started, my body awakened, and I clasped my staff firmly. As I spoke under my breath, the crystal adorning it began to shine with a brilliant purple glow. Once the incantation was finished, with one hand, I swung the staff forward. A quick streak and a flash emitted from the tip, and a burst of dirt and muck tore away at a mass of Gilded soldiers. The archers, though briefly bewildered by my magic, felt a swell of encouragement and hastened the frequency of their arrows leaving their strings.

Another incantation later and my staff became a ranged weapon. The crystal shone a bright orange as if within the hardened stone itself was a flame. As I held the staff with both hands, I let fly several fireballs, great spheres of rolling flame, hurling into the outer ranks of Gilded soldiers, trying to thin the herd and lessen the threat toward the duke and his men. The tide was beginning to turn, as more and more Caliphate soldiers were smote by the red and blue of Ensalor.

In the chaos, from the hills to the west, there came a mighty roar—not the roar of any beast, mind you, but a swell of sound shaking the land to its core. It was as if thunder became physical and pounded the ground ferociously. I drew my gaze to the southeast beside the mountains, and a twinge of hopelessness erupted at the empty hills. But then I heard the mighty roar again, this time closer than it was before. It dawned on me at that moment. It was the sound of horns, great, deep, bellowing horns!

Reinforcements!

Over the southeastern hills, there came a mass of riders dressed in hooded cloaks, some with swords and others with bows. It was clear to see that these were not humans. No, these were the Purloinians of Londror, and there among the front ranks of these riders was the grand warden himself! He rode upon a spotted gray stallion as fast as the wind. Beside him rode the Purloinian baron with his greatsword trained to kill.

Swift was their clash with the Gilded ranks. Like a broken dam, the Purloinian riders flowed through the wall of soldiers, streaking from end to end. The forces of Ensalor cheered as they paused, watching the riders' work.

"Skeef is watching over us! Advance! Advance!" cried the duke, a gleam of ambition twinkling in his eyes.

His loyal men followed him, for they had not suffered too many losses.

Another clash of swords with shields struck the air. I could see Nahla dispatching rider after rider, dismembering and decapitating some of them in one swing. I remembered that she was still a large target. I began to mutter another incantation, one that even she could not avoid. I held my staff's crystal close to my lips, and with each word uttered, it once again began to glow.

When the last of the incantation was over, I raised my staff high. There, in the air, appeared several spears of green light primed and aimed. With a brandish, I let them fly and find their marks. Each of them was like a comet leaving green trails as they flew. They struck some of the Gilded and continued through the ranks, piercing more and more of the gold-and-black enemies. Those who were struck were instantly killed and collapsed with a cauterized hole in their chests.

I watched the sole spear that was meant for the Caliph. I watched it descend from the parapets and curve around soldiers and even our men, for it knew they were not its target. I watched it climb high into the sky once it sighted the armored woman and fall fast toward her. But she was quicker. No, she was not only quicker, but she was also aware of the spear.

She caught the spear in her grip, clasping it tightly with one hand as the spear gave off a greenish hue. Her gaze found mine, and stunned was I to see the recoil of the spear leaving her unscathed, but the dirt and soldiers surrounding her were thrown like rag dolls behind her from the spear's flight suddenly being cut short.

Impossible, I thought. *No one can stop the Seeking Spears of Lorcrish.*

I was horrified when the spear was broken in her grip and disintegrated like shattered glass. But my trepidation was short, for I was already told she could not be thwarted.

The rain began to lessen and eventually stopped altogether, leaving the grassland a dirty, muddy mess as the battle raged. Minutes and minutes passed, and the Gilded Legion never faltered. Nahla continued to wipe out swarms of our men and Purloinians as she rode. The sun began to peak through the murky clouds, thin rays of light shining down on the crowds of men from above. The battle felt like an eternity with neither side giving in.

There were times when it seemed it was in our favor, only for the Caliph to come in and defeat more and more of our troops. I watched as Pinner cast an incantation in which three soldiers made of purple light were conjured and began fighting back more Gilded. These soldiers' weapons were merely literal extensions from their bodies. Each swipe and stroke had a thin trail of purple haze behind it.

But even then, those magical constructs did not last long, for Nahla found them in the crowd and ousted them. I signaled to the archers.

"The Caliph is your new target!" I cried. "Focus your arrows on her!"

I figured it was the best option with Purloinian soldiers fighting back with our men.

Soon, each arrow began its flight toward the armored despot. But with the raising of her scepter, whose reddish glow never fizzled out, a narrow wall of fine mist appeared and repelled each try for her life.

"Irksome imbeciles!" she cried.

I watched her scepter glow the brightest it had since the battle began, and she raised it to the highest point her arm could reach. That was when I knew the fight was moot.

There, in the sky, as if they were coming straight from the ether, were large and terrible owls as big as trees. Each flap of their wings nearly stirred the air itself; their cries were deafening. They dived quickly and began to swipe away battalion after battalion of our men and the Purloinians. Those who were not taking away troops on the ground were swiftly plucking archer after archer off the parapets. One alighted on one of our towers and flapped wildly.

"Begone with you," I ordered, waving my staff in defense. "Servant of that cursed mother, I command you to begone!"

I struck the stone beneath me with my staff. The beast squawked loudly once more and reared up to take flight. Before its talons could leave the tower, I released another fireball from my staff, and the beast fell away in cinders, smoking all the way down.

I heard a voice cry aloud from somewhere in the folds of battle.

"Retreat! Retreat!"

I knew it at once to be the duke himself. More and more of the winged beasts took and took from their feasting ground of men. The Gilded began to advance as what remained of the Purloinians began to retreat.

Soon after the evacuation began, I went back to the duchess's chamber and found that she had given birth to a beautiful baby girl. I informed her of the situation, and the duke soon returned as well, sweaty and panting, urging everyone in the room to come quickly. We hastened and found ourselves heading through the halls of Ensalor. As we ran and ran, the very walls of the castle rang with the calamity of Gilded voices running rampant. I warded some away with a blinding flash, and we sought the southeastern exit. Before we could depart, more Gilded forces arrived, and we were separated. Carrying the duchess, the duke urged me to take the baby and keep her safe.

"What is her name?" I asked, taking the swaddle in my arms.

"Her name," the duchess cried through sobs of sadness and terror, "is Willow."

That was the last I saw of them before I was forced to make haste to the western shore, riding hard and fast on a borrowed steed from a Purloinian.

Chapter 13

Hidden

"Why didn't you warn them when you came back?" Willow asked.

She yawned and covered it with her hand. She and Merlin were still sitting by the bank of the ford in the Garmouth. The others were fast asleep in the bivouac.

"Because," said Merlin, "even if I told them, they would have denied that those were Skeef's words. They would have laughed and carried on. Besides, the duchess giving birth was the duke's priority at the time, and I did not want to bestow further stress upon him."

Willow gesticulated as she spoke.

"So all this time, you kept me hidden from the Caliph?"

Merlin nodded, his eyes closing, then reopening.

"Now you understand why your childhood predicament was what it was. I had to keep you hidden. She would have come for you eventually," said Merlin. "I will say, though, that before I stepped into the mouth of Balaen, I spoke with Skeef for the last time.

"'Remember the prophecy of the first priests. Tell it to the realm,' he said. 'I've not long for this world now. I will return, but no man knoweth the day or hour.' Those were the last words in my head from his voice. Then I, in a loud voice, loud enough to be heard from coast to castle, spoke the prophecy into the air. I knew they had heard me, for those who had followed us came riding out of the small forest beyond us."

Willow had taken in the wizard's words, but they were not processing well. It was a huge shock to her to hear of her disastrous birth and an explanation of what Skeef had shown her briefly. She returned to the bivouac, used her cloak to cover herself, and found a place on a blanket next to Rowan, who was snoring mildly. Sleep then overtook her, and her dreaming began.

CHAPTER 14

Rocks, Arrows, and Talons

Willow awoke, panting, to find that Rowan was missing. She had shifted with her closed eyes and flinched when she found that where he should have been was only air; she had rolled over unexpectedly. The rest of the bivouac was asleep. The Gnomes were huddled close together; Racer and Juniper. together. Her eyes could see their chests rising and falling with steady breaths. Even Merlin's face was covered by his pointy hat, his beard streaking down underneath as he lay on his blanket with his hands folded over his abdomen. But it was Rowan who was missing.

Willow decided to go look for him. She rose and threw on her cloak, making sure that Pnevma never left her hip. The air itself had a cool effect. It was like stepping out into the street when summer had taken its first light. The sun played hide-and-seek with the clouds, periodically revealing itself in phases. All round her were the same she had seen yesterday—the two peaks she was between, Ittermount and Mount Quall; the black oaks with their gentle swaying; and the shallow ford running briskly downstream.

She drew away from the bivouac, thinking, *I shan't be gone long. I'll find Rowan, and we will both return soon.*

Taking a few steps along the riverbank, she noticed some bubbling in the ripples of the stream. Seconds later, a little green nose poked out, lingered, and then sank back below the surface. Willow had never seen anything like it. She paused and crouched, waiting to see if the nose would poke out again. Steadily, she eyed the same spot where it first emerged, drops of anticipation dripping in her veins. More seconds passed, and then farther down the stream, the same little nose broke the surface, stayed, and then sank once more. It was almost like a game of cat and mouse.

She continued to follow the little nose as it poked up and down farther and farther down the stream. The pebbly shore crunched under her boots, and she told herself to tread lightly so as not to scare off whatever she was observing. Her short travel along the bank soon came to an end when she watched the little nose rise again, only this time, more was revealed.

The nose soon began a head, which grew a neck. The head had beady black eyes that sank into its skull; the neck was a rubbery green with yellow stripes running into the body. The body, however, was surrounded by a dense oval-shaped brown exterior. Four greenish limbs protruded from the armor on its back. The creature crawled onto a log that was lodged in the riverbed and was sticking above the surface.

Suddenly, she remembered what happened in Al Wafra, the scary Kappas that were tasked with hunting her down and slaughtering her. She remembered that they wanted her for a feast! She placed a shaky hand on the wrapped hilt of Pnevma, her conscience telling her to be ready for an attack. She began to draw…

A hand tapped her on the shoulder. She shuddered and quickly drew Pnevma and turned about-face, gripping the sword. To her surprise, it was not a Kappa or any sort of enemy come to claim her. It was the face of a friend, a damp friend.

"It is only a turtle," the voice she knew as Rowan said. "Completely harmless."

Willow saw that he was without a shirt yet kept his boots and trousers on. Draped across his forearm was his black tunic. His blond hair was heavy with dripping water, drops of which still clung to his pale skin.

"Oh," said Willow with relief. "There you are."

"What are you doing this early in the morning?" asked Rowan, slinging on his tunic.

"I was…looking for you," said Willow. "Why did you leave camp?"

She sheathed Pnevma with a click into the sheath on her hip.

"A bath," said Rowan. "It had occurred to me—and with some critique from Racer—that I'd not cleaned myself in a week."

He slicked his hair back again since his tunic ruffed it a bit.

"It was quite refreshing, I must say."

They began to walk the short distance back to the bivouac.

"Did you have any dreams last night, Willow?" Rowan asked, putting his hands behind his back and his head forward.

Willow was hesitant to answer. Usually, her dreams stayed with her. But sometimes, they ended up nothing more than a vapor in her mind's eye. She began to recall Merlin's story of her birth and how the images she visualized from those words matched with the images shown in the vision given by Skeef. It was something that had not settled comfortably yet like indigestion. She wrung her hands together in a pondering gesture. The words were there, but they would not come out. Her eyes darted back and forth between the ground and the path ahead. Finally, she felt she could trust the young man with the details.

"I did," she croaked. "One."

She paused.

"Ah," said Rowan. "Enlighten me."

The command came with a sincere grin.

"Okay. Last night, Merlin told me what happened ten years ago. When we were called by Skeef in the Shriveled Forest, he showed me what I guess were memories of those involved."

"What does this have to do with your dream?"

"Well, when I eventually got to sleep, I could not get it out of my mind. The words and memories kept flooding back. The men dying in the fields, the rain making a muck of things, and the siege of Ensalor—it all kept coming back."

Her breathing began to quicken, her cheeks flushed.

"I don't even understand how I was able to sleep!"

Rowan noticed her panicked state.

"Peace, Willow!"

He placed a hand on her, trying to comfort her.

"Peace. Perhaps the old wizard should not have told you."

"No!" said Willow sharply. "It was not that."

She started trembling now, an anxious shiver overcoming her. Her eyes were wide when she turned to Rowan.

"I saw…"

The words began to feel like cotton in her mouth.

"I…I saw…"

"What?" said Rowan. "What? What did you see? What was it that has caused this trembling?"

He placed both hands on her upper arms.

"I saw *her*."

Willow's words were drenched with dread.

"I saw the Ninth Mother!"

Rowan backed off, aghast.

"I saw her red eyes and wild hair! She was sitting on that wretched throne!"

The vivid description and the mentioning of the events were enough to cause a relapse in Rowan's memories. Quickly they came—his flight from Ensalor, the burning of his village, and the swarms of Gilded soldiers marching and marching to the north and across Kastallon. Those were the parts of his mind he kept under lock and key, repressing them. They were nothing more than a thorn in his side, a stain of sorrow on his soul. He did not want to feel the emotion attached to those images and quickly shoved them back down again.

"Hush now, child," said Rowan, taking Willow in his arms like an older brother consoling his younger sibling. "'Twas nothing but a dream, naught else."

He began a comforting stroke with his hand on her upper back, up and down in gentle repetitions. She was weeping with fear.

"She knows not where we tread," he continued. "We have safe passage through the Garmouth."

Willow looked up at him with damp eyes, tear trails lining her cheeks.

"That may be," she said, wiping them away. "But why were they coming to Onolon? If she couldn't find us, how did she know we were there?"

Rowan released her.

"I had not thought about that."

He rubbed his chin pensively.

"Perhaps it was just mere coincidence. Sometimes, you just get lucky."

His tone was light, trying to ease her mood so the others would not ask questions when they returned. It worked…slightly.

Willow sniffed.

"Lucky?" she asked. "The knowledge of impending danger does not sound in the slightest like luck to me."

"Ah," said Rowan. "It is when you've the advantage. It was three wizards and the One Who Unites against a band of expendable grunts. They stood no chance."

Rowan patted his chest with a fist in a triumphal gesture.

Willow thought for a moment, then asked, "What does *expendable* mean?"

"I'll tell you later," said Rowan. "Come now before the sun discovers us."

It was not a tedious thing to mosey back to the bivouac since only several minutes passed before they reached it again. It was still the same camp as before. The fire was ashes, the animals were still snoozing, and the grass held the morning dew comfortably. Very few clouds crowded the new dawn, which from the horizon began as a warm golden haze that gradually blended into a cool cerulean canvas. Upon viewing, Willow was sure that the sunrises she had seen in Earthrealm could not hold a candle to those in Kastallon.

As for the bivouac, the Gnomes had not awakened yet. Valner was on his back, his breath whistling through his nose; Rossa was slumped on her side. They were greeted by Merlin, who was meditating by the river, his eyes closed and his back facing the camp.

"I see you've taken the liberty of exploring," said Merlin, his staff lying plainly against his shoulder. "Or perhaps you have been giving Willow a tour."

The old wizard's mouth moved, but his eyelids were locked tight. The wind began to blow, sending a breeze through his long beard.

"Actually, sir," said Willow, "I went to look—"

"From now on," the wizard interrupted, "I am not sir to you. It is master."

"Master," Willow corrected herself. "I went to look for him. I slept next to him, and he was gone when I awoke."

"It is true, master," said Rowan. "I went to bathe in the river so I would not slow the company down. May I join you?"

The young man approached the still-sitting mage.

"Both of you," said Merlin, his eyes still shut, "find your places."

Willow and Rowan sat on either side of the sorcerer on the pebbly shore. Rowan was not unaccustomed to meditation and quickly followed his teacher's actions. As calmly as he could, Rowan closed his eyes and steadied his breathing. Seconds later, he crossed his legs and placed his hands on his knees. It was a very tranquil action—in and out through the nose, relax your mind, and focus on your feelings. Before the invasion, this was a daily practice in the halls of Numalosh.

For Willow, this type of thing never happened at the orphanage. The closest thing to it was sleeping in her bed. To her, it was like sleeping sitting down instead of lying. She figured it was something those with magical abilities did. But she wondered, why did he want her to join if she did not possess these abilities?

When Willow was situated, Merlin began.

"This is something called meditation. One does this to clear the mind and to relax the body. It is good for when things are stressful or negative thoughts begin to intrude. It is also a perfect way to embrace the world around you. Now since we are near the river, let your mind unwind to the sound of the water. Focus on it, and understand it.

"Listen to the wind in the trees. Listen to the birds and the fauna. Allow yourself to find solace in their indifference. They function on one sole instinct: survival. The happenings and circumstances of us humans do not matter to them. Each day, they tackle the constant threat of hunger and predators. But to them, we are simply irrelevant until hunters come along.

"My meaning, should you be inclined to inquire, is that when the time comes a decision must be made, do you run, or do you stay? Do you bend the knee and cower, or do you stand your ground and fight?"

Merlin's eyes opened, and his gaze drew to the heavens.

"It was no coincidence that Gilded troops were moving on Onolon," he continued. "They may be following us at this very moment. But for the life of me, I cannot pin down how they caught sight of us. The Strix are only vigilant when dusk breaks and just before the dawn rises. We've done our best to keep out of sight, so it is a head-scratcher as to how they knew where we were."

"I haven't been hearing them at night," said Rowan, his eyes opening.

Willow did the same.

"That does not matter. They are like owls—silent hunters. They are spies sent from the Caliph's Seers. Nasty witches, those. But we only travel at daybreak and until the evening sets in."

"Perhaps one of the Gnomes has been leaving a trail. You know how centered they are with their foods. Would not be a surprise to me if crumbs have been spilling from their pouches."

"No, no, no, they are far more careful than that. Do not take these Gnomes for traitors."

"I did not mean to imply that, master."

"Regardless, they are our own. They would not betray even the meanest of their own kind. Gnomes are built on community. They help and care for one another. Besides, these two are still young and impressionable. Caflan would not lead them astray."

There came, seconds later, a rather pleasant and savory scent in the air. The three near the river turned back toward the stone wall on the Ittermount side of the Garmouth. There, Rossa was cooking breakfast; Valner was fishing by the riverside.

"Mornin'," he said with a wave. "Fish'll be caught and prepared momentarily."

Merlin, Rowan, and Willow returned to the bivouac and found their places on their blankets from the night before. On a makeshift cook board made of tree bark and a cloth from her rucksack, Rossa was rolling out pieces of dough to be placed in the pot hanging over the fire. She formed them into soft, fluffy, moderate dollops. She took a small knife and sliced off thin slabs of butter from the crinkly paper on her knee and smeared the light-yellow lard on top of them. Then one by one, Rossa placed them in the black pot over the fire.

Minutes passed as the company sat in silence. The breakfast was soon finished when Valner had caught and cooked a few trout from the ford: lightly browned filets sitting next to the bread rolls on their wooden plates. The Gnomes ate with their hands, which left their fingers rather greasy; the rest, with their forks.

"A fine meal. Well done," said Merlin after swallowing the last of his trout. "If there is anything to rely on a Gnome for, it is most certainly their cooking."

"I wish you were the cook at the orphanage!" Willow said, then took another bite of her bread roll. "This stuff is great!"

"What is an orphanage?" asked Rossa.

Her face was pensive. The word had never crossed her lexicon before since Gnomes were very family oriented. Each Gnome family had at least two children, and those children were always taken care of. When they came of age, the girls were trained in cooking, cleaning, and nurturing; the boys were trained in hunting, fishing, and baking. But one thing that all Gnomes were trained and told to practice was singing.

"A question for another time," said Merlin. "For now, it appears that Pinner has not returned from his morning walk. Normally, he reserves the first hour of each day for a tranquil stroll. The sun is getting higher, and morning soon becomes afternoon. He should be here by now."

The wizard held a hand over his brow and looked behind to where they had first come to the Garmouth. The air above the pebbly shores and even above the thinly grassed dirt was rippling from the heat. The trees still swayed in the gentle breeze, and the sky remained cloudless.

Then from somewhere beyond or perhaps above in the mountains themselves came a shriek the likes of which they hadn't heard in days—a shrill, ear-piercing cry worse than any red-tailed hawk or horned owl screech. There came also several *thwump*, *thwump*, *thwump* like the flapping of heavy wings. The company took a reluctant gander up to the peaks of the mountains they lay between, and once they saw what appeared, their very souls shivered and quivered. They were huge, gargantuan owls as big as buses. Ten of them!

Strixes!

At once, the company sprang into action. Willow dropped her things and drew her sword, Rowan rushed to Racer and stirred him, the Gnomes, Rossa and Valner, began collecting the cookware and stomping out the fire, and Merlin stood his ground, staff in both hands.

"It's an ambush!" Rowan cried, saddling up a groggy Racer. "How did they find us?"

"Leave the food and take the blankets!" Merlin ordered the Gnomes. They understood.

"What do we do?" asked Willow, for she had never fought a giant bird before.

"Stick 'em with the sharp end!" Rowan said, finally aboard Racer.

Juniper scrambled to Willow's shoulder as Willow widened her stance and gripped Pnevma in her hands. Merlin spoke something under his breath and then raised his staff high. Fire came quickly, billowing from the crystal tip of his staff and blowing like breath into the fray of Strixes. Some of them avoided the flames. One of the larger owls had cinders fleeting from the tips of its tail feathers as the crowd of them dispersed, circling around the company in the air. In the motion of it all, a drizzle of black, blue, and gray feathers fell, and these were not simple feathers like those found in Earthrealm; they were sharp and fell like knives sent from rain clouds.

The feathers impaled the ground next to Willow's feet, recoiling from the impact. She turned and saw that Rowan was swiping and brandishing his shamshir atop Racer, the Strixes that drew to him squawking and shrieking in anger. Their large, lifeless eyes were filled with both a livid rage and insatiable hunger. The thought crossed her mind, and it was one that was just as startling as seeing the Caliph in her very dreams: Did these large birds—or rather, could they—eat one of them whole? She shoved the thought down.

"To me, friends!" hailed Merlin, his staff raised high. "Farther into the Garmouth we must go! The gorge may be enough to cut them off!"

With his last words, a bright light beamed from the crystal in his staff, an attempt to blind the flying monsters. The Gnomes, who were surprisingly successful with the complete pickup of their belongings, hastened toward the wizard and clung to the hems of his robe. Rowan led Racer over to Merlin; Willow retreated as well.

"Go! Go! Fly fast!" cried Merlin, pointing his staff toward the path leading farther into the gorge.

The Strixes then began to take turns, each swooping down in a fast glide to try and scoop up one of the company, but with each attempt, their talons were met with sword strokes. These served only to increase their umbrage.

"Master!"

The shout came from Rowan.

"Look there!"

His shamshir then pointed toward the entrance to the Garmouth yards and yards away.

As their gazes shifted, the Strixes still circled. But even when it had seemed the weather was rather clear in the morning, now a looming shadow of storm clouds formed and quickly festered. The wind began to pick up, almost to the speed of a hurricane. This sudden whirlwind threw off some of the birds, but most of them flew against the current. Was the weather really this unpredictable? Had the Caliph summoned it? Could she do that? Or was it Skeef watching over them?

Their questions were soon dismissed as something, a figure, began to creep into view in the distance, walking beside the ford. Its features were not entirely perceivable, yet the thing as a whole was there, a silhouette almost. As it crept closer, the angry birds began to fly toward it, their screeching sounding once more.

Upon the perceived head of the silhouette came two bright orbs shining and flickering with magical light like small tendrils of lightning emerging from them. Soon, it could be seen raising a staff, and a fell voice proclaimed a spell in a language unknown to Willow, followed by a streak of yellow lightning raining down from the storm clouds. Though it was merely a scare tactic for the Strixes, some of the discharge struck one of the birds, and down it descended, smoking like a roasted pheasant. Its limp, lifeless body smacked the earth with a crumpled thud.

The rest of the owls glided back to the company, who now knew the figure to be none other than Pinner Vemtal, the grand warden of Ensalor. They began their swiftness in the gorge with the Strixes in tow. They ran with all the haste their legs and feet could muster.

"Pinner has returned!" cried Willow, a tidbit of joy in her tone. Her feet carried her next to Merlin and the Gnomes.

"Took him long enough!" Rowan scolded, gripping Racer's reins. "That was quite the distraction, I must say. An impressive display, no doubt!"

"He was always one for grand entrances!" replied Merlin. "Let us speed on! He will catch up with us in due time. For now, we must outrun these spies!"

The Gnomes huffed and puffed. (They still were not used to all the running.) Their rucksacks, specifically Valner's, jingled and jangled with the various cookware and camping tools hanging from them. It was no wonder the birds knew where they were! But to Willow, she gathered that it could not have been the Gnomes who gave them away. They were not singing on the way, and certainly, their danglings were not loud. Even their singing by the ford could not have been heard miles away. Perhaps the Strixes had been lying in wait? She did not know and cared not.

They continued their retreat through the Garmouth, which now began to become more narrow, and the ford widened. What formerly were pebbly shores transformed into low, rocky crags with several boulders of various sizes. The only indication of the way forward was by following the ford. They had to be careful now and be sure not to misjudge their steps. If they stepped on the wrong rock, it could shatter; and they would either slip into the ford, or their pace would lessen, and whoever did would instantly become an easy target for the birds.

Of the remaining Strixes, there were seven still making for the company. One was struck by Pinner's discharge; two were swept away by the storm's whirlwind. One might think they were less of a threat, but seven were dangerous.

Several seconds passed of climbing over large stones and maneuvering between sharp crags and loose rocks. The wind was still picking up; the company was thankful, as the Strixes were slowed by it. They were right in the middle of the Garmouth, the most treacherous part of it. The breeze howling from the peaks of Ittermount and Quall felt to them a lot like laughing, laughing at their foolishness and futile determination. Perhaps they were overlords or despots cackling at their silly attempt at navigation, their inane hope of making it out alive. Soon, the trees were left behind, and the ground began to grow steeper.

Then suddenly, at the crest, the climax of the incline, large, bulbous stones came tumbling down, several of them, in fact, as if they had been carried up the other side and pushed down straight away. Willow gulped as a flood of adrenaline seeped in like an intravenous drip.

"Ho! There come boulders!" cried Valner in terror. "The gorge is working against us!"

"Could it be the Caliph's magic?" Willow asked in a loud voice.

The sound of the earth cracking under the momentum of the boulders mixed with the continuous shriek of Strix made for a cacophony around them.

"Nay!" shouted Merlin. "She has no control over the natural world! This is just a bad stroke of luck! Keep out of their way!"

The wizard then swiftly shifted away, out of the path of an oblong boulder, and watched as it broke away on a lower cliff.

Rowan, it seemed, was struggling the most. He dared not pause to dismount lest he became a target for the birds. Instead, he opted to fly perpendicular to the incline. He, too, shifted away from a boulder. He could feel Racer's ever-quickening heartbeat in his thighs.

"Steady now, boy. We must reach the top!" he said, patting Racer's mane.

The Strixes flew high above the falling, rolling stones and once again took up trying to snatch one of the five. Valner barely avoided their sharp talons, throwing himself to the ground. Willow heard Merlin utter something under his breath, and he waved his staff shortly thereafter. The crystal within began to glow a faint green, tiny blips of light forming around it. Willow remembered the tale that Merlin had told her the night before and knew it could only be one thing.

The Seeking Spears of Lorcrish, she thought. *He's going to cast them!*

"Willow!" called the wizard, staff primed. "Get behind me while the spell is still arming! Once the spears fly, run like the wind!"

Willow nodded quickly and took shelter behind Merlin, peeking round to see the Strixes screaming with sharp, open beaks. Getting a better look at them, she could see the false horns created by feathers just above their eyes, which were cold black orbs with a sheen of white. Their wingspans had to be yards apart, wide enough to carry their massive bodies. They were indeed horrific beasts to any who had the misfortune of being their prey.

The green haze of the crystal on Merlin's staff intensified.

Almost there, Willow thought again.

The shards of light around it were thickening, molding into cylinders, and extending. Along with their emerald tinges, they were nigh transparent, as though they were made of pure light.

Almost there, she thought again, the pointed ends of the spears becoming apparent.

"Get ready to run!" Merlin warned.

Willow felt her body tense up in preparation. She slowed her breathing and released from Merlin. She backed a bit, not too far away. She told herself to head straight up the hill. There was no time to stop and watch the spears do their work. Once they flew, the only thing that mattered was getting away.

Almost there…

Crack!

Suddenly, one of the larger Strixes flinched as if an invisible hand had wrapped itself around the beast's throat. Willow took a sharp look back and noticed that the verdant spears had not flown. Upon glancing at the falling Strix, a large, purely wooden arrow pierced one of its eyes, the tip lodging itself within the head and sticking out the back. The Strix had been grounded! But by whom?

Soon, more arrows followed the first, a hail of wooden nails zipping from the crux of the hill. Black, fetid blood spurted from the wounds inflicted to the Strix, leaving an unpleasant odor in the air as the birds were finished off. Willow watched in awe as each bird was grounded, and their shadowed eyes rolled back.

When she glanced back up the hill, she saw Racer galloping down with Rowan still at the reins. Behind him, a line of strange riders rode into view. Willow had never seen such peculiar clothing before. Each of the archers—for they were equipped with large bows—donned a grassy cloak; their helmets were crafted from tree bark. Their faces were painted with shades of black, green, and gray dyes. What covered their bodily extremities and torsos were smocks made of animal hide. It appeared that they knew not what shoes or boots were.

Merlin came to meet them with Willow.

"Greetings in the name of Skeef!" hailed Merlin, an ooze of relief binding the words.

But the people who had saved them drew back their bowstrings once again atop their steeds.

"Do not speak his name!" one of them said. "It does not merit proclamation."

"What is the meaning of this?" said Rowan, soon meeting the threat of arrows too. He held up his free hand in an act of surrender. He did not wish harm to their saviors.

"Peace, archers!" a voice called from beyond the incline's crest. "Stay your bows. They are not our enemies."

The voice was soon accompanied by a face and a body, a woman's body. Her smock was red unlike the hazel of the archers'; her cloak was a bluish drape of fine cloth instead of a grassy pelt. A shortsword hung from her hip, sheathed in a leather scabbard. When she removed her hood, the face revealed, albeit beautiful, was a caramel visage with white paint in ceremonial patterns. Her face, though aged slightly with mild wrinkles in her cheeks, was the very definition of determination. Her eyes were dark, but her countenance gleamed. Long charcoal locks were kept behind her with a single bone. When the line parted to let her through, Willow almost gave in to an urge to bow before her. She trod down the slope to meet Merlin and the others.

"We are in your debt, my lady," claimed Merlin with a subtle bow. "I am the wizard known as Merlin, magistrate of Châte—"

"Yes, yes," interrupted the woman. "I know who you are. I am Cho, captain of the Gallantinels and shaman of the Da'iini. We came to investigate the many cries and wails heard from the valley. I take it those demons were after you."

"Yes, Lady Cho," said Willow. "They are spies sent from Caliph Nahla, cursed be her name, to eliminate us. Thanks to your swiftness, we are unharmed."

Willow bowed.

"It seems no one is safe anymore," said Cho. "The Caliphate has those foul avians staying increasingly more vigilant lately. Why would they suddenly target the likes of you all?"

Rowan dismounted once the Gallantinels backed off.

"We are the company of the One Who Unites, Lady Cho."

He pointed toward Willow, who sheathed Pnevma.

"And which of you might that be?" asked Cho, who put her hands on her hips.

All their eyes turned to Willow. She was used to being the one at the center of attention since most of the other young girls at the orphanage made her the butt of most of their jokes, so the combined gazes of the company and the Gallantinels were no different.

"The girl?" said Cho, surprised. "My, she is young. Are you sure she is the One? What proof have you?"

Cho crossed her arms, the stance most gave when in doubt or disbelief.

"Show her your sword, dear," said Merlin.

Willow drew Pnevma slowly so that the archers would not perceive it as a threat. The blade gleamed in the sunlight; the crystal in the hilt was bright and violet.

"This is Pnevma, my mother's sword."

She held it higher.

"It was preserved by the grand warden and passed to me."

"It may just be coincidence," scoffed Cho. "To me, it is unlikely that a child would be the downfall of an entire institution and savior of the realm. It may be aligned with the prophecy heard across the land during the Conquering, but it does not make her the One Who Unites."

"Clouded by doubt, are you?" said Rowan.

The Gallantinels drew closer to block him.

"Tell her what we saw in the Shriveled Forest days ago," he continued. "Tell all of them. Perhaps that may change their minds."

At the orphanage, it was common in the classrooms to stand and answer the teacher's questions when he or she called on your raised hand. Said student would stand, present their answer, and return to their seat. As for said student's classmates, they would sit and listen quietly and either affirm or deny the validity of the given answer. This circumstance was no different. The archers were the classmates; the captain was the teacher.

"Speak, child," said Cho.

"Well," began Willow, "I should probably start from the beginning."

Willow cleared her throat.

"Days ago, Merlin brought me here in a Wayfinder whale named Balaen. I was introduced to this new world I did not even know existed. I was not sure what to think, but I could tell something was wrong with it all—the dreariness of the sky, the desolate plains of the landscape. Even the people were unsettling. I had a run-in with a baker in Al Wafra, nearly lost Juniper there. I ran for my life from horrendous walking and talking turtle fiends. That's where Rowan came in, and he saved me from them. We came across some bandits on the road from Al Wafra, and Rowan used Shimmer to blow them all away. There was, however, some strange old woman with them, leading them. I don't know if she, too, could use magic, but she was after us. She was the last thing I saw as we entered the Shriveled Forest.

"When I awoke, the forest was dark and spooky. I wanted to go home, so I tried to look for a way out, a way that could lead back to Balaen. I searched and searched, but I was getting more and more lost. Then I encountered a Strix! Menacing it was, as large as the trees themselves. I ran and took cover inside a cave next to a stream, where eventually, Rowan came to find me.

"Soon after we talked, I heard an uncanny voice in the wind, a whisper actually, long and slow. Then golden streaks like pathway guides appeared and took us to a glade, a bright light in a sea of darkness. There we saw the White Lamb, Skeef. He was the one who confirmed my being the One Who Unites. He showed me visions, memories even, of the Conquering. His very presence was the definition of comfort and of peace. Never had I felt such calmness, a quiet of the soul. The last we saw of him, he was fading away into those golden streams. That is all."

The Gallantinels and their captain stood like fence posts—quietly. Soon, a jumble of murmurs ensued, but it was Cho who remained speechless.

A moment later, she raised her hand for quiet and said, "It seems my doubt has been shaken. If two people have seen it and the girl possesses the sword, then the world changing around us is not a coincidence. The prophecy is true!"

"My lady, we must make haste to Londror before sundown lest the excursion becomes exponentially more dangerous," urged Merlin, drawing nearer. "Will you escort us there?"

"Nay," she said. "The sun now begins its descent to slumber, and night shall bathe the land in darkness. We must make for Hrinthas, our village in the Gallant Valley. It is safer there."

Most of the Gallantinels began moving farther through the Garmouth, down, down the slope.

"We shall travel all that way?" said Rowan. "With all these fiends about?"

"You've better idea, prentice?" the captain said, turning.

Her glare was serious, a visage of commanding respect. She meant business. Her words were final. Out in the wilderness, she was the highest ranked, and she was nobility.

Rowan stood silent and followed the company as they trailed the Gallantinels.

Chapter 15

Runes

Night fell, and the ford began to show signs of infection from the black blood of fallen Strix. The man could even smell it in the air. Large shards of reddish-brown rocks lay on the banks of the stream, crumbles of the boulders thrown down the hillside. As he approached the base of it, he could see the steadily decaying corpses of the Strix, wisps of silver energy wasting away like smoke on a grill.

They are but shells of the Caliph's magic now, he thought, taking a long look at the dead spies.

He saw the feathers jutting up from the ground, quills using the soft earth for parchment. He made a slow pace around the scene, stepping over feathers and avian cadavers. But then something caught his eyes, a sharp, thinly feathered stake lodged in the skull of a Strix.

The man wrapped a firm hand around the shaft of the arrow and yanked. It came free with ease. Black bile was already seeping into the layers of the wood. It was a damn good shot. As he examined it, wheels of thought turned in his head, and he brought the arrow closer. There on the shaft were several runes that had been finely carved in by knife.

Enchanted arrows, he assured himself. *Clever. Very clever.*

He then crunched the arrow in his hand in a single squeeze.

"Damn those savages!" he said in a soft yet angry voice.

With his head down, he paused in mourning, spoke a soft prayer to Fikra, and placed a hand on the gaping beak.

"So," the man said, "that is where they are headed."

Chapter 16

Intruder

Before the Conquering, when the land was lush with greenery and teeming with all kinds of fauna, the Gallant Valley was profoundly the most alluring area in all of Kastallon. Its multicolored flowers blossoming brightly in the spring, its grassy plains interposed with layers of dense greenwood, and even the rolling camel-hump hills were a pleasant sight for travelers from wanderers to pilgrims. When the curse of Nahla festered, the Gallant Valley, like all other paradigms of abundance, fell to recession and became nothing more than empty husks of a previously joyful ecosystem.

With the arrival of the One Who Unites, or Willow, the very landscape itself began a slow and steady revival of color, life, and strength. By now, most of the southern regions were back to their original states, but the northernmost lands, the epicenter of the curse, were still locked and imprisoned by wretchedness. As for the company, they still walked as the others rode.

"How much farther?" Valner asked as he nursed his swelling knees. His beard still had a few crumbs from his breakfast nestled in between curls.

Rossa kept an arm around him so that if one knee gave out from all the walking, he would not falter and drop everything in his rucksack.

Captain Cho rode closely beside Merlin, and the Gallantinels protected the rear, marching behind the company. Rowan kept

Willow atop Racer as a precaution should another ambush catch them by surprise.

Cho leaned over to Merlin and spoke with a low voice.

"Do the little ones always complain?"

Merlin held back a chuckle.

"Only when they are hungry," he said. "Gnomes have quite the appetite. It's a wonder they've not expired their rations."

He watched a faint smile quickly come and fade from Cho's painted lips.

They had been marching at a consistent pace for at least three hours since the descent from Garmouth's peak. They had not spared any moment for breaks, to the despair of the Gnomes.

To her surprise, Willow's energy kept up, and she did not feel sleepy at all. She reasoned it was the shock of it all. The attack of the Strix, the boulders being hurled at them, and even the defense of the Gallantinels with their makeshift arrows—so much happened in such little time. She swore she could still hear the bloodcurdling screeches of those terrible birds. Such a sound left her aquiver.

As the marching continued, she began to think about Leo. She began to remember that all this time, he was still there at the orphanage, waiting for a day that would perhaps never come. She wondered if the unfortunate truth that he might spend his entire childhood there would, in fact, become reality. The sound of his boyish laughter and the childish movements of his hands as he ate came flooding back as she clung tightly to Rowan. It seemed that Leo was her only friend, someone among the children in that glum place who didn't take it for what it was: hopeless.

She began to think of all the questions she forgot to ask him: "What do you think of Mrs. Veraminta?" "How long do you think you will stay here?" "How in the world are you able to stomach that food?" As the questions lingered, a tear formed in her eye, and she blushed with sorrow. The biggest question that rocked her conscience was also the question she hoped she would never have to ask: "Will I ever see you again?" Even with assurance from Skeef, somehow, she still felt a morsel of homesickness. It was like the feeling you got when you left for a vacation, and the vacation did not seem to be what you thought you would enjoy. It was a longing for a return home.

There had been a day, an afternoon rather, where she found a peculiar book in the orphanage library—when Veraminta took the girls for a period—about a girl a tad younger than herself who followed a pocket watch–sporting rabbit into its hole, only to discover a magical, estranged world of weird, humanlike creatures ruled by a mad ginger queen. She felt she could relate to her now.

When the thoughts of her friend dissipated, she was reminded of the statement from earlier. "Do not speak his name," she remembered. "It does not merit proclamation!" Did they doubt? Had they lost faith? What in all of Kastallon had made them refuse to utter his name?

"Captain Cho," Willow began, "as the One Who Unites, I must ask, why do you disclaim Skeef? One of your sentries denounced him back there. Is something wrong?"

Lady Cho looked over from atop her steed.

"I'm sure the wizard has told you of the events that have led to now. The Conquering."

"Yes, I am aware of what happened when I was born."

"Then you know how he abandoned us."

Willow considered her words before speaking.

"I do not see it like that. Perhaps Skeef had to go. Perhaps it was part of the prophecy."

"The prophecy mentioned no necessity of his departure," said Cho, "only that you would one day come and save us."

"Then does that not bring back your hope? Your faith in him?"

"Your arrival is beneficial, yes, but the grudge holds. Had he not withdrawn, perhaps we'd have no need of you, and perhaps we'd still have our many villages and the people we lost along the way."

She sniffed.

"Can you bring them back?"

Her tone was suddenly strict.

The rest of the while, silence surrounded them. Willow dared not stoke the captain's already tense patience. Even with the One Who Unites being the perfect proof of Skeef honoring his word, she still refused to raise his name. She thought about calling on him and asking to show the captain the same grace he showed her, but as she considered the possibility of her believing in his return, she figured she would deny it anyway. She closed her eyes, prayed softly, and rode on.

*****

Hrinthas was walled within the seclusion wrought by the valley's dense woodlands. Oddly enough, there were many woodlands here, scattered randomly. If one were a bird, they would see the forests like balls on a billiards table. Some were closer than others, and it seemed as though where one ended, another began, but one would not know it if they were inside.

Willow felt a feeling she had not felt before. Inside the village, she felt as though everything was too tightly packed together. The paths were barely three men wide. If you breathed fire, you would surely burn your neighbor adjacent. She and the company had to walk with the riders in the middle and the rest on the outer ends. Greening trees took up spots between places of interest.

"So," said Rowan as they walked through the stone wall's gateway, "this is Hrinthas. A sorry excuse for sanctuary. Everything is so close. Too close, if you ask me. I don't even see any war barracks."

Lady Cho chimed in.

"We have no intention of fighting on a grand scale. Fighting in the dark and in the shadows is the only way to take any ground."

She paused for a moment, taking in the view of builders repairing a broken wall, workers carrying buckets and tools, and vendors negotiating the sale of their goods.

"It is not much, not nearly as much as we had before. But we get by. We have scouts that ride each evening to scavenge from other towns, taking what they can from the people who are foolish enough to leave a door open or present themselves unarmed."

"So you're a village of thieves?" said Rowan, his tone rather judging.

"Aren't I speaking to one?"

Lady Cho dismounted, and a servant led her steed away.

"Nay, this life chose me. My actions are not my choosing. I am not willingly stealing from good people. You haven't lived life on the run."

He had dismounted from Racer.

"They are not good people! They kowtowed to the Caliphate, not us! They are no better than the wretched Caliph herself."

"Well—"

"Peace, both of you!" Merlin interrupted. "We all have had our struggles. Bickering and trying to claim higher victimhood is not going to restore the thrones."

The captain and the prentice backed off.

"I suggest that we wait in Hrinthas for Pinner. We will need all the help we can get."

"I don't trust him," said Rowan. "If he walks so early, he should have been back by now."

"Be still, my boy," said Merlin. "The man has always had such an appreciation for nature. Now that its wonder is returning, it makes sense in my book for him to lie back in awe."

Night was closing in. The hot sun was but an orange streak just above the horizon. Heavy clouds were thickening in the sky. No stars would shine tonight. No moonlight would they bask in. The only light to find their way around Hrinthas would be the scarce torches hanging from the poles lining the pathways. Some of them hung on either side of the thresholds of doorways. Maybe that was why all the buildings and structures were arranged in a narrow fashion: to hide the firelight from any soldiers lurking with vigilance.

The company was led into a marketplace, a town square almost. To their left were several yurt-like structures built on a hill as more spruce trees climbed it; to their right was a garden mixed in with other gated areas where moist dirt provided a fertile womb for crops. Small, verdant saplings were in their early stages of life. Willow assumed it was a byproduct of her return and smiled. She looked up and could see that some of the trees within the village had wooden platforms staked into their stalks, rope-and-plank bridges running between them, an intricate and efficient way for sentries getting from one point to another. She had never seen anything like it. In between it all, she could see the strength of the stone wall surrounding the village.

"You are dismissed," said Cho to the Gallantinels. "But keep an open eye."

The sentries gave a salute by bringing their forearms to their shoulders before crossing them.

"Go."

They fled with their bows in hand and grassy cloaks bobbing behind them.

No sooner had the Da'iini people begun to gather around the company than the Gallantinels made their retreat. They were a murmuring people of the same color skin as their shaman. They wore the same smocks, though the women had rings on their arms and the men had braces on their wrists. Some wore sandals; others laced flats. Children clung tightly to their parents, some of whom were younger than Leo. Willow tried to look friendly.

Minutes later, a large man wearing a riveted iron helm approached. Menacing ivory tusks protruded from under the ear slots like an elephant's nose. A breastplate of iron rested above a kilt-like cloth garment tied together by a leather strap. Gold studs lined the sections of the kilt and tossed about as he walked closer to them. Two pauldrons from the breastplate adorned his shoulders. He appeared to be the only one of them all who was wearing gauntlets.

Merlin, remembering the Gallantinels' response to his original greeting, instead said, "Hail, mighty warrior! We are the company of the One Who Unites. I am Merlin the Magical, magistrate of Ensalor."

The helmeted man said nothing.

"Um, this is she we speak of."

He gestured to Willow, who tried not to quiver at the beastly man.

"Willow, the One Who Unites."

Willow placed a hand on Pnevma's hilt, and there was a slight gasp from the gathered peoples; the beastly man was unmoved. Slowly, she drew it, keeping her nerve still; and once the end was loose, she kept it perpendicular and, with her other hand, laid the sharp end in it, a presentation of her weapon.

"This is my mother's sword, Pnevma," she began. "It was present during the siege of Ensalor, the period of turmoil I was born in. As the prophecy goes, I am destined to wield it."

The company sat still with both anxiety and confusion, perplexed as to why the burly, armored man had not spoken a word. The tusked helmet was not inhibiting his speech, nor did he appear to be a mute. He simply crossed his thick, massive arms across his chest.

"He doesn't appear amused," said Rowan, leaning toward Merlin.

"Perhaps he does not understand?" the wizard said back.

"Ob is a man of very few words," said Lady Cho. "He understands the common tongue but prefers to let his physique do the talking."

The man named Ob grunted in agreement.

"It's effective," Rowan told Merlin.

"Ob is our sheikh, a title passed down by his father and father before and so on. I am privileged to be his wife. We have lived in the Gallant Valley ever since the Conquering."

"I'm assuming you hide because you do not accept her religion?"

"You have quite the observation, prentice."

"You shall hide no longer," Willow spoke up, sheathing her sword.

Ob's visage from underneath the helmet turned sour, and his dark eyes glared at her.

"Skeef has not abandoned you."

Cho's countenance fell too.

"Why do you doubt me? Why do you cast aside the prophecy when it has been fulfilled? Am I just a shadow on the wall? Another limb on the countless branches of life? What must happen for you to see that all hope is not lost? I have the sword, and the very world itself is changing around you. What further proof need you?"

"Willow," Merlin began, "I do think she does not mean an offense—"

"Not now!" Willow stood her ground. "Unless you intend to aid my cause, keep your pleasantries to yourself."

Merlin backed off, shocked by this newfound demanding attitude from the little girl he had watched over so long ago. She had only been in Kastallon a few days, and her mother's grit was coming out.

You certainly are your mother's daughter, he thought.

Willow directed her spark back to Ob and Cho.

"If only you could feel what I feel, see what I have seen. I assure you that it was never his intention for this to happen, for you to renounce yourselves and fade into seclusion. What then? Will the names of Ob and Cho be proclaimed through the valleys and peaks in triumphant celebration, or will they be forgotten and tossed away like spoiled children do with dolls?"

Despite her bile, the young girl's face was not stained with crimson emotion. Instead, a gaze of unfailing determination burned in those sapphire orbs.

"I will leave that decision to you," she finished. "Whether you are with us or not, my company will leave for Londror at dawn."

She whistled for Juniper, and the bird alighted on her forearm gently as she walked into one of the structures, the fine threshold curtains dropping behind her. Seconds later, the crowd of Da'iini began murmuring once more.

"My lady," said Merlin, "forgive her. She is only a child."

He bowed.

"A child with a sword for a tongue," said Rowan, grinning.

Merlin shot him a look.

"I like this new Willow! Passion, just like her mother!"

"Passion will not save us," said Cho. "Only we can do that. The girl has spunk, true, but spunk alone will not withstand the hordes of Gilded when they eventually find us."

Ob, behind his tusked helmet, grunted once more in agreement and crossed his arms.

*****

Rowan sat alone at one of the wooden tables inside the large pavilion somewhere next to the main longhouse in Hrinthas. He held a clay cup of something hot, wisps of steam rising, in both hands and let it warm them. They had not been near a fire in quite a while, and this was the closest similarity to it. With the world changing, the very nature of cold returned. As a nomad, he was used to arid nights and sweltering days as he took shelter in his tent.

Now he found himself both amused and somewhat upset inside Hrinthas—amused because there was a semblance of safety within its walls, a sense of security one attained when settling in from years of temporary homes, but upset because despite the safety, he was not acclimated to one place. In his heart, he knew this was only temporary too. By morning, they would be off again and on the road. He tried to savor the moment as best he could and sipped.

The pavilion was a large structure of wooden beams capped with tiles of mud and rock. It was large enough to house the entire village. From end to end, a basin of hot coals provided the necessary temperature to cook the evening meal. Slabs of rabbit, bird, turtle, and squirrel lay simmering on the iron grills. The smell of freshly cooked meat was a rarity for nomads like Rowan, who survived on jerky, wildflower, and water. His mouth watered like a hungry dog to a bone. Beyond the structure, a wildly large bonfire was ablaze, and several of the villagers were gathered around it, their clothes rent and tattered. It was a mourning ceremony.

Lady Cho had told them hours ago that tonight would be the annual mourning ceremony for those who were slain or taken by the Caliphate. They paid tribute to them by tearing their clothes and crying out, ways of putting themselves in their places. They took on their spirits and dined in remembrance.

If a person was chosen to participate, they would be given a name, the name of a fallen villager. The chosen would wear their clothes or clothes similar to what the fallen would have worn and apply any special features unique to the fallen, such as scars, tattoos, or blemishes. The chosen would then spout lamentations around the fire and throw the torn clothing into the blaze before claiming their meals in honor of their represented fallen. In Hrinthas, it was a high honor to be chosen. But Rowan was still confused about the taking on of their spirits idea.

The lamentations concluded, and the chosen began making their way to the pavilion after receiving a thin djellaba. Lady Cho held a ceremonial staff in one hand and waited for the chosen—and the rest—to be seated. Seconds later, the pavilion was full.

"My beloved people," she began, "tonight, we honor those who have sacrificed everything, given their lives so that we may have ours. We thank those who were chosen."

"We thank those who were chosen," said the Da'iini who were not.

Merlin and the Gnomes came in and sat with Rowan, the tiny ones' legs hanging off the benches.

"The chosen shall eat first, and when they have swallowed their last, the rest of us may partake. We shall now feed the chosen."

"We shall now feed the chosen," said the Da'iini who were not.

They began to pass clay plates from the back to the front, where the chosen were seated. Rowan could see that the chosen sat in almost a trancelike state, bobbing their heads subtly with closed eyes. It was as if their movements were not their own. Once the plates reached them, the Gallantinels served them a slab each of bread and meat. They ate at their own pace. They gulped down the same warmness that Rowan held in his hands. Seconds after their meals were finished, the chosen opened their eyes, and Lady Cho painted their faces with blue streaks, signaling that the other Da'iini could now eat.

Rowan had never seen anything like it. In all his months of life on the road, nothing compared to the procedure of it all. Sure, he was a wizard's prentice, but this magic was unlike that of Shimmer users. This magic was supernatural, if it could be called magic at all. He began to wonder if Skeef had anything to do with it, or perhaps they were all faking it, an illusion cast upon the tribe by the spiritual leader herself. Were that to be true, his trust in the captain would wane, and his wish to stay would transform into a wish to leave.

"Any word from Pinner?" asked Rowan before biting into the crispy skin of a rabbit thigh.

The meat was tender and cooked perfectly. Valner's was gone the minute it was placed before him.

"Should be along any second," said Merlin, gulping down the warmth in his clay cup.

The feast was solemn, full of silence. It was surprising, especially for the Gnomes, that a village of this size could accomplish a feat like that.

"Don't you think that's a bit suspicious?" asked Rossa quietly. "If one of my gnomish friends, perhaps even a good, trusted one, disappeared in the night and had not returned by nightfall, I would certainly feel worried for them."

"Oh, come now," said Merlin. "Neither of you know him as I know him."

He bit into his bread roll and spoke between chews.

"He is a good friend, and he will be along shortly."

He gulped.

"Give him time. He does admire the beauty of nature."

"Master, forgive me," said Rowan, slapping the tabletop with restraint. "But I do believe you are making excuses. He has abandoned the quest, forgotten it entirely. I should have known he would leave. Lousy old geezer that one. How could we have been so foolish?"

Merlin rose from his seat, a decision that commanded looks from the entire pavilion.

"I will not sit and listen to this slander!"

He paused, glaring at his prentice, but then he turned to catch the doubly disappointed and offended eyes of Lady Cho.

He said to her, "Apologies, my lady. My prentice and I were just leaving."

His glare returned to Rowan, and with it, he motioned him and the Gnomes to exit the feast.

*****

They sat somewhere in the midst of the many spruces inside the village. Merlin was seated at the foot of one with his hat beside him, his long gray hair resting on his shoulders. His staff stood erect as he held it in one hand. Rowan and the Gnomes sat at the foot of the tree opposite, slouching with embarrassment.

"Master?" said Rowan softly. "I would like to apologize—"

"No," put in Merlin. "I should be begging pardon, my boy."

He put his head back against the tough bark of the spruce.

"Perhaps you are right about him. He has never been gone this long."

"Perhaps they got him," suggested Rossa anxiously.

"Not probable. They are too undisciplined to take him on their own. It would take all five of the Caliph's Vexes to withhold him. But they'd never leave the Caliph, let alone Ensalor, for fear of a weakened morale."

"Cowards, all of them," said Rowan. "I bet they're there just to spite us, to be nothing more than a deterrent."

"Have you ever seen them?" asked Merlin.

Rowan paused. "No," he said. "But they better pray to their phantom goddess that I never do. I'd lay a mighty blow to any of them should they try and test us."

"I admire your confidence, Rowan, but these men are not childhood bullies. They are well-trained, well-learned soldiers selected for their extreme piety and loyalty. A Shimmer user barely compares to their faith. I would not be so arrogant."

"It shouldn't matter since we have Willow, and she has the sword."

"True, yes, but would you depend your life on Willow's capability?"

"Fair question. My answer is no still," said Rowan, crossing his arms in defeat.

He wanted to be right about the girl, to be sure she could restore it all. He had never known children to be saviors or world-shakers. But one thing he could not deny, because Skeef himself professed it, was that she was the One Who Unites. Though his conscience believed it, his mind wanted to doubt.

"She would not have made it without us," Rowan began. "Those Strix would have taken her if it weren't for Lady Cho and her Gallantinels, if it weren't for you and I. She got herself lost too in the

Shriveled Forest in the same situation. She cowered in fear inside a cave."

"Lucky she had you there," said Merlin, smiling as tears welled in his eyes. "I should not have left her when we landed. I should not have let a bird make her decisions."

"An unwise yielding for sure, master."

"I'm serious." He sniffed. "Had you not saved her in Al Wafra, Skeef knows where she'd be by now. What a poor excuse for a guardian!"

He began to weep.

This was new to Rowan. Never had he seen his master shed tears. It was an idea he never let himself entertain. Seeing it now, he felt sorry for the old man. As for the Gnomes, they were emotional beings, who began to weep with Merlin and console him.

"Oh, my boy!" wept Merlin. "If I never gave my thanks to you, I give it now! Thank you for staying by her side and bringing her back!"

This consolation was cut short by a sudden flash of light not far from the walls of Hrinthas. Tears dried, and feet were found almost as quickly as the light itself. A din of clamoring men and desperate women followed. They watched as the women took the children into the yurts, and the men gathered around Lady Cho and Ob. They were unarmed, except their leaders, but some of them fled to the barracks to fetch weapons. To arm each man, they would need time.

"By the White Lamb, whatever is happening?" said Rowan, drawing his shamshir.

"I don't know," said Merlin, replacing his pointed hat. "But we need to move."

Merlin, Rowan, and the Gnomes, who carried their small knives, rallied with the Da'iini, making their way to the front of the crowd. Whatever discord stood between Cho and the wizard was temporarily put aside.

"Any ideas, Magistrate?" asked Lady Cho, prepping her shortsword.

The Gallantinels finally took their place on the walls above.

"I've one," said Merlin, "though I don't know why he'd choose spontaneity."

"Goran!" called Lady Cho to one of the Gallantinels. "What do you see?"

The Gallantinel's voice was loud and brave.

"Only a man in black robes, my lady."

Merlin shot forward and banged on the heavy stone door with a fist.

"Open the door! It's all right! Open the door at once!"

The door didn't budge an inch. Merlin turned around.

"Tell them!"

He pounded with a balled fist.

"It's all right! Let him in!"

Lady Cho considered for a moment just what might lay behind the door. She glanced at Ob, who began to repeat the motion of fist to palm as if he was ready to fight. She glanced at her people, the Da'iini, and saw the nervous faces of most of them, even those who were brave enough to equip themselves. Her lips turned inward, and she looked at Goran, who stood with other Gallantinels, grasping the rope in the door's winch.

Lightning doesn't strike in the forest without a fire. This must be a Shimmer user, she pondered.

"Open the door!" commanded Lady Cho, her shortsword tight in her grip.

The Gnomes held fast next to Rowan. Merlin stood back and felt the low rumble of the heavy stone doors as they slowly swung open outward. Anticipation set in as the doors flattened the blades of grass beneath them, creating an arc from the door's motion. It wasn't long before the doors were wide open, and the many forests and glades of the Gallant Valley could be seen. But there, in the dirt path leading from Hrinthas, standing as still as stone, was Pinner Vemtal, unscathed.

Not a soul moved.

Merlin locked eyes with the old man in black robes, both seeming to give the other quite the scowl. The whole village seemed honed in on what might happen next.

"Took you long enough, old friend," Merlin said, laughing.

Pinner embraced Merlin.

"I had some catching up to do since *somebody* decided not to wait for me."

He smiled back at Merlin and walked with him.

"Halt!" Lady Cho crowed.

The Gallantinels atop the high stone wall drew their bows and aimed at Pinner. Merlin's joy faded to confusion.

"What is the meaning of this?" he said. "Do you not see he is a friend?"

"A friend to you perhaps but a stranger to Hrinthas."

"You said yourself that you used to be subjects of Ensalor before the Conquering. Do you not recognize the former grand warden? He served the duke and duchess."

"May they rest in the clouds with their Creator. But if he is with your company, explain why now he shows his face? He could be plotting against us as we speak."

"Oh, come off it! You have hidden yourselves for so long that your paranoia is beginning to catch up with you. You trusted me. You trusted the rest of us. Why not trust someone who trusts us too? I've never known Pinner to dabble in malevolence. You must see that this hostility is surely not needed."

"Do not take me for a fool, Magistrate! I do what is best for my people! Hiding away has kept us safe, kept us healthy. One bad egg could spoil the dozen. Either turn him away, or let him speak for himself."

Lady Cho accented her words with her sword.

"Do not fret, friend," said Pinner, waving off his friend. "I've always been the better with words between you and I. I can handle this."

The wizard in black stepped forward with a stride of confidence.

"What would you wish of me?" he asked Lady Cho.

"State your business," she replied.

"What my friend here has said is true. I am Pinner, former grand warden of Ensalor, and I do not wish harm upon you and your village. Quite the lovely place you have."

"Flattery will not suffice."

Pinner nodded subtly.

"Apologies. I am simply here to rest and recuperate with my company. They have come a long way, and I am in need of nourishment. Won't you grant an old man sanctuary in these changing times?"

Lady Cho withdrew her sword.

"I only have one final question, and it is the most important question for what happens next."

She took a few steps forward. Merlin held his breath as witness. The Da'iini, Rowan, and the Gnomes stood in suspense.

"Do you denounce Fikra?"

Her question was firm.

"What?" said Pinner, tilting his head.

"Do. You. Denounce. Fikra?"

"I don't understand. If Merlin has vouched for me, then I—"

"Answer the question, or we will be forced to shoot."

Pinner paused briefly again, choosing his next words very, very carefully. He could see the look in Lady Cho's eyes, the look of tenacity but also of fear—fear for the safety of her people and her village. He began to feel a slight tug at his heart from knowing he would watch the entire village burn down.

"The time has come," he said. "You can reveal yourself now."

It seemed the very tone of the wind itself changed. Behind Pinner, something stepped out of the tree line. Darkened from lack of sunlight, a massive rider approached and stopped next to Pinner. Heavy was his iron armor, and riddled with red feathers was his helm. A sprawling crimson cape flowed behind him and draped over the horse's behind. The steed was as dark as night, and its head was adorned with an iron covering. Steam trickling out of the mount's nostrils created the imagery of an angry horse.

"It can't be," said Rowan, gazing upon the powerful rider in both awe and terror.

"What have you done?" said Merlin, backing away from Pinner.

"What I had to," replied Pinner, taking his twisted staff in both hands. "I'm sorry, old friend, but a deal had to be made."

With the uttering of a strange word, Pinner then blasted a burst of bluish energy from the tip of his staff. Merlin was knocked back against the stone wall from the burst, and when he tried to rebound, he found he could not move his limbs. He was still conscious, but his arms and legs refused to cooperate.

"Let that serve as a warning to any who should be so foolish as to resist," said the rider upon the dark horse. "Lay down your weapons now!"

He drew a black steel longsword from the sheath by his side—black steel was normal steel dyed black—and held it at the ready. The cowards among the Da'iini threw their blades and axes to the ground.

"Traitorous dog!" cried Rowan, a squall of anger rising like a well bucket being raised. "I knew something felt off! How could you betray us?"

"You forget, both of you," said Pinner, "what happened a decade ago. We were outmatched. The Caliphate cannot be beaten."

He turned to Merlin, who was still paralyzed.

"When you decided to take the child with you, I made a deal with the Vexes."

"A rat remembers where to find the food," said the dark rider. "Follow the rat, find the food."

He seemed to scan the crowd of people at the stone doors.

"However, it does not seem to be here."

He dismounted.

"Where is the girl?"

None of them answered. As the rider trod forward, the crowd tightened. Rowan clambered over to Merlin and helped him to his feet. The spell had worn off.

"Where is the One Who Unites?" the rider exclaimed.

Again, the crowd remained silent. The caped rider brandished his sword.

"I will not ask again."

"I would listen if I were you," said Pinner, the tip of his twisted staff beginning to glow a hazy scarlet. He turned to Merlin, who was supported by his prentice.

"If she is hiding, call her."

The hazy glow deepened.

"I know she trusts you."

The rider revealed a talisman from under his armor, a circular token fastened to a thin but fine chain. Rowan could see there was something embossed on the iron amulet, and whatever it was, Merlin could tell it had affected him in some way, for Rowan suddenly dropped his master at the sight of it. His breath began to pick up.

"So it was you, Sal the Caped Vex," he said tightly. "You were the one!"

Sal, though stoic, was confused.

"I know that symbol. It was burned into the fields of my village the day your kind decided to move in."

He readied his shamshir.

"Then you must know what it is capable of," said Sal. "Tell me where the girl is, and perhaps I may allow you to see another sunrise."

He then raised an armored fist burning in a ball of fire. Scorching, blazing flame engulfed his chain mail fingers.

"I'd rather die than relinquish her."

Rowan prepped his footing. Years of practice led to this moment. Years of fighting bandits and city guards and years of scars and broken limbs—each served as a reminder of his progress.

"So be it," finished Sal. He yelled as fire surged forward from his smoldering fist.

The crowd of Da'iini retreated back into Hrinthas to avoid the inferno. Rowan dodged to the right and sprinted forward, shamshir gripped with both hands. A shout left his lips, a shout full of anger, as his shamshir made contact with his enemy's longsword.

Back and forth they exchanged blows, each guarding the other. Rowan swiped for the head, but his foe ducked and made for his torso. But swiftly, he swerved and guarded once more. Each strike of their swords let out a clang and twang of metal.

"Impressive, boy," Sal said and swiped again, and Rowan dodged. "But this resistance is futile. You will die here."

Swipe. Clang!

"As will your master."

Clang! Clang!

"And when I find her, I will kill your precious savior too!"

"To do that...," a voice called.

In the midst of their clash, both fighters turned, only to see Lady Cho brandishing her shortsword.

"You'll have to kill us both."

Then the duel became a battle of three, two against one. Lady Cho was swift, landing several strikes on Sal's armor as he guarded Rowan's aggressive blows. From one to the other, Sal blocked and blocked, occasionally using his gauntlet as a shield. Sparks flew with each clash of their blades. But the Caped Vex was barely breaking a sweat. Each time Lady Cho's sword edge made contact, he compared it to a spoiled child throwing a tantrum.

"You should not have come back," said Pinner, who watched as Merlin supported himself on his staff.

The graybeard in purple steadied himself. He had been betrayed, and to add insult to injury, it was by a close ally. Many thoughts and emotions swirled in his head—anger, frustration, sadness, and even regret. He could see that Rowan was busy engaging the Vex alongside Lady Cho.

"We will find her," Pinner continued. "And we will take her to Ensalor ourselves."

He raised his still-glowing-red staff and aimed it at Merlin.

"The Caliph will decide her fate."

"She won't b-be going any...anywhere," Merlin said, catching his breath.

"Is that right?" Pinner said.

A second later, he conjured a beam of burgeoning red energy hurling toward Merlin, who quickly retorted with a swish of his staff that conjured a sturdy blue screen. The red beam dissipated upon contact, transforming into a grainy mist.

"Give it up, Merlin!"

He shot another beam. Merlin made the screen.

"You cannot win, not against me!"

Beam. Screen. This cycle continued for a few seconds, a skirmish of red and blue, the flashes from each illuminating the forest with brilliant light. Beam. Screen. Beam. Screen. With each impact,

Merlin felt the recoil vibrate in his bones. In his psyche, he was uncertain if he could withstand the cycle.

Then as if the leaves and branches of the trees all cried out at once, the deep note of a horn could be heard at the heart of Hrinthas. Scattering people halted, the flashing of magic bursts ceased, and the clanging of blades finished. All heads turned to see a brave hazel-headed girl blowing into a corkscrew horn atop a majestic zebra.

"There you are," Sal muttered to himself.

"Get your people to safety!" the brave girl said to the beastly man known as Ob. "Take them out of the valley! Fly quickly!"

She shouldered the horn and drew her sword, a fine blade with a purple gem integrated into its hilt. She turned toward the duel of three near the stone doors.

"Hey, you! It's me you want! Leave them be, and face me yourself!"

Sal, caught in a clash with both rivals, broke away from them and used his flaming fist to fire a lob of blazing fire toward Willow. Seeing the fireball, Racer skidded sideways, and the fireball made contact with one of the yurts, setting it ablaze!

Merlin then took the offensive and cast a bolt of lightning toward his former friend. Bolts of sky blue cascaded from the tip of his staff, crackling and sizzling the whole way. But with a swish of his hand, the sorcerer in black waved them away, and the bolts slammed into the stone wall of Hrinthas, chunks of grayish rocks breaking away.

"Again with your useless tactics," said Pinner. "Give me a real fight!"

He raised both of his hands high, and like it had been in the Garmouth, the winds began to bluster. Limbs, leaves, and other bits of rock swirled and whirled around him. It became intense enough to free himself from the ground beneath him. He sent a chunk of tree bark hurling toward Merlin with a gesture of his staff. Merlin countered by burning the bark with a brief throw of flames. Pinner's wind lifted a chunk of fallen wall and hurled it toward Merlin, who again countered, but with a single charge of lightning.

The fire was now spreading through Hrinthas. From the single burning yurt spawned numerous blazes that began to engulf their crops, trees, and other yurts.

"Take the children and go!" some of the villagers cried.

"Save the cattle!"

"Don't leave without me!"

"Wait! Wait!" they cried.

They headed for the eastern exit.

Willow, her attention focused on the duel of three, readied herself, sword in hand. There was no way one man could handle three opponents at once no matter how much armor he applied. She kicked at Racer, and the zebra started forward.

"Rowan!" she cried. "I'm coming!"

Racer picked up the pace. The stone door was not far now. If Rowan could just hold out longer, they could escape, and Lady Cho could focus on her people. Along with Rowan, she tried to out-speed the Vex with quick thrusts and slashes, but the mighty knight's stamina never faltered. Again, he broke away from the duel and sent a seething mass of flames ahead of him from his burning fist. Willow pulled Racer's reins, and the zebra lurched backward, his hooves digging into the soot-filled grass.

"No, Willow!" said Rowan when he wasn't blocking the long-sword. "Stay back! Get yourself out now!"

He blocked another strike. Sparks.

Willow didn't listen. She strode forward again, digging her knees into Racer's ribs. She pointed Pnevma forward like a cavalry rider.

"Get back!" Rowan said, brandishing his shamshir.

But his guard was down, and before he knew it, Lady Cho had been knocked away.

"Enough!" demanded Sal, his blazing fist writhing.

The once orange glow intensified into a ghoulish blue hue. With a hefty swing, the Caped Vex introduced it to Rowan's upper back, and the young prentice was blown away. Limply, he was flung back through Hrinthas's stone doors and landed before Willow, a cindering wound freshly made where his tunic was burned up. Racer whined and reared up, his front hooves thrashing wildly!

"Bastard!" he cried.

But Willow pulled at his reins.

"We need to go now!" she said, her voice on the verge of collapse. "Run, Racer, run!"

Racer turned and started for the eastern exit. By now, most of the Da'iini were through, but a few stragglers still waited for the women and children with hatchets in hand.

"Clear the way! Clear the way!" said Willow, her sword still in hand.

Soon, she heard a dreadful sound from behind her, a sound like an out-of-tune string instrument. Sal was pursuing her! She kicked at Racer's again, and his hooves moved as fast as they could. Something hot passed by her and landed against the inner side of the stone wall. All around her, the village of the Da'iini burned. Years of time spent building and cultivating were incinerated and thrown up in smoke.

Soon, she was through the stone door and into the wilderness once again. It seemed as though the very forest welcomed her with their branches like open arms, relieved that she had made it through the chaos.

She looked back and found that the Vex was gone. Something—or someone—must have stopped him. Only one thing mattered now, and it was the only thing Merlin and the others would have urged of her in this very situation.

Get to Londror safely. Finish the quest!

Chapter 17

Warrior-King

The flight from Hrinthas was not an easy one, for the sun had refused to rise, and the path itself seemed unfollowable.

An hour had passed since Willow escaped the inferno. Cold sweat blanketed her skin, the feeling you get when you step out into the cold night from inside a warm home. A jumble of emotions danced around in her mind with each gallop forward. She tried to focus on the task at hand: getting to Londror. She tried to remember the map she had been shown in Tel Pata, but it was naught but a hazy dream by now, nothing but tan with black lines. On top of emotions, questions lined up right behind them.

How could I just leave him? What in the world happened? Who was that caped rider?

She hoped answers would come soon.

The stars were shrouded by dark clouds, and barely any moonlight revealed the path ahead. Racer galloped hard and fast. Willow remembered that this was not only affecting her. Racer had watched as his friend was wounded, potentially killed even. She knew this flight, this retreat, was better than sharing his fate. Still, neither of them saw him move or even make a sound. The cindering wound still bore itself to the forefront of her memories.

Then she began to think about Merlin. After she stormed away from Lady Cho, she took up residence in one of the neighboring yurts. She stayed there because, one, she didn't feel like arguing with someone whose mind was already made up and, two, because she didn't want things to escalate and risk losing protection for the others. But after she hid herself away, a while later, she heard voices and the smell of cooking food. It was almost enough to lure her outside, but her appetite disagreed.

Then moments later, there was disarray. She began to hear cries of despair, clanging metal, and shouts of aggression. When she stepped out, she saw former friends fighting in a very one-sided duel—Pinner against Merlin. There had never been feelings that she had felt in that moment like she had ever felt before—the feeling of betrayal, of spite, of lividity. The appearance of Pinner turned from someone she thought she could trust to the very figure of malice and evil. Pinner had turned against the company. She looked farther and saw that Rowan had engaged with the menacing rider. Lady Cho was fighting too.

In the spur of the moment, she decided to help. She was tired of running, of being on the sidelines while the others did the heavy lifting. She made haste toward the stables, where Racer had been taken and saddled up. She was thankful that Rowan's things were still strapped to him. She had both her sword and her horn with her, and when she found the words to say, she spoke them after having no other choice but to blow the horn. At that time, she remembered what Merlin had told when she received the horn: "One blow of this instrument will, without a shadow of doubt, bring help from somewhere in the user's immediate surroundings or farther." After the deep note concluded, nothing immediately happened. So she had taken it upon herself to aid her friends.

But now she thought of herself with regret. She had tried to help, and look at her now. She was running through another dark forest with no guide and no allies. She was alone again like she had been for a decade at the orphanage.

Minutes later, she noticed that Racer's pace had decreased. She felt his ribs expanding with each strong puff. She was regretting not finding sleep inside the yurt.

"Okay," she said, patting his mane. "Let's rest up for the night. Rowan's things are still here. Maybe I can set something up."

She reached back and unlatched the rolled cloth behind the saddle.

"Stop over there. That spot looks fine."

She pointed toward a tree with several of its leaves dangling like hair strands from its branches. In the dark of the night, she could not tell if its leaves were green, but it didn't matter. As long as they kept the morning sun off her as she slept, they could be brown or orange or red for all she cared.

Willow dismounted. As she worked, trying to make a suitable tent, her loneliness felt different now, worse than before. She was thankful, though, that Racer stayed closer. He nuzzled her with his snout, trying to comfort her. But the zebra only made her think more and more of Rowan and what had happened. She began to weep, sniffling as her face reddened.

Eventually, the tent was made, a shoddy triangular thing constructed with a drape and poles. She only felt cramped as she settled inside. Sleep took its time finding her, but it came.

*****

The tree had done what she had asked of it. The morning sunlight was dimmed against the drape of the tent. Shadows of the dangling strands swayed against the olive-green canvas. Willow awoke and rubbed her eyes. They ached from all the tears. With a fingertip, she dug out some of the tiny bits in the corner of her eye that you got sometimes in the morning. She flicked them away. She took a deep breath in, held it, and sighed.

When she had slipped her boots back on and thrown her cloak on, she stepped out of the tent and gasped. All around her were the same trees that she had taken shelter under, tall, wide bright-green trees, all with dangling hairlike branches. She looked up and saw that hers had a winding trunk, curved yet sturdy. To her left lay Racer, his white underbelly rising and falling peacefully. She went over and sat in the space where his front and back hooves did not meet. Seconds later, she watched his eyelids blink open. He lifted his head and rolled over onto his stomach, folding his short legs under him.

"Good morning," she said softly.

Racer shook his mane.

"You too."

There seemed to still be a hint of mourning in his voice. He blinked as he looked around. A brief moment of peaceful silence followed. Willow relaxed against the zebra's warm, striped body.

A few birds chirped. The breeze was gentle. For some reason, these niceties felt undeserved for her, this...peace. She had failed her friends, so why was it all still so calm? Even the sunlight twinkling in and out of the dangling branches was gently warm on the parts of her it shone on. But she felt she deserved none of it.

"You know, I have never seen a horse like you," she said, breaking the silence. "I don't think I have ever seen anything like what you are."

The words felt awkward, uneven. The zebra did not move.

"I don't mean to seem rude, but what are you?"

Racer, though still deep within his depression, was polite.

"I am a zebra."

He breathed in and sighed. Willow petted his salt-and-pepper mane.

"Merlin said you were one of a kind here."

"Did he now?"

His voice was bland.

"Yes. He said you were gifted to Rowan. That you came from across the sea."

"That's right."

"So you too are a stranger here."

"Too?"

"Like me."

Racer snorted.

"You and I are not the same. You were born here and taken to a different place. I was born in a different place and taken here. Complete opposites."

"Still," said Willow. "Do you ever miss your...people? Your pack?"

She cringed.

"I don't know what a group of zebras are called."

"A herd. It is called a herd. The same as normal horses."

"Oh. Well, do you ever miss them?"

"To be honest," he began, "I have little knowledge of them. One of the faintest memories I can recall is the moment I first met Rowan. He was a chipper little boy, full of enthusiasm and hope. He accepted me, cared for me, played with me. We were almost siblings. But as I grew and he too, things began to change. Instead of the back-and-forth of being it, we practiced riding, scouting, and fighting. He said that it was Merlin's idea. All the same, however, I never once felt out of place. Rowan and his family gave me a home, a place to stay and belong. So I would say my answer is no. I have always belonged here."

Willow nodded.

"After all that has happened, this world doesn't feel like home. Sure, I've got friends. But what good are they if I've no home, no place to fall back on?"

"Rowan would agree with that. I've realized you're both alike in that way."

"Yes," said Willow. "You both have been through so much together. Oh, thinking about it now is just making it worse!"

She rolled over, facing away from the zebra. She felt her face getting warmer, her eyes making the shape of crying, but no tears came.

Racer rested his head on the ground away from her and breathed gently.

They sat for a period, letting the tranquility around them make its attempt at bringing some calm to them, but the scene from the night prior still clung to them like cacti spines. The more they tried to do away with it, the more it dug itself deeper, worsened. Bad memories were often like that, especially the first time they happened. They stayed with you, and no matter how many good memories we put on top, the bad ones stuck around, waiting for you to be alone with your thoughts. They haunted, and they depressed. Motivation went down, and what was left was the shell of someone formerly happy.

But something began to change in the glade they sat in. It seemed the sunlight shone brighter, the wind blew slightly stronger, and the grass grew greener than before. Trees whose flowers had not appeared yet began to blossom around them, bringing shades of white, pink, blue, and yellow to their surroundings.

Racer looked up and looked from side to side at the sight he beheld. Never had he seen anything like it!

"What's happening?" he said.

He found his feet, and when he did so, Willow slumped over and turned back, becoming aware of the wonder.

Soon, when they were both standing, there upon the air were golden streams as if the wind itself had become opaque. Suddenly, all negativity and despair was relinquished, all sadness was dissipated, and all anger or frustration was banished. A wave, therefore, of positivity, joyfulness, and serenity washed over them, clothed them with radiant delight. There was an overwhelming sense of elation all around. They peered deeper into the forest and saw something coming toward them, the golden streams flowing into whatever it was.

A familiar sight revealed itself.

"My children," the voice in their heads spoke.

Willow's eyes widened at the sight of what the streams were flowing into. She smiled when she saw a lamb with fleece as white as snow and a nose as pink as a rose trotting slowly into view. The streams flowing into it were likened to that of a sun's corona.

"Skeef!" she cried gleefully. "Skeef, it's you! It's really you!"

"Master!" said Racer, rearing his front hooves to the heavens. "At last!"

"It is good to see you again," Skeef said, his voice in their heads. "But it appears I have come at a rather sorrow-filled time. Why do you fret? Why do you worry? Why do you allow yourself to become wrapped up in what is wrong when you know that I am with you every step of the way? I who gave you life, and I who have delivered you out of the hand of evil? What are you sorely afraid of?"

"Failure," said Willow. "I don't want others to be hurt because I messed up. Rowan, Merlin, the Gnomes, even Juniper! Oh, Juniper! What have I done? I've left them behind!"

"Peace, my child," his voice said, the lamb drawing nearer. "It was the only way. They would not have wanted you to be captured or, worse, killed. They were ready to lay down their lives for you from the very beginning. There is no greater admiration than those who would sacrifice everything for the people they love. Worry not for them should they be alive. Fret not for them. They've played their parts, and now you must play yours."

"I don't know how to," said Willow. "I've never had so much responsibility. I don't even have my parents here to guide me, let alone Merlin."

"In time, child, you will find strength in their sacrifice. Be proud of those who have helped you every step of your journey, though it may not be finished. Alas, I will show you the way to Château Londror. You will find all the help you require there."

Skeef turned gracefully and began to wander through the woods, golden wisps of light trailing behind him in a moving line. Willow could see that where the wisps began was exactly where the lamb had been standing before.

"Come on, Racer," she said. "We have a baron to call upon."

*****

Soon, they were out of the Gallant Valley, and the landscape had shifted from a dense taiga to hills sparse with conifers. Willow rode atop Racer with a newfound courage, holding her head high and forward. She watched the world around her continue its rebirth of color. The very grass under the zebra's hooves grew green and healthy; the sky above was nearly back to its normal pale blue expanse.

With her eyes focused, she saw that the golden streams wound around a cluster of trees and across a small stream and continued eastward. They blinked every so often.

"Ride hard, Racer," she said. "Keep up with him!"

Racer whinnied and picked up his pace. His black hooves clopped loudly on the ground, picking up bits of dirt behind him. In his swiftness, Willow could feel the wind flowing through her hair as her cloak flew behind her.

The sun was reaching its summit now, and the wind had kept the sweat from staining her hair. She held a hand to her brow to shield the sunlight from her eyes. In the distance, a rocky escarpment rose, and at its base was a yawning stretch of ginkgo, oak, and dogwood trees.

To her surprise, nothing adorned the top of the cliff save for several stone constructs resembling statues of people she did not recognize. One gave an outstretched hand, another held a shield, and the others carried various tools. If she squinted long enough, she could make out that all of them had thin, noodle-like tails protruding from their lower backs. They were made of a mixture of stone, clay, and plaster. They were unlike any statue she had ever seen, even in Earthrealm.

They continued their haste toward the escarpment as the golden streams led them. But overhead, a group of native birds flew in a group like geese. As they dived, they split apart and scattered into different trees before them. Willow heard a familiar chirp that prompted an upturn of her head. Whatever it was must have recognized her, as its chirping continued to a rather annoying frequency. Then the chirping became a voice!

"Willow! Willow! Wait!" it said, urgency in its tone. "Slow down!"

Willow pulled back on Racer's reins, and the zebra stiffened, pulling up dust and dirt.

There's only one bird I know that talks, she thought.

A small puff of dust wafted past Racer's hooves. He shook his mane and caught his breath. They were at the crest of a hill.

"Hey!" he said. "Why are we stopping? We're so close! The golden streams won't last forever, you know."

He snorted.

Something black, white, and sunset orange alighted on Racer's pate. Willow nearly shed a tear at the sight of it. Its beady eyes closed as it hopped up and down. It was the toucan Juniper, flapping her wings wildly!

"Thank the Creator! Oh yes, thank him unto the highest!" she said, nuzzling Willow as she lay in her arms.

Her feathers were still soft, to Willow's surprise.

"It is good to see you too, Juniper!"

Willow's smile was genuine. But their elation soon foundered, their mood dropping to a rather sorrowful level. There was silence.

Willow broke the quiet and said, "I'm sorry. For everything back there."

"What?"

Juniper blinked rapidly in confusion.

"I ran away…like a coward."

"You had no other choice."

"I abandoned you…Merlin…Lady Cho…Rowan. I let everyone down."

She dropped her head, her nose inches from the tip of Juniper's beak.

"I thought that help would come by blowing the horn. That's what Merlin said after all. But seconds, minutes, passed, and no one came. This is all my fault."

She felt tears coming back.

"Hey now," said Juniper. "Don't you go feeling sorry for yourself when you would have done the same for the others were you in their position. They *wanted* you to run away, to protect yourself, to protect the entire realm. You getting yourself captured or, worse, killed would have made the entire campaign moot, pointless. What you did was the right choice, girl. And look at us now! Here we are in open country, mere minutes away from our objective. I'm alive. Racer is alive. More importantly"—Juniper looked straight at Willow—"you are alive. Restoration is still possible, because you slipped through their fingers."

Willow sniffed and wiped her face with a sleeve.

"Yes, you're right. Like Skeef said, I mustn't fret for them. How did you get out anyway?"

Juniper looked at Willow with a countenance of slight contempt, a look that she had possibly never given anyone before.

"Look at me," she said. "What do you see?"

Willow was not sure if it was a rhetorical question or a serious one. Either way, she answered, "A bird."

"And birds have…what?"

"Beaks?"

"Yes, but not the answer."

"Feathers?"

"Close."

Willow thought a bit harder.

"Oh!" she said. "Wings!"

"Correct. So how did I get away?"

"You flew away," she said blandly, thinking herself dumb for not thinking that. "I didn't guess it was that simple. I wondered if you met any resistance."

"Oh, surely I saw the treachery of Pinner and the tenacity of his acquaintance. I did have to dodge fire and smoke the same as you. I think we were separated after the first fireball was lobbed at our heads."

"You answered my next question before I could ask it. But were you able to see anything before you fled? Rowan's condition? Merlin's status? The Gnomes?"

"All I remember is Rowan still lying limp on the ground, the back swathe of his tunic still smoking from that punch. As for Merlin and the others, nothing. One can only assume he was successful in his escape. Skeef help us if Rowan was taken."

Willow tried not to imagine it. If they took him, who was going to rescue him? How would they find him? A girl, a zebra, and a toucan was not the most ideal search party. She tossed the possibility into her mind's figurative rubbish bin.

"If he was," Racer butted in, "then we can get him back. Should it be revealed that my partner was captured, I'll not stand idly by and let him suffer. But we need to get moving. The golden trails are beginning to thin."

"Make haste!"

Willow used the back of her heel to jab Racer in the ribs—not hard enough to hurt but enough to get the command across.

Racer dashed down the hill, leaving more dust and dirt behind him. Juniper held tightly to the back of the saddle as Willow gripped the reins in both hands. Air rushed by as she rode, creating a blowing effect in her ears. They passed through some of the conifers, splashed over the small stream, and ducked under any low-hanging branches, all while following the golden streams provided by Skeef.

Willow felt the zebra's strong lungs drawing in breath on her feet, in and out deeply.

He's giving it everything he's got, she thought. *He shouldn't overexert himself. He will need all of his strength soon. I can feel it.*

The statues that adorned the tall escarpment like a crown soon disappeared from her view and were replaced by treetops of green. There was shrubbery and foliage here and there on the forest floor, and the branches of the dogwoods created an odd resemblance to fingers on a hand. Around here were shades of green, yellow, and even some browns. One could easily get lost should they be without a guide. Luckily, the golden streams lingered. They weaved and curved between stalks and shrubs. In the distance, the growls and yowls of animals could be heard. Willow acknowledged them but kept her focus forward. She knew they were too far away, and the forest concealed them too efficiently for them to target them.

Soon, the forest began to thin, and the seam between sunlit grass and shaded forest bed was clear. Ahead, the tall, rocky wall of the escarpment loomed over a sturdy stone behemoth of a castle. Londror stood solitarily on a mass of ground within an abundant lake as if the fortress itself had risen from beneath the water. Its forward wall was sizable, stretching between its two parapet-capped towers.

Two narrow semicircle windows faced outward from each tower. At its center, for a door was a wide portcullis that could only be lifted from the inside. Expanding out underneath the portcullis was a stretch of ground, a straight path leading into a hexagonal platform. From this platform, a fixed wooden bridge connected to the forest side of the moat. It was the main path to reach the castle.

"May I present," began Juniper, "Château Londror, the fortress."

"It's huge!" said Willow. "Far larger than Al Wafra. Far larger than the orphanage."

"Yes, it dwarfs that ragged place."

Willow gathered herself, breathed in, and let it go, saying, "Okay. Here we go."

They proceeded forward slowly. As they emerged out of the forest, a realization was made: the forest surrounded the watery expanse and blended into the looming cliffside. Drawing closer to the beginning of the bridge, they could see long, sharpened spikes protruding out of the water in clusters throughout the lake, even close to the other parts of the surrounding forest. These were meant to deter a direct flank from anywhere other than the main bridge. The entire scene was a triumph of strategy and construction.

"Whoa there!" a voice called out from somewhere at the castle.

Willow brought Racer to a halt before his left hoof could be placed on the first plank of the bridge. She looked up and saw six figures atop the parapets looking down at them from afar.

"None shall pass."

Though they were yards away, Willow could see their pointed helmets, cloth and mail armor. Two were standing atop the towers; the other four were across the middle parapet. Each of them carried a broad bow with arrows trained on her, Racer, and Juniper.

"Come no farther. State your business in Londror!"

The voice was harsh, raspy, and seasoned. Whoever it was behind the voice obviously meant business, was serious. She couldn't exactly pinpoint which of the six archers was speaking.

"We seek to see the baron!" shouted Willow. "We have been riding through the night, fleeing with our lives! Let us pass! We mean no threat!"

"Are you armed?"

Willow placed a hand on Pnevma's sheath.

Lying would get me nowhere here, she thought. *Should they let us in, they would see the sword on my hip, and I'd be caught. Better to tell the truth.*

"Yes. I have a sword. But I shall not raise it against you. You have my word."

"Words are words, lass. Actions speak louder. There has been smoke rising from the direction you've come from. Have you anything to do with that?"

"No, sir! That was a rogue rider with a red cloak. He burned Hrinthas to the ground."

"A cloaked rider? Hrinthas? Are you of the Da'iini?"

"I am of Ensalor, sir, before the wretched Caliph seized it. My name is Willow Drinith, daughter of the late duke and duchess of Kastallon. I have met with the Da'iini, for it was they who rescued us in the Garmouth. There were eight of us, but they were lost in Hrinthas. We are what remains."

The guard considered her tone of voice—slightly urgent, not quite filled with terror. Even from his position on the tower, he noticed the toucan, the symbol of House Drinith. She could be telling the truth, or she could have taken the toucan prisoner. No other toucans existed in the wilds of Kastallon. He considered then the zebra, an animal someone like him had never encountered before. It was not as tall as the common horse, but it was a steed nonetheless. But one term stood out in the girl's words: Drinith.

"How can I believe someone who claims to be of noble blood? What do you have to make me believe you are who you say you are?"

Willow figured the question would be raised. People, especially dissenters, were paranoid of the Caliphate and its spies. "Those who did not submit to their way of life were burned to the ground, every last one of them"—those were Pinner's words. Knowing what she knew now about him, his true self, she couldn't prevent the very thought of him carrying out those orders from entering her mind. She focused and allowed herself to calm.

"Here," she said. "I am going to show you."

She gripped Pnevma's hilt with her right hand and held its sheath with her left. Slowly, she drew the blade so as not to seem like she aimed to assault. When the blade was no longer concealed, she held it high.

"This is Pnevma, the duchess's sword. It was kept by a former ally and passed down to me by my guardian, Merlin the Magical."

The blade and its gem flashed in the early sun. The guard squinted, honed in on the blade in the girl's hand, and withdrew his bow.

To the others, he said, "See that purple gem, boys. She's not lying."

"It could be a fake, a copy, sir!" one of them said.

"Impossible," the guard retorted. "There has only been one to exist. I doubt the wicked Caliph herself knows about it."

"I don't trust it," another said. "I'd have to see it up close."

"Fine," said the guard. Then to Willow, he added, "A decision has been made, lass. Bring the sword to the wall so we may inspect it from here. You will proceed forth, but at a leisurely trot. Any faster will be taken as a threat. Understand?"

"I understand," said Willow, still holding the blade high.

"Proceed!"

Willow flicked Racer's reins gently, and he began a mild stroll across the bridge. His hooves against the wooden planks made a satisfying *clop-clop* as he went. Soon, they were at the hexagonal platform, and it became clearer that the archers on the parapets had strange, angular ears protruding from beneath their helmets. Thin fur covered them like felines.

She paused in the center of the platform, the rest of the path lying before her with the entrance to the castle shut tight. She waved Pnevma slightly, trying to reflect the sun off it to make it clearer to see. She saw two of the guards' heads pop out, leaning over the parapet's square gaps. Their faces were humanlike, but their ears and long hair threw her mind for a loop.

They have…cat ears? she thought. *How strange. So these are the Purloinians that Merlin spoke so highly of. I need a better look.*

"Ah yes," said one of them. "Authentic, wouldn't you say?"

"Seems legitimate to me," the other replied. "Up close, I can see she has her mother's hair and her father's eyes."

"You needed that much proof?" Juniper squawked, realizing she was less believed than a sword.

Willow shot her a look.

"Open the doors!" the main guard said. "Let in the daughter of Ensalor! Let her pass!"

The huge wooden doors standing tall lurched forward with a low rumble, the stone underneath crying out with a loud scrape. It was then revealed that two more catlike guards dressed the same as those above had been pushing the door outward.

The girl, the toucan, and the zebra strolled in.

*****

Château Londror was a spectacle, especially for a ten-year-old girl. She had compared it to the many historical pictures she had found in several of the books in the orphanage library. But seeing one up close was a whole other experience. She, along with her animals, had passed through the huge wooden doors, witnessed the stone staircases up to the parapet walls, smelled the aromas of different herbs, and gazed upon the town surrounding the towering main structure of the castle, all within the security of its moat and walls.

As they followed the guard and his bouncing noodle tail, many of the common Purloinians stopped and stared at her in uncomfortable silence. Each of their thin pupils gaped, and she felt all of them following her every move.

"Who is this girl?" "What kind of horse is that?" "What a peculiar bird!" and "Do you think the baron knows her?" were some of what she picked out from the many murmurings from the crowd.

"Keep up now," said the main guard. He still held his curved bow in hand as he walked.

The other guards walked rank and file behind them. Willow kept her left hand tight around Pnevma's sheath.

They look upon me like I'm something scary. Why?

"Through here," he said, stopping short of the maroon entrance to the main structure.

The path leading up to it was full of people trading things, buying things, stabling horses, carrying goods, and even some children playing in the street. But she was glad to escape the multitude and walked with purpose through the doors.

The foyer was a mixture of tapestries, elaborate painting, and carpets. It was obvious that the Purloinian nobility had sophistication and elegance at the forefront of their priorities. It could be seen from the ground floor that about ten feet up the wall, extending around the room from the top step of the grand staircase, there was a second floor gated by banisters. Parts of the wall on the ground floor were occupied by heavily stocked bookshelves. It made the orphanage look like an abandoned shack. Then again, she already considered it as that.

"Wow," Willow murmured, looking up side to side. "Incredible!"

She looked to the right of the grand staircase under the banister and saw furniture set by a fireplace—a circular wooden table, wooden stools, and a faux throne with pointed tips.

"Why don't you have a seat? Make yourself comfortable, heiress," said the guard. "Someone will be along with provisions. I shall fetch my lord."

He bowed and made for the stairs. Willow and Juniper, who was perched on her arm, exchanged glances.

Heiress? she thought. *Why does he call me that? What even is that? Some kind of title or moniker?*

She sat down on one of the stools near the table and let Juniper climb down. She let herself smile when the toucan settled and let its eyes droop slowly close by the fire. A deep sigh later, she found herself standing by the fire, looking into the orange light. Her hands were wrapped around her arms. It was hard to ignore the pain in her body and the rumble of her stomach. It had been hours since she last ate, which was only a few tears of doughy bread inside the yurt. Adrenaline began to recede, and the warmth of the fire made it harder to keep her own eyes open. She was on the verge of slumber when she heard the paced stepping of someone coming down the stairs. Her head jolted up.

He was magnificent, a Purloinian purebred. His eyes were a sparkling dandelion with thin pupils under relaxed eyelids. His reddish mane was tied back at the top of his head, revealing his furry, earringed ears. Darker mail under a green tunic and black boots made him appear like a warrior-king from the days of old. Exposed under his top lip were two short fang tips, white as fresh snow. Like the rest of his people, his face, neck, and hands were absent of fur. But the parts of his body that were hairy were bronze with stripes; his tail was ringed with brown streaks. The guard from before trailed him.

"Welcome, heiress of Ensalor," said the warrior-king. He strode over to the faux throne near the fireplace.

Willow felt paralyzed in his presence. It was not magic, only anxiety. He was unlike anything she had seen in the world yet, far better than those Kappas and much prettier than Lady Cho.

"Replenish yourself."

As he gestured, a maid with the same feline features entered from the door next to the fireplace, carrying a tray with an assortment of fruits, nuts, cheeses, and breads. She placed it on the table beside Willow, who began to take bits of the bread and combine it with slices of cheese.

"Heiress, may I present the baron of Château Londror and ruler of the east, Zohar, son of Avidar," said the guard, bowing once more. "You will address him as sire or Lord Baron."

He then gave them privacy.

"It is good to finally meet you, Lord Baron," said Willow, nodding.

"Likewise, Willow," said Zohar, sitting on the throne. "I've been told that Hrinthas no longer stands."

He paused to chew on a nut, then swallowed.

"A shame, it seems."

"It's true, s-sire. It was one of the Vexes. I was betrayed."

"Never a good feeling."

He thumbed another nut past his lips.

"It was Pinner Vemtal, Your Majesty, the former grand warden of Ensalor. He has sided with the Caliphate. I thought we could trust him."

She ripped a piece of bread from a loaf and ate it, chewed it, and swallowed it.

"Quite the travesty of his character. I've heard stories in the past of his bravery, especially during the Conquering, how he led my people against the invasion."

"Now he serves them. Merlin tried to stop him, but I do not know if—"

"What?"

Zohar paused and leaned in.

"Merlin is…alive? Here in Kastallon?"

"You didn't know, sire?"

Ah, I see, she thought. *His father must have told him about his disappearance a decade ago. He was probably told something different from the reality of it. That is why he is surprised to hear his name.*

"Clearly not! Back from the dead, it seems. The things wizards are capable of…"

The maid returned, carrying a glass flask of something runny and red. She placed it on the table next to the assortment tray and retreated back through the door. Zohar took one of the grails and filled it with some of the liquid, supped, and held the grail still.

"What have you heard about him?" she asked, popping a grape past her lips.

"Before he passed, Father told me stories of his miracles," Zohar began.

He supped once more but left the grail upright on the table.

"Countless they were, and wonderful."

"Miracles?"

"Yes, quite. Father claimed it was divine magic, but the old sorcerer said it was 'honed discipline of the natural world,' whatever that means. One story, though, sticks with me to this day, and I will never forget it as long as I live."

Intrigued, Willow took up the other grail and filled it halfway. She wafted it just below her nose. The crimson gave off notes of different bases, cherry and raspberry among others. She took a sip, swallowed, and was surprised by how it tasted the same as it smelled.

"What is this? It…it's very good," she said, then proceeded to sip again.

"Ah, you are tasting the finest wine in the east. We call it lendryma, berry brew. It is crafted from the fresh berries handpicked in both our personal gardens and the surrounding area. Those who receive it are considered honorable guests. You will never find a lowborn drinking this tincture."

"W-wine? As in alcohol?" she asked, a twinge of regret rising.

"What is alcohol?" the warrior-king asked.

Such a word was not among Purloinian lexicon.

"Some kind of elixir?"

"Never mind. I would much prefer to hear that story you mentioned. About one of Merlin's miracles?"

Willow supped again, assured that what she was drinking, however much it resembled Earthrealm wine, was zero proof.

"Precisely."

Zohar emptied the contents of the grail and placed it back on the tabletop.

"When I was but a cub, Merlin visited this castle in the days of the Brown Goat, bringing sack after sack of a powder he called Shimmer. My father was still the baron. He allowed the wizard to give a lesson in his magic, through which we were able to turn the purple crumbs into fizzles and sparkles. For children, this was quite amusing.

"Ever since then, I have developed a curiosity for Shimmer. But alas, the Caliph's curse has drained all the mines in the north and southwest, preventing any insight to magic, perhaps because she did not want competition or resistance when it came to her phantom sorceress's power."

"That is why she is here," a voice from the staircase beckoned.

They turned to look, and down the stairs, with a paced stride, walked two more Purloinians in ball gown dresses, one red, the other a dull cyan. From their longer lashes to their braided manes, Willow assumed these were female. For like humans, they exhibited bosoms and slender faces. She could tell the one in red was older by the slight grayness in her roots. Hooded cloaks adorned their shoulders, but they kept them down.

"Have you forgotten the prophecy?"

"Of course not, my lady," said Zohar firmly.

"You should consider it a blessing that she has come all this way, let alone returned to the Land Where Castles Lie."

The elder Purloinian turned to Willow.

"You honor us, heiress."

She suddenly remembered the manners Merlin taught her in their private lessons together.

"The honor is all mine."

"I present to you Lady Marandasia, chief physician and apothecary of Londror."

The eldress curtsied.

"And this is her daughter, Faoma."

"A pleasure," she said and curtsied.

Willow nodded back.

"My ladies, this is Willow Drinith, heiress of Ensalor," said Zohar.

Willow stood and curtsied, a gesture she recalled again from her private lessons.

It must have something to do with my parents' former nobility. Does this make me a queen? Or a princess? Maybe nothing until the Caliph is gone.

"It's good to match a name with your face," said Marandasia. "Calling you the One Who Unites every time would become dreadfully exhausting."

"Now," began Zohar, "that the formalities have been addressed, we can proceed to business. There must be a reason as to why the One Who Unites would visit the east first. She could have gone south or northwest, but she chose my kingdom. Please enlighten us, Willow."

He propped his boots up on the table.

"By the order of Merlin the Magical," said Willow, "I was brought to this land via a Wayfinder whale. We touched down on the western shore, where I encountered foes at Al Wafra. A friend saved me. He was a former apprentice of Merlin, and his name was Rowan. We escaped an old witch in the desert and took shelter in decayed woods, where I met with the White Lamb. It was he that confirmed my prophetic title and sent us on our way.

"In Tel Pata, we met with our now enemy Pinner Vemtal and conceived the plan to find His Majesty and take back Château Ensalor. We were saved by Da'iini when we engaged Strix in the Garmouth, as His Majesty has been told. Since then, Hrinthas was burned down by a member of the Five Vexes. I, along with my companion, the toucan, escaped. That is the story. It was told that you have an army worthy of defeating the Caliph. Merlin himself declared it."

Zohar rubbed his chin. It was a great thing to have the prophecy being fulfilled right before his eyes. It was an even better thing to be told that Merlin had returned. He considered the skirmish that took his father from him.

Things have been getting dicey as of late, he thought. *Perhaps now is the time to take up arms. She has the sword and bears the duke's name. She has also met the White Lamb, who has affirmed her. Hmm…*

"What is your decision, sire?" said Willow.

Zohar remained silent.

"My Lord Baron?" said Marandasia.

Nothing.

"Lord Baron, as your friend, I urge you to accept," said Faoma. "Think of your brothers, Torlan and Matai. You wouldn't want them to sit and cower for the rest of their lives, would you? Our forces are ready. The people, they yearn for battle! How long do you wish to remain hid—"

"Enough!" Zohar snapped. "Know your place, girl. You may be the apothecary's daughter, but you are still under my roof. Mind your tongue. I did not permit your residency for counsel."

He turned his attention to Willow.

"As for the One Who Unites, what of your time with the Da'iini? Will they fight alongside us if you call them?"

Willow felt a faint drip of sweat from her temple.

"About that, sire. I never received a straight answer from her. She persists in her wish to remain hidden. But she cares deeply for her people, and I'd bet on her being a risk-taker. After all, she fought by Rowan's side to protect me."

Zohar rubbed his chin again, even scratching it lightly.

"But," she continued, "I do not know her status since I left Hrinthas. However, I do not think she would be taken in lightly. A fierce woman, her."

"Then we can only assume she has refused," Zohar said.

Then after standing, he added, "Fine. Let her sit in the shadows like cowards. We have power on our side. We have the One sent by the White Lamb."

"Yes, Lord Baron!" said Faoma.

Willow could hear the joy in her voice.

"I will alert our generals."

She turned for the door and exited.

Marandasia crossed to the table near the fireplace. Zohar stood near the flames, letting the saffron wisps dance with a warming glow on his face. He felt a gentle grasp on his shoulder and the tender mezzo-soprano of the apothecary.

"Lord Baron, we are with you every step of the way. Have faith, and nothing will stand against us. The Caliph's time is cut short. We will return the world to its natural order. The girl is the key, and we are the hands that will turn the lock."

"I appreciate your advice, apothecary. Show the girl to her room."

"At once, Lord Baron."

She turned to obey.

Chapter 18

The Wasp Flies

Red orbs reflected off the faded panes in Ensalor's throne room as the Caliph watched another battalion of gold-and-black soldiers leave the castle gates.

They were headed for Falmeuse, the field that bridged the land between the northern and southern regions. It was a rolling, abundantly grassy field, which had now been restored to its former viridian glory, expanding from the outskirts of the vast woodland hiding Château Londror to the bases of the northern peaks. Before the Conquering, many faunas would graze upon its gentle stalks as they blew in the breeze. But even now, none dared to make the return to it, as encampments were being erected with barracks for troops and forges for weapons. The whole process seemed to have begun overnight.

Nahla, cursed be her name, gripped her scepter tightly in a closed fist. Even outside of use, its red crystal displayed a dim vermilion glow. She felt her brow furrow and her lips curl downward into a frown of sorts.

I will show them the full might of Fikra, she thought. *Nothing will stand in my way. They will bend and break like twigs over my knee.*

Behind her, in that moment, the throne room doors opened, and in strolled the witches known as Cliona, Kestrel, and Sabrine with their eerie, trancelike walks. Nahla turned and tightened up, then turned her chin up to them in a gesture of power. The witches, who stopped a few yards from the Vexes, bowed in greeting.

"Your Ladyship," they said.

"An unexpected visit," Nahla spit. "Make it quick while the armorer is busy."

"Why, of course! We daren't waste your time, Ladyship."

Kestrel's voice was raspy, ripe with wizened grain.

"It has come to our attention, Ladyship, that the One Who Unites is in Londror, safe with that savage Zohar."

Sabrine stepped out.

"Our Strix have seen Purloinian banners rising in the east, hanging from the trees and blowing in the wind."

Nahla growled behind her teeth.

"We know not when or where they plan to attack, but one is certainly coming."

This was Cliona now.

"Our estimate is that they are two thousand strong, a feeble force in comparison to your legions!"

"Do not underestimate them," said Nahla. "If it were not for your Strix, they may have bested us a decade ago at the height of their power."

She sat on her wretched throne.

"Ah," said Sabrine, "but that was when the land was filled with the armies of each region—north, south, east, and west. Now there is none save for the cities subservient to you, Your Ladyship. No one will be coming to help them."

"A futile assault indeed," said Kestrel.

The witches chuckled and cackled briefly.

"Spare me your laughter, witches," said Nahla. "You forget that they have the one the prophecy has foretold. She allies with the baron. If the prophecy is to be believed, she could hold untamed power. Her family was akin to their teacher, this Merlin Numalosh, and we must consider that she knows herself by now. Perhaps she understands how men like him harness this Shimmer crud and use it as a weapon. Perhaps she could be more than him, more than the likes of you."

She gazed into her scepter, and her eyes, scarlet as rubies, matched its glow. Her sharp nails caressed it, and her gaze returned to the witches.

"Which is why I will be joining the Gilded Legions," she finished as a vengeful grin slowly widened across her visage.

The witches, exchanging glances back and forth in a frantic manner, said, "Your Ladyship, how bold of you!"

"What a brave gesture!"

"Oh, how magnificent!"

"Enough! Go. Continue to gather what you can on them. I seek every advantage."

"With haste, Your Ladyship," said Kestrel.

"It will be done, Your Ladyship," said Cliona.

"At once, Your Ladyship," said Sabrine.

Each witch bowed and simultaneously, in step, strolled out of the throne room, the doors closing behind them with a thud.

Nahla drew in a breath and released it. A moment passed where she sat with her eyes closed and head relaxed on the head of the throne.

She then opened them and called out, "Raj, my Stoic Vex."

The weird man holding a black box carved with strange symbols turned around and knelt before the Caliph, saying nothing.

"I seek counsel. Summon her."

Without hesitation, Raj walked to the middle of the throne room. The long sleeves of his robe swayed with his stride, and he placed the box at his feet. The Vexes, except Sal, proceeded to gather around in a perfect circle and dropped to their knees. Each man raised their arms in an acute fashion. Strange words echoed out of their mouths.

> Londala, Hextila, uth Nokitha
> Acto don luthrin nox, twii furi coma sin Nahla
> Remona ot thaa Dominoth, hocasa uri prudix
> Hocasa uri prudix!

With each chant of the strange words, the ebony box that one might consider symbolic or artificial began to glow, the symbols and writings carved taking on a menacing vermilion radiance. Seconds passed, and the box's corners shifted. To the unfamiliar, the cracking on its surface that followed might be considered a sign of destruction, but it was meant to happen, an indication that the ritual was proceeding correctly.

"Hear my call, O Great Mother! I summon thee as counsel!" cried Nahla.

The black box, cracks and all, exploded!

In a haze of velvety maroon smog, a spherical mirror appeared. It was transparent, as Nahla could see two of her Vexes trembling with effort behind it. Soon, two eyes black as night appeared and then a nose and then a mouth and so on until a shadowed face with skin as gray as charcoal could be witnessed in that crimson mirror.

The face spoke with a chilling voice, a voice constructed of endless voices.

"You dare to command me when it is I who hath power over thee?"

Behind her, Nahla could feel the Synod's shivers.

"You assume control of *me*?" said the face in the mirror.

"I would never dream of such impudence, Great Mother," said Nahla, who rose from her wretched throne, only to drop to her knees like that of the Vexes.

"Then why have you disturbed me?"

"I do not intend to keep you long, Great Mother. I only seek advice, wisdom of the highest intellect only you can provide!"

"Get on with it."

"Before he was defeated, the deity known as Skeef proclaimed a prophecy over this land, a prophecy foretelling the coming of a savior who could supplant us and retake your land, your kingdom. That savior is here in the east, and I fear she will be too great. What must I do to ensure victory, O Great Mother?"

She stooped to groveling.

The face sneered and hissed.

"Is that doubt I sense in my creation?"

Nahla, as if the act itself was risking disrespect, peered up from her bow and gulped.

"Nay, Great Mother, simply caution. Nothing more."

"You were created to be conquerors!" the face boomed. "Crusaders! I did not conjure you from the depths of the abyss for you to be cautious! Caution implies weakness! Weakness guarantees defeat! You had best snuff out this savior or make her submit!"

"Yes! Yes, Great Mother!" cried Nahla, her forehead stuck to the floor.

"Now begone with you! That is my command!"

As quickly as it arrived, the face dissipated, the mirror shattered, and the smog fizzled away. The Vexes, panting and exhausted, rose to their feet and returned to their positions ahead of the wretched throne.

Then almost as though they had been waiting for something to be completed, a group of men waltzed into the throne room behind a single burly man clad in iron armor. The men carried polished steel pieces and a midnight cloak. The Caliph brushed herself off as she stood. The burly man was the armorer, and he bowed before her.

"Your Ladyship, the armor you requested has been completed."

"Bring it forth," she said and used her hand to signal them to come forward.

In a way that seemed rehearsed, the Caliph girded up her loins by taking the bottom back of her dress and tucking it into the fine belt wrapping her waist, revealing attractively slender gray legs. She stretched her arms out beside her with the scepter still in hand. One by one, the men came and equipped the Caliph with a piece of the steel armor until the only thing unarmored was her head, which remained adorned with the gold antennae diadem. Finally, two men came and clipped the midnight cloak to rungs on her pauldrons.

"Call the stablemaster," she said. "Ready my bukavac."

CHAPTER 19

Falmeuse

No light but the moon shone through the rather large open window in Willow's room, illuminating whatever lay in the darkness. There were no candles and no lamps, for obvious reasons.

She found herself peering through the window at the landscape in the distance. Her eyes bounded from the waters of the moat below to the woods crowding the edges of it to the grassy plains and mountains ahead of it all. She looked up and found that the black canvas had been painted with dots of burning ivory. Then the realization that the last time she had gazed at the stars was the first night in the Garmouth set in.

Tears formed and fell as she remembered that she had shared the moment with Rowan, and now…now she couldn't conceive any thought of where he might be. She shivered at the thought of him being taken by the Caliph. Or was it just the cold of night? Then her thoughts shifted to Merlin and his whereabouts. Last she had seen of him, he was sparring with Pinner, the sorcerer they believed they could trust. A fat lie that was.

A fluttering made her turn, and there, alighting on the foot of the bed, was Juniper. Her presence was comforting now, as she was the only being in Londror that wasn't just an acquaintance. She was her friend, her companion, and her symbol of a royal heritage.

"How are you feeling, Willow?" the bird asked, tilting her head the way avians did when they were inquisitive or curious.

"Fine, I guess," said Willow. "Perhaps reminiscent."

She turned her eyes back to the stars. If she looked well enough at the parts of them not clouded by moonlight, she could pick out the same Y-shaped constellation that Rowan had shown her: Norlik. She perused again, trying to find the trapezoidal imitation Vida, but it must have been blocked by the moon.

"I know you miss them," said Juniper, fluttering over to the windowsill. "As do I."

"Do you think they're all right? Still alive?"

"Your guess is as good as mine, though I will say, if that brute saw his prize escaping, he would surely follow. As for the wizards, well, Merlin can handle himself."

"But the Gnomes? A-and Rowan?"

"Hard to say, child. They're so small I lost track of them in the chaos."

"I hope they are well at least. It was very brave of them to join us so willingly."

"That it was," said Juniper. "That it was."

She flapped and returned back to the bed.

"You should sleep while you can, Willow. You'll need all the energy you can muster. I've the right mind to expect a big, very big, day tomorrow, and strength will be crucial. Come now. Rest your head."

Her beak pecked at the soft pillow at the headboard.

Before she had spoken with the bird, she had changed out of the garments that Merlin had packed her in the adult-sized suitcase on the night they stepped aboard Balaen and slipped into the most comfortable of linens in nothing more than a sleeved pale gown. Normally, at bedtime, she would have kept her hair somewhat up. But seeing as Veraminta was not here to bark at her to do so, she kept the hazel locks dangling behind her shoulders. They bounced as she walked over to the midsize bed of wood and sheets and climbed in.

"Juniper," she called to the toucan resting at the foot of the bed.

The bird lifted its beak as an indication that she had been heard.

"How long were you in Earthrealm? Merlin said I wasn't able to see you until I turned ten, so I'm curious."

Juniper shifted and found her feet and waddled over to meet Willow's eyes.

"Ever since the wizard and I stepped off the whale all those years ago," she began. "I waited in old shacks and treetops until he gave the signal. He told me that when the time came, he'd mark a certain window of the orphanage with silver light. Days passed where I wondered if it would come at all. Sometimes, I would wait on that same lamppost you found me on, watching different girls pass by, wondering if one of them was you. A blonde one here and a black-headed one there. Several brunettes, the ones with brown hair like yours, passed by.

"But it was not until that night with the moon full and the stars vast that I saw a girl bearing the resemblance of my former masters—the blue eyes of the duke and the thin nose of the duchess. I knew at once that this girl was the one Merlin had carried away with him, the one I was sworn to protect and guide. So it seems the answer to your question is just as long as Merlin was. We were there, watching you grow."

Willow heard most of what the bird said, but as the words continued, exhaustion arrived, and she sank slowly into a somber slumber.

*****

Morning came, passed, and transformed into the afternoon. During that time, Willow had dressed herself, eaten, spoken with some of the maids, and found her way to the stables close to the outer wall of the fortress. There she found several majestic-looking stallions, each of different colors, all the same size and structure. When it came to horses, Purloinians settled for nothing less than strong, adept specimens. They were well-fed and, more importantly, well-bred in order to maintain their physiques. Most collectors or breeders across Kastallon would pay a very pretty price to get their hands on equines raised by Purloinians.

With Juniper on her shoulder, Willow went from stable to stable, looking over the half doors on either side of the extended barn.

Where is he? she thought. *What have they done with him?*

She looked into the fifth stable on the left side and nearly retched from the stench inside. The horse must have heard her wincing, as it turned around mid chew to glare at her with a brown eye full of curiosity.

"Sorry, sorry," she said and moved on to the next stable.

One by one, she stopped by each half door, only to find the opposite of what she was looking for. These horses were natives of the land, chosen from all corners of the realm to be brought to the east.

All her searching and scurrying caught the attention of the stablemaster, who was a fit farmer type. He shared the same Purloinian resemblance as the rest of the fortress, but he wore brown linens tied with rope. His mane was greasy, and he had a scar across his nose. After tossing another scrap of hay into one of the stables near the corner, he made his way over to the inquisitive girl who had wandered into his domain.

"Lookin' fer a certain mare, girlie?" he said, his voice gritty with a drawl. He balanced himself with a pitchfork under his elbow.

Willow turned to him and felt the redness building in her cheeks. She had met almost everyone in the castle, but when it came to the rest of the fortress's citizens, they were all strangers. But this sense of alienation somehow felt different from her time in Al Wafra. The people were warmer, brighter, than the dread and hastiness of the desert town.

"Um…uh…not a mare, no," she responded. "I'm l-looking for a male zebra. He was brought into the castle yesterday?"

She blinked rapidly at the man scratching the thick hair under his chin, which made it hard to distinguish where his hair and beard separated.

"What the nob's a zebra?" the stablemaster said. "Hadn't heard o' that before."

"It's a striped horse, black-and-white?"

The shaggy man's countenance didn't change.

Seeing that he was still perhaps confused, she cleared her throat and said, "Were you aware of a girl, a bird, and a striped horse coming in through the gates when the sun was high yesterday? Has the baron made it clear that they were his guests?"

Suddenly, the man's eyes widened with disbelief and a shade of embarrassment.

"By the stars, forgive me for my ignorance!"

He dropped to a knee.

"Word passes 'round quick, and pray, tell me that you are the heiress of Ensalor."

"I am," she said.

"Please have a horse. I insist! Any that you like!"

He backed up and gestured to the many steeds chomping on their food and drinking from their tin basins.

"As I said before, I've need for but one horse. My zebra."

"You said 'striped horse, black-and-white,' correct?"

"Yes."

"Then I am afraid it is not in this particular stable, heiress. The other stablemaster took him to the stables near the barracks, where the warhorses graze."

He bowed.

"Apologies again, heiress, for my incompetence."

"You are forgiven," said Willow, curtseying to him. "Thank you for your help."

"A pleasure," he said, bowing once more.

Willow departed from the stables and made her way through the town surrounding the castle inside the fortress walls. As she walked, rising high above the stone and wood buildings were the great cobblestone parapets lined between a tower at each corner. But if she looked behind the castle, she could see the massive escarpment she had seen the day before. She began to wonder how it wasn't all crumbling down onto them.

Following the wooden signposts around the street, her path began going around the castle itself. Two guards stood watch at the main entrance, the same as yesterday, but she could see more around its many balconies and towers too. As she trod the cobble path, much of the scenery reminded her of Al Wafra, only this time, the buildings were much more appealing to the eyes. Most of them were the same, being constructed of sturdy stone and topped with wood and straw.

Of the buildings she passed, she recognized the oval sign hanging just above one of their doors. The Laughing Flute was posted as its title. From how close she was, she could faintly hear the merry sound of mugs clinking, voices laughing, and violins singing. It sounded like a joyful time. Perhaps there would be time enough after it was all said and done, and she could take the Gnomes inside. When the thought came, she put it aside in her mind. She wouldn't let herself be discouraged now. Time was drawing near to fight, to be strong. What would Merlin think if she had come all this way now just to cower and quit?

She passed several Purloinians on the street. Most were just out and about, doing their daily errands or simply taking in the day. There were young ones, old ones, tall ones, and short ones. Some of them appeared like tigers; others appeared like lions. Some had spots, and others stripes. But it seemed the default appearance was that of a tabby cat. Like the baron, their faces were quite humanlike with it, their necks and hands being hairless.

There were other buildings down the street from the tavern. From the looks of them, there was a blacksmith, a cobbler, a tailor, several vendors for different foods, and even perhaps a theater. It was like a city within walls. Perhaps if the upper area of Staten Island where the orphanage was were barricaded with walls, it would feel the same.

Within the crowds of ordinary Purloinians were pairs of soldiers standing by at different parts of the street and city. Some even walked down the street with their swords on their hips. When she passed two of them, they nodded to her in respect. She nodded back. For once in her life, she felt a strange sense of belonging.

Everyone seems nice here, she thought. *Even that stablemaster was kind before he realized who I was. I could get used to this. Leo would have a ball if he came here, though I imagine it would take great effort to keep him from petting them all like the cats from Earthrealm.*

She chuckled silently at the thought.

It was only half an hour walk to the barracks, and sure enough, she noticed a barn very similar to the previous one, only this one appeared more sturdy and kept. The stablemaster here was, as expected, dressed in a more official garb than the previous. He wore linens, but they reflected the colors of the soldiers. His mane was shorter on top, but his beard was tailored to his jawline. A Purloinian of a discipline, this one.

"Good morning, sir," said Willow, bowing.

"And to you, heiress."

The stablemaster reciprocated the gesture.

"How can I assist you this morning? Perhaps a warm-up ride? Or would you like to feed one? They are very gentle, I assure you."

"That won't be necessary, but I thank you. I'm looking for a zebra. The stablemaster on the other side of this fortress claimed he was taken here yesterday afternoon when I arrived. I am the baron's guest."

The stablemaster bowed again.

"Precisely, heiress. Right this way."

He turned to enter the stables, and Willow followed. They passed the same scene as before: several half-door stables with strong, healthy stallions eating, drinking, or simply admiring their homes. She was led to the very back of the stables, where a plot of land had been sectioned off and gated. Here was where the horses were trained or let out for recreation. Luckily, Racer had indulged in the latter.

Willow saw the zebra prancing about near the back gate. Moments later, he began to roll in the soft grass like a carefree dog in a field of dandelions. The sight warmed her heart, as it was the first time she had seen him enjoy himself since Rowan's incident.

She thought, *Better not remind him of it. Wouldn't want to rob him of this newfound joy.*

The stablemaster whistled, then made a clicking noise with his tongue. This sound got Racer's attention, and he began to trot over back to the stables with a happy tiptoeing almost.

"Willow!" he exclaimed. "Juniper!"

He nuzzled Willow's face with his warm snout.

"Good to see you too, Racer," said Willow, patting his striped neck. "Glad to see they are treating you well. Did you sleep all right?"

"Are you kidding? I haven't slept this well in ages! These people sure take their horse care seriously."

He whinnied happily.

"Easy now. Easy," said Willow, calming him. "Did they tell you what this place is?"

"No, but don't say it like that. You make it sound like a horrid place."

"It's where the warhorses are kept. The Purloinians mean to face down the Caliphate in a few hours. They're meeting at a place called Falmeuse."

The zebra shuddered, and it seemed his white stripes became paler at the mere mention of the name.

"Falmeuse?"

His lower lip trembled.

"Yes, Falmeuse. It's the field between the southern and north—"

"I know what it is. I've heard stories from the towns I've been to detailing the uneven landscape and the rolling hills and how it is not the best place for a battle. Getting caught in the slope is a death sentence."

"What's the slope?"

She tilted her head and raised a brow.

"It's the space between hills. Getting caught there means you have the entirety of two armies crashing down on you from either side. Not pleasant."

"If it be of any comfort to you," butted in the stablemaster, "you and the heiress will not be descending the hill. You will stay with the reserve."

"What do you mean, good stablemaster?" asked Willow, turning to him.

"I mean that given the nature of your status, you will be a last resort. We cannot afford our best fighter to be thwarted so early. By order of the baron himself."

"But she is your champion!" cried Juniper, raising her feathered black wings. "She is one of your best chances of victory, and you keep her off the battlefield?"

"Should we be overtaken, the baron insists she and the others to defend Londror—"

"Honestly, Juniper," said Willow, "I like that plan."

"What?" she squawked. "But…in the Garmouth?"

"Yes, yes, I know. But I barely even scratched one of those birds. If it weren't for the others, I—we—might not be here."

The stablemaster's feline ears perked up, and his nose twitched.

"The Garmouth?"

He drew nearer with fresh curiosity.

"You went through the Garmouth? And lived?"

"That's correct," said Juniper, who then proceeded to turn her beak up at the man.

"We had to make a shortcut to avoid Gilded soldiers. We went around the Ittermount and through the pass, where we were ambushed by Strix. Thankfully, we were saved by the Gallantinels, Da'iini militia."

"Amazing," said the stablemaster. "Just amazing. Ne'er a soul has been through and escaped close to unscathed. You should consider yourself lucky, heiress."

"She is the One Who Unites after all," Juniper commented again. "You shouldn't expect anything less from her."

"My, what an…interesting bird, heiress."

He turned and entered the stables.

"My apologies, sir," said Willow.

She turned to the toucan, embarrassment seething, and said, "What has gotten into you? I might be who Skeef said I was, but I am not this great warrior! I thought about running back there, but Merlin stepped in. I ran away from Hrinthas as it burned to the ground. Sometimes, I can barely hold Pnevma as it is. I'm not war-ready."

"Have you learned nothing from what I told you?" Juniper raised her head. "From what the White Lamb told you?"

"What?"

"You *are* strong. You *are* ready. All you need is to trust that he will bring you through it. He said himself that he will always be with you. That is all you need."

"I blew the horn too. No one came."

"Perhaps someone heard it but was delayed. Patience, dear girl. You did leave Hrinthas before anyone came. Don't forget."

"You're right. I'm just…distracted, I guess, from all that's happened. I wish I'd the knowledge of their safety."

"Knowing Merlin and Lady Cho, I'm sure they made it out. But right now, it would be wise to find Baron Zohar."

She settled down.

Willow took hold of the reins drooping from Racer's cheeks.

"Come now," she said and began to lead him away through the stables to the entrance. "We can probably find him inside the barracks over there."

She pointed to a large cabin-like structure with a rather enormous chimney, ashen-gray smoke billowing from its mouth. Purloinian soldiers came and went from the place, some carrying swords and shields, others with gourds of arrows or wooden arcs intended to be fixed into bows.

They really are preparing themselves for a fight, she thought, peering at a pair of soldiers prepping each other's armor.

When both were equipped, the one on the left took a swing with a dagger at the right's torso. The blade struck the chest plate with its flat side, and because it was metal clashing with metal, a thin clank sounded. The right looked up at the left with what Willow assumed was a look of anger birthed from an unexpected strike. But the two men broke into hearty laughs and clasped hands.

At least it works.

Swiftly as they left the stable's gates, they made a path to the barracks, passing by a soldier carrying a wide keg in both hands, nearly knocking him over. Willow looked back and apologized before entering the wide threshold. Racer obliged to stay outside.

Seconds passed inside the barracks, and she could tell it was not what she was expecting. She expected, with soldiers about in abundance, many to be fighting or drinking like some of the Da'iini, but what she found was quite the opposite. Plenty of seating with several picnic-like tables was arranged neatly from one side of the room to a few feet from where the hearth of the fireplace began. Soldiers were conversing in a pleasant manner akin to what children were taught to be inside voices, and none of them seemed to be lollygagging or drumming up any fusses. They all seemed attuned to the matter at hand yet chose to remain calm and collected.

As she looked around and up, she could see the upper level to the barracks as other soldiers leaned against the railings of the second floor, their hands hanging over illuminated and made clear by the firelight.

At one end of the room were several troughs filled with burning coals, and atop these troughs were grated platforms carrying slab after slab of cooking meat, among which included venison, chicken, and pork. Each platform was sectioned out. The first, meats; the second, vegetables, which included potatoes, carrots, cucumber, and zucchini; and the last section, pans filled with boiling grains, oats and rice to name a few.

With all the food cooking and the aromas attributed to such, Willow began to remember the Gnomes and their love for this sort of thing. She could almost visualize Rossa and Valner drooling over each section of the cooking troughs with an undying impatience to satiate their stomachs. Again, she put the thought aside so as to not let herself be discouraged by their absence. She was here on the idea that the person she was looking for, the baron, would be inside.

Suddenly, it seemed that all the chatter and clinking of mugs and utensils ceased, and Willow felt hundreds of eyes over her, a feeling not quite pleasant for someone used to being overlooked. She felt a warmth coming to her cheeks, and she folded her arms as if to cover herself from invisible beams from their stares, but they looked on.

A voice called out from across the room, a man's voice, which had not yet been afflicted by age.

"The One Who Unites!" he said, and the perpetrator was quickly found to be a Purloinian in military garb pointing at her from his table.

It was this that caused all the eyes of all the patrons inside to shift their glances to her. At that moment, another voice called out from the second floor, and their glances shifted upward. Nothing followed it, not even footsteps or the rattle of dishes, save for the crackling in the fireplace.

"At last, she arrives," a familiar voice said.

Willow joined the soldiers in their gazing upward and recognized who it was who had spoken in the heights. It was the baron himself. He carried an iron helm under his right arm and steadied his left palm over the pommel of his sheathed sword. Those below who weren't sitting knelt while those who were bowed their heads in allegiance. Willow, who didn't feel the need to stick out, bent the knee as well. After all, this was the first monarch she had come across.

"Rise, brothers and sisters. Enjoy yourselves for now. When the sun touches the treetops, we will descend upon Falmeuse. And with the aid of our savior, we will thwart the Caliphate then and there. Skeef be with us all."

"Skeef be with us all," rang all the soldiers' voices, a unity of sound that seemed to reverberate within the walls of the barracks.

Willow heard her stomach grumble again and clutched it softly with a hand. The food did smell and appear appetizing, and she swore she could hear her conscience—or was it Juniper's whispering?—telling her to eat before the battle. It was merely a series of steps to arrive at the cooking area, where a serving soldier placed a chunk of meat on her clay plate followed by others serving the vegetables.

Thin wisps of steam wafted away from the skin of the food items as she found a place near the fireplace, sitting comfortably with crossed legs. Quickly, she found herself putting piece after piece past her lips before she realized she had been eating with her hands, something that she figured the wizard would have scoffed at if he had joined her. She also realized she had nothing to wipe the grease from her face too.

The warmth of the fire's light on her back was enticing her to sleep. Drowsiness nearly prevented her from acknowledging the pair of boots stepping toward her and stopping just within the scope of her gazing at the floor.

A voice spoke, and it said, "I think you'll be needing this."

The voice belonged to the baron. Willow shot her gaze up, and the kingly Purloinian was presenting a small cream cloth to her, clean and soft.

"T-thanks," she said, accepting the cloth and blotting away the messiness.

The baron sat down beside her and matched her sitting style.

"I imagine you are unprepared for what's coming."

Willow kept eating but nodded, not wanting to speak with a mouthful of food.

"Don't worry. You'll be with the reserve at the top of the hill. We'll need all the defense we can muster should the forward ranks be diminished."

"I know."

"You know? Who told?"

"The stablemaster just down the road."

"Ah, that's understandable. You need a good horse for war."

"War?" said Willow after she swallowed, looking at Zohar.

"Yes," said the baron. "This is war. Has been for a decade. But this could be the deciding battle. We have two thousand capable bodies with another thousand in the reserve. Our spies, though very little of them, tell us we match the legions. At that point, it all comes down to discipline and dexterity. Even better, we have you, the One Who Unites. By the White Lamb, we might just prevail."

Willow could hear the smile in his tone without looking up from her plate, which was finally spotless.

"What's dexterity?" she asked, putting the plate aside.

"Just a fancy word for skill."

He crossed his arms across his chest.

"Doubtless they've forgotten ours. Though as tough as it is to admit, this war has been quite the one of attrition. That just means both sides fight to weaken the other. But now the tides have turned."

"Because of me," Willow said rather matter-of-factly.

"Correct," the baron said. "That being said, one could infer that a girl of your age has never swung a sword before. Most boys your age have already mastered it."

"Hey, I used Pnevma in the Garmouth, thank you!"

She patted her sword's pommel.

"But have you ever stared down an enemy with unfathomable determination and certainty of victory? Ever watched a man bleed from your blow?"

He saw the girl shake her head, embarrassed.

"I thought as much. Now in the hours we have before the sun begins to set, we must give you a basic overview of dancing."

He stood and stretched, standing over her.

"Dancing?" said Willow, who stood up and had to actively look upward to speak to the monarch. She felt as if she would have to resort to standing on her toes.

"Ah, I see. They don't call it that in Earthrealm. Dancing simply refers to fighting with swords, as you could compare the footwork involved with both. Understand?"

"Yes," she said.

The baron then proceeded to call out a strange name across the dining hall, and a man rose accordingly, placed his dining accoutrements down, and walked over to the baron to kneel. This Purloinian was balding yet still bore bushy whiskers on the sides of his head and had pockmark blemishes dotting his nose and bags under his eyes. Willow looked away to try and find a better sight without seeming rude.

"Fetch two training blades, one for myself, the other for the heiress. I shall be giving our savior a proper demonstration, which she will use should she have to defend the east."

The pockmarked man gave an affirming grunt, rose once more, and dashed out of the barracks with haste.

*****

The arena where soldiers rehearsed their dancing was nothing more than frail posts hammered into the dirt connected with smooth planks of oak in a rectangular fashion. One might even compare it to an elongated boxing ring. Of the many things she acknowledged when she arrived, Willow noticed the plethora of boot prints and skids in the soft dark dirt. She could see specks and long streaks of something darker than the dirt itself scattered about the area of the ring.

Is that what I think it is? she thought, a sick feeling welling in her core.

Before she continued to think about it, her attention was grabbed when Juniper alighted on one of the posts of the arena.

The same odd-looking, balding Purloinian returned, carrying two thin rods of wood, one in each hand, over to the baron. When the monarch thanked him, he repeated the action he performed inside the barracks.

Willow stood in the center of the arena since, to her, it felt wrong to occupy one side of it.

"What are those?" she asked, rubbing her hands nervously.

She could see the worn nature of the rods by the dents and chips among the scarce smoothness of them.

"Training blades," said the baron, swinging one of the rods.

With each swish and brandish of the rods, there was a quick *whoosh* in the air.

"Will it hurt?"

"Only if you get hit," he said and smiled.

Tossing one of the rods to Willow, the baron firmed up his grip on his own.

"The first lesson, heiress, is stance."

He widened his feet, centering himself.

"See how my feet are not so close together? See how my knees are locked and steady? This gives me the support I need for each swing. Without balance, your blade will falter and miss its mark. Let me give you an example."

He placed a hand behind his back and aimed the wooden rod at Willow, who gulped.

"Make your best effort."

Willow could tell it was a test, but like most beginners to new things, she was unaware of the correct next move. She held her rod tightly in both hands and ran toward the baron with a scratchy yell in her throat. Swiftly, the baron utilized his anchored stance to block

Willow's rod and kick her feet out from under her. When she opened her eyes, the dulled, dirty tip of the baron's training rod was ogling her like a Cyclops. She knocked the rod away with her own and stood quickly, finding the sudden instinct to block the baron's incoming blow. When she did, seconds later, she found herself wagging her hand. Shaking it off, she charged at the baron again, but she was blocked and thrown down. Her eyes closed, then opened and saw the dirty tip.

"Understand?" he said, looking down at her with an upturned chin.

"Yes, sir."

She found her feet and brushed off some of the dirt on her tunic.

"Next lesson, heiress, is parry."

He brandished his rod once more and began a steady orbit around Willow, who took his advice and widened her own stance.

"Parrying is the repulsion of an enemy's blow and countering it to throw them off. This is a move crucial to getting the better of your enemy. If their stance is broken, you can dispatch them quickly."

So that's why I was so easy to beat, she thought. *That was how he was able to get me to the ground so quickly.*

She kept her eyes trained on him, focused.

"If their blade aims in the center, block it and push them away with your body weight, like this."

He motioned her to make another attempt. Seeing no other option, she thrust her rod horizontally as if to pierce his armor. As expected, one swift stroke of the baron's rod swiped her own away; and with the full weight of his body behind the stroke, she was nearly thrown down again. When she found her balance again, it was too late. The dulled edge of the baron's rod was approaching her neck.

"That is a parry."

He retracted the rod.

"Now I want you to try. Use your stance to your advantage. Throw me off."

Willow never considered herself to be a strong girl. Sure, she had been taller than the rest of the orphans her age, but that did not denote a higher strength. She was far too lanky and not nearly as bulky as a man with Zohar's physique. To her surprise, however, the rod she used now felt identical in weight to her mother's sword.

Maybe it's possible, she considered.

She turned to look at Juniper, whose feathers ruffled and eyes blinked rather mindlessly. Her attention returned, however, when the baron's voice cried aloud, and she found herself using her instinct to block once more. But as her rod met his, it was overcome by his adult strength and sent to the ground, even while she was holding it.

"Quick!" he said. "Pick it up!"

He readied his sword. Willow obeyed.

"Parry!"

The baron swiped, and Willow dodged. Another swipe came from her right, the opposite side, and she blocked. She wobbled, though, when she tried to revert the energy of the blow back to him.

"Again! Try again!"

Another fury of swipes ensued. She dodged half of them and stopped the rest. Each contact of the baron's rod with hers sent a rattling tingle through her hands and up her arms. A crisp knock clacked with each kiss of their rods, drawing the attention of other Purloinians around the barracks. Soon, there were many onlookers, who watched the duel with careful eye. Most peered with anticipation; others peered and began to make bets, murmuring between all of them. Was it that much of a spectacle to them?

The baron swung his wooden rod once more, and though Willow still had strength to block it, the blow was enough to unbalance her, and she tumbled to the hard dirt with a thud, her wooden rod rattling to a stop beside her. The murmuring stopped.

"It's hopeless," she said, bringing her knees to her chest. "I'm sorry."

She felt tears welling in her eyes not because of her performance but because she imagined the disappointment that would have followed had Rowan heard about this fight. Then again, she wondered if he expected anything less from a ten-year-old with no prior fighting experience. After all, he had been trained in both physical and magical combat. She put the thought aside.

Instead, she thought, *Hopefully, the baron will keep this to himself when Rowan shows up.*

"Nonsense," replied the baron, extending his hand. "Nothing is hopeless while you're here. I've trained plenty of men and women, and no one gets it the first time. Give yourself some grace."

Willow took his gloved hand and pulled herself to her feet.

*****

The quickly dimming afternoon sun made contact with the tallest treetops in the west, and the sky, though finally at its deepest, normal blue, began to change to a somber navy. The clouds, too, turned from happy white to anxious gray.

Atop Racer, Willow followed the baron's convoy third from him—behind Faoma, behind Marandasia, and behind Zohar. Behind her was the entirety of the east's forces on their stallions—men with spears and shields and others with bows and swords. Each of them wore the green and silver of Purloinian fatigues over their mail. The ones with bows, the archers, wore a cloak of brown that draped over the rumps of their horses. It was all like a rank-and-file army from the early days in Earthrealm. She learned about them from a lesson in her classes at the orphanage. But that didn't matter now.

They were riding and traveling on the natural path to Falmeuse that ran from the moat, through the forest surrounding the escarpment of Londror, and into the open plains between the north and east. There were lots of hilly sections and scattered trees. Here and again, a bounding deer crossed their path, or a pack of wild horses held races in the distance, going Skeef knew where.

Willow was just happy to see them regardless. It was not every day that a girl from the city got the chance to see horses, the one animal most young girls adored, roaming wild and free. Then again, she thought, most people didn't get the chance to visit another realm and make friends with Gnomes and cat people. She considered herself lucky.

As the legion proceeded, various conversations were underway from the many, many soldiers behind the convoy. Willow heard some chatter about favorite foods or past experiences with women or aspects of childhood that stood out. But one conversation was loud and clear, and it came from three of the soldiers a few rows behind the first.

"How many do you think they have?" said one of them, a male voice.

"I dunno. I'm betting we outpace them," replied another male voice, deeper.

"You think so? What if their numbers have increased since the last battle? Remember how many there were when they first came here? They—"

"It doesn't matter how many they have," butted in a new voice, this one female, alto. "The One Who Unites is with us. It's a guaranteed victory."

"You don't know that," the first male said.

"One person can't take on an entire battalion of Gilded," said the next, "even if Skeef promised her coming. He said nothing of power or strength, just the person."

"She is also just a little girl. Did you consider that, Rantha?"

"No, but even so, she must be powerful," Rantha said. "Or is it too much for your thick skull to comprehend, Djollo? A little girl with the strength of adult men?"

"That's not what I'm saying!" Djollo said, and Willow could hear the man's desperate attempt at hiding his embarrassment in his tone.

She took a hand off Racer's reins and looked at it pensively. It was scarcely wrinkled and still pink; there was not much sign of wear.

A little girl with the strength of adult men, she thought, examining the short digits of her fingers.

Never had she felt powerful enough to be seen as strong, but she wondered how much these soldiers were told.

They must be extremely faithful to him if they believe that someone like me can take on the Caliph and her armies by myself.

Had they not seen the duel hours prior?

"You must not have seen her fight the baron," the second male voice said.

Willow felt the warmness return to her cheeks, the same as she had felt then. Were her ears burning too?

"What are you on about, Wenst?" said Djollo.

"I heard that the One Who Unites faltered against the baron in a training duel. She was disarmed several times and seemed shaken with each blow."

"She was probably holding back because she didn't want to harm His Excellency. Surely he, too, knew her power," said Rantha, rubbing her nose.

"I dunno," said Wenst. "I heard it was quite clear how wobbly she was."

He shared a laugh with Djollo, and both men quickly snuffed it with one look at Rantha's annoyed gaze.

"Fine," she said, holding tightly to the reins of her horse. "Mock her all you want, but when the Gilded begin to overwhelm you, don't come crying to me."

The soldier known as Rantha went quiet, and the two men began to talk quietly enough to where Willow couldn't hear more of their conversation. But what she had overheard was enough for her to question herself. Did she really have that much potential? Was there something she hadn't unlocked yet? What could they have been told for soldiers like Rantha to be so convinced that she was more powerful than the Caliph? She barely affected the Strix when they attacked, and she was powerless against the bandits too. Sure, she had a magic sword, but what good was it if she couldn't use it properly? To make matters worse, she ran at the moment when her friends needed her most. How could she be their savior?

But she remembered the words of the White Lamb: "Why do you allow yourself to become wrapped up in what is wrong when you know that I am with you every step of the way?" They rang like a whisper in her ear, and at once, she was somewhat comforted.

Suddenly, the convoy came to a halt. All chatter and discussion among the soldiers ceased, and Willow felt their eyes looking past her. The baron Zohar of Londror rode forward a few paces and turned around to face his subjects. From what she could see, they were at the crest of a hill, and the expanse of the plains was around them. To the west, the summits of Ittermount and Quall and the surrounding peaks looked far and away at them like spectators eager to bet on the outcome. To the south, it seemed like all of Kastallon was waiting, watching, and hoping. Willow kept her eyes on their warrior-king.

"Men and women of Londror! The hour has come!" he began. "Beyond this crest lies danger, ruin, and for some of you, death. All the battles in the decade since have led to this moment, friends. Remember, they are not men. Though they wear armor and walk like us, they are not men. They are animals and have been from the very beginning! Show them no mercy! Give them no quarter!"

At this moment, he drew his handsome sword, and it gleamed in the fleeting sunlight.

"Form ranks! The first thousand, with me. The rest will protect the girl!"

He watched as his army began to spread out across the back end of the hill and divide itself in two. Willow stayed back with the reserved thousand.

When the first thousand formed its ranks, Baron Zohar, atop his horse, stood ready.

"Do not advance until I say. May the One come forward."

He pointed his sword to Willow, who gulped and passed through the reserve as it opened a way to him.

"Today, the Caliphate meets its end!"

Zohar's army released a bellow of agreement.

"Today, we take back the north!"

Another bellow.

"It has been a privilege to lead you all, and I consider it the highest honor should I fall among your ranks."

He turned his attention to Willow and spoke softer.

"I know that you have been told to stay back, but I want the Caliph to see exactly who you are. Follow me."

With that, he turned and descended.

As she watched the baron cross over the crest, Willow leaned down and whispered into Racer's blackened ear, saying, "Are you ready for this?"

She felt her own voice become shaky, her breaths shallow, and her heart like a hopping joey.

"No time like the present," the zebra replied.

He felt the girl nudge him with a boot tip, and he began a slow trot forward a few feet behind the baron's steed.

At the crest of the hill, nothing could have prepared them for the sheer size of the legions sprawling across the landscape—multitudes of human-esque figures wearing gold-and-black armor carrying spears, swords, halberds, and battle-axes. They seemed endless, infinite.

Willow gulped again, trying to slow her breathing. Racer kept walking, edging closer and closer to the enemies—no, to certain doom. Something inside her, gnawing and clawing, was trying to persuade—no, demand—the zebra to turn around. But a stronger will never wavered and repressed the anxiety, locking it away. Something about the confidence of the warrior-king and the validation from Skeef kept her head high and her focus strong.

Finally, the baron came to a stop a few yards from the massive sprawl of men-imitates, turning his royal steed to the side so they could see his kingly sword. The light in the sky was fading, and soon, there would be nothing but moonlight to greet death's ugly grin. But the baron's resolve was in full display as he stared the Caliph down behind his helmet's eye gaps. She was in full war regalia—a set of silvery steel armor with a flowing gold cape to match her horse's war helm. A fine gold scepter found its place in her right hand, its pate glowing as red as the most seething anger. Three hooded witches stood behind her.

"Here at last, the baron of the east arrives, and he brings the cowardly, weak proclaimed savior of the realm to watch him die."

Her voice was the same stern contralto she had heard in her vision, a voice harsh enough to wither flowers and freeze sunlight.

"Brave, I must say, but terribly lacking in judgment, I'm afraid."

Zohar took the verbal blows and refused to let it sway him.

"Fear shall not deter us, your foulness. By the time the sun rises and casts its light upon the land once more, it will be your blood in the dirt, whether I join you or not. To bear witness, I have brought the One Who Unites, someone whom I assume you have grown to loathe."

Seeing the Caliph here and now in the present sent a shiver of fear through Willow's body, a brief tingling shock of terror like an invisible arrow from an invisible bow. Though she felt it, she tried to appear unfazed.

"Thus," continued the baron, "hear this proposition I give. To avoid any further loss of morale and manpower and to simply put this war at ease, I suggest a duel. You against me. Baron to Caliph. Should I fall to your blade, my kingdom is yours. Should you to mine, your armies will return at once to whence they came and never return. Do we have an accord?"

The sentence was spoken, and his words were not said shakily or timidly. Willow saw the Caliph consider them or perhaps create a false attempt at doing so. She waved her scepter in a circular motion and then let the arm carrying it droop.

"No," she said. "We do not."

What? Willow thought. *How could she not accept? No disrespect to the baron, but it would have been an easy fight! But what about me? If she had accepted, I'd be done for!*

"Before you ask a question you already know the answer to," the Caliph said, "let me be clear: your death would simply not be enough. But it will come, and hers to follow."

She pointed her angry scepter at Willow.

The baron kept his stoicism.

"Very well, then. Let it be known that Caliph Nahla, the Wasp of Kastallon and Ninth Mother of the Gilded Caliphate, refused an offer for peace. Come, heiress."

And he turned to gallop back up the hill, Willow in tow.

So it begins, she concluded. *The time has indeed come. Nothing can stop what happens next, not even me, their chosen one. Oh, Merlin, Rowan, where are you? I need you to be alive. I need you to help them, help him. I cannot do it alone.*

She put her head down and closed her eyes as Racer neared the crest of the hill they had descended before.

Skeef, White Lamb, if you are there, give them strength. Help me aid them. I know you are with us, but I cannot help feeling useless.

The thoughts trickled away as drops of sweat fell from her brow, and like a gust of reassurance, something about the way the wind blew in the coming night sky felt comforting, bringing temporary ease.

The baron had not sheathed his sword and probably did not plan on doing so until the Caliph's life was claimed with it. By now, the stars were out, but the moon was blocked by a hedge of gray streaks.

"The Caliph has refused peace," said Zohar valiantly. "Show her the true might of Londror. Ready the flames!"

In confusion, Willow looked around, wondering what he meant. But as if they had rehearsed it several times over, the Purloinian wave of green and silver began to withdraw thick sticks whose tips were coated in a sappy substance. One by one, the soldiers took daggers and created sparks by swiftly striking them with others around them. In mere seconds, the lot of them appeared to have will-o'-the-wisps hovering about them, but these were makeshift torches to light their way, burning orange and hot.

"Archers in the reserve," he continued, "man the hilltop, and let none pass. It is likely that she will have her Strix in the air. Use your arrows conservatively by choosing your targets frugally. As for the riders, there is a horde of evil waiting for us in the valley. Though they outnumber us five to one, they've no mounts. Use it to your advantage. Do not let honor or fear prevent you from helping your comrades."

Then the baron turned and readied his helmet by lowering the face guard, keeping his sword steady beside him.

Willow and Racer stood a few feet away from them, near the archers. From here, she could see the warrior-king in all his kingly glory.

He is prepared to die, she thought. *A confidence like that is sure of it. That look and that stance, he means it.*

"Fight for Ensalor!" he said, holding his blade high. "Fight for the White Lamb!"

And with this, he let fly a righteous cry louder than the most intense eruption, a cry that could have been heard across all sides of the realm from Numalosh to the upper mountains. The warrior-king sprang down the hill, followed by his riders, who let forth a flurry of hearty yells and shouts, their torches fluttering in the wind as they rode. They were a swarm of ants marching with the strength of elephants toward a hive of hornets.

The black horde lying in wait was not shaken, and soon, the galloping swarm collided with them, dust and dirt and blood flying as the sound of steel rang in the air, the sound of anger and fear!

Seconds into the battle, Willow saw the riders making their rounds, dispatching several of the Gilded as they rode between their ranks, swiping and carving away. Some of them fell, however, from a precise strike to their horses, which was followed by a lethal stomp or thwacking.

Beside her, she heard the quick twangs of bows in succession. Almost every single arrow to fly met its mark, and another Gilded was defeated. This back-and-forth of Londrorian and Gilded tug-of-war went on for the first few minutes of the battle. The fields of Falmeuse felt the first drops of bloodshed and, though it was just the beginning, seemed ready to bear the full brunt of war.

Willow, from the safety of the hilltop, watched as the warrior-king, with every fiber of his being, parried and finished any foolish troop who defied him.

He's doing what he showed me! Keep it up...please!

For a moment, it seemed that the horde would be fully overtaken slowly and surely with how easily it seemed the Gilded were being defeated. But if Willow had learned anything from the story Merlin had told, the Caliph would not let her army be so quickly defeated, certainly not by a regiment of lesser size. Another shiver of fear tingled up her spine as she looked on.

The Caliph, even without her helmet to shield her head, was sending off brave Purloinians who got too close with a blast from her scepter. Angry, agile bolts of scarlet were released, and each victim was blown away. The fear turned to terror at the sheer scale of her power.

This is the might of Fikra! I have to do something! Now!

Terror stopped her. Soon, she saw a sight she wished she could interfere with.

Seeing his men be torn apart by the blast, the warrior-king brandished his sword and began with haste toward the Caliph's position, cutting down any Gilded who dared. One, two, three were dispatched! He edged closer and closer to her. Four, five, six more went down!

Stop now! Turn back! You can't win! Please, go back!

Willow knew that even if she shouted with every vocal cord, it would be futile to assume the baron could hear her. His path did not change, nor did his velocity.

The Caliph turned away after eliminating another brave Purloinian. The world seemed to slow as she witnessed the warrior-king charging her from the west. Her scepter glowed once again, and a rain of crimson bolts emerged.

Thoom!

The ground under the baron's steed shook, sending mists of dirt upward as he felt himself dismount. Finding his feet, his eyes caught the figure of the towering woman before him. The scarlet glow reflecting on her steel armor intensified in the darkness.

She dismounted?

He cared not and rose to meet her.

"Seems you will get your aimless duel after all, my lord."

Her tone was mocking, a tactic she knew would get to him.

"Meet your death!"

"In the name of Skeef, lord and protector, I will not fall this day!" said the baron, taking a readied stance. "His light will shine upon your folly!"

He made the first blow, and to his surprise, the scepter withstood the burden of his sword. A clash kept them together, pushing against themselves in a struggle of strength.

Zohar clenched his fanged teeth and flashed them in a hissing manner, and his striped bronze hair stood on its ends. His pupils widened, and his veins seemed to inflate. The Caliph looked at the man, unflattered by his performance, almost as if she was bored. She pushed away from him, but he was not shaken, his feet planted and sturdy. He made several more attempts to land a strike on the Caliph's armor, trying to find a soft spot to rest his blade, but the Caliph was more than ready and blocked each sideswipe and cleave.

He readied himself as the scepter began to glow bright red once more. Looking at the position of the weapon, he began to contemplate. If the trajectory was correct, the bolt was aimed for center mass. Instead of handling the sword with a single hand, now the baron gripped his steel with tight fists. He knew the sword must not leave his hand, or it was over. He shifted his right foot in the sand, preparing to put his weight forward. The timing had to be perfect. Once the bolt was free, there would be a moment open for counter-attack; he just had to survive it.

Thoom!

The baron saw it coming, and his contemplation served him well. With a precise guard, the ejected bolt was deflected and sent hurling away across the battlefield. But when the bolt was far from them, something then felt off. The weight in his hands was lighter, much lighter.

He looked down at his sword, only to find that what was once a fine, handsome blade forged by the best blacksmiths in Londror was now destroyed, broken, cradled in his loose grip. Where the blade gave in remained but a jagged break still glowing hot from the bolt. He cursed under his breath and tossed the hilt away, drawing the dagger from his belt to replace it. It was curved and serrated; the blade itself was littered with fine indentions to give the resemblance of a feather. It was like a carving knife, at least seven inches in length. It was his last defense against a foe like her.

I need to keep her close, he thought. *No room for scepter bolts. But her armor is dense, tightly wound. It would take several hits to be effective.*

He tightened his grip on the hilt of the feather-blade.

So be it.

Another flurry of scarlet bolts flew, and the baron saw them coming, avoiding them by jumping or skidding to a side. This was easier to achieve with less weight to handle. With each desperate release of red energy, he steadily closed the gap between them. Soon, the armored Caliph was upon him, and he held the feather-blade raised, ready. Her crimson eyes, red as rubies, were distinctly reflected by it.

"Die like the worm you are!" she exclaimed and tried for a bashing, wearing an evil sneer on her face. "Suffer!"

Zohar blocked the scepter with a gauntleted arm, feeling the immense burden of her strength weighing him down. Using his armed arm, he thrust the blade forward, but the cursed Caliph took his wrist in her grasp.

Skeef alive, the sheer brawn of her! If she holds on any longer, she might break my wrist!

Luckily, her aim was to disarm, and her grasp was effective. The warrior-king felt his fingers forced open from the pain in his wrist, and the feather-blade fell to the grass.

Damn it! Damn it! Damn it!

He considered the only options he had now. He could try to break free and reclaim the blade; he could go for her face and strike with a fist, hoping to stun her; he could use his feet to push off her and spring away. His strategizing was cut short, though, as he felt his feet leaving the gritty dirt beneath him. The Caliph, still clutching the baron's wrist, held him the way a hunter held his prized pheasant. Her glaring eyes seemed to pierce the very armor her squirming prey was using.

"Such spunk for a dead king," she said, grinning. "It's almost saddening."

She lifted the scepter, glowing as red as seared metal, and pressed it against the baron's breastplate. She watched him writhe and land a few ineffective kicks on her armored bosom.

"Goodbye, ruler of the east."

In that moment, the baron told himself he had tried and that he was prepared to die. He knew that upon his death this day, his generals and reserve army would come crashing down upon her legions and make one final stand to achieve victory. More brave men and women would be maimed, injured, or dead because of it. And if indeed they failed too, the realm would be lost to the darkness and wickedness that was Fikra, her phantom sorceress. All would be folly.

But it wasn't, and his army didn't come. Something withheld the scepter.

Chapter 20

White Wings

The battle had begun, and all Willow could do was sit and wait for the baron to signal the reserve army to advance. She had watched as the riders of the first wave began a successful streak across the legions of Gilded, but now the tide was turning. The forces of Londror were dwindling.

Of the thousand souls sent down the valley, she estimated that only a quarter of them remained.

There's simply too many of them, she thought.

Her eyes widened when she saw the baron, the last hope of the east, riding hard and fast toward the Caliph. Every red light and warning began in her head, signs she wished she could project to him.

Stop now! Turn back! You can't win! Please, go back!

She knew and had seen how powerful she was. In her dream, she had been at her mercy. But when it came to her actions physically, she knew mercy would be out of the question. The Caliph had known of her presence and had begun every precaution to stop her. Merlin was smart to raise her outside of the realm, knowing that it would be out of her reach. Willow knew that she had longed to kill her since the words were proclaimed at the height of the invasion a decade ago, and now that she was in the same field, in the same land, she knew Nahla, cursed be her name, would be out for blood. She would finish the baron first, and soon, she was next. She had said it herself!

If the journey itself had not been stimulating for a ten-year-old, war surely was. In the brief span of time that passed since it began, there were moments when she wanted to look away and other moments when she couldn't, moments when she had to keep watching. Her nerves simply would not allow her to miss anything. The chaos, the turmoil, all of it was both horrifying and mesmerizing—trauma and glory.

But it wasn't the first she had seen of violence. She began to remember the trouble she and Rowan ran into on the outskirts of Al Wafra with the witch and her bandits and how their bodies were maimed in the magical explosion Rowan made, sand and blood spattering. She could swear now that one of the witches on the battlefield—there were three, and they were controlling the Strix's reign of terror—had to be that very witch that night. Maybe Rowan would have told her.

"Aren't you going to help them?" she heard Racer speak. "They're getting hit hard out there. I don't think they can keep going at this rate."

"Don't say that!" she replied, giving him a restrained pat. "They can do this!"

Willow looked once more at the valley, which could have been painted and displayed in a medieval history museum, men and women in silver fighting against their enemies in gold and black, a tug-of-war between kittens and lions. Indeed, she felt helpless just waiting at the top of the hill. She wondered if the reserve army felt the same.

Suddenly, there was a tickling in her ear, a breathy, flowing tickle.

Willow.

She turned her head toward the Purloinians, who were beginning to grow restless as they watched their comrades slowly be overtaken, and saw no immediate culprit. Whatever it had been, it was the same feeling she had felt in the Shriveled Forest when she was lost and chased by a Strix. She looked around the landscape past the reserve army and found that no golden streams of opaque wind were present. None was shining through the scattered trees or shrubbery. What was it? Then she heard it again.

Willow. Go to the trees. Hurry!

The voice was shallow, barely above a whisper. Whatever—or whoever—it was needed her and called to her. She looked once more at the battle in the valley and saw that the baron had engaged the Caliph, and blips of red were popping in and out like fireworks. He seemed to be doing fine, she thought as much, and flicked Racer's reins.

"Hyah!" she said, and he took off, flying past the multitudes of soldiers, who looked on and gasped or murmured at her leaving.

His hooves kicked up dirt and bits of grass as he cantered away in the night.

*****

"Ride, Racer, ride!" Willow said, flicking the zebra's reins as if they were a throttle, one that could somehow make the striped horse's legs move at a speed higher than average.

Racer, who thankfully was accustomed to trekking, galloped and galloped as fast as the wind across the plains. In the distance, faint glimpses of the sequoia trees in the heart of Onolon caught their eyes—tall, tall stalks with bushy evergreen leaves.

"I see them!" she continued. "Those have to be what it was meaning!"

Racer spoke between breaths.

"Are...you...sure?"

"Has to be. The Gnomes said they were special. And immune to the Caliph's curse."

Perhaps there's more to them than just immunity, she thought.

She stole a glance at her wrist and saw the wooden rosary jumbling about in the motion.

Wonder what Rossa would have to say. I really hope they're all okay. Please, Skeef, let them be alive!

They were crossing the river now. Splashes danced around them as they trudged through the knee-deep—for Racer, that is—water in seconds. The banks of them were still overgrown with drooping flora. To the west, prying mountains watched when Racer picked up his speed again. Urgency was of the utmost importance. A battle was being waged, and the fate of important people—nay, the entire realm—would be decided. Willow felt guilty for ditching and departing at short notice, but she had to be sure it was him. He was the only one who could make the wind speak to her.

The lack of the golden streams had assured her they were going to the right place. She remembered how they showed her the way out of the forest, how they showed them the way to Londror. They only appeared when she did not know her way around. Because she had been to Onolon before, they weren't needed. The voice told her trees knowing full well she knew what it would be talking about. But would he be there? The White Lamb? She had to be sure. Whatever was there, Skeef needed her present.

It wasn't much farther now. The bubbly waters were a few miles away, and the mountains began to grow larger as they neared Onolon. Mist streamed down from their peaks and hovered as it did in the heart of the Garmouth, light ivory tufts of puffy vapor. They almost appeared like cotton candy, a rare treat for orphans in Earthrealm.

Soon, the plains transitioned into woodlands.

"We made it!" said Willow, feeling somewhat relieved by familiar sights. She was anxious to see the Gnomes again.

Maybe they were sent back here as a warning?

A few gallops more, and they arrived at the very same open glade where the large stone dwelling had given them shelter.

"Whoa, boy."

Racer came to a halt, snorting and heaving for breath. Willow looked around, confused and slightly afraid. No one was here. It was empty, totally empty.

"Hello?" she said in a cautious tone. "Where is everyone? Caflan? Rasmorn?"

She dismounted and patted the zebra with a gentle thrum.

"Hello! It's Willow! The One Who Unites?"

No response, not even a ruffle or a shuffle or a scurrying of tiny gnomish feet. It was as quiet as a graveyard. She looked back at Racer with worried countenance.

"Where could they have all gone?"

Then she broke down, weeping and mourning.

"This is all my fault. I know I should be strong, and I know I should have faith, determination, all that. But it keeps getting worse! People have suffered because of me. Probably died too! How could I be the one to save them? I'm not even there with them! They are all going to die because of me!"

Willow slumped to her knees, drawing ragged breaths between sobs of grief. She sniffed a few times to keep the drippings from streaking to her lips. Of all the bad things she had found, this was the worst. It was almost as if the words the White Lamb had spoken were false and in vain—empty, superfluous verbiage meant only to cheer and uplift regardless of truth or verification.

Racer took a few steps and nudged her with his snout, ruffing her hair a tick. He could see the red flushing her cheeks and eyes. It took everything in his animal being not to join her and let the negative thoughts surrounding Rowan's whereabouts consume him.

Then it happened. It was as if a thousand bright suns opened up from the path ahead, the path where the trees lay. Night nearly turned to day. Great luminosity lit their faces, drying up Willow's tears. Racer nudged her like a bored puppy would its owner and turned his head to show her what he was seeing. Willow gasped and clasped her hands over her mouth in both awe and disbelief at the thing that had appeared.

And it spoke to her!

"Do not be afraid, child."

Its voice was gentle, majestic, and angelic.

"Rise and take up your sword. Fret not. Your friends are safe. I have seen them. The only thing you must be concerned with now is eliminating the enemy."

It lifted part of itself up on its hind legs and flapped its white wings in excitement.

"Come now. Take flight! We must hurry! The One Who Unites belongs on the battlefield."

The being's words were encouraging, and Willow did not feel any ounce of dread at the mention of being on a battlefield. In fact, what she felt was quite the opposite.

"Who are you?" said Willow, still in awe and drawing closer.

"I am known by many names," said the being. "Feathered One, Lightbringer, Shadowslayer, Pale Flier, or Dayglider. But the name bestowed to me by the Numen of Ufton is Cosma. I am at your service, O uniter."

"You know who I am?"

"Of course," said the being. "You are Willow, a daughter of Kastallon, heiress of Ensalor, and the One Who Unites. I was meant to find you."

Willow considered for a moment, gazing upon the heavenly thing in the glade. It was the embodiment of purity, full of light and radiant. It seemed that even the night could not quiet its majesty, and it burned brighter and brighter by the minute.

The prophecy did mention a 'winged being of white.' This must be it.

"How did you find me? I was so far away, and yet...it was you who called."

"Was it not you who called me with the horn?"

The being's eyes drifted to the corkscrew horn slung over her cloak.

Oh, she thought.

"I understand now," said Willow. "Wait. You said my friends are safe. What did you mean?"

She trod nearer to the being. Racer shied away.

"I will take you to them. Come now. Quick!" said the winged being.

"But—"

"There is no time left for questions! At once!"

The being reared up and pranced. Willow turned back to Racer one last time, a touch of sincerity on face. With solemnity, she spoke like a heartbroken child to their dying parent.

"If I don't see you again, then I want to thank you, Racer. For everything."

She moved and embraced the zebra's striped neck, tears slowly streaming.

"I could not have asked to meet a finer horse."

She pulled away, wiping her face.

"Now go. Find Rowan. I release you."

Racer was hesitant. He made a few steps in place in contemplation. How would he find him? The winged being said he was safe, so why was he so anxious?

"Go, Racer. I will be okay," said Willow, grinning. "You can follow us to find him."

At last, she clambered aboard, and her legs wrapped around the being as if they were always meant to. It was seamless, nonchalant, as if she had rehearsed it thousands of times. Yet this would be their first flight.

With a grin never fading from her face, Willow unsheathed Pnevma and held it high in a royal fashion, a knight upon her mount.

"Okay," she began. "Here we g—"

"Just a moment there, girl!" a sinister, raspy voice called out, halting the performance.

Racer shifted like a surprised squirrel and turned behind him, as this was where the voice had come from. He lowered his head in a defensive stance and used his left hoof to kick up dirt for intimidation. There was no backing down now. The knowledge of Rowan's living had reinvigorated his confidence. He would let nothing stop him, not this time.

Someone emerged from within the bushes in the glade, someone familiar. It was a man, a man dressed in black rags and hobbling on a twisted cane. His fingertips were chipped and nasty; his eyes, bloodshot and piercing. Willow remembered him and began to wonder how in all the Land Where Castles Lie had she seen him as trustworthy, this ugly, wrinkled, traitorous sorcerer.

"Pinner," she hissed and pointed her sword at him. "How dare you show your face to me again! Do you know how much pain you've caused? All the worry and doubt and—"

"Oh, do quiet down, girl," he said, waving her off. "Do not speak to me as if you have any place over me. I do not believe in you, and therefore, you do not command me. I have waited a decade to find you and bring you before Her Ladyship. And now that Merlin is gone, there isn't anyone left to save you."

His staff began to glow.

"I would advise you to stand down, wizard," said Willow. "I am the One Who Unites, and Skeef himself is on my side. You cannot win. Now return to the Tels. I will deal with you once the battle is won."

She spoke with pride, but in the back of her mind, she was worried, thinking, *Merlin is gone? But this being said...*

"You think I would listen to you?" Pinner scoffed. "You who cannot wield Shimmer properly. You who are young and naive with no battle experience. Without your pathetic friends, the Strix would have finished you early. But it seems I will have that pleasure myself."

He began to raise his staff as a phalanx would a spear behind his shield.

"She has warned you, man," said the being. "Do not allow yourself to be so easily defeated. Lay your weapon down and walk away. I fear there will not be another warning."

Pinner felt his sweat cooling in the chill of the night. Although his level of knowledge about Shimmer had allowed him three ports a day, he had used up his final one to get from Ensalor to Onolon. Even if he were to succeed, his journey to Falmeuse would be long, arduous. He knew that with his energy drained, there was the possibility he would never make it there and would find himself sleeping in a dell. But he had come prepared.

With a careful movement, he reached into the satchel at his hip with a trembling hand and revealed something that stirred the majestic being, driving it into a restrained frenzy. He watched as it stomped its front legs, and its body tremored.

"W-what have y-you d-done?" said the being, using its incredible willpower to resist the thing glowing red in the sorcerer's hand.

"What she has asked me to do," replied Pinner, gazing into the red object's haze. "I've taken the power of Kastallon and perfected it."

In that moment, Willow could see what exactly the wizard had. It was a crystal, similar to the violet one in Merlin's staff, but this piece did not radiate purple, as she had seen before. This one was writhing, seething, roiling red, quivering to the point where it might have been considered alive. There was a whitish core to it like a simmering bubble. Around the bubble was the mass of crimson boiling.

He's taken a Shimmer crystal and...

She didn't want to think of what abomination he had committed.

"You've corrupted it!" cried the being in a voice loud enough to let all sentient things in the glade hear. "I cannot abide this. You have submitted fully to the enemy. You have desecrated the very essence of this land. For this, you must perish!"

Pinner began to grip the crystal tighter and tighter, growling as he did. His eyes looked away from the crystal and darted at Willow. They were scarlet, a bright, burning scarlet, full of rage, anger, and fervor. He was a man desperate to gain power through any means necessary even if it meant sacrificing his loyalty and his morality.

Atop the being, Willow noticed a sharp point on the being's face between its eyes near the beginning of its mane.

It's a horn! she thought.

She tightened her grip on Pnevma, not fully knowing what was going to happen next.

The horn of the being began to shine, glow the same glow she had seen earlier when it first arrived, a bright sparkle building and building. Before she knew it, there was a great flash, and the world went white as she shielded her eyes.

Something screamed but was cut short.

When the world returned and the flare dissipated, she rubbed her eyes with the sleeve of her tunic and checked back where Pinner should have been. She saw the red crystal on the grassy forest floor, sizzling and charring the earth around it, slowly sinking. But her eyes widened at the realization that hit her when she found the twisted wooden staff lying next to it, alone and broken in two, a remnant of a former ally. Nothing else remained, no clothes or shoes.

"Quickly now," said the being with a shaky voice. "Both of you!"

Chapter 21

The One Who Unites

Hanging from the hand of the enemy, the warrior-king gasped at the brilliant luminescence streaking across the sky. Lines of glorious golden light like comets in the night came flying, and in the center of it all was a great violet dot. The chaos around ceased, if only for a brief moment, and watched as there in the infinite canvas of darkness speckled with stars a heavenly rider on a majestic winged unicorn flew toward the swarm.

In that instant, the baron felt his arm released; and being a Purloinian, he dropped to his feet with perfect balance. The Caliph had turned and was distracted by the entrance. He took his chance and grabbed the feathered dagger, raised it high, and jammed it into a crevice between the armor pieces of her long leg. She howled in pain, turned back to face him, and heaved her scepter at him. It collided with his breastplate, and the sheer force of the blow took the ground from him, sending him a few feet away. As for the Caliph, drops of crimson seeped onto her iron armor from the wound. Without flinching, she withdrew the blade and cast it into the ground, feathered blade first. She then sent a bolt of red lightning toward the heavenly rider despite the cacophony of cheering, hollering, and praise.

Aboard Cosma, Willow saw the lightning coming and shifted to the side. The Pegasus felt it and weaved away from the bolt, which crackled and dissipated behind them. The two of them flew closer now, enough to stir up dust from the earth into the eyes of the Gilded. Another pass once more, and Willow swiped away any foolish attackers, their armor giving way to Pnevma like a hot knife through soft butter. It was too easy.

"To arms, fighters of the east! The One Who Unites has arrived!" cried the warrior-king atop the hill he and his first reserve had descended.

The second reserve, mounted on their stallions, raised their swords and spears high, bellowing with a triumphant outcry loud enough to give any Gilded shaky knees. With a rallying cry from the baron, they charged forth and descended the hill once more.

"Avidar!" he cried and joined the fray of Londrorian riders.

Soon, they collided once more with Gilded forces, and the Caliph fought back.

It was to the advantage of the Purloinian archers that Willow had returned. The Strix had been inflicting severe losses to them and to their brethren in the valley. Now they had a new target. But this target was armed to the teeth. Willow gritted her teeth and began to remember all the times she had encountered them, and each time, they were a nuisance; nothing but a roadblock in her journey.

"You will see no mercy from me!" she cried, summoning every ounce of hate and anger she had been saving up since she arrived, but not toward her peers; it was awakened by the Caliph.

She used this newfound lividity and ensured that it flowed through her sword as she struck each Strix that met her in the pass. Cosma also used her horn's power to disintegrate any of the black owls that had the misfortune of getting too close. One touch from the rays, and they were filled with yellow cracks that shattered like a broken mirror. She whinnied with each little victory she claimed from them. No matter how many there were, she kept them at bay, as each ray of light created a domino effect, taking multiple birds in its wake.

On the ground, the baron fought without ceasing. Someone had thrown him a greatsword, taken from a fallen ally, and with it he avenged their death with each defeated soldier. He hissed and snarled at the Gilded knight he turned to, who wielded a fiery fist and donned a vibrant red cape. This one's helm was plumed.

"Baron Zohar," said the knight. "It would be my highest honor to claim your life in the name of Fikra."

The plumed knight beat his balled burning fist on his breastplate. "Give me a challenge!"

The knight began to dash toward the warrior-king with all his might, and the warrior-king stood his ground. With each stomp of the plumed knight's greaves, there was a faux quake vibrating ever closer. The baron readied his sword to prepare for the incoming attack.

No more mistakes, he thought. *This blade will not shatter this day. I am Zohar, son of Avidar and Grismilla, baron of Londror, christened by Skeef, and I will not fail! In the name of the White Lamb, lord and protector, this demon shall fall!*

He raised his greatsword, taking in a breath and holding it, and steadied himself as the knight charged forth, right gauntlet unscathed by the blue-hued flame.

Closer, closer, closer, and…

The knight suddenly halted and produced a gurgling sound in his throat; the flame was suddenly extinguished. Still holding his breath, Zohar watched as the knight's head slowly slipped away from his shoulders, the sound of hooves close by. As the head fell, he released his breath, watching the scarlet flowing from the neck stain the armor.

He turned his head to look behind him, all the uncertainty of the world falling in on him at that moment with the unbearable fear of the unknown. It could have been anyone. Perhaps one of his riders or Willow had come down from the sky above and claimed an easy kill. But when he turned and took in the view of the one who had slain the charging knight, he was both confused and joyous. It was a complete stranger, a stranger in black on a zebra.

"I don't know who you are, but you have my thanks," said the baron, putting his greatsword to his chest, bowing.

When he rose, he said, "You must have a name. I must know the title of the one who overcame Sal, the Caped Vex!"

The stranger clopped over to the baron, shamshir in hand, and grinned. He was not a Purloinian, and he was not Willow. His hair was a fine blond, and he was not much younger than the baron himself.

"Rowan," he said. "My name is Rowan. We have a battle to win."

"Rowan, the realm shall remember your name. When this is all over, you have my blessing. Whatever you desire, it is yours. My word is my life."

"My desire now is to win this thing and go home. Shouldn't be an issue."

Rowan sliced an oncoming Gilded who was shorter than the rest and dispatched him. The soldier fell at once and hit the stained grass with a thud!

"You're welcome again."

"So it seems. Many thanks," said the baron, who parried a threat, tripped him, and drove his sword through his breastplate. "What do you mean shouldn't be an issue? Are you talking about the girl on the horse in the sky?"

He looked up briefly before his attention was redirected to the ground, and he clashed with a Gilded in two strokes before ending him.

"No, my lord," said Rowan, who allowed his shamshir to pierce a Gilded as it ran toward him.

The dying Gilded hadn't realized he had been stabbed until he was falling over. Rowan saw his eyes roll back as the soldier fell to the grass, clunky and quite dead.

"Look to the southwest peak, where the Ittermount looks down on us."

He pointed his shamshir toward the small peak of a valley. It was true. The summit of that great mountain could be seen from their location. But more importantly, it was that hill that concerned them.

Several fizzling balls of light, red and green and blue, came sizzling up from the very ground. They flew higher, higher, and higher before eventually exploding in a dazzling display of sparks and flares. Around the stranger and the warrior-king, the battle was distracted by this mighty flourish of magical prowess. The baron stood in awe.

As the flares continued, it became known to the whole valley of Gilded what was causing all this ruckus. There, coming down the southwest valley, was another army, a massive army, an army of size unfathomable to the Caliph, who roared with despair at their arrival. The black wave of Gilded began to withdraw, but it was already too late. They were already trapped in the valley with no escape.

Leading this army were two familiar figures, and Willow began to cheer and cry tears of overwhelming joy at the sight of them.

Merlin and Lady Cho had returned!

Behind them, in a screaming horde, came a legion of Da'iini, Gnomes, and other humans dressed in combat garb she had not seen before. They were carrying a variety of weapons—swords, spears, clubs, knives, daggers, bows, and arrows, to name a few. As one unit, they descended upon the Gilded troops and overwhelmed them. Some were even trampled by the sheer strength of them. Most cried and ran, only to be mercilessly extinguished. There were those who took their loyalty to the Caliphate to extremes. They held out longer than the others, gnashing their teeth and taking a few foes with them, but ultimately, they met their demise all the same.

"For Ensalor!" Willow cried.

She instructed Cosma to descend, and the winged unicorn blasted more Gilded with her horn ray. They made rounds, slashing and blasting away at the multitudes. Victory on the grounds of attrition was more than certain. Eventually, the threat was reduced enough that Willow decided to dismount.

"To the ground please!"

Cosma glided to the ground, and each flap of her feathered wings was a hurricane that tossed any stragglers about like rag dolls. Stardust as pure as moonlight sifted off them as she touched down at the edge of the battle.

Willow dismounted and stepped forward to meet Cosma's eyes.

"Stay in the air. We'll need cover, and you're our best bet. Better yet, watch over the archers on the ridge."

She pointed to the hill the baron's armies had descended. In obedience, Cosma flapped her wings once more and took to the skies.

The time had come. Every single step in her journey from Al Wafra to Londror and every instance in between had led to this moment. She had never felt more powerful in all her ten years of life. She felt it flowing through her, surging with a feeling close to euphoria. It made her believe she was unstoppable, and truly, she was.

She stepped into the fray, and without moving her blade, enemies bounced away, smashing themselves against an invisible barrier surrounding her. They did not distract her, and her gaze remained focused on the desperate Caliph, that tall, armored, yet frail woman knocking back Gnomes and demolishing Da'iini with one stroke of her scepter. She watched her send furious bolts of crimson toward the Purloinians, but now they were too perceptive to be reached; they dashed away from them.

Across the battlefield, Merlin and Lady Cho had regrouped with Zohar and Rowan.

"Seems the battle has already been decided," said Merlin, putting his weight on his staff and smiling that ever gracious smile. He winked at his apprentice, who returned the favor with the opposite eye.

"Not yet," said Lady Cho with her hands on her hips. "She has one more victory to claim."

She paused for a moment, taking it all in. At last, she turned to the wizard with an apologetic countenance.

"Perhaps I was wrong to put my faith in our people. Skeef has not abandoned us after all. I see that now. I hope he can forgive me."

"Don't trouble yourself with worry, my lady. You were looking out for your people, and that is honorable. But what good is a leader if she's not bound to righteousness? Skeef cares not for what you've done, only for what you believe. Do you trust him?"

"I do," said Lady Cho. "I proclaim him, to the end."

"I don't believe we've been acquainted," said the baron, bowing to Lady Cho. "I am Baron Zohar, ruler of the—"

"I know who you are," Cho interrupted. "Word spreads fast, my lord. I am very sorry to hear about your father. You have my condolences."

She nodded to him.

"I thank you for your humble welcoming of the girl."

"As do I," said Merlin.

"I concur," said Rowan.

"The kingdom of Londror will surely be rewarded for its kindness and contribution to the reclamation of the realm. Your father would be proud, son," said Merlin. He clasped a hand on the warrior-king's young shoulder and smiled.

Then the four of them looked on and witnessed Willow reach her target. She was splendid. Nothing stood in her way. Before long, the Gilded recognized her glory, her indomitability, and withdrew from her. It was a chain reaction that opened a clear path to the Caliph, and soon, a circular arena was created, forged by bodies of rivals on either end. Although these enemies were close, they were too awestruck by Willow to fight one another.

The Caliph remained and raged at the realization that her power no longer had any sway over the minds of her minions.

"Cowards!" she shouted. "All of you, cowards! I command you to fight!"

None of the Gilded moved a muscle. They all looked at their former leader without a shred of fear of her wrath. They had been transformed, revitalized by the One Who Unites. They threw down their savage weapons and held firm to one another. This ensured that the open space they had created with their former enemies was compact.

"It's over!" yelled Willow. "Your army has turned their backs on you. You have lost."

"Nothing is over!"

She raised her scepter and unleashed a vehement beam of venetian fury toward Willow, a continuous stream prolonged by the Caliph's immortal anger and strife, a swell that had built up over the years finally awakened by the inevitable threat to her throne. Her voice reverberated and dripped with a fusion of desperation and agony.

The beam, despite its visual strength and resolve, was powerless against the invisible barrier shielding the One Who Unites.

Rowan found himself whispering as he watched, if not to Merlin, then to himself, "The power of Skeef is within her."

His volume increased to a yell.

"She will not be moved!"

And he raised his shamshir high!

Willow began to close the gap, which, as she trod, slowly began to reduce the length of the roiling beam. Closer and closer she came, the Caliph never giving in. At last, she was a few yards away from the Caliph, and the beam dissipated as she took time to catch her breath, panting. Willow stood firm, calm and collected. It was her who looked down on the Caliph.

This was the moment she was sent here for—to eliminate the Caliph. There was an overwhelming temptation gnawing at the back of her mind, a feeling of hatred for this person, this person who had made her return to her homeland a hardship, this person who killed her parents, enslaved her people, and sent witches to kill her too.

Now is your chance to kill her. Finish this once and for all!

It was her conscience talking.

This is what you've been waiting for. Do it! Do it now while she is down!

But then she remembered the warmth and comfort she had received from the White Lamb, the feeling of forgiveness. Oh, what a feeling it was! Then a thought popped into her head, and she began to wonder. She considered…

"This does not need to end in violence," said Willow, her voice gentle yet firm. "The battle is over, and you have fought with all of your strength. I offer you peace under terms. Submit to our lord and protector. Give in to his grace. Let him satiate you."

The Caliph looked up at her, and her scepter fell from her hand, rolling away. Then she did something none of the crowd expected, not even Merlin and the others. She began to weep—terribly.

"I have known nothing but anger, nothing but strife and hatred. I was created to oppose his light. I am a servant of Fikra, the very embodiment of everything opposite to him! How could he accept me? How could he forgive me?"

Willow smiled at her, and the words came as if she had always known them.

"It does not matter what you've done. I've heard the stories about you. How you invaded this realm when I was born. How your army chased my parents down while I escaped. Skeef said I was to come when you arrived, and so I did. His prophecy claimed that I was the realm's savior. But was it really the land that needed saving?"

She extended a hand to the Caliph.

"Come to the light. Bask in his mercy, and you will feel the same peace I feel."

The Caliph looked up, her eyes still watery and red. Her grayed skin was stained by the price of violence, dried and black. Her armor was dented from the many blows she had sustained through the skirmish. In her mind, she was frightened—frightened by the outcome of her choices. If she accepted, would Fikra find her? If she refused, her death was certain. She looked at the scepter on the ground a few feet away from her boots. There was still a glimmer of red in its fading crystal. She closed her eyes and drew in a ragged breath.

"Will you protect me?" she asked.

Willow's brow furrowed. Then she realized whom she was referring to and drew closer to the Caliph.

"Yes. By the White Lamb, she will never hurt you again."

A single tear formed and dripped down the Caliph's cheek. A thankful smile began to grow across her lips, and she began to strip off her armor piece by piece. She threw off her gauntlets and tossed them aside. Her shin guards she removed and kicked away. She called over a few of her Gilded, and they helped her remove the cape and breastplate, throwing it down onto the stained grass. Underneath all her armor, her former gown had been girded, which she unwound now.

"I am ready," she said with open arms.

Now the wind began to pick up—not enough to be a gust or bluster but enough to feel the tug of it like a sail blowing in the breeze. Golden streams began to form upon it, and they rounded in the air, curving downward to a single point. In a mere matter of seconds, it was apparent that something was appearing, something small, about the size of a small dog. It took shape, and as the golden light faded, the thing was revealed.

It was a white lamb whose wool was as white as morning snow. It was grinning, and its ears flopped on the sides of its head. It was Skeef, lord and protector of Kastallon, in all his divine glory. The crowd that had formed the space now knelt in submission to him. There were even some spouts of joy and exultation from them.

The lamb made a few steps over to the Caliph, who fell to her knees and curled up.

"Master," she said, on the verge of tears once more, "I submit myself to you. I renounce who I was, my wretched self, and proclaim you lord and protector of the realm. I no longer wish to suffer under the burden of my servitude to Fikra, cursed be her name!"

"And suffer you shan't," the lamb's voice said in the Caliph's head.

Willow heard it too.

"As long as you trust in me and believe in my design, you shall know peace. No hand of evil shall befall you. None shall pluck you and take you out of my will. Do you trust me?"

"Yes!"

Skeef clopped forward and pressed his nose against the top of her raven hair. When he withdrew, there was an immediate change. The former Caliph's locks began a transition from black to a delightful orange. Her once gray skin turned a fresh, new cream color, and her eyes went from a threatening ruby to a serene sapphire.

"Then rise anew," said Skeef. "From now on, you will be called Hahla, not Nahla."

She stood and found her trembling feet. At once, she was overwhelmed by the amount of color that surrounded her. She looked to the east and saw the vibrant yellow sun beginning its waking ascent above the horizon, turning the dreadful night to a hopeful day. Streaks of red surfaced above the valley as she saw the thin rays of sunlight dance within the whitening clouds. She closed her eyes and let the warmth bathe her with its solace. Tears of joy fell.

She was redeemed, no longer a slave to wickedness.

Chapter 22

House Drinith

Willow awoke to the familiar smell of lemongrass and a touch of mint as if the very walls had been slathered with the bold, citrusy aroma.

She was back in her room inside the château, the same room she had been shown and slept in two days ago. It was homey, more so than the enormous room full of other children in Earthrealm, and it still contained the same furnishing as before, almost as if she had never left. She sat up and rubbed her eyes gently, taking in a deep breath, then letting it go in a long, whispered sigh. When it was all out, her whole body ached with a subtle yet annoying pain. Her arms, most of all, were weak. Even raising them to stretch was less than easy.

She began to recall everything that happened leading up to this afternoon. She remembered the flight of the horned unicorn Cosma, the annihilation of Pinner the traitor, and the sudden transformation of the very enemy of the realm. Nahla was no more. That name had been thrown out, cast in the ether. Instead, the autumn-haired Hahla took her place. She remembered seeing Rowan and Merlin and Lady Cho in the fray and how they came crashing over the hills and down onto the Gilded with a mass of soldiers behind them. That was what had surprised her the most. Where had they come from? Were there more people living hidden from the Caliphate than just the Da'iini?

But something struck her that unnerved her. She did not remember returning to her room.

Someone must have carried me, she thought. *But I don't recall that either.*

A knock came to the door, a rhythmic rapping of knuckles on wood.

"Come in," said Willow, moving her legs out from under the sheets.

The door opened, and in strolled someone who made her heart nearly burst from relief-fueled joy.

"Merlin!"

Up jumped Willow with outstretched arms that wrapped around the wizard tightly, nearly knocking him over.

"Thank the White Lamb, you're alive!"

"Of course," he said gleefully. "Why wouldn't I be?"

He released her.

"But Pinner? You and he…you fought."

"Oh, that whole squabble? Nonsense. I was letting him give me a good thrashing, letting him think his knowledge was greater than mine. In the end, the big man Ob forced him away, using his size to deter him. Even as the grand warden, the old coward will always be exactly that—a coward."

The wizard winked his signature wink. Willow smiled, but it left and was replaced by a look of almost sorrow.

"He betrayed us. I thought he was on our side. I trusted him like a fool. But he was on Fikra's side from the very beginning."

"My dear, do not feel regret for him. His actions were his responsibility. He made the mistake of denouncing our lord and protector, sowing evil and deceit, and he wrought the fruit of those choices."

The scene of Cosma's blinding horn ray in reaction to Pinner's presence came back into mind, and she gulped. Did Merlin know about what she had done, about the twisted staff lying lonely in the glade, and about the strange scarlet jewel sinking into the ground? It was still a mystery to her what might have happened had the now erased sorcerer completed whatever process he was beginning at that moment.

Perhaps it is better that he is gone, she thought. *I should still tell him even if he does know.*

"Master?" said Willow. "Do you know where he is n…"

Merlin waved his hand briefly.

"You no longer need to call me master, heiress."

He gave a smile.

"As to where my former friend is, it matters not. All that does now is getting you to Ensalor. I'm sure our friend Hahla can help us with that."

"But, Merlin, Pinner is dead. Cosma, my steed, destroyed him."

"As I said, he wrought the fruit of the choices he chose to make."

"There was nothing left," said Willow, "not even his clothes or boots, just that sickening, twisted staff of his. And there was another thing, and I don't know what to make of it. He said it was something Fikra ordered him to do."

"What are you talking about?" Merlin asked, stroking his beard in the way old philosophers did when deep in thought. "Tell me of this thing."

"It was a Shimmer crystal, but instead of the normal violet sheen, it was angry, boiling with pure red hatred. Cosma said that he'd corrupted it somehow. But what I can't make of is the fact that after she killed him, the crystal survived and began to sink into the ground. One thing I noticed was that it burned the newly greened blades of grass around it. I remember the disgusting smell it gave off."

"Hmm," murmured Merlin. "It seems Fikra is stronger than we assume. We can no longer pretend that this is over now that the Caliph is reformed. That is, if she sees herself as the Caliph still. Regardless, the threat of Fikra remains, however close or far she is."

"You said they were from the Isles Far and Wide. How far or close is that to Kastallon?"

Willow sat down on the Purloinian bed.

"It is unknown, not charted on any regal or official maps," said Merlin. "But there are legends that say it's out there, and it is full of things no ten-year-old should dare set their minds on. So I've been told, that is. For now, let us celebrate a victory! The prophecy has been fulfilled!"

He raised his hand and staff in the air in a celebratory fashion.

Willow smirked again, left the bouncy bed, and hugged the wizard once more. For once in a long while, she felt the joy of true happiness. From the time she stepped off the whale into this once cursed land to now, it had been a roller coaster of emotion. Most days were nerve-racking with the constant threat of capture between different havens throughout the land. She thought for a moment and decided she hadn't felt this way since Onolon. In fact, this euphoria was something that was not present before the whale. She cherished it and hoped it would last forever as she held firm to Merlin's embrace, letting the sunlight from the afternoon sunbathe them through the window.

Another knock came, and this time, it was Merlin who granted access. Willow was taken aback by the man who stepped over the threshold. No sign of ailment or injury befell him. No sign of fatigue or tiredness either. He held himself the way most politicians held themselves: high and proud. He was unarmed, which surprised Willow, and he was alone.

With tears beginning to form in the corners of her eyes, Willow ran to him, and the man knelt down and embraced her warmly. It was tight, warm, almost as if he was reuniting with a long-lost young sister.

"Rowan! Thank Skeef! Oh, thank him!" cried Willow, burying her face in his shoulder.

"Willow," said Rowan.

It was true, he had missed her. But it was also true that he missed his horse, Racer, even more. But for now, she was on his mind; and finally, they were together.

He pulled away and said, "What a relief!"

"I could say the same of you," she said with a smile as pure as a true love. "But...how are you still...walking? I saw that punch you took from the Vex. It was f-fiery a-and...and..."

"I believe I can explain," a voice called from the threshold.

Willow looked toward the door and saw a familiar figure not quite illuminated by the sunlight. The woman walked in, and she was still wearing her fine red smock and grassy pelt cloak.

"It is good to see you, child."

She crossed her arms comfortably.

"Lady Cho!" Willow cried again.

"It was Ob who scooped up the prentice when he fell, after, of course, running off that nasty, no-good sorcerer Merlin was fond of—"

"Formerly fond of," broke in Merlin.

"Formerly fond of," continued Lady Cho. "We took him to another haven of ours to the south, Udguei. We were grateful it hadn't been ransacked yet."

"Wait," Willow said, stopping her.

She could do that now since Cho had accepted and respected her as the One Who Unites.

"I thought Hrinthas was the only hub for the Da'iini?"

Cho chuckled slightly.

"Oh, the naivety of children. You think we as a hidden people would stay in one place?"

Willow shrugged, not trying to ruin the mood.

Cho continued.

"It was hard to leave Hrinthas. We had built it from the ground up, and to most of my people, it was home. But Ob's brother Obe accepted us posthaste. From there, we found that your prentice had only had the wind knocked out of him."

"But what about the wound on his back?"

"About that," began Rowan. "It was mostly cauterized from the flames. They didn't need to do that much treatment other than bandages and burn relief. I am forever thankful to Obe and his apothecaries."

He nodded to Lady Cho, who reciprocated. He rubbed the top of his right shoulder.

"It will take time to fully heal."

His tone was awkward.

Willow shrugged it off and gave him another hug gently. When she was released, Willow came to the center of her bedroom and gazed at her grinning comrades around the room. It was hard to contain her excitement. It felt like a balloon on the verge of popping, like a volcano ready to erupt. It was clear from the mile-long smile on her face. She was just happy everyone had made it through to the end. Merlin, Rowan, and…

"Wait!"

Her countenance fell. Her eyes made a scurrying motion.

"Where are the Gnomes?"

A jarring vision entered her brain, and she gasped.

"Oh no! Have they fallen?"

She looked at Rowan.

"Did they come up with you?"

He shook his head.

"What about you?" she said to Merlin, who shrugged. "Well, then, we have to find them!"

At that moment, she saw Lady Cho and Rowan shoved aside as if they had been pushed by an unseen force. Something did move them, and whatever it was made loud steps coming into the room. In strolled two people only three feet tall, one bearded, the other not. Both of them wore their pointy hats with pride. One carried a frying pan; the other, a lump of something. But hanging from each of their belts was a small dagger.

"You'll not have to look far, girlie," said the bearded one, who presented the lump of something wrapped in a thin cloth.

"Valner!" cried Willow.

"We aren't hiding this time," said the one without a beard, who rested her frying pan on her short-stocked shoulder with ease. She winked at her.

"Rossa!"

"Eat, girlie. You earned it," said Valner, dropping the cloth-wrapped lump into her palms.

Willow felt the slight weight of it and the texture of it. It was spongy and slightly warm. She unwrapped the cloth and revealed what was hidden. She nearly lost moisture once again, but her lip curled through the elation. It was a perfect cube of delicious brown gingerbread, the same that she had shared with the Gnome in the Garmouth.

"Thank you," she said. Then to all of them, she added, "A thousand times, thank you!"

"We should be saying that to you, my dear," another voice chimed in, and the whole company turned back to the threshold.

Still shadowed by the sunless hallway, they all saw the shape of someone. From the looks of him, his hair was shaggy, but it covered his entire head save for his face. It was bronze with stripes. Though his face was bare, his ears were pointed and furry like those of a feline. In he walked, and Willow knew exactly who he was, except he was no longer wearing his green-and-silver armor. He took the liberty of dressing in a very regal olive-green gown with an auburn cloak. Atop his pate rested a finely woven crown of gladiolus flowers, light pink and orange. He was still as majestic as the first time they met.

"Zohar," said Willow. "It is good to see that you're alive. I wasn't sure that you were going to make it when I saw you take on the former Caliph like that. I was afraid for you!"

"I was fearless," he said, "because I knew you were there. If you weren't, I knew it would have been a death sentence, suicide even. I will say, I was not expecting an entrance like that. When the prophecy said a beast with wings, I predicted a bird of sorts. Instead, I beheld something exponentially greater—a flying horse! Of all the things to imagine! Incredible! And then in came the Da'iini with their people. And Gnomes too!"

He extended a hand to the Gnomes present in the room.

"All of you have my utmost thanks. Because of you, my father's name remains through me. Forever am I indebted to you."

He bowed a most regal bow in the most kingly fashion.

"The feeling is mutual," said Merlin. "Without your armies, the enemy would not have been distracted enough for us to garner reinforcements. You are a fine leader, Baron, and your father would have been proud."

He clasped a hand on the warrior-king's shoulder.

"Speaking of which," said Willow, turning to Lady Cho, "what changed your mind? If I remember correctly, you were against leading an attack on the Caliphate. You even denounced our lord and protector too. But it seems—and thankfully so—that you've decided to come out of the shadows."

Her eyes met the Gallantinel leader's.

Lady Cho thought briefly, reflecting on her inner pride. She remembered what she had said to the girl days ago when Hrinthas was still standing and thriving.

Soon, she said, "You did. When I saw the fury in your eyes as you called out that Vex, something had changed in you. I know not whether it was raw, unadulterated will or the very essence of Skeef that I witnessed in your eyes, but nonetheless, I was inspired. I knew my choice as leader of the Da'iini to hide us away was the wrong action, and therefore, I used your name as a call to unity to all surviving tribes of Da'iini.

"When they'd heard that the One Who Unites was in the Land Where Castles Lie and had resisted the Caped Vex, their zeal was stoked, unmatched. Quickly they came to Udguei by the thousands, rallying behind your name. Never have I seen quite the likes of it."

Willow had no words for their actions. In all her ten years of life, she had never expected anyone to look up to her in that way other than the orphans, whom she was mostly taller than. Grasping the idea that thousands of souls rallied and proclaimed her was something she figured no ten-year-old could comprehend, let alone deal with. But in all its metaphorical size, it did not feel burdensome. One could imagine that with all that popularity instilled within a child, that child might have quite the active personality, but not Willow. Never Willow.

The orphanage had trained her against pride. Mrs. Veraminta made sure of it. If any of the children was caught mocking others or uplifting themselves, their punishment was a quick slap on the wrist with a meterstick or, depending on the severity or frequency, a one-way trip to the room at the end of the hall, that unlit place where light never blossomed. It was quite clear that Veraminta was aware of every child's first fear: the dark. But it worked. It was enough to prevent Willow from ever having a sense of self-worth. Even now with the overwhelming joy of being the chosen one, the feeling of confidence, of strength, and of importance was still very much new to her.

"So this is it, then," said Willow, putting her hands behind her back. "The journey is over. The Caliphate is gone. The realm is restored."

She turned to Merlin.

"What comes next, master?"

There was a warm, true smile on her face.

"Oh, my dear, my dear, my dear," he said. "The journey is not yet over!"

He strode closer to her and knelt.

"There is still one more thing to do."

"What?"

Merlin let his staff rest on his shoulder and took Willow's hands in his.

"You already know what it is. Think back to what I told you when we first arrived, even before then, in my office."

He smiled that same warm, comforting smile, and she was taken back to all those days ago before she knew there was another plane of existence. She remembered the little bookmark she had with her birthday on it and how it sat between the pressed pages of a book she realized didn't matter anymore, yet it was an interesting book at the time. She remembered all the times she visited him, or he would call her to tell her about the world and its many facets. Sometimes, it was even to check in with how her day was going. But then she remembered the night when everything first began. It all started when…

There was a fluttering outside the window of the room. Everyone then looked to the sill; Willow turned completely around. There perched upon it was a black thing shaking its feathery head and polishing its sun-yellow beak on its wings. Its beady eyes widened with both elation and surprise.

A toucan!

"Juniper!" said Willow, rushing over to the sill.

The bird began to hop with delight!

"Willow! Oh, Willow!" the bird replied when the girl took it in her arms, dancing around the room with it.

The toucan squawked happy chirps and coos. When the dancing paused, the bird flew around the room excitedly before perching once more on Willow, using her arms as a faux branch.

"Where have you been?" Willow said, stroking the toucan's feathers with a bent finger. "I did not see you last night during the battle."

"No, I was there," said the bird. "Before you ran off."

"Oh, right, yes. I must have thought you were with me."

"Don't you remember? When the first army went into the valley, I flew up to watch and keep an eye out. Next thing I knew, you were gone."

Willow frowned.

"Sorry," she said. "I thought I heard Skeef's voice and rode Racer all the way to Onolon to meet the winged unicorn, Cosma. I'm sure you saw us in the air when I returned. It was...hard to miss."

She hoped it was not rude.

"Yes, it was spectacular!" said the toucan.

Internally, Willow breathed a sigh of relief.

"Never have I seen a more brilliant display of majesty. You were where you were meant to be. I am so proud of the person you have shaped up to be. There is no one else I'd rather be the companion of."

With that, the bird gave a gracious, feathery bow. Willow nodded accordingly, a gentle smile adorning her lips, genuine and heartfelt.

Willow then turned to Merlin again, letting Juniper alight on the sill once more. Before she spoke, she took in the sight of her new friends all standing there together. They were almost like a family—a weird, exotic mash-up family but a family nonetheless. Tears formed in her eyes; joy rose in her heart as if a bellows was placed in the flame of her heart, stoking it with each pump heightening the emotion.

She summoned the words from her throat, commanding them.

"The land cries out for a new leader. The Two Thrones must be restored. I am Willow, heiress of House Drinith, ruler of Château Ensalor."

As she paused, her new family knelt, each taking a valiant knee. Merlin then tapped his staff on the stony floor.

"Yes, Merlin?"

"With permission, heiress, I would like to say something."

"Granted. Go ahead."

"It is of the utmost importance to name your council. Whoever you name shall be with you to help guide your decisions or simply offer advice in life."

Willow considered. She liked everyone present in the room, and as most ten-year-olds thought, she wanted them all to play a part. But then she realized she did not know who belonged on a council!

"Um, is there, um, names for the council?"

She tightened her shoulders, trying not to give away this new-found sense of importance and respect.

Merlin obliged.

"Oh. Well, of course! You have the magistrate, the person in charge of law, and the captain of the sentries, the person responsible for all security of the castle and your safety. Next is the ambassador, the representative of your authority and law, and lastly, you have the lord commander, the person responsible for all military or wartime efforts. They will be your second-in-command."

Although Willow weighed her options, it was quite clear to her which of her new friends was the best fit for each position. Each of them had a niche unique to them. Zohar was a natural leader, Lady Cho was a great fighter, especially one-on-one, and Rowan was one of the best riders she had ever seen, even among the Purloinians.

"I understand," said Willow. "I think I've made my mind up."

"Exemplary," said Merlin. "I expected nothing less. Now draw your sword."

He eyed Pnevma propped against the dresser beside the feathered bed. It lay waiting to be wielded, longing to be drawn from its sheath. Willow noticed her master's look and went over to retrieve it. Upon drawing it, there was a crisp *shing*! She held the scabbard in her left hand.

"When you have made your choice, say their name followed by 'I dub thee…' and give them their title."

Willow peered at the shimmering blade, pure and unscathed, even after the slaughter hours earlier. It was a fine sword, just the right length for a girl of her height, and it was not too heavy, as one could expect. It was light enough to be held with a single hand. She held it up, straight and strong.

"Merlin," she said.

The wizard stood, came forth, and knelt again in front of the heiress of Ensalor.

"I dub thee magistrate of Ensalor."

As she spoke, she tapped one shoulder with the sword, crossed over his head to the other, and tapped it. Merlin grinned and exchanged a bow with her before replacing himself among the others.

"Lady Cho," said Willow again.

The Gallantinel leader came forth and knelt in front of the savior of the realm, the One Who Unites, with all the strength and gratitude of her people.

"I dub thee captain of the sentries."

She made the same shoulder-to-shoulder movement that she had done with the wizard.

"I shall not fail you," said Lady Cho. "As Skeef as my witness, it is my highest honor to have the privilege of your protection. I shall wear this title proudly."

She stood, bowed, and replaced herself all the same.

"Next, Baron Zohar," said Willow, still holding the sword.

This is pretty easy, she thought. *I know each of them will fulfill each role they're given dutifully.*

The warrior-king came forth from behind the others and, out of respect for the true monarch, bowed with his head down.

"I dub thee lord commander. Never was there a finer warrior or braver king."

The baron stood with pride, not enough to be prideful or lacking to be cowardly. It was just the precise balance between humility and dignity. In his eyes, Willow could see the spark of his people and their commitment to bettering the realm. She was appreciative and knew inside her heart of hearts that he was the best possible choice for this role on the council.

"You honor me, heiress," he said. "But I shall never forget the honor that you hold. I wish that you could have been able to meet my father, Avidar, in his prime. He loved the duke and his duchess, so by extension, he would have loved you."

He bowed.

"I will do everything in my power to ensure the victory of Ensalor, the Citadel of Kastallon."

He replaced himself all the same.

"Finally," said Willow, ready for her last naming, "we shall have my ambassador."

Knowing there was naught anyone else left but Rowan, the prentice, the others stood aside, leaving him to solely stand between them. Instead of calling him forward, Willow strode to him. She looked up at him, he who had tears welling in those blue orbs, and wiped his eyes. She had an idea of what he had to be thinking at this moment: his parents.

She remembered that at the time of her birth, Rowan's parents were slaughtered by the forces of the former Caliph at the hands of the Caped Vex known as Sal. He had been on the run ever since. Perhaps he was missing them. Perhaps he was melancholy at the thought of how proud they would have been knowing that he would be a member of Ensalor's council and that they were unable to see him be sworn in. It was a likely possibility, and Willow respected him for it.

If they had survived, she would have thanked them for raising a fine son. In her mind, she imagined it would have been awkward for a ten-year-old to be thanking adults for their child, a gesture uncommon in most places. But she was the heiress, and soon, she would be the duchess of Ensalor. She had dominion over them, and they would have been grateful that the monarch had even the thought of them, let alone had chosen their son for a highly respected title.

Through tears, Rowan knelt deservingly. Willow spoke gently and kindly.

"I dub thee ambassador of Ensalor. With a fast horse and an indomitable will, I've no doubt you shall be the finest representative in our history. Rise, friend."

When he rose, they shared a warm embrace. After Willow sheathed her sword, that is! Merlin then came to Willow's side with arms open to the new members of the council.

"In the name of Skeef, a new era of royalty begins in the Land Where Castles Lie! May he bless us as we serve and give us the strength to uphold his will."

*****

In the hours that passed after their reunion, the whole company had loaded several Purloinian carts and wagons and horses with supplies ranging from cookware to tapestries to weaponry to ingredients and more, all to take with them on the journey north to Ensalor. It was a magnificent parade, far greater and more convergent than any throng or gathering led or forced by the Caliph's influence. Trumpeters trumpeted, drummers drummed, flutists fluted, and a mighty sound was produced therein. It was unlike any celebration the realm had seen in past eras, perhaps even since the First Bleating.

Willow sat nearly napping in the stagecoach as it rocked her into a lull. Its grand wooden wheels created narrow treads in the grass beneath. The cushions inside were clouds constructed of feathers and fine amber cloth, enough to make a young girl sleepy quickly. She tried to stay awake, however, as her curiosity sparked and began to grow and grow with each passing second.

Merlin was in the coach with her. He was still her guardian after all. Juniper, who did not feel like flying all the way to Ensalor from the east, lay snuggled and asleep against Willow's thigh. The windows of the coach were open, which made for a pleasant, cool trip as it went. It was horse-drawn, led by the finest and strongest stallions the eastern kingdom had to offer.

Willow covered a yawn with her hand, then spoke.

"Magistrate," she began.

Merlin turned to her from the window.

"Yes, heiress," he said with that same warm, gentle smile.

"I'm curious."

"A good thing, that. What of, my dear?"

"How did the realm Kastallon come to be?"

Willow moved in closer to the old wizard in his purple robe, his staff resting on his shoulder. Merlin's brow pricked up.

"A fine question," he said. "I do believe it will be long enough to last the entire journey north. But as is the nature of younglings, do mind that your attention does not waver. It would do the duchess-to-be a good turn to listen carefully."

With that, the wizard began another of his eloquent orations, told in the way of his kind: with plenty of detail and careful verbiage. Willow felt her eyes' will to remain open dwindling.

Chapter 23

The Bleating

"Before time itself began to tick, there was only a bright, luminous light. This light was unlike any light known to beings of any kind, more bright than the sun and thousands more hot. Shapeless it was, and abstract. Its radiance was unquestioned. It is known only as the Primordial.

"From this Primordial, it is written in the sacred scriptures of Massax and Pilloc that three beings came to be. Though they are not what the word means, I shall call them children of the Primordial. It shaped them and gave them part of its light—or its ability to create, to take from nothing and create something. These three beings were named—and might I add that we as servants of one of these children were told by him their names—Skeef the Ever-Changing, Ephod the First-Gifted, and Ghetrix, the Hard-Hearted. They are the Numen, personifications of order, morality, and discipline respectively.

"At their inception, the Primordial tasked them with taking on the challenge of creating their own realms and filling them with beings to subjugate. This was a test, a test of discovery. The Primordial wanted to see if they would use its power for good or for evil, to see if one of them were worthy enough to be given free range of their abilities. Naturally, each Numen went to work. Note that while I've met with Skeef, I do not know the realms created by Ghetrix and Ephod. From time to time, I find myself grateful for that lack of knowledge.

It frightens me to wonder just what may have been birthed from their loins. I digress.

"Skeef, being the ever-changing of the Numen, began to craft the very world we stand on. The very road we travel, the very air we breathe, and even the very water we drink—everything came from Skeef. But it all began with a sound, a bleating.

"Why Skeef chose to only appear as goats or sheep, I do not know. Perhaps I never will. Nevertheless, it was his song that sang the world into existence. Through melodies of radiant grace and harmonies of melancholy woe, he bound the world by his own threads, shaping and molding and piecing it all like a glorious puzzle. Each leaf of each tree is his. Each vine in the ground is his. Every hopping hare and gliding gazelle is his. It was he that sang them alive. He knew exactly who they were before he created them. All he had to do was sound the Bleating.

"According to him, this process only took mere minutes to finalize. When the last bird was flying high, the last fish swimming low, and the last beast grazing upon the land, his song was finished. He looked upon it all and was satisfied. With his realm established, Skeef took rest for a while, a few hundred years, inside the mountains of his own creation. As for the others, well, perhaps he'll tell us when he finds out.

"When Skeef awoke all those years later, he found that even though his realm was finished, it was still lacking something, something…more. In a burst of creativity, Skeef sang forth the shape of a human and began to make more and more of them to occupy the land. He gave them the knowledge of craftsmanship and farming in order to sustain themselves. He was very, very proud of these beings that he'd created and found that, in response to their gifts, they worshipped him without needing the concept of worship. For this, he was thankful. But with this knowledge, this revelation that the beings began to think for themselves, came dire consequences.

"More time passed since the dawn of humanity. By now, the realm, which they called Kastallon, was flourishing. Cities were constructed, ways of life were maintained, and even the beasts began to tolerate the new beings. Then everything changed when a man by the name of Naic changed everything by smiting his father, Leba, with a jagged rock.

"Apparently, Naic had had enough of his father's punishments for his son's wanting to be a kid. Each day, Naic was given chore after chore to complete with very little time to enjoy much else. It was constantly 'Son, do this' and 'Son, do that.' 'Feed the sheep,' 'Water the gardens,' 'Make your bed.' On and on, Naic worked and worked until he could stand it no longer. His mother, Argia, tried to make things better by offering him extra food when the time came for nourishment, but food would not quell the growing anger inside her son.

"One evening, when the moon shone dimly on the shadowed grass and Naic's parents were asleep, the boy left his home and hatched his plan. He would cry out with a loud voice 'Help! Help! Father, please help me!' to try to stir his father from his slumber. It was a sad thought knowing that even though the boy was aware that his father loved him, it was not enough to overcome the desire for an end to hard work and busyness.

"Like any good father, Leba thrashed awake and darted for the door. He looked out over the hills and saw his boy standing amidst the stalks of wheat in the fields. Despite the low light and visibility, Leba knew—nay, felt—something was wrong. He ran up to meet his son, who lie in wait with his weapon. With the element of surprise, Naic smote the back of Leba's head, drawing blood quickly. After his father's body collapsed, he continued to bash in its head, leaving nothing but bone and blood behind.

"Naic, breathing heavily with adrenaline coursing in his veins, knew he could not return to his mother. So he decided to leave his home and roam the land, taking shelter inside caves and caverns, eating and drinking whatever he could get his hands on—fish, insects, birds, anything. He'd kill them with a makeshift sling.

"Eventually, Naic grew into an adult, a wretched, ugly, twisted adult, who was balding and lacking teeth. He'd lived in his sorrow and hatred for so long that it had consumed him. Each time he caught a glimpse of other families enjoying themselves or even a lost traveler, he would spit and curse at them. 'Suffer!' he would say, launching pebbles at them.

"There came a time, however, when Naic was visited by the Silver Shag, one of the many forms of Skeef. It was inside one of the wretch's several craggy dwellings one evening. Naic heard the Shag calling his name, and in fear and shame, he fled to hide himself. At first, the Shag could not see him. He knew he'd come to the right place, for Skeef knows all things. He clopped atop one of the larger boulders, where just ahead was a large pond, gray and sterile. Not a ripple befell its surface.

"'Naic? Naic, where are you?' The Shag surveyed the rock-filled dwelling. Nothing stirred. Nothing responded. Nothing, perhaps, even breathed. 'My child, come where I can see you. I do not mean any harm. I am simply here to talk.'

"Naic heard the Shag's voice in his head, for that was how the Numen, or at least Skeef, communicated. He held his hands over his ears, desperate for the noise to vacate, but to no avail. The Numen's voice was simply much too strong, louder than any buzzing of bees or shriek of scavenging things. He strained and gritted his teeth.

"'Away!' he said, revealing himself by falling away from the boulder and writhing, flailing like a fish out of water. 'No more! Please! Away with you!' His shrill cries were none the more comforting than the scraping of nails on sandpaper. The Shag spotted him and crossed the minor crags to meet him. In his divine heart, a twang of pain befell him, a soreness unlike any sadness once and forever, the deepest sorrow that cut true to the soul. There, in the Numen's eyes, was the frailty, the vulnerability, of his creation.

"'Poor creature,' said the Shag, its voice dripping with remorse. 'What have you done? Where is your father? Why have you retired to this ugly place? This place reserved only for those who cannot tolerate light? What has transpired?'

"Naic dared not to look upon the Shag. He knelt with his hands covering his face, for he knew in his position that he'd done this to himself. Acting on instinct—nay, on malice—had led him to lose what could have been a life of peace and possibility. Instead, he inherited the life of a hermit bound to his malignant ways, destined to live and die on fish and insects in the very cave that had swallowed him. But as always, something burned within him, a scorching, searing, enveloping feeling.

"'I have done nothing,' said Naic. It was a lie, but he tested the Shag. 'This is the result of living in your world. See my teeth. How they rot! See my skin. How it wrinkles! Thus is my reward as a being made by Skeef.'

"'I have done not this, my son. For a transformation such as this, something far worse had to have happened. I have not seen something this dreadful since Kastallon's birth. Please, tell me what you have done that has earned you such a visage as this.'

"A pang of regret sounded in Naic's heart, a pang that resonated and began to wrestle with the burning feeling that ate away at him. There was a side of him that wanted to tell the Shag what happened and beg forgiveness, and maybe perhaps he could be spared. But simultaneously, the hounding tug of that charring feeling overcame any desire for mercy. He succumbed to the darkness inside him, wrought from years of forced servitude to his father.

"'I killed my father! There! Is that what you wanted to hear? Did you want to hear me confess to my evil deed? There, I said it! I killed him! And it was plenty fun, I'll have you know. I'd smite him again and again if it meant seeing that slaver fall away each time!' Naic cackled a most sinister, bone-crunching howl. 'I also defile my meals, leaving naught but the bones! Tasty, tasty flesh!' His mad laughter filled the bowels of the cavern he'd made his home. The Shag was mortified.

"'Look upon me, servant of darkness!' the Shag bleated. Suddenly, the laughter ceased, and the being that was once Naic gazed upon the wooliness of the Numen. Golden light radiated forth from the tips of his fleece. His very essence seethed with divine judgment. 'I have tried to be benevolent, to be a Numen of peace. I know not what has consumed you or why you have chosen to oppose me, but I will not allow you to corrupt my world. You, like the others of your race, were made to worship I, who have given you shelter and the means to produce life-sustaining food. Yet you mock and scorn me with this deed, this murder! I cannot allow it. Depart from this land, wicked wretch, for never did I call you mine own! Go forth and away from here, and ne'er shall you sojourn back!'

"The Shag let out a mighty bleating, louder than any he'd bleated before. From where he stood, Naic felt immobilized, yet a crooked smile still remained. In his mind, this is what he wanted—not the Naic from before but something more sinister, dark. The ground beneath him quaked and began to crack.

"'I have taken him,' a voice came through Naic's lips that was not his own, a voice made of multiple voices, echoey and vile. 'He is to be my vessel! Long have I tempted him, and fruitful have his labors been.'

"Through the bleating, the Shag called to the being within Naic's shell. 'What are you? I command you to reveal yourself!' The bleating intensified. With feeble arms shielding its face from the sound, the creature responded—not through choice but from a sudden will outside of its power. 'I am she who was made from the loins of a failed creation. I was made to serve the Cosmic Blemish, the Defiler of Worlds, the Eater of Light, the Thing of Darkness himself! But I rejected him and stole a fraction of his power. I am Fikra, and I will have my reign! This world shall be mine!'

"On the final word, the Shag had had enough. With a mighty cry, the stony ground still cracking beneath the body formerly belonging to Naic opened wide, and down he fell into the depth of the very earth he was made from. It was as if the earth was alive and swallowed the wicked whole.

"With the creature gone, the Shag rested upon the very boulder it stood on tiredly. Skeef wept. With this new knowledge of a phantom evil that had penetrated his grasp of supervision, Skeef felt it was time the realm had a protection of its own, a means for its people to take up arms themselves and stand against anything that should threaten the realm once more. Away he went to the center of Kastallon, the heart of his realm. His presence beckoned forth all of his creation to his side. Around him, they surrounded in groups—people, air beasts, and land beasts alike. They awaited his words as if they were nourishment everlasting. All was quiet and calm. All were eager to hear what the Shag had to say.

"'Inhabitants of Kastallon,' they heard in their heads, 'it is with a heavy heart that I regret to inform you that something has threatened the realm.' There were some gasps and murmurs of uncertainty. 'You've nothing to fear, however, for I have sent it away, never to return. For now, your homes and ways of life are safe.' Stomps and claps and cheers sounded briefly before the Shag raised a hoof for quiet.

"'But it is because this force came without alarm, without my knowing, that I have made the decision to give the realm protectors. I will make among you kingdoms to stand united should another threat to your dominion arise. Four domains shall there be, and four domains shall work cohesively. This land is your land, and you must defend it at all costs. Therefore, I shall bring forth into the land a saving grace to be used only as defense and a last resort.'

"At this moment, Skeef called forth strong-willed and worthy men and women among the humans and Purloinians to be rulers of the four domains. He named them Ensalor, Londror, Nessongor, and Delnor—the Citadel, the Refuge, the Oasis, and the Stronghold respectively. It was here that the first age of dukes and barons was established. They were crowned and given Skeef's blessing. As for this saving grace, it is the crystals we call Shimmer. They are microcosms of Skeef's divine capacity. As time went on, these crystals were harnessed and studied. And thus, the Astrons were founded—wielders of Shimmer who came to the aid of kingdoms.

"So that is the answer to your inquiry, heiress, a paraphrased but truthful history of the realm. It was quite the honor of the dedicated Astrons before me, who transcribed these events into the many volumes found in Numalosh. Of course, as previously stated, they credit this knowledge to Skeef, our lord and protector. May he bless us as we serve and give us the strength to uphold his will."

Chapter 24

Dawn

Willow felt the stagecoach come to a complete, sudden stop. The shock of it triggered her awakening, gentle but still sudden. She rubbed her eyes with balled fists and moved over in her seat to peer through the window. What she beheld was unlike any building she had ever gazed upon, even Londror.

It was a massive castle, larger than Londror, larger than Al Wafra! Its many parapets and towers and battlements were a sight to behold indeed. At the corners of the forward wall lay a sturdy tower, windows spiraling up and around it. Across the parapets between them, hanging off the sides, was a grand tapestry sporting a midnight hue behind an ivory toucan silhouette. Armored men stood watch armed with bows and hoods over their helms. They were sentinels, ready to strike at a moment's notice. But Willow knew they were there for her protection.

The length of the castle was larger and much grander than Londror. Instead of being surrounded by a moat underneath an escarpment, it was a wide-open field with many plains and ferns, among other attractive flora. It certainly added to the majesty of it all.

Lining the sides of each of the huge wooden doors to the entrance were crowds of different beings, ranging from humans to Gnomes to Purloinians to animals, all ready to receive the heiress for her coronation with accepting arms and hearts. But their presence was quite odd to her. She did not remember there being this many people in the parade. She looked over at Merlin, who had a smile of pure joy streaking his face.

"How did they all get here?" she asked. "There weren't this many people with us when we left, were there?"

"Indeed," said the wizard. "They are what remains of the siege last night. I was not among them, but I did receive word from a rider just this morning. I'd been waiting to tell you until we arrived and until you were awake. When the conversion was resolved, the Caliph accepted bindings as a precautionary measure. She was then transported to Londror, same as you.

"But as for the multitudes that remained after the battle, including those of the Gilded who recanted and joined our ranks, they marched north and took the castle. From what I heard, it was very one-sided—men, Purloinian, and Gnome alike all fighting to free its majesty from the dwindling grip of Caliphate remnants. Then when it was all said and done, the castle itself underwent a fantastic, wondrous transformation."

"So it didn't look like this when we got here?"

"Certainly. Rowan tells me it was not the most pleasant sight on the rare occasions that he passed by it in my absence. I'd rather not pass the time trying to imagine that dreadful sight, for it would be a burden upon my heart to see the Citadel so wrought with wicked darkness. For now, let us celebrate its healing."

Merlin then unlatched the stagecoach door and stepped out. When Willow followed suit, there was almost instantaneous rejoicing around her—a welcoming cacophony of stamping hooves, sounding instruments, joyful cheers, and wave upon wave of clapping louder than any baseball stadium ever mustered. She felt a few gentle flutters on her shoulder and saw that Juniper had found her place. They exchanged smiles, and the toucan raised her feathered wings in celebration.

"Welcome home," said the bird. "You don't know how long I've waited to say that."

With her excitement taking over, the bird jumped from her shoulder and soared into the air, gliding on the very wind itself, squawking and chirping quite cheerfully. It seemed that the triumphant commemoration was infectious enough to overcome the bird's willpower. Never had she seen the bird so free, so happy. It brought a warm feeling to her heart. It all did—the happy people and the delightful sounds of jubilation, all of it.

For the first time in a long time, Willow finally, truly felt like she belonged. This was her home, her true home, her birthright. She considered herself lucky when she thought of those still trapped in the orphanage on Earthrealm. All the times the other young girls chastised or criticized her and her appearance were now meaningless. She had found her place, and they hadn't. Yet she felt no sense of superiority over them. In fact, she was quite sorry for them. It was, as she had seen before, quite the unhappy life for orphan children. Maybe their day would come. Maybe.

Merlin guided Willow with an arm around her as they trod through the path of people. Willow found herself darting her eyes back and forth between one side and the other in awe of just how many people had come to see her arrival. Perhaps even the entire realm was in attendance. Imagine the whole country lined up to see the most famous person in the land. That was how Willow felt at this moment. All the attention was focused, centered, right on her.

She looked behind her and saw that her newly bestowed council members were tailing. They stopped just before the massive wooden doors of Ensalor. With a closer few, Willow could see the embossments stretching all the way up and across them. Carved into the doors themselves were brilliant, intricate designs of flowers ahead of a shield.

Willow glanced at Merlin, who knew her question before she asked it.

"Your parents were always fond of botany," he said. "That is the study of plants and plant matter. Their reasoning was that one could find an appreciation for the world that our lord and protector created simply by examining and caring for it. As you can see, they also chose a shield for the flowers to reside on. This was your father's touch. His explanation was that Skeef created the precious world around us, and we must defend it."

Willow stood in awe, both because of the masterful design of the door and because she felt a slight tug at her heart knowing she would never get the full explanation from the designer himself. She turned to Merlin with wells in her eyes.

"Marvelous," she said. "I wish he was here."

Merlin's eyes began to join hers in their saturation. Each year that had passed, when he looked out for her at the orphanage, he saw a bit more of her parents each and every day. He began to recollect all his experiences with the former duke and duchess and restrained a sob.

"As do I, my dear," he said, drops of grief in his tone. "He would have been tickled to death to see the girl that you have become, and rightfully so. He would have gladly passed on his title to you. It would have been his highest honor. I can hear him say it now."

His smile, though retaining the gentleness of his character, hid the grief well. Part of him was still mourning, even to this day. Willow could tell he was just thankful to have kept her safe through it all and brought her to exactly where she needed to be.

After sharing a brief embrace, Merlin called to have the doors opened, and in strolled the heiress and her newly named council members. Once through the threshold, it was clear that whatever spell the Caliphate had placed on the castle had been lifted. The windows were no longer foggy; the thick pillars lining the throne room now appeared stronger and sturdier than ever. The whole scene was vibrantly and brilliantly made, forged by the masterful minds of the first monarchs.

But one thing remained still cursed: the throne. It sat before them, wicked and twisted into a gruesome, horrific chair. Blacker than night it was and seemed to ooze with an evil aura. Little spindles emerged from the body of the throne, implying a crown. It was conjured from the original two thrones that were obliterated during the Caliphate's invasion. It was a mockery of its original owners, a spit in the face of their culture. Willow tried not to feel a sense of hatred when she eyed it.

By now, the multitude of beings from before had piled in and stood patiently watching the actions of the council as they unfolded.

Each member, save for Merlin, found his or her place on the steps leading to the throne. The Gnomes, Rossa and Valner, stood where the wizard would have, and not in the slightest did they feel even somewhat out of place. They stood proud knowing they were immediate friends of the duchess-to-be.

Valner nudged Rossa with his elbow.

"You know, I'll never forget this moment."

"That's understandable," replied Rossa, keeping her eyes forward. "I of all gnomish peoples should know that Valner the Hungry has never stepped foot in the Citadel. Of course you will never forget!"

It was all said in a whisper so as to not potentially interrupt the ceremony. In fact, she, too, had never seen Ensalor in all its glory. She was just as awestruck and excited to be among them as he was.

Merlin led Willow up the stairs as they walked between the council members. The wicked throne was now before them, and it was even more grossly wicked up close than from afar. It was no wonder the Caliph was as devious and malignant as she was; the very chair she sat upon was imbued with malice. It was all Fikra's doing. But now the time had come to make things right, to fulfill the sole purpose of her return.

Merlin turned around and faced the good people of Kastallon. He raised a firm hand to indicate his need for quiet from the murmuring guests. In a clear, celebratory voice, he spoke.

"Citizens of Kastallon, we are gathered here today in this magnificent house of royalty this morning to make the land right again. Skeef himself prophesied this very moment. All of our waiting has finally paid off. It is my highest pleasure, as a servant of Skeef and member of the council, to affirm the heiress. But first, we must undo that which has been done."

He then turned back to Willow, and his voice was suddenly a whisper.

"Calmly now," he spoke softly. "This is the moment everything has led to. Take up your mother's sword and look."

He gestured at the glowing purple gem in its hilt.

"It is a Shimmer crystal, pure as the first one ever spawned. Use it. Raise it toward the throne."

Willow, unsure of what would happen next, understood and obeyed her master's orders. Carefully, she raised Pnevma and pointed its sharpened point toward the wicked chair, soaked in midnight.

At first, there was nothing. Then suddenly, seconds later, there was a minute vibration arising in the hilt. The hand that held it was buzzing with energy! The gem in the hilt glowed brighter than it had ever glowed before. A slight panic birthed in her chest, an anxiety that something might go wrong and the wicked chair would remain unscathed, as it did right now. Did she believe she could do it? Was it enough just to believe one could? She closed her eyes and steadied the still-buzzing sword.

A short cracking sound was heard, and the crowd gasped briefly. Willow opened her eyes, keeping the sword focused on the wicked throne. There, in the body of the chair, was a glowing fissure, as if something had thrown a metaphysical stone at it and cracked it. She looked to Merlin, who nodded and urged her to keep going. She drew in a breath and moved the sword slightly forward again. The buzzing intensified, sending small vibrations up to her elbow. She clasped her forearm with her free hand and centered herself like the baron had shown her.

Keep going, she told herself. *It has to shatter. It must be done!*

She began to step toward it now, keeping the blade honed to the throne like a magnet. With each step closer and closer, more fissures erupted, glowing with bright white light. When she was inches away from the throne, the buzzing was at its highest point, its climax. The vibrations were now all the way to her shoulder! She gritted her teeth behind closed lips as she slowly raised the blade above her ahead. The whole room was quiet with anticipation. Everything, from the moment she had stepped off the whale to her journey through the land and her victory at Falmeuse, had led to this moment.

"By the power of Skeef, I demand you to shatter!" she exclaimed, bringing the sword down upon the seat of the throne.

In a flash of golden aura, the entire throne room was illuminated, basked in divine essence, as if the sun had descended and welcomed them personally. All except Willow shielded their eyes from the majestic light the explosion had caused. Some merely closed their eyes tightly and turned away. But Willow stood and watched as the light began to dim, fade, and finally dissipate.

There, in place of where that wretched, cruel seat originally stood, was a wreckage of several ordinary-looking pieces of rubble. She had done it! The last remnant of the Caliphate had finally been demolished, never more able to bring darkness to the land.

"Skeef's fleece, you've done it!" said Rowan, a smile of pure elation on his face revealing pearly teeth. It was the happiest Willow had seen him since she met him.

The crowd beyond the pillars erupted into applause, a mixture of praise and cheering, all for her. Merlin let them have their moment briefly, then raised his hand once more to settle them down. They listened.

"This is but half of the deed we must complete. Now the thrones must be made anew, made stronger by the trials of adversity and the strength of our lord and protector. Only then can we crown our new duchess."

He turned back to Willow.

"Heiress, if you would do us the greatest of honors."

Willow nodded and raised her sword once more. Again, the vibrations returned, but they weren't as unstable as before. Her arm was used to it now, and it was easier to manage. In a waving motion, she commanded the rubble to combine themselves together piece by piece. Everyone watched as the individual shards of rock began to merge as they swirled around before them. In a matter of seconds, what used to be a pile of broken stones now floated above as two elegant, beautiful stone thrones, which Willow guided to the floor. Gently she placed them, and they stood in a way that seemed as though they had always belonged. Neither of the two felt out of place, and it was quite pleasing to see them both in their rightful places. And when she turned to face her people, an even louder uproar of appreciation met her gaze. As if she had rehearsed it a thousand times, she curtsied as a gesture of thanks to them all.

When the cheering and clapping had finally settled back down to an appropriate level of polite watching, Merlin turned to the crowd once more, this time with a feeling of wonder unlike any he had ever felt before.

"And so begins the dawn of a new eon," he proclaimed, then turned to the heiress of Ensalor and bowed. "I would name you duchess of Kastallon, but as you are quite aware, my lady, there are two seats of power. Two must rule, just as your mother and father did. Tell us, my lady, is there anyone who you would name to reign alongside you as your duke?"

Willow had but one answer, and it was the easiest decision she had ever made.

Chapter 25

Ever After

It was a bleak, quiet day in Earthrealm. Not much had happened today, for it was scarily similar to the last two days that had passed. The rain rained, the wind blew, and Leonard Leobo sat alone on the orphanage swing set.

It had been a dreary day. The clouds never seemed to leave, and as such, the sun never cast a happy shine upon the land. Even the cars passing by that used to fill him with curiosity didn't seem to affect him anymore. It was bad enough that no one else cared to push him on the swing. All his former friends had found their happy family.

Hank, a boy taller and older than him, was the most recent adoption today. It was a sad moment to watch him go. He could still hear the last words he said to him.

"I guess this is goodbye," he had said. "Thanks for making this place a little brighter."

But it didn't feel bright to him, not one bit.

Although there were other children on the playground, none of them seemed to take notice of the frail boy of eight swaying lightly on the swing set. He watched as they cherished this brief moment of freedom they had as orphans. They were allowed to play as they liked so long as they didn't go near the fencing of the play area.

Promptly, there was a ringing bell, the signal to indicate that playtime was over. He heard the shrill voice of Mrs. Veraminta, who was now headmistress of the orphanage ever since Mr. Linmer disappeared, calling them all back to go inside. Everyone began to line up and march back to the orphanage's back door, everyone except for Leo. Seeing that he hadn't moved a muscle, Veraminta approached him, ready to scold him with every strict bone in her body. The boy did not look up as her footsteps approached.

"Mr. Leobo, have you no ears to hear my instructions?" she ordered.

No response from a sulking Leo.

"Mr. Leobo, I order you to..."

She was about to say something more, but there was a blast of thunder from above that followed a flash of light. The old crone looked around, wondering why the rain had not started yet. After all, in Earthrealm, most of the time, if there was thunder, rain would follow.

But it didn't, for something else was in the wind, something far scarier to a strict administrator than any roar of sound or falling water: a rebellious student.

"Don't talk to him that way, Veraminta," a strange, confident voice announced.

The elderly admin turned around and was frightened by what she found. There, at the bottom of the steps that led to the back door, was a figure in a hooded cloak blowing in the wind.

Veraminta raised a finger to speak, but quickly, the figure intruded.

"Don't bother. You will find that your words have no effect on me. Might I suggest keeping quiet and returning to your quarters? After all, it *is* suppertime, isn't it?"

Mrs. Veraminta, uncertain of who this small, shadowy figure was or why it knew her name, looked back at Leo and then at the figure once more.

"Who are you, and what do you want?" begged the haggard woman, her tone still striking in the same commanding voice she used on the children. "Take off that pathetic thing at once!"

She said this when she realized the figure was no taller than her chest. The figure then raised its arms carefully and removed the hood that obscured its face.

Upon seeing just who was under the hood, Leo exclaimed, "Willow!"

But before he could leave the swings, Veraminta turned and cast a frightfully menacing eye at him, an act that meant, "You had better stay put, or else."

"I come for Leo," said Willow, confidence still in her voice. "You will relinquish him to me at once, and I urge you to comply."

She put forth a beckoning hand.

"You dare to give me orders?" shrieked Veraminta, stewing with rage. "Mr. Linmer is gone because of you! Because of you, I have to run this miserable place! Come here at…"

Her words were cut short by the raising of Willow's sword, whose influence bade her to freeze. Leo looked upon it, agape and in awe. After all, he was an eight-year-old lad who fantasized about swords and magic. He had read it in some of the books from the library and became hooked immediately. Seeing now was like a dream come true.

"Should have complied," said Willow with a slight smirk. "Now what is going to happen next is that I will release you, and you shall be on your way. Understood?"

The frozen Veraminta was able to make a few restrained grunts in agreement.

"Good," said Willow, who then withdrew her sword.

Veraminta thawed and, without a single moment of hesitation, began a full sprint up the stairs and away from the play area.

With her gone, Willow waved Leo to come to her from the swing, and the boy quickly ran to her side. There they embraced, fulfilling a long-awaited act. Finally, Willow was able to see him again, and she was happy nothing about him had changed. He was still the same plucky little boy who had sat with her at lunch, eating the kitchen's food like he had never had a full meal in his life. Her stomach still wrenched a bit when she thought of it.

"Where did you go?" asked Leo, who was too excited to cry. "You have been gone for so long, I thought that you went to a new home."

Willow smiled, because in a way, he was not incorrect.

"Actually," she said, "I have, and I came to get you because I want you to be a part of it."

"What? Me?"

"Yes, you, silly!"

"But…but why?"

Willow knew he would ask, but she was confident enough that he could handle the truth. She knelt down to meet his eyes and placed her hands on his arms.

"Because I am part of something much larger and much grander than this old place. Far and away, there is a place where happiness blossoms, where the sun always shines and sadness never comes. There is no sickness, no fear, no tears to fill our eyes. And if you can imagine, it is overseen by a white lamb!"

"Like Mary?" Leo asked.

"Yes, just like Mary! But unlike this world, where grass withers and flowers fade, nothing in this land shall end. There I am like a queen, only it isn't called a queen."

She drew him in closer, keeping her gaze fixed on his.

"I want you to be the king, but it isn't called a king."

She paused to give him time to process.

"What do you say?"

Leo thought for a moment.

King but not called a king?

He wondered what else a king would be called, but that was not important. If there was anything he could want more than being a king, it would be to leave the orphanage.

"I don't understand," he said, scrunching a bit.

"Come," Willow said, standing. "Let me show you."

About the Author

Matthew Joe Blackburn is an American author from Lillington, North Carolina. When he is not working as a middle school English teacher, he is writing and reading and plotting stories of fantasy, science fiction, and horror that have been stewing since he was young. In his academic years, he spent countless hours both in and out of school brewing storylines and crafting characters from the depths of his imaginative mind, characters inspired by the many iconic and memorable stories of his generation.

Blackburn's upbringing was founded in reading and writing. His mother would read him *Peter Rabbit* as a child, thus stoking his passion for books and the art of storytelling. In elementary school, he was selected from among his peers to read to the lower grade levels and was praised by his teachers for his writing prowess. In high school and university, Blackburn began to take his love for writing seriously and would write for leisure on his days off.

The son of a shop clerk and a principal, Blackburn was raised in a Christian home and soon found a fascination for the many biblical stories of the Old Testament. He was spellbound by the miracles and spectacles documented by the prophets. His brother was the one who introduced him to the genre of fantasy, and it has hooked him ever since.

Blackburn lives with his wife and dog. He enjoys reading and cooking in his spare time away from his writing. In 2023 alone, he read a total of twenty-seven books. His debut novel, *Daughter of Kastallon*, is a result of his everlasting love of magic, heroism, and faith.

Printed in the USA
CPSIA information can be obtained
at www.ICGtesting.com
LVHW090046210624
783561LV00001B/131

9 798892 215299